LONDON LODGINGS

THE QUENTIN QUARTET I

LONDON LODGINGS

Claire Rayner

MICHAEL JOSEPH

LONDON

MICHAEL JOSEPH

Published by the Penguin Group
27 Wrights Lane, London W8 5TZ
Viking Penguin Inc., 375 Hudson Street, New York, New York 10014, USA
Penguin Books Australia Ltd, Ringwood, Victoria, Australia
Penguin Books Canada Ltd, 10 Alcorn Avenue, Toronto, Ontario, Canada M4V 3B2
Penguin Books (NZ) Ltd, 182–190 Wairau Road, Auckland 10, New Zealand

Penguin Books Ltd, Registered Offices: Harmondsworth, Middlesex, England

First published 1994
Copyright © Claire Rayner, 1994

Typeset by Datix International Limited, Bungay, Suffolk
Set in 12/13.75 pt Monophoto Palatino
Printed in England by Clays Ltd, St Ives plc

ISBN 0 7181 3668 3

The moral right of the author has been asserted

For Julie

with a mother-in-law's love!

Acknowledgements

The author would like to thank: London Library; Victoria and Albert Museum; Museum of London; Harrods Ltd; Transport Museum Covent Garden; Public Records Office; GPO Archives; Meteorological Records Office; Kensington and Chelsea Library; and other sources too numerous to mention.

Prologue

TILLY DIDN'T KNOW how long she'd been sitting underneath Mamma's special small table, the one with the long lace cloth that touched the floor all round. She couldn't tell the time yet ('and neither can you,' she whispered to her doll, Charlotte, who was as usual tucked under Tilly's arm with her head dangling down. 'So don't you laugh.') which was a terrible thing to admit when you were as old as seven. Dorcas had laughed and laughed at Tilly when she'd found that out, because she'd been able to tell the time for ten years now, she'd said scornfully; which meant she'd learned it when she was two.

Tilly had sighed when she'd heard that. How could she ever be as clever or as accomplished or as — well, *everything* — as Dorcas? And she peered again through the lattice of the tablecloth to see if there was any sign of Dorcas. Not that Dorcas came into Mamma's boudoir when Mamma was there, usually, but you never could tell with her. If she got in a temper and made up her mind to find Tilly and punish her, she'd not care a whit about Mamma being asleep on the sofa. She'd just come and —

Tilly shivered and drew back again into the shadows in the middle of her lace tablecloth tent. She didn't like thinking about Dorcas in one of her tempers, when she would twist Tilly's arm behind her back or stamp on her feet and throw Charlotte about. That was why Charlotte's head had to dangle

1

downwards. When Tilly held her up the right way she looked like that horrid picture of the man hanging on a tree that Dorcas had shown her and which was the worst picture Tilly had ever seen. Dorcas had done that to Charlotte, twisting her head round till it nearly came off altogether. One day maybe Dorcas would do it to Tilly, if she got really nasty. And inside her head Tilly whimpered at the thought and wondered again what the time was. If it was after five o'clock Dorcas would have had her supper with Mrs Leander, her mamma, in the kitchen, and she was always in a better humour after supper. Dorcas in a happy mood was wonderful. She told the best stories, dreamed up her best games and was the nicest person in the world.

Tilly heard the clock tinkle again and knew that all she had to do to tell the time was count the chimes, but she also knew it would go all wrong if she tried. She could count as far as four, easy, but after that it got tangled in her head. Sometimes six seemed to come next and sometimes it didn't, and when she tried to remember what it should be, she forgot how many she'd already counted and by then the clock would have stopped chiming anyway; so she never could be sure of telling the time that way. It was awful to be so stupid, she thought forlornly. She could just hear how Dorcas would laugh in her loud cold way if she knew.

The clock had stopped chiming by now, and Tilly hadn't even begun to count and she could feel tears collect inside her throat, deep down, where they could prickle at her and make her feel horrid, and she tried to swallow them away. But they wouldn't go. She hugged upside-down Charlotte close, to see if that would help. It didn't.

It was getting darker now, and she could barely see anything under the lace cloth. Just a sort of dimness on the other side of the pattern, a dimness where Mamma breathed her rather thick, bubbly breaths as she slept, while downstairs in the basement kitchen Mrs Leander rattled dishes – Tilly could hear her easily all the way up here – and outside in the street horses and wheels went rattling and creaking past.

2

Not past; Tilly cocked her head to one side and listened hard, the forgotten tears sliding away down inside her and leaving her throat comfortable again. Horses had stopped outside; she could hear the jingle of a harness and a man's voice as footsteps rattled on the cobbles, and now Tilly tried to make herself very small indeed, wanting to shrink away till she was smaller even than Charlotte and no one would ever be able to see her, even if they looked under the lace cloth, lifting the edge to peer under at her. No one, not even Papa . . .

If only she'd been able to tell the time, she'd have gone long ago. She'd have known when it was safe to crawl out, in that special little time between Dorcas having her supper and Papa coming home. It was dreadful to be caught between them both, Dorcas and her laughing and stamping on feet and Papa with his shouting and bigness and well, general Papaness. If only Mamma hadn't been frightened of Papa as well; then Tilly would have had someone to help her; but Mamma was and, Tilly sometimes thought, she was also frightened of Mrs Leander. She certainly let her say very saucy things sometimes and never complained. Tilly knew they were saucy, because she'd heard the housemaid tell the bootboy so, giggling about it, and Mrs Leander had heard her and thrown her out into the street, bag and baggage. Tilly had wondered about that; she knew what a bag was, and indeed saw the one the housemaid had, but she hadn't a baggage, which Tilly expected to be an even bigger bag; and she had almost asked Dorcas about it, until she'd seen the way Dorcas was looking at the weeping housemaid, with her face all still and staring and sort of laughing, so she'd said nothing.

No, Mamma wouldn't help. All Tilly could do was stay very still and hope Papa didn't think to look under the edge of the lace tablecloth. She would have to stay and think her own thoughts and not listen to Papa.

But it was impossible not to listen. He talked too loudly.

The light lifted suddenly as he pushed open the door and

3

came in and Tilly peeped through the lace cloth and saw him holding an oil lamp in each hand, standing there by the door and staring across the room at the sofa. He looked even bigger from where she was. It was like looking up at a mountain. She knew about them from the pictures in her story book about saints who were killed because they loved God and were martyrs. Lots of the martyrs seemed to spend all their time walking about in places where there were mountains, and she tried to imagine people, very little people, all martyrs of course, walking about on Papa. It almost made her giggle out loud, and she put her fist inside her mouth to stop it. It wouldn't make Papa laugh to find her there.

'Good God, Madam!' he shouted. 'Asleep at this hour of the afternoon? Have you no better way to occupy yourself?'

He came in, marching across the room and putting down the lamps, one over Tilly's head on the small table (and the lace cloth shivered as the table rocked under the impact, and she tried again to make herself very small; but it still didn't work) and the other on the table beside Mamma's sofa. Then he stood there with his hands in his breeches' pockets and his boots set apart on the red Turkey rug staring down at Mamma, who had woken up and was looking up at him, wide-eyed and startled, and murmuring in a mixed-up sort of way. Tilly could hear her voice, soft and jerky, like a lamb bleating. She often heard the lambs in the yard behind Mr Spurgeon's butchers shop across the other side of the village, bleating sadly. Dorcas had told her it was because they knew Mr Spurgeon was going to cut their throats and turn them into cutlets for her Papa's dinner and that was why they cried. Mamma sounded just like that. Was Papa going to cut her throat? Tilly wondered suddenly and then shivered. Of course not. All he was going to do was shout, and bad as that was, it wasn't as bad as making a person into cutlets.

He was shouting again now. 'If you were to bestir yourself about your affairs, Ma'am, you'd be a sight less given to sleeping your days away! Is this why you are never ready to come to my bed when I call you of a night? Always ready with reasons to be busying yourself then, are you not? But in the afternoons when there is no risk I shall speak to you of your duty as my wife, why then you are able to sleep well enough!'

'A headache, Austen,' Mamma murmured. Tilly couldn't see her, for Papa's back was in the way, but she knew how she looked, staring up at Papa with her big pale-green eyes shining wetly and her hair soft and loose on her forehead, catching the light like wisps of yellow sewing silks. 'I had such a dreadful headache.'

'I'm sure you did,' he said and went stamping away to the other side of the room where Tilly couldn't see him so easily. She could see Mamma now, stretched out under her pale blue shawl, her face rather pink as though she was very hot and her mouth a little open and pouty. She looked as worried as Tilly felt, so Tilly knew how it was to be Mamma, and was very sad for her. It was horrid when people shouted at you. 'It's as good as any other reason for being so useless. You and your megrims!' And he made that snorting sound that Tilly most hated, and she put her hands up to her ears, but Charlotte got in the way and she couldn't reach them and was forced to listen. 'It's enough to drive a man to drink! You be grateful, Ma'am, that I remember my responsibilities and continue to work for your upkeep, yours and the brat's – and what a brat it is, to be sure! No better than you are yourself, Ma'am, as milk and water as any mewling cat. May God help the man who marries her more than he helped me when I took you off your father's hands. Much the worst bargain I had of it. Where are they all, for the love of Heaven? The house is like a morgue! Even your brat should be able to make itself felt as some sort of life about the place. Thank God for Mrs Leander is all I can say – without her a man could die of starvation in his own home, and not just for want of decent victuals either. I tell you roundly, Mrs Kingsley, you have only yourself to blame if I do turn to wherever I must to get a decent day's

5

provender and a decent night's care! If you were any sort of a woman it would not be necessary for me to look beyond yourself, but what sort of a woman are you? A puling milk-and-water miss is all you have to show for six bites of my apple, and a fair healthy apple it is! Why, any cow in Spurgeon's yard has done better than you! Six pregnancies and not able to rear more than one and that a heifer runt? It makes no sense to me. What's a woman for? I ask you, what's a woman for?'

He was stamping about the room now, his boots passing in front of Tilly's face and then moving away, only to come back again and she sat there with Charlotte clutched beneath her arm and stared out as they went by her line of vision, and she couldn't move, not at all. She wanted to come out, to tell him to stop shouting, wanted to be like Dorcas and not be afraid to be pert and to shout on her own account; Papa would roar furiously when Dorcas stood up to him, but he laughed too, and he always laughed and was very happy when Mrs Leander did the same. They were forever laughing, Papa and Mrs Leander and Dorcas, but never Papa and Mamma and herself, Tilly. It made Tilly wretched to think of it and she tried not to, and sat and watched the boots go by and wished and wished she could be Dorcas instead of being Tilly.

She must have said something aloud or moved or breathed or something while she was wishing, for suddenly there was Papa's face peering down at her as he pulled the lace tablecloth out of the way, and he was staring at her and his face was twisted with anger and his mouth was opening to shout —

Tilly always remembered as far as that, always dreamed the dream to that point, but then it would all be black and she couldn't recall another thing. She would lie in bed and stare into the darkness of her room as she tried to continue the memory, would try to push the barriers down and climb over and into what happened after that, but she never could.

Not even tonight, the last night of her life as Miss Matilda

Kingsley, only daughter of Austen Kingsley Esquire and his wife Henrietta, of this Parish, in the Village of Brompton, not far from London. Tomorrow, 15 September 1855, she would become Mrs Francis Xavier Quentin and it wouldn't matter any more what had happened to the small Tilly all those years ago. But she wished she could remember, all the same, though she could not for the life of her have said why it was so important. It just was. She lay awake for a long time trying to recall it all, but it was no use.

Chapter One

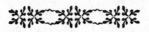

SHE MUST HAVE fallen asleep eventually, for suddenly there was Dorcas, opening her bedroom curtains and whistling through her teeth the way she did when she was feeling particularly sharp, and Tilly stared at her, puzzled, and then remembered suddenly and sat up very straight.

'Making the most of your last night of peace, were you?' Dorcas came and looked down at her. 'Poor wretch – what *do* you look like? As blotchy as the drayman's horse. A fine handsome bride you'll make and no error!'

'Oh, I'm not, am I?' Tilly's hands flew to her face and she felt her cheeks all over; but they seemed to be much as usual, and she scrambled out of bed and ran over to her washstand to peer into the mirror. Her eyes, as green as Mamma's but rather darker, stared back, round and anxious, and her brown hair lay in an unlovely tangle over her forehead, but there were no blotches that she could see and she peered closer and said with what indignation she could muster, 'There's nothing there!'

'None so blind as those that won't see!' Dorcas said blithely. 'But don't you fret, I'll make some sort of fist of you, see if I don't.' She came and looked over Tilly's shoulder into the mirror and Tilly shifted her gaze to Dorcas's bobbing dark curls and wicked brown eyes and the way dimples punctuated the corners of her rich mouth and wanted to weep, as she always did when she compared Dorcas to herself. Dorcas was so merry and lively and so altogether all a wench should be; Papa had said so ever since she and her mother had first come to the house all those years ago; and Tilly was so meek and quiet and stupid, as Dorcas had been telling her ever since — as indeed Papa had — and she could see for herself it was true.

But not today, she told herself then and moved away from the washstand. Today was her wedding day, not Dorcas's. Today she, not Dorcas, was to marry Francis Xavier Quentin, though Tilly knew that Dorcas would be glad to have him. She had seen the way Dorcas looked at Frank when she stood at the front door pretending to be the perfect demure servant while giving him his hat, had watched her waiting at table when Frank came to dine, and she knew. Oh, yes, Tilly knew. Dorcas would gladly have Frank Quentin for herself, she would, and knowing that had made him even more interesting to Tilly. Not, of course, that there would be any chance of Frank being interested in Dorcas; she was after all only a housemaid, and never did aught but say meekly, 'Oh, yes sir,' and, 'No sir,' when he addressed her, which was not very often. When Frank came to the house in Brompton Grove all his spare attention was paid to Tilly, as it should be of course, for they had been affianced ever since Tilly's sixteenth birthday. Papa had arranged it, and she had been entranced by the plan. He was so tall and handsome and so romantic, for he had no relations in all the world, being an orphan who had been reared by a friend of Papa's, a man who had but recently died; a circumstance which Tilly found very touching and which gave Frank an added glow in her eyes. Yet in spite of such a sad history he was rather jolly when he sat with Papa and they shared their claret and laughed loudly. Above all, she was comfortable with him. When Frank was with them, Papa was positively benevolent and Mamma looked happy and not so peaky and all of them were so kind to Tilly it made her feel better than she ever had. Being sixteen and affianced to Frank had been the best time of her life. This morning was wonderful, of course, for it was her wedding day, but it would be a little sad to see this year end. It had been such a happy year. Papa being so – well, not affectionate precisely, but at least not angry all the time, and Mamma being quite lively sometimes. Oh, it had been a wonderful year.

'And today will be a wonderful day,' she said aloud and suddenly felt so light and bubbly that she twirled on the spot, letting her nightgown lift into a frill around her waist and Dorcas roared with laughter and said, 'Save your wares to show the buyer – don't waste them on me!' And Tilly went scarlet with shame and felt dreadful as she realized how badly she had behaved, and at once pulled down her nightgown and scurried to the screen in the corner.

'I shall take a bath at once,' she announced from its anonymous shadows, 'and you can fetch my breakfast while I am doing so. Get on with it, now!' And she quaked a little, amazed at her own boldness. It was rare she dared to speak so to Dorcas; but today, after all, was special.

Again Dorcas laughed and for a moment Tilly heard an echo of the anger and contempt that was so often in her housemaid's voice and shook again; but Dorcas seemed biddable this morning and went away. Tilly heard her drag the enamel bath across the landing and into her room, and let her tense shoulders relax. It was all right. She wasn't going to be hateful. Everything would be all right.

The bath wasn't nearly hot enough, for Dorcas had been too idle to bring up more than one can of really hot water, but it didn't matter. Tilly soaped and rinsed herself happily enough, imagining Frank doing the same in his lodgings on the other side of the village, almost in Knightsbridge in fact, not a very nice place for the dear man to live. Then she blushed a little at the road down which her thoughts went leaping.

Dorcas had told her, long ago, in great detail all the things that brides and grooms did and had frightened the small Tilly almost senseless, especially when she told Tilly that her Papa did it with Dorcas's mamma, Mrs Leander; that had upset Tilly

11

most of all, even though she pretended not to believe it. Papa with Mrs Leander? Ridiculous. As ridiculous as thinking of Papa with Mamma; dreadful, so not to be imagined. Ever. And she had almost succeeded in banishing it all as just more of Dorcas's lies, until at last Mamma had told her, amid many tears, that what Dorcas had said about brides and grooms was, after all, quite true. But nowadays the grown-up about-to-be-married Tilly wasn't frightened by her thoughts in the least. She was in fact a little startled by the pleasure they gave her: but they were secret thoughts after all, so who could know of them? Perhaps she should be frightened, but she could see no reasons for finding Frank alarming. He had always been so kind to her, had sat with her and held her hand and kissed her very sweetly, all this past year. No, there was no need to be afraid of Frank, however hard Dorcas tried to make her so.

Nor, she thought as she dreamily rubbed up handfuls of bubbles in the chilly water, need I feel ashamed, surely? I am to be a wife, am I not? It is Dorcas who makes these things sound coarse and ugly, but it cannot be so for a husband and wife who love each other as Frank loves me and I love Frank; we have no need to pay any attention to the foul talk of Dorcas Leander. She felt very brave, very Miss Matilda Kingsley and not at all anxious Tilly as she sat in her bath thinking on her wedding-day morning.

But her fears came back in a rush when Dorcas returned, for she had her mother with her; and Tilly scrambled out of her bath as quickly as she could, reaching for her wrapper and very aware of Mrs Leander's mocking and appraising stare at her nakedness, and pretending not to care. She had long ago learned to pretend about everything in front of Mrs Leander; it was the only way she could deal with the way the older woman made her feel. I wonder, she thought suddenly, if Mamma has to pretend with her as well?

'Your Mamma has sent me with this, Miss.' Mrs Leander held out a flat blue velvet box. 'She says you're to go to her as soon as they are on and you are dressed and ready, so that she may see you and judge if you should wear her earrings as well.'

Tilly took the box and opened it gingerly and then sat down at her dressing-table a little abruptly. The box contained a string of pearls; large and creamy, a little uneven in their shape and knotted into a single rope. They lay on the rather faded satin lining in a sumptuous tangle and she caught her breath with delight at the sight of them.

'Oh!' was all she could say, and she held them up to her face with slightly shaking fingers and stared at the way their cool gleam was set off by her flushed cheeks.

'Though for my part, I can't see what the woman's thinking of.' Mrs Leander went on to Dorcas in a conversational tone, as she turned away and helped her to lift the bath to one side of the room. 'Seeing as pearls means tears, as any one of any sense knows. It's not what *I* would give *you*, my dear, to wear on your wedding day!' And she and Dorcas both laughed, making it clear in every note that they expected Dorcas to have a much better time of it altogether when she should wed.

It must have been her guardian angel, Tilly decided later, who had sharpened her tongue, or it could have been her anger at the insulting tones Mrs Leander used in speaking of poor Mamma; but whatever it was she lifted her head and looked at the pair of them very directly and said in loud clear tones, 'Well, whenever that will be, of course. You must be quite set about, Mrs Leander, that Dorcas has reached two and twenty and not turned off yet! Now, if you please, Dorcas, I will have my breakfast and then we shall set about my dressing. I wish only some tea and a sippet of bread with some strawberry jam. Be about it, if you please.'

They went, neither of them saying another word, and with her hands shaking more than a little, Tilly picked up her hairbrush and began to deal with the tangles in her hair. She would have to make her peace with Dorcas, of course, for she was the only person who could dress her hair right, but never mind. For the present she felt amazingly pleased with herself.

13

Not only was she to wear Mamma's pearls, but she had dealt with the servants as they should be dealt with. She felt very much the married lady already.

She had managed to put on her own underwear by the time Dorcas returned with her tea and bread and jam, leaving only her stays to be tied. Her drawers, trimmed with deep French lace, looked very fetching above the white satin wedding boots (which also needed buttoning) and her crinoline frame lay ready, heaped beside her bed. Her chemise, with its matching trim of French lace, drooped on her shoulders and she stood there clutching its front as Dorcas came in and with an ill grace set her breakfast tray on the dressing-table.

'You had better lace me first,' Tilly said, trying to maintain her authority, and standing very straight. Dorcas turned and stared insolently at her for a beat, and for a dreadful moment Tilly was afraid she'd gone too far; but then Dorcas relaxed her shoulders and laughed.

'Oh, what you look like, you poor wretch! Trying to be the madam with me what knows better than anyone what you really are – oh, give over! You don't have to be something you ain't with Dorcas, now, do you? Me as has been your best friend all these dunnamany years! Come here, do. You look like you're afraid the cat'll walk by and gaze at you –'

With expert fingers she started work on the stays, looping the strings through the hooks and tugging and twisting, and slowly Tilly's meagre bosom began to take some sort of shape as the stay busks came together and pushed her chest wall into the fashionable concave shape, until she could hardly breathe, and her breasts lifted poutingly above the French lace; and at last she could let go of her chemise, for it was firmly held in place now. Dorcas tied the strings with a flourish and then set to work on the white satin boots, talking busily all the time.

'Now, you eat your bit of breakfast and then we'll get your hair dealt with. And I've a rabbit's foot and a hint of rouge here – no, don't you fuss. You'll be glad of it before the day's

14

out, take my word for it — and then I'll advise you to take a nip o' daffy. It'll give you a bit of courage, will a drop o' gin, and you'll need it I've no doubt when you see the sort of set-up your Pa's arranged. They've been running around in Ma's kitchen since before dawn, you never saw the like! There're tables set all over the drawing-room as well as the dining-room and your Pa's study, and your Mamma'll be hard put to it to find a place to lay her head if she gets her megrims today. So, you have your daffy and I'll fetch you more if you give me the wink.'

She stopped then and looked up at Tilly, staying crouched at her feet. 'You can trust me, you know, Tilly. I'm your friend, you know that. Who's been your closest and dearest playmate these dozen years and more? Why, I have! You'll not cast me away now you're to be a married lady, will you? It'd not be in your nature and I'd be surprised if your Mr Quentin would admire it in you, for all I'm just a servant —'

Tilly was all remorse at once and reached down and took Dorcas by the shoulders. 'Oh, Dorcas, of course I shan't! It's just that — well, you can be so cruel sometimes —'

'Cruel? Me?' Dorcas got to her feet and began to dust off her skirts. 'I'm not cruel. I just speak as I finds, and I'm honest. If that's a sin, then of course —'

'Oh, no, it's not a sin. But you can be so — well — so *heedless* sometimes, and say such cutting things.'

'Oh, such stuff!' Dorcas said lightly and shook her head and then hugged Tilly roughly. 'You shouldn't be so foolish, missy, and so I tell you! You need to grow a skin or two more to make yourself a little less of a goose. That's what makes your Papa so cross, you know. You shrink away from him and stare at him with those great cow eyes and irritate him beyond measure. If you spoke up for yourself more as you did to Mamma and me — well, let it be. You are as you are, I dare say.' And again she hugged her and then half pushed her, half led her to the chair beside the dressing-table.

'You sit there and brush your hair, now, and eat your

breakfast and I'll make your bed. Who knows who'll be up here afterwards to see you?' Then she giggled. 'Look at it, Tilly – the last haven gone for ever! From now on he owns you, bed and all. You'll be lucky if you get half the sleep you need, looking at your lusty lad! Now let me tell you –'

And she was off, talking in such farmyard terms that Tilly couldn't bear to look at her and buried her face in her tea cup and chewed her sippets of bread as loudly as she could to keep the words out of her ears. But she said nothing to stop her. It was too comfortable to have Dorcas being friendly again to take such risks as that.

By the time the wedding breakfast was only halfway through, Tilly had a most powerful headache. It was partly due to the tightness of her stays – for Dorcas had managed to lace them even more just before putting her into her dress – and partly because of the noise and heat and the fuss of it all.

She had blushed all the way to Holy Trinity Church hard by the corner of the spanking new Ennismore Gardens, which Mr Elgar was building in Brompton New Town, for the workmen who were putting up new houses had shouted at the bridal carriage, and waved their hats and building tools and sent up mocking huzzahs. The church itself had been very hot and full of people, for Papa was a well respected business man, in partnership with so many – including Mr Elgar, the building contractor – and they had all come to see his daughter turned off, and Frank too had many friends with the same ambition. Tilly had stolen glances at them as she had walked slowly up the aisle on her Papa's arm, overawed to see so many dashing and elegantly dressed young men in the first stare of fashion looking at her, and feeling very grateful for the veil which hid her blushes and kept out the dust that made her eyes feel hot and sandy.

She had hardly been aware of the ceremony, so alarmed was she by the need to remember all she had to remember and when she found herself walking back down the aisle on

Frank's arm, she clung to him almost desperately, not sure she could manage to walk all the way out, and that had made her shoulders very tight and painful. And then there had been the rice which stung her now-unveiled cheeks and which Frank's friend had thrown with such abandon, and the squealing of the young ladies who had accompanied so many of Papa's friends, and then Mamma had almost fainted in the crush – oh, it had been dreadful.

And now she sat between Papa and Frank at the long table which had been set up in the drawing-room with its wreaths of smilax and stephanotis, by the great vases of lilies which filled the air with their heavy scent – so heavy it made her head feel quite swimmy – and all she could think of was the steady throbbing in her temples and her aching wish to be out of her stays and lying down somewhere quiet where she could sleep.

She was grateful then for Dorcas. She had been everywhere, ever since they had come back from the church. She had welcomed her back into the house at her Mamma's shoulder as Mrs Leander stood at the front door, very splendid in purple silk and quite out-shining Henrietta Kingsley in her blue taffeta as she greeted every arrival with a glass of champagne wine which had been kept on a block of ice in the cellar this past three days, and then bustled about serving them all with more wine the moment a glass was half empty. And when she had done that, it had been Dorcas who had helped Tilly to her room to cool her burning forehead with lavender water – which she urgently needed to do – and to use her chamber pot – which she had needed even more, with her stays being so tight and all. It had also been Dorcas who had powdered her crimson cheeks with some concoction of her own, thus making her more presentable to her guests, Dorcas who had half carried her downstairs again to take her place beside Frank (who was getting boskier by the minute as he threw back a prodigious quantity of champagne wine) and it was now Dorcas who leaned over and murmured in her ear and pulled back her chair so that she could get to her feet and escape.

Her Papa seemed not to notice her going any more than Frank did, for he was sitting silent over his wine looking as blank eyed as the glass which held it, and clearly perfectly happy to be alone in the midst of the general hubbub, and Tilly leaned on Dorcas and let her lead her away.

One or two of the guests did look at her with some pity, but it didn't seem to matter. Brides were expected to have a fit of tremors on the afternoon of their wedding day; it was, her Mamma had told her on one of those rare occasions when she and Tilly had any sort of conversation, a sign of gentility in a girl to show anxiety as the night of her nuptials approached. Indeed, it would show a sad lack of feeling not to be alarmed, and Dorcas seemed to know just when to allow Tilly her chance to show she had such feelings.

She took her upstairs and with swift fingers took off the veil — now sadly crumpled — and the wedding dress and set them to one side and then released the stays which had been biting more and more cruelly, and Tilly sighed with deep gratitude and lay on her bed as Dorcas, with rare solicitude, drew her curtains and tiptoed away.

She woke suddenly to stare round the room in terror, not sure where she was or why. She knew it was daytime because of the light coming round the edge of the curtains, but she never went to bed in daylight, so why was she here? And then she remembered and took a deep breath of relief. It was her wedding day and she had suffered a dreadful headache — and she lay there for a moment, wondering whether this was the first thing that happened to females when they were married. They got headaches like Mamma. And then sat up gingerly, to test how she felt.

It was wonderful. Her headache had quite vanished and she felt alive and energetic again and to her surprise, remarkably hungry. She had eaten nothing of the wedding breakfast which had been spread before her – again much to onlookers' approval, for brides were supposed to be above such common matters as food – and now her belly rumbled in protest.

She slid out of bed and reached for her silk wrapper which lay over the foot of it and pulled it over her half-unlaced stays, and crept to the door. She needed Dorcas to get her back into her clothes so that she could return to the wedding party, and perhaps find some food; and she pulled on the door gently; not sure what she would do if by any chance any of the guests had found their way upstairs.

Below her she could hear music, for Papa had hired a violinist as well as a lady to play the pianoforte for the dancing, and her spirits lifted even more. It would be very agreeable to dance a little, to be in Frank's arms and whirling round with all of them looking at her and admiring her being Mrs Francis Xavier Quentin. She gazed down the long corridor, which was rather dim, for all the bedroom doors but hers were closed, and wondered how she was to find Dorcas. It would be a waste of time ringing bells, for she would never hear anything in the kitchen above all the hubbub, even if she was there. Perhaps if Tilly crept to the head of the stairs she could peer over and catch the eye of someone friendly who would go and find Dorcas for her. After all, there was nothing strange in a bride wanting the attentions of her maid.

She slipped out of her room and crept towards the stairhead. In her haste she forgot the creaking board that lay outside her door until it gave its usual protesting little squeal and she heard, from inside the empty room that lay alongside her own, someone say sharply, 'Sshh!'

'Wassa matter?' someone else said, and there was a soft giggle and the 'sshh' came again. 'Stop it – Stop it! –'

Tilly froze and tried to think what she had heard. Someone in the empty bedroom? Why? There should be no one there – and again there was laughter, a deep rumbling sound this time, and suddenly Tilly was angry. Guests had no right to be in these rooms. Papa had arranged a very fine party in the drawing-room below and provided lots of extra space on the floor below that in the dining-room and his study. There was no need for strangers to be in this part of the house. And emboldened by her deep awareness of her new status as Mrs Quentin rather than Miss Kingsley, she marched to the door and knocked on it sharply.

'Oh, Christ!' someone hissed behind it and the other person laughed again as the first speaker hissed, 'Hush, you idiot!' It was more than Tilly could bear, and she pushed the door open.

It was not difficult to see what was to be seen, with the late September afternoon light flooding in through the half-drawn curtains.

The big bed in the centre of the red Turkey carpet was piled with blankets and uncovered pillows in heavy striped ticking, but these had been pushed to the back, by the brass bedhead, and Tilly stared at the shiny rails and remembered, absurdly, the day the bed had been delivered. It was after Papa had seen all the new designs at the Great Exhibition four years ago and had decided that his house would be the most fashionable in all Brompton Grove. He had changed the furniture in all the rooms, even the servants', but this one had never been used by a guest or anyone else; so the brass rails were still partly wrapped in calico strips. Tilly stared at them, and then at the piled blankets, anything rather than look at what was happening at the foot of the bed.

But she had to look eventually, and she let her eyes move, painfully and draggingly, till she was staring at the whole scene. Dorcas, lying crossways on the bed with her skirts up around her hips in a ripple of white petticoats, and Frank, his coat and waistcoat on the floor at his feet, kneeling between her parted legs and fiddling with his trouser buttons.

There was silence and then Dorcas, who had been peering at Tilly between the bars of the foot of the bed with her eyes bright and mocking, said, 'No need to look like that, Tilly! You've lost nothing, take it from me – the man's too far gone in his cups to be of any use to anyone! This is how they are, Tilly, my little friend. You wore pearls to be wed in, and pearls is tears — which is what comes to all who wed. You might as well be used to it sooner as later.'

Chapter Two

BEING MRS FRANCIS QUENTIN was not, Tilly discovered, any better than being Miss Matilda Kingsley, though it was sometimes more tedious, if that were possible. In the old days she had at least been able to slip away on her own to hide with a novel and a bag of apples filched from the kitchens to dream the dull hours away and re-emerge composed and better able to deal with Mrs Leander and Dorcas. In the old days when things had gone wrong, Papa had blamed Mamma, shouting at her about domestic disasters and bad dinners, but now he shouted at Tilly, telling her she was a married woman now and must take up her responsibilities. In the old days there had sometimes been outings with other young ladies and visits to other people's daughters; but now she was Mrs Quentin her calls had to be more formal, and much, much more dull. It was altogether wretched, because of course there was also Frank.

She did occasionally allow herself to wonder if things would have been different if she hadn't found him with Dorcas on the afternoon of their wedding day. Would she have enjoyed the excitement of the train journey to Brighton for their honeymoon, happy to be going to her Frank's arms, instead of spending it in tears, to his embarrassed fury? Would she have shared his bed in their boarding house overlooking the sea with gladness and pleasure instead of lying curled up into as small a ball as she could, terrified of his approach? She still shuddered when the memory of that dreadful week came back to her, as it often did in great waves of unbidden, unwanted images, so vivid that it was like reliving the whole experience. He had been annoyed that first night, she knew, but had tolerated her weeping fearfulness as probably inevitable; she was, after all, a carefully reared young lady, and such persons were expected to find the necessities of the marriage bed distasteful. When, however, her shrinking behaviour continued for the next three nights, despite any amount of cajolery and pleading, his patience had snapped, and he had stamped out of the boarding house in a rage to go to an alehouse in the rougher part of town where he became morose and even more angry on copious draughts of rough brandy.

That had been the cause of his dreadful behaviour upon his return, she had tried to tell herself ever since. He had insisted on his husbandly rights, hurling himself on to her with the stumbling heaviness of an enamoured bull, forcing her legs apart and his own body into her in a way that had hurt excruciatingly. She had been left bleeding, burning with deep pain yet with her muscles half-numbed, half-leaping with pins and needles, and wept herself to hiccoughing sleep; and he had regarded that as acceptance on her part, and had tried again and again in the succeeding days of their honeymoon, leaving her dull with misery and unable to resist.

However, it wasn't just because he had come to her drunk on brandy that she had found those first experiences so dreadful. It was the way, again, that her memory had been triggered. Would it all have been better, she asked herself miserably, if he had been more patient, more loverlike, as he had been in the days of their engagement? Could she have responded more happily if she hadn't had that vision of Dorcas in her froth of petticoat frills, peering at her between calico-wrapped bed rails, to torment her? Silly questions, all of them, because the truth was as it was; from the start their married life had been a disaster. She hated his touch, hated his brandied breath on her cheeks, hated the taste of his tongue thrust into her mouth, and above all she hated the cruel invasion of her body by his, finding no joy at all, but only pain and shame and blood and disgust in something that had once been so agreeable to imagine and dream over.

Perhaps if she had tried speak to him of what she had seen in that unused bedroom they might have resolved their differences, but she had not been able to put her hurt into words, and could never say Dorcas's name to him; and he for his part acted as though nothing untoward had happened. He behaved as though *he* were the wronged party, deprived of his husbandly rights by a missish wife who should know better, and became permanently changed. The young admirer who had been such a cheerful and attractive fiancé became a morose and sulky husband. The evenings he used to spend laughing and joking with Papa as she and her Mamma sat contentedly watching them had gone for ever. Now Frank sulked in his dressing-room, on the rare occasions, that is, that he was in the house in Brompton Grove. Mostly he went out and that made Papa curse and shout at him, roaring that he saw no reason why the man should treat his house like an hotel; at which Frank would roar back, 'You know perfectly well I had rather have my own establishment. It's you who are too mean to pay up as you promised and enable me to take your daughter away from here! It is your own fault if you object to my being here – you know the remedy!' And out he would go, slamming the door and making Papa even louder and angrier – oh, it was no wonder Mamma never ventured out of her room these days. No wonder that she drank ever more daffy and sometimes sherry wine and became pinker and moister and more glassy-eyed and – well, generally more useless. Tilly had never felt so alone in all her life as she did now she was Mrs Francis Xavier Quentin.

It was not that she minded Papa's assumption that she would take over the running of the household now that Mamma was an invalid (which was the polite way everyone spoke of her these days). In fact she would have enjoyed doing so, and often read books on household economy and cookery in order to instruct herself against the day when she would at last be free to run her own home as she would wish. She wanted her own house as much as Frank did, but knew better than to discuss the possibility with either her husband or her father; but she hoped all the same, and planned for it. It would have given her much satisfaction to go to the kitchen and order the dinners, and to check the household books to see that money was being spent economically, but there was no hope that she would ever be able to do that while Mrs Leander held sway.

It was Mrs Leander who employed the cook and the housemaids, she who gave the orders for dinners and dealt with the tradesmen, she who supervised the cleanliness of the house.

'What else is a housekeeper for?' she had said firmly on the first and only occasion Tilly tried to involve herself in the running of the house. 'You go and do your sewing, Madam —' (and she put an insulting emphasis on the word 'Madam' that made Tilly's cheeks redden) '— and leave the rest to me.'

Tilly had tried to explain to Papa that she could not run the house as she wished because of Mrs Leander, but that made him shout again and indeed become quite purple with fury, and she still hadn't the ability to stand up to him, and doubted she ever would; and so gave up trying. So her days were spent in lonely solitude nodding over the interminable making of lace-trimmed nightgowns and chemises for herself (she already had enough to last her for years) and her evenings in trying not to think about what Frank might be doing.

For although she found no pleasure in the core of her marriage, she was determined to be happy in every other way if she could. She longed to go about on visits with her handsome young husband and preen under the eyes of the still unmarried girls who were once her friends, and had started out with great hopes of one day being able to do so; but as the weeks pleated into months and Christmas came and went and the year turned into 1856 in a flurry of bitter weather, she was forced to realize that her chances of persuading Frank ever to live the sort of life she wanted were very slender indeed.

Even when the snow and ice lay thick in the streets of Brompton and veiled the rawness of the many building sites that littered Knightsbridge and the land in between, as London's suburbs crept ever westwards, Frank went out. He belonged to a club in a small street off Belgrave Square at which he spent much of his time, and Tilly had rapidly learned not to speak of being neglected for its greater attractions. He was very direct with her when she asked him to stay at home in the evenings sometimes to keep her company.

'It's no use your complaining to me,' he said, sitting in the small armchair in his dressing-room to which she had followed him when he went up to dress to go out. 'If there was any pleasure to be found in staying here, you may be assured that stay I would. But I have no wish to sit and watch your Papa get bosky and then go wandering off to the housekeeper's bed, and —'

'Frank!' Tilly cried, scandalized, her face scarlet with shame, but he would have none of that.

'Oh, don't come the milk-and-water missy with me, Madam!' He bent to pull on his boots, and for a moment she considered kneeling down to help him but then thought better of it. He was much too red-faced and irritable to risk that. 'Your Papa is a libertine and should be disgusted with himself. He uses that woman shamelessly — do you hear me? Shamelessly. A man may have mistresses and welcome as far as I am concerned —' He had looked at her sharply for a moment and then let his glance slide away. '— But he should show some discretion! To use one of his own servants and under his own roof . . .' He shook his head in revulsion and got to his feet to start buttoning his shirt and collar before arranging his cravat in careful folds.

'It's the outside of enough. It disgusts me,' he went on with a great air of virtue, 'to have to live in the same house as such a one. Had he kept his word and paid over the sums he promised me on my marriage to you, we'd have a house of our own and you would have less cause to complain.'

He stopped then and turned and looked down at her as she stood in her usual nervous way just inside the dressing-room door. 'Oh, Tilly, I am as sorry as I dare say you are that things are not — not all they might be for us.' He hesitated and waited as though he expected something and she thought briefly of moving forwards and putting her arms about him, and wondered what would happen if she did; but she let her gaze at his face slip away this time, and looked down at her feet instead; and after a moment he went on brusquely, 'But until we have our own home I see no help for it but to be out and about my own affairs as much as I may be. If you object, then don't complain to me. Tell your father. Or send him a message via your Mrs Leander.'

And he shrugged on his coat and pushed out of the room past her and went thumping down the stairs. She stood in the doorway and heard Papa's voice rumbling as he came out of his study and saw Frank, and heard Frank snap back at him and decided that she would be like Mamma tonight and remain in her room with a megrim. She had no headache yet, but she would be sure to get one if she went downstairs and spent any time with Papa.

She went to bed at nine o'clock, having by this time a very thorough-going headache indeed, and cried herself to sleep. There didn't seem anything else she could do.

By the time the snow and ice at last melted into a muddy spring and the first crocuses were showing in the raw earth that lay around Mr Elgar's new streets and terraces, it was March, and Tilly had become as accustomed as it was possible to be to life as Mrs Quentin.

She spent her mornings with her Mamma, who lay most of the time half asleep, or at best muttering to herself. Tilly had long ago given up trying to prevent her from drinking; she became alarmingly distressed if she was forbidden her much-loved daffy and Tilly had not the heart to sit and watch her weep and tear at her hair as she did when it was withheld. All she could do was give her glassfuls with as much water and as little gin as she possibly could, though Henrietta always knew when it had been diluted and fussed dreadfully until her glass had been topped up from the gin bottle. Tilly would then watch her until she fell asleep, which she did fairly soon, to snore stertorously until roused at noon. Then, with gentle insistence, Tilly would make her eat some luncheon, though she rarely took more than a little soup and bread.

It was pitiful to see her so, but Tilly hardly noticed any more. The once fair and pretty hair had faded to a thin and colourless single layer through which the scalp shone dingily and her skin had taken on the slightly bluish tinge of the habitual gin drinker, but there was no one but Tilly to see it, for no one came near her these days. Austen Kingsley certainly did not, having given up any pretence of being any sort of husband. He spent most of his free time in Mrs Leander's cosy room below stairs when he was not out and about his own affairs, about which Tilly knew remarkably little, for he was a secretive man and never spoke of his business interests. Mrs Leander didn't go to Henrietta's room either, only sending one of the most junior maids to give it a cursory cleaning from time to time, which meant that only Tilly cared at all for Henrietta's well-being, and she could do little to help her mother apart from allowing her to have her gin.

She would watch her sleeping and worry about that; should she be stronger with her, tell her she may not have it? Should she fetch the apothecary and see if he could help her to get better? But Tilly shrank from even considering that; Papa had shouted amazingly when she suggested it once before, saying he was not going to be shamed all over the town by gossip about his drunkard wife; that Tilly should be ashamed to suggest such an exposure of her own mother to the calumny and disgust which would surely be theirs if any outsider saw her and discovered how deep her habit ran.

Tilly had seen at once what he meant, for the apothecary, the only one in Brompton with whom her father had not quarrelled, was famous for being a dreadful gossip. No, it would never do to call in Mr Fildes; so she did nothing. There was nothing she could do. But she felt ashamed of her uselessness.

The afternoons were not quite so bad; Henrietta was contented enough in the afternoons to sit alone, sleeping lightly from time to time, but mostly with a book on her lap, and Tilly could escape to be alone, which she had actually come to enjoy. It was better to retreat into her daydreams over her sewing than to do anything else, and so she would sit most afternoons until it was time for dinner.

On the last day of March the weather was seasonably windy and the air had a breath of freshness in it that had warmed Tilly's feelings a little, and she came back from an afternoon walk with her cheeks tingling and a new sense of hope in her. She did not know why, but it was there, and it felt good. Perhaps it was the way the builders had been so jolly as she had picked her way over the mud-streaked pavements, and had called after her about the good news about the War. Everyone knew that the Crimean adventure was over and done with at last, and the soldiers, such as had survived, could come home again from the horrors of Sebastopol and Bala-clava. Perhaps it was that Papa had been unusually quiet this morning at breakfast, and not complained about anything; and even Mrs Leander who had been quiet even when Tilly suggested she send someone up to clean her Mamma's room thoroughly, for it was showing the signs of winter grime in the thin spring sunshine. Or maybe it was the fact that last night Frank had come to her bed and she had managed to tolerate his attentions without letting him see, as she had so often in the past, how much she disliked them. In fact, she had not disliked them nearly as much as she usually did; it had not hurt and that had helped, and he had not been quite so filled with brandy fumes as he usually was, and that too had been a blessing. Tilly had allowed him to do all he wanted without once crying out, and so she was pleased with herself. All of which added up to a general sense of well-being as agreeable as it was rare.

She put away her pelisse and bonnet in her room and then looked round her Mamma's door, as she usually did, to see her sleeping quietly and comfortably and without that deep heavy breathing that was so distressing, and that helped strengthen Tilly's happy mood and when she went downstairs in search of tea and some cake, for the wind had sharpened her appetite, she was actually humming under her breath. Life was not so dreadful after all, and soon it would be her birthday and perhaps Frank would take her out for it. It was a possibility and one to look forward to.

She settled herself in the morning room – she hardly ever used the drawing-room these days, for few people came to call; not surprising as she herself so hated paying formal calls that she never did if she could avoid it, and therefore of course no one called on her – and rang the bell. She would ask little Eliza for tea and settle down to reading a new novel she had borrowed from Mudie's; that would be a treat on a cheerful day like today.

The answer to her ring sent all her fragile contentment spinning away in shards. She lifted her head as the door opened and felt her face stiffen with anger and surprise, for it was Dorcas who stood there, looking at her with expressionless eyes.

Tilly had not seen Dorcas for several weeks. In the early days after her wedding Dorcas had tried to carry on as though nothing had happened, as though she had never been caught in a spare bedroom with her mistress's bridegroom, but Tilly was having none of that. Frightened of her father and of Mrs Leander she may be, and easily alarmed by Dorcas's sharp tongue, but she was not going to tolerate any sort of insult from her ever again. To Tilly it was as though Dorcas was

30

invisible; and so it had been all these months. She would pass her in the hall, on the rare occasions she saw her, and ignore her totally. If Dorcas spoke to her, she behaved as though not a sound had entered her ears. It had been a masterly performance and it had worked very well. Long before winter had set in Dorcas had seen that Tilly was not in a forgiving state of mind and had given up. She had disappeared, in fact, from view, and Tilly assumed that she lived the life of a lady of leisure below stairs, with her mother. Certainly she was no longer one of the housemaids. New ones appeared to take over the care of the house and, as far as Tilly was concerned, that had been that regarding Dorcas.

Until now. Sitting with her back very straight and her hands folded on her brown taffeta skirts she stared at Dorcas, too surprised to treat her with the icy indifference she usually offered.

Tilly noticed at once that Dorcas looked older and that pleased her. Her face was pale and rather thinner than it had been, with no dimples to be seen, and her curly hair, once so carefully dressed, was lacklustre and lay on her shoulders in a way that once would have been attractive but now looked merely unkempt. She was wearing a gown of dark green merino with white collar and cuffs but they looked crumpled and a little grimy, and Tilly felt her brows close in a sharp frown. Dorcas looked ill; but then she pushed down the wave of concern that had, to her surprise, risen in her. Why should she care about Dorcas, ill or well?

'I have to speak to you,' Dorcas said gruffly and closed the door behind her. At once Tilly lifted her book and opened it at random and bent her head and purported to read. But it made no difference. Dorcas ran across the room and almost collapsed at her feet in a rustle of skirts and tugged the book from her grasp. 'Oh, don't behave so, please! I have to talk to you. This is no time for old grudges — you must forget the past and hear what I have to ask you —'

Tilly had not meant to speak but the words came out in a

splutter of indignation. 'Forget the past? Old grudges? You behave like a – like a street drab and you tell me I must forget the past and – and –'

'Oh, Tilly, do be quiet and listen to me! I have so little time! She'll be here and will – oh, she's done enough! *Look*, will you!' She pulled at her grimy collar and it opened at her throat and she dragged back the fabric to expose her neck and upper chest. 'See what she did when she – oh, do be quick and listen or she'll be here and then heaven help me!'

Tilly stared at Dorcas's skin, appalled. There were vivid blue bruises there, and long red lines of scratches and she put both hands to her head in horror. 'You – what happened?'

'She –' Dorcas jerked her head at the door and both knew she meant her mother. 'She did it. She found out – Tilly, you must help me! I have to get away, somehow, but I have no money and –'

'But Dorcas –' Tilly shook her head, dazed. It was as though the silence of the past months had never happened, as though the two of them were conspiring again as they had as children, though in those days it had always been Tilly begging Dorcas to help her. 'What can I do to help you? You are the one who knows everything and can do everything –'

'Except what I want to do.' Dorcas was bitter. Her voice was thick with it. 'If I do as she wants, then I am all that is good. If I don't – you know what she is –'

'But how can I help you? I have no –'

'You have money, though, haven't you? Now that you're married. You must have money, especially as you live here and don't have the expense of your own establishment.'

Tilly felt her face smooth out with the shame of it; she tried to sound as expressionless as she could. 'I have no money of my own,' she said, after a moment. 'If I need anything, I have to ask Frank or Papa.'

'Well, your Mamma has,' Dorcas said urgently and got to her feet and went back to the door to listen for sounds from the house beyond. 'Hasn't she? Where do you get her gin if not with her own money? Can you not let me have some of that?'

'I get the gin from the dining-room,' Tilly said with what dignity she could gather around her, ashamed to admit she was stealing it for her mother, ashamed to admit her mother demanded it. 'The only female in this house who has any money to handle is your Mamma, as far as I can see. Even the maids are better off than I, I imagine, in that they can put their hands on their own wages. I don't even have that.'

'Oh, God!' Dorcas said and closed her eyes. 'Oh, God, what shall I do? What shall I *do*?'

Tilly sat and stared at her. She had never heard Dorcas so despairing, had never seen her so woebegone and bedraggled, and the anger and ice of the past months melted out of her until all she could remember was the time when she was small, when Dorcas had been the centre of her life; unpredictable, often bad tempered, sometimes cruel, but at least alive and interested and knowing as no one else did that Tilly too was a person with feelings and dreams and ideas. It was almost more than she could bear to see her so unhappy and she got to her feet and hurried over to her and put her arms about her.

'Oh, Dorcas. I'll do what I can, I promise. I will try to get some money. What do you need? How much? And how soon, and –'

There were footsteps outside and then the door handle rattled and Dorcas's eyes dilated with terror, and for Tilly the last vestiges of doubt about Dorcas melted away. Whatever she had done to Tilly in the past, she was a fearful person now and that was something Tilly understood very well. And could deal with.

She pushed Dorcas sharply so that she was back against the wall behind the door, and then pulled it wide to stand firmly in the opening with her hands folded against her skirts and the crinoline of her afternoon gown more than filling the space. Anyone trying to get into the room would have to push past her boldly; and Tilly was in no mood to be pushed aside.

Mrs Leander stood staring at her with eyes as black and round as boot buttons, and she moved forwards as the door opened and said smoothly, 'You rang, Mrs Quentin?'

Tilly didn't move though Mrs Leander was standing very close to her now, her sharp eyes peering around behind Tilly, trying to see into the room. 'Indeed I did, Mrs Leander. You will fetch me some tea, if you please, and some of the cake that Cook sent up yesterday afternoon. I found it agreeable. At once, if you please.'

'Tea?' Mrs Leander said and moved closer still, trying to make Tilly give way. But she didn't, even though the woman's face was so close to her that she could feel her breath hot on her face – an unpleasant sensation.

'Tea,' Tilly said firmly and reached behind her and took the doorknob in her hand and tugged. Then she stepped back sharply and closed the door in Mrs Leander's face, calling loudly as the latch clicked down. 'At once, if you please.'

And then she turned back to Dorcas and helped her to her feet, for she was crouching down behind the door, and half pulled her, half led her to the window that looked out of the morning room into the garden.

'Out you go,' she said urgently. 'Go on. I'll be in my room after I've had the tea – come to me there as soon as you like. We'll sort something out for you. But you'll have to tell me all the whys and wherefores, you understand. But be on your way now – quickly. Leave your mother to me. I'll deal with her.'

As Dorcas obeyed, startled but silent, Tilly went back to her chair feeling remarkably pleased with herself. Whatever Dorcas's problem might be, one thing was sure; because of it Tilly had been given the strength to stand up to Mrs Leander in a remarkable way, and for that alone Dorcas could be forgiven almost anything.

Chapter Three

TILLY ACCEPTED WITH equanimity her tea and cake from the housemaid sent by Mrs Leander and enjoyed it, taking her time, before making her way out of the room. She was aware as she walked across the hallway that Mrs Leander was standing in the shadows beside the green baize door that led down to the servants' quarters, watching her, but she pretended she didn't know, and hummed softly to herself as she went; and then, on an impulse, stopped beside the occasional table at the foot of the stairs and ran a housewifely finger along the edge of the rosewood. She looked at the dust on her finger and then at the track left on the table and shook her head and sighed in exasperation; and went on her way, smiling to herself at the anger she was sure she had left behind her, and went into the dining-room and closed the door.

Once inside she stood and listened a little breathlessly, then, feeling ashamed of the guile but quite determined none the less, bent and looked out through the keyhole to the hall beyond.

She heard Mrs Leander's heels clack on the black and white tiles of the floor, and watched her come into view, and stop by the occasional table. Then Tilly wanted to laugh aloud, and had to cram her fist between her teeth to prevent it, for Mrs Leander took her handkerchief from her pocket, and with deft, angry movements dusted the table and each of the gewgaws on it.

'I won!' thought Tilly gleefully, as happy as though she had won a vast wager, and listened as Mrs Leander clacked away to the baize door and beyond, leaving the hall silent and empty.

Tilly straightened and looked about her at the heavy mahogany furniture, also a little filmed with dust, and the great sideboard with its many cupboards and drawers, and after a little more thought, moved purposefully towards it. There were things she had to consider before she went upstairs to Dorcas, who anyway needed time to return to the house from the garden and thence upstairs, without her mother seeing her.

Ten minutes later, Tilly went quietly upstairs to her room, so quietly that Dorcas nearly jumped out of her skin in terror as Tilly closed the door behind her. That made her marvel a little. Fearless, outrageous, brave Dorcas to behave so? What had happened to her to make her so anxious? And she looked at the other woman huddled at the foot of her bed with a combination of pity and concern and triumph and revenge that made her feel as though her chest would swell up and burst out of her gown; it was an exhilarating sensation, if a touch shaming.

'Well now, Dorcas,' she said and sat down tidily on the small round chair that stood at the foot of her bed. 'You had better tell me all about it. First of all, why have you no money of your own? You've been paid wages all these years, I imagine? And have few expenses, living here —'

Dorcas looked at her sharply and for a moment the old edge was there in her glance, but then she looked away, and shook her head. 'Oh, I got some wages, I suppose. Not much — your father's no fool when it comes to hard cash — but I like pretty clothes and there was none coming the usual way —'

'The usual way?'

'Other ladies' maids get hand-me-downs from their mistresses,' Dorcas said with a flash of spite. 'You never gave me nothing — not so much as a kerchief.'

36

'I couldn't,' Tilly said with what dignity she could. 'You said yourself my father's hard with cash. I have few clothes, and what I have I need —'

'Well, anyway, I spent what I got, and there's an end of it. I've not a penny behind me now when I need it — say you'll help me, Tilly. Just five pounds is all —'

'Five *pounds*?' Tilly's voice rose to a squeak. 'But that is a vast sum! What can you want with so much?'

'To get married, that's what. I've done the computations very carefully, and I'll never get Walter turned off without a bit of a blowout and —'

'Walter? A blowout?' Tilly frowned suddenly. 'Are you asking me to provide for a party of some kind, Dorcas? For if that is the case I have to say —'

'Oh, please *listen!*' Dorcas curled up again into the small huddle she had been in when Tilly came into the room, seeming to find comfort in the posture. 'It's much more than that —'

'I'm listening,' Tilly said and folded her hands on her lap in her favourite pose.

'It's Mamma — she wants me to marry well,' Dorcas said. 'It's what she's always said, "Money's money, my girl, and don't you forget it." And the only way to get it, she reckons, is on your back. Women don't get no other chances, after all. You never saw a woman yet with a business of her own except what she got from under her pillow in the marriage bed, did you? No. Ma always wanted to have her own public house, you know. A superior kind, in a decent district, none of your nasty alehouses, but my father was useless and would not help her to it. Indeed —'

Tilly was startled. She had never considered the possibility of Dorcas having a father. Mrs Leander was so powerful that it had never occurred to Tilly that she wasn't capable of producing a daughter without help from any mere man. But obviously there had to have been a Mr Leander once.

'— my father brought her nothing but trouble and debt,'

Dorcas was saying. 'She thought he had money, for he came of a good family but he was a younger son and anyway they didn't like Ma and that was that. He disappeared before I was born and there she was with just her wits to keep us. And she told me as soon as I could hear the words and make sense of 'em that I was to wed money, for she had not managed it and since no one of fortune would have a woman with a brat in tow, it was my duty to her as had borne me and raised me –' Dorcas sighed suddenly, a deep intake of breath that made her whole body seem to swell, not just her lungs. 'And I saw the sense of it, I swear I did. I'd set my sights on a better life than we had – I turned away a dunnamany likely lads, for they weren't good enough. Not a penny between them, apprentices and so forth. Any worthwhile ones were soon taken up by the likes of your father seeking matches for their daughters.' She peeped sideways at Tilly, but then buried her head again and went on quickly, 'I wanted a man of substance – and then –' Again that huge sighing breath shook her, '– well, I got one. Walter Oliver's a big man, a lot of substance there –' And she managed a sort of giggle that became a sob almost at once. 'Past six feet and with shoulders like one of Mr Spurgeon's best oxen. All beef, my Walter –'

'But not a rich man,' Tilly said.

'Rich? And him a soldier? No, he's not rich. But he's beautiful. Oh, you should see him in his regimentals, Tilly! He throws your Frank into the shade entirely.'

Tilly stiffened, hearing the spiteful tones of a much younger Dorcas teasing her about her dolls, but Dorcas seemed unaware of her reaction and went on, almost dreamily.

'As handsome and exciting a man as ever stepped. I never thought I'd be so milk-and-waterish as to fall in love, but I did, Tilly, oh I did – I saw him in the park, by where the Crystal Palace was – back when your Ma used to be took out in her Bath chair, after she had that fall and broke her leg, and I used to push her there on sunny mornings. It was a wicked long walk, and she as heavy as lead and whining all the way, but it

was worth it. I saw Walter with all the other guardsmen and –'
Dorcas sat up, holding the bedpost '– it was wonderful. All
those nights when we met, and the parties at the Barracks and
all. Wonderful – and you sitting here at home being the high-
up married lady, and me having all that fun and – well, it
helped. I felt so left out when you wed.'

'Left *out*?' Tilly was agape at her. 'You felt –' She stopped,
unable to find another word.

'Well, so I did.' Dorcas was gazing at her now. 'I had no
one to talk to and laugh with any more, once you were wed.
But I found my Walter. And we were so happy. Until –' Her
eyes glinted with tears, or seemed to. 'And then he had to go
away to the war, and I cried bitterly. I thought he would be
killed but he came home after the fall of Sebastopol, injured,
you understand, but safe. He has the most romantic limp and
is still my dear handsome – oh, Tilly, what shall I do if he
won't have me? I shall have to spend the rest of my days like
Ma, putting up with the sort of life she does with your Pa,
and I couldn't bear it, for he treats her so dirty and evil –'

Tilly found it hard enough to accept Dorcas's view of
herself as abandoned by Tilly on the occasion of her marriage,
but this new tack erased all consideration of that from her
mind. She went cold, staring blankly at Dorcas, who suddenly
seemed aware of the impact of her words and stopped. Dorcas
then said awkwardly, 'Well, it must come as no surprise to
you – he is not a – well, he behaves as gentlemen do, I
suppose, only a deal rougher than some.'

'Rougher?' Tilly said in a small voice and Dorcas lifted her
brows at her, almost irritably.

'Oh, come, Tilly, I know you are a soft, silly creature and
can't see what's in front of your eyes half the time, but why
do you think your Ma's the way she is? There was no other
way out of the strange practices and the hateful things he
demands as far as she was concerned, but to pickle herself.
And it worked for her, for he has such disgust for her now
that he uses my Ma instead. But she is made of harder stuff

39

and can deal with him. Though I've heard and seen a few things –' Her voice hardened. 'And I shan't be like that, I *shan't*. No man shall use me in such a manner! Not even to wed a rich man would I bear it. And I can make a rich man of my Walter, I swear to you, once we're wed. Only get him wed I must, and soon, before he realizes and takes fright –'

'Realizes what?' Tilly whispered, seizing on the question, needing to ask something, anything, to take her mind away from what Dorcas had said about her father, and what was happening inside her head. What had he done to her Mamma to make her as she was? And what did he do to Mrs Leander and – she swallowed and said again in a louder voice, 'Realizes what?'

'That I'm knocked up,' Dorcas said, her voice muffled, for she had curled herself into a ball again. 'That I'm in the pudden club. He'll run a country mile if he knows that, for all it's his.'

'Pudden –' Tilly said and Dorcas let out a sudden whoop of laughter.

'Christ, but you're green! Increasing, you idiot! With child.' And she sat bolt upright and smote her belly hard. 'I've got a brat in here, God help me, and unless I'm safely wed this month and no later, I'm in the gutter for sure, for not even the bloody Hearne would have me – and before you ask, he's the man Ma's picked out for me and I'll not have him for all his gelt. I'd rather work myself to death to make my Walter rich than take on a fifty-year-old death's head like him.'

Tilly sat silently, trying to understand and to think at the same time. She felt much older, suddenly, as though she had put on years between coming into the room and this moment, and she could not be quite sure what had made her feel so. Dorcas's pleading need of her had to be part of it and was enough to upset her equanimity, of course, but it was more than that. She felt now the old married woman in a way she never had, and she tried to push away her growing awareness of why that should be.

40

But now she knew. She had always feared her father for his loudness and roughness but had thought it was no more than that. Now, however, there was something else pushing at her memory, somewhere deep inside her, a place she had locked up and never visited again; Dorcas's words about the way her father had used her mother and Mrs Leander were shaking the padlocks she had set on her secret place. It was the dream she had so often, the memory dream in which she sat under the table in Mamma's boudoir and listened to Papa shouting, until he came and found her under the cloth. In the past when the dream came at night that moment had been followed by blackness and her waking, but now the blackness was thinning and there were shadowy movements in it, and she didn't want to see those movements or even think about them, she didn't, she didn't, she —

She took a long shaky breath and said carefully, 'So. You need five pounds.'

Dorcas sat up sharply and gazed at her. Her face was flushed and that gave her back some of her old beauty, and in the late afternoon light her bedraggled hair and clothes softened and looked better, almost seductive. It could have been the old Dorcas who looked hopefully at Tilly, but it was the new Tilly who looked back, waiting. She was holding on to herself very tightly, for fear she would weep; 'yet why should I weep?' she asked herself in the secret recesses of her mind. 'Why should I, when it is Dorcas who is in trouble, not I?'

The control held, to her deep gratitude, and went on holding as Dorcas scrambled off the bed and came to crouch at Tilly's feet to hold on to both her hands and look up at her pleadingly.

'Say you will help me, dearest Tilly. Say you can give me the money I need. I can't say when I will give it back but one day I will, I swear it. Just get me out of this tangle now, I beg you, so that I may be married to Walter and start our new life, and as soon as I am able to repay you, I will, truly I will — only I beg you —'

41

'I can give you no cash,' Tilly said calmly and pulled on the string of her reticule, which was attached to the waist of her gown. 'But I think you may raise what you need with these. I can't say if they're worth five pounds of course, but – well, if not, we must think again.'

With remarkably steady fingers Tilly pulled the reticule strings open and turned it over on to her brown taffeta lap to spill a little shower of silver and colour; the set of twelve enamelled silver teaspoons her mother had once told Tilly were her favourite wedding present. She had collected them from the dining-room on her way upstairs.

'They came all the way from St Petersburg in Russia and are worth a great deal of money,' her Mamma had said, turning them lovingly in her hand. 'My Uncle Patterson gave them to me and told me they were worth much money and would be a useful standby for me. But I would not sell them for the world. They will be yours one day when you are a bride –' And Mamma had bent and kissed small Tilly, let her touch them and stroke the jewelled colours, the red and green and blue and purple and yellow that adorned each of the handles and the backs of the bowls. The inner parts of the bowls were yellowed with tarnish now, though Tilly remembered them being sparkling silver, but that didn't matter. It did not affect their value, and she held them out to Dorcas in both hands.

'If you take them to a jeweller well away from Brompton – in town perhaps – you should be able to get a good price for them,' she said in a steady voice. 'Mamma will never know they have gone. And she told me they would be mine one day. So I have but taken them a little sooner.'

Dorcas looked down at the spoons with calculating eyes and then took one and turned it over to peer at the reverse of the bowl, and after a moment got to her feet and carried it to the window where the failing light was strongest. After a while she came back and nodded and took the rest of the spoons from Tilly's hands.

'Thank you, Tilly. It's a help — I'll go now into town and see what I can get for them — and if it's not enough then perhaps you will find me something else. There are always your Ma's pearls — the ones you wore on your wedding day —'

'No!' Tilly flared and reached for the spoons, suddenly regretting her action, but Dorcas had already tucked them into the hidden pocket in the skirt of her merino gown and they were not to be seen, let alone touched. 'No — those are — I will never sell them. But there is some other silver that is never used as far as I can tell.'

Dorcas was standing by the door now, pulling her gown straight and running her fingers through her matted hair as she set her untidy cap straight on it. She was all business now, practical, cool and not at all the sodden frightened heap she had been, and Tilly sat and stared at her and confused feelings were again tangled inside her. The pity had gone, for there was nothing pitiable about Dorcas now, and so had the concern, for once again Dorcas seemed in full control of herself. As for the triumph — that had a hollow ring, now Tilly thought about it, and she felt flat and a little sick as she watched Dorcas rearrange her appearance.

'I need to slip out quietly,' Dorcas said. 'Lend me a cloak, dearest Tilly —' and without waiting for an answer she was across the room digging into Tilly's big press, and was pulling out one of her dark stuff cloaks, one with a wide hood inside which she could easily hide her head and face as well.

She came back to Tilly and again crouched at her feet, staring up at the still white face above her. 'I'm truly grateful, Tilly. You mustn't think, because I have ceased weeping, that I have ceased fearing and feeling. You always were much too beguiled by surface appearances — I can imagine you now thinking I am ungrateful, for I am in such haste to be gone, but I am not. You will see — I will always stand your friend. As you have mine. Believe me.' She reached up and kissed

Tilly's cheek and hugged her briefly, and then went, closing the door behind her so softly that no one could have known anyone had left the room at all.

Chapter Four

TILLY'S FIRST THOUGHT when she woke after a restless, dream-haunted night, was the spoons. She lay with her eyes still closed against the early spring sunshine that poured in through her window and saw them against the orange glow there behind her lids, vivid in their rich colours, with the delicate ribbed traces that highlighted the perfect enamel work of the handles and the backs of the bowls, and regretted their loss as keenly as she had ever regretted anything. Even, she remembered suddenly, as much as the loss of her doll Charlotte. When she had been eleven, Mrs Leander had pronounced her to be an insanitary rag and thrown her on the kitchen fire. Why had she done it? Why, oh why had she parted with her Mamma's precious spoons, her own precious spoons come to that, for weren't they her promised inheritance?

The anger lifted in her and she snapped open her eyes and sat up sharply with her arms round her bent knees and her eyes fixed unseeingly on the dead grate of her fireplace where last night's ashes lay cold and cheerless. *Why on earth had she done it?* what had possessed her to give so special a possession to Dorcas, of all people?

She shivered involuntarily as she tried to answer her own question; realized how cold she was now that her arms were outside the bedclothes and frowned. Her bedside clock announced that it was past eight o'clock; the housemaid should have come long ago to light her fire so that she could dress in decent comfort. It was all due to Mrs Leander's laziness that the girls who worked under her neglected their duties so sorely and Tilly, luxuriating in the anger which had started with the spoons and now encompassed cold arms and a dread of having to expose the rest of her shrinking body to the cold air of her distinctly uninviting bedroom, reached across and seized her bell pull and tugged hard.

She couldn't hear it pealing far below in the kitchen, of course, but she could imagine the third bell from the left in the second row on the board above the back door dancing and jangling on the end of the complicated series of loops and ropes that connected it to her bedroom. She could imagine Mrs Leander looking up at it from her favourite place beside the fire in her little sitting room, from which she had an excellent view of the whole of the kitchen, and ignoring it; and that made her angrier than ever and she tugged even harder and went on tugging until she was sure the bell below stairs was dancing in an ecstasy of constant movement. She should not ignore her. She could not!

She was still tugging in rage when the door opened and Eliza the housemaid peered in, her face flushed and dirt-smeared, and her cap askew. Eliza stood there gaping at her and Tilly, who hardly ever raised her voice, opened her mouth and let out a shriek of fury with all the strength she had in her. It felt wonderful.

The girl gawped at her and her face crumpled and that added fuel to the flames for Tilly. She was not used to having people stare at her with fear-twisted faces and brimming eyes, and she was amazed at how much she liked it, and she shouted more loudly than ever as the girl stood and shook her head, openly crying now.

The tide of fury ebbed away as fast as it had risen and Tilly stopped and looked at the girl who gulped and looked fearfully back at her, and suddenly felt a wave of shame.

'Oh, Eliza, I did not mean to be so — well, I am very cold! You cannot blame me for being angry when it is so late and there are no fires set and lit yet. Where have you been? Why is my fire not yet dealt with?'

'Oh, Missus, I'm sorry, Missus, really I am, only I couldn't, what with the kitchen to get done and Mrs Cashman not fit to – I mean – well, I had to do the kitchen fire first for the breakfasts, and it wouldn't draw not for no one, and it's been such a battle, though it's going now, Missus, and I'll be about your fire right away, that I will.'

'Mrs Cashman?' Tilly frowned. She hardly knew the woman, for she had been employed as cook only a month ago; for some reason which Tilly did not fully understand no cook remained in the house for very long. One after another they came and went, and Mrs Leander would mutter to Austen Kingsley about them and demand more money for a better one, and he would roar back and refuse, and yet another cook would appear and the dinners were never any better. Mrs Cashman was just the latest in a long line of such women and it was not surprising to Tilly that there were kitchen troubles again.

'She had a – um – she had a bad night, Missus.' The housemaid looked over her shoulder as though expecting someone to pounce on her from behind. 'There's only me stirrin' and the master'll be shouting for his fire and tea soon and – oh, Missus, I'm that sorry and I'll be about it right away, that I will.'

She was a country girl, still with the soft roundness such girls brought with them from their homes in Sussex and Surrey and Kent when they came into service with families in London, but there was the beginnings of the familiar city pallor about her and Tilly was filled with compunction. She wasn't much more than a child – thirteen or fourteen, perhaps, no more – and small for her years at that, and Tilly said, 'Oh, it's all right, Eliza. Go and see to my Papa's fire and tea first, and then see to Mr Quentin's. Once they are settled you may come back to me. I shall manage well enough. But tell Mrs Leander when you go down to –' She stopped, not sure what to say to the housekeeper, wishing she had the courage to send a very waspish message indeed, and as she paused Eliza said quickly, 'Oh, but she's not – I mean –'

'She's not what?' Tilly demanded. She had braved the cold and swung her legs out of bed, and was sitting with her toes curling against the chill, and as the girl swallowed and muttered, anger stirred in Tilly again. 'Well? What?'

'Oh, Missus, please not to tell her I was behind, like!' The girl's face was once more crumpled in a mask of terror. 'I got that tired I couldn't wake up this morning and that's why I'm all at sixes and sevens, and the only good thing is she's not up yet so she don't know and if she finds out she'll tan me again and I don't think I –'

'Not up yet?' Tilly looked at her clock. Half past eight and the housekeeper not yet out of her bed? 'What's going on down there? And Mrs Cashman, you say –'

'They was both the same last night,' Eliza said. 'They had their suppers and a lot of porter and –' She reddened. 'Well, it's not for me to say, Missus.'

'A lot of –' Tilly nodded. 'I see. Drunk, you say?'

'Oh, no, Missus, I never said nothing – oh, Missus, please not to tell her I said nothing. She'll have the skin off my back again, and I couldn't bear it, and my Ma says I'm not to come running home again or she'll just send me back like she did last time.'

Tilly was no longer aware of being cold. She was staring at the girl in amazement. 'What do you mean, running – you went home from here? When? Why? What happened?'

'Oh, please, Missus, I won't do it again, only don't tell her, please don't tell her. She'll –'

'I won't,' Tilly promised. 'Just explain, will you, what this is all about.'

'Mrs Leander, Missus. She beat me for being stupid like and I went home to my Ma and she said I had to come back because of the money she'd paid over, Missus, and –'

'What money? You mean your wages?' The girl looked miserable and once more on the verge of tears.

'It was this 'rangement they made, my Ma and Mrs Leander, Missus. Mrs Leander promised to teach me to be a proper cook and then a housekeeper and my Ma pays her the money, Missus, and –'

Tilly shook her head, mystified. 'Your *mother* gave money? Why?'

'My apprentice money, Missus. To teach me, like Mrs Leander says. For five pun' she'll teach me to be a lady cook and housekeeper what'll get positions in dukes' palaces and all that, and my Ma finds the five pun' and it ain't easy, Missus, that I can tell you, for a widder woman, and I've three little sisters at 'ome to come after me but like Ma says, once I'm apprenticed and taught right, I can teach them and we can all get into good positions with the real gentry, and off I go and that happy to do it. And then it all –' Her eyes filled again. 'It ain't what I expected, Missus, and there's the truth of it. And when I tried to tell my Ma she says I'm just being lazy and won't hear me and says she's got to have value for her money and sends me back. So don't tell Mrs Leander, Missus, please not to tell for she'll –'

Tilly was sitting very still now, staring at her and trying to get her head clear. It wasn't easy.

'It's all right, Eliza,' she said after a long pause. 'Go about your business. See to the gentlemen. I shall be well enough. And do stop crying. I shall cause you no mischief at all, be sure of that.'

The girl looked at her like a scared kitten and then bolted and Tilly sat and thought a while longer and then very purposefully got out of bed and set about getting dressed. The water in her jug, cold as it was, would do well enough for washing. She would add no further burden to Eliza's already overladen shoulders by asking for hot. But she would have to do something about Mrs Leander, that was for certain. Not only was the woman a shameless abuser of her mistress's household and no better than a bawd, she was robbing everyone in all directions; Tilly's Papa and by extension, Tilly told herself, me too. She was robbing that child Eliza and her simple-minded mother.

'And there's my spoons!' she thought illogically, and again rage rose in her like a tide and she welcomed it, for it gave her strength and sharpened her wits. She knew exactly what she was going to do, and do it she would. Today.

By the time she got herself downstairs the household seemed to be in some sort of order. Her father was in the breakfast room shouting about coffee and Mrs Leander was in there dealing with it. Tilly went into the breakfast room herself, summoning all the dignity she could and looked at the older woman sharply; she was a little pale and perhaps a touch puffy about the eyes, but otherwise looked much as she usually did. She nodded frostily at Tilly as she went out, leaving her to serve herself with coffee and to find a piece of toast that was not too badly burned. It would appear that Mrs Cashman was also in circulation at last; for there was bacon that was burned and poached eggs, though they were leathery, while the cold dishes — the ham, the ox tongue and the collared beef — on the sideboard looked decidedly tired and quite ungarnished, as though they had been hurried there directly from the larder and not even set on clean plates. Once again Tilly let anger rise in her and she relished it.

Her father ignored her, sitting hunched over his coffee and his large plate of ill-cut ham as he peered at the *Morning Post*. It was not a journal he particularly enjoyed, Tilly had long suspected, but it was necessary for any gentleman in business to know of its contents, so read it he did, and she knew better than to interrupt him while he did so.

She sat herself quietly opposite with her toast and coffee — which was, she decided, definitely muddy. Her father looked red about the eyes, as he usually did, and more jowly perhaps than he had this time last year, but much himself in other ways. The things that Dorcas had said about him yesterday afternoon came unbidden into her mind, and she immediately dropped her gaze and tried to think of other things. Think about the spoons, she admonished herself; think about Dorcas and your spoons.

The door opened again and Frank came in and she looked up almost eagerly. Perhaps today he would be in a better humour. Last night he had come late to bed, stamping about in his dressing-room and choosing to sleep in there rather than come to their bed. Not an unusual act for him, of course; he rarely spent more nights in the week in bed with her than he spent on the dressing-room truckle bed. But he had been noisier than usual and she suspected he had been drinking too much again. His behaviour this morning made that seem even more likely, for he was sulky and irritable and threw her a withering glance and only grunted when she said, 'Good morning,' as brightly as she could.

Her father ignored him as he went to the sideboard and looked under the silver covers and grunted his disapproval of what he saw before loading his plate and coming back to the table.

'Coffee,' he snapped as he sat down. 'And be quick about it.' Tilly frowned, once again aware of the anger that was simmering in her. How dare he be so ill-mannered to her? It was he who owed her a bright good morning, he who should try to heal the silence between them, since he had left her alone all evening again and returned to the house in his cups. She tightened her mouth and used her new-found courage, and displayed it by paying him no attention at all. It was quite extraordinary, really, how everything was having an effect on everything else, she thought. It was like that silly game Dorcas had played with her all those years ago with dominoes. Tilly, with great effort, would stand them on edge and set them up in long rows like soldiers and then, just as she put the last one in place, Dorcas would flick her forefinger at the front one and over they would all go in a row. Tilly had wept bitterly the first time Dorcas had done it, but then had learned to find it funny. She did now as she contemplated how her early morning anger at Dorcas and her spoons had spilled all down

51

the line so far; she was still going to knock Mrs Leander over – oh, indeed she was – but here she was first tilting at Frank. And she lifted her chin and waited to see what he would do as she sat with her hands unmoving on the table on each side of her plate.

'Coffee,' he shouted. 'Are you deaf, you stupid creature? Coffee, for Christ's sake –'

'There is no need to blaspheme,' Tilly said stiffly and still did not move her hand towards the coffee pot and Frank gawped at her and said, 'Eh?'

'I said you need not blaspheme,' Tilly repeated, though her courage was beginning to ebb because now her father had become aware that something was going on and had lifted his head from his journal.

'Stop being a fool,' Frank said sharply. 'I've no head for it this time of the morning. Give me my coffee and be quick about it.'

'I shall not,' Tilly said bravely. 'You may pour your own coffee if you need it.'

'Pour his own –' roared her father and slammed his paper down. 'What are you about, girl? What are you sitting there for if not to deal with the coffee? Give the man his cup and let's have a bit of peace here. Can a man not read his paper in decency at his own table? You make this house sound like an alehouse, the pair of you.'

'I have not raised my voice,' Tilly said, not sure when her bravery would run out. It was already seeping away through her feet. 'Only you two are,' for Frank had roared, 'Coffee!' again, even while Austen was speaking.

And still she sat with her hands idle on the table before her, and stared at them both with her lips compressed.

'Oh, for God's sake!' Austen shouted and slammed his fist on the table. 'What's bitten you, you fool? Are you running mad all of a sudden to make such a drama at the breakfast table?'

'I hope only for a little politeness,' Tilly said and her words were clipped, making her sound fierce, she knew, when in truth she was simply terrified of her own temerity. '"*Please* may I have my coffee," perhaps.'

'He asked for his coffee, you idiot! What more do you want? A written order?'

'He *demanded* it,' Tilly said. 'I wish for politeness, please.'

Frank threw up both hands. 'Please, please, please,' he bawled. 'Coffee, coffee, coffee. Will that do?'

'No,' Tilly said in a small voice. 'You continue being impolite, Frank, and it is not becoming to either you or I —'

'Becoming!' Frank shouted and jumped to his feet. He reached across the table and seized the coffee pot, pulling it off its small spirit lamp where it had sat bubbling sullenly. 'So much for becoming! See how becoming this is!' and he slammed the pot down on the table so that it tipped over and the streams of thick brown fluid splashed everywhere. Austen joined in, shouting at the top of his voice, and outside there was a clatter of heels and Mrs Leander appeared at the door. Still Tilly sat, her face white now with a mixture of shock and determination and sheer cold terror. She was sure that someone would hit her next; but she sat tight and waited, trying not to flinch as Frank loomed over her and her father went on shouting.

'You're out of your mind,' Frank was bawling. 'You hear me? I've not just got a wet dishrag who's as much use as a wife as a dead codfish, and saddled myself with Christ knows what sort of misery, but I've got to deal with madness into the bargain! You mind your manners, Madam, or by God, I'll —'

'You'll what?' Tilly said as steadily as she could, and lifted her chin to stare at him. Her neck was shaking uncontrollably. Could he see it? she wondered. But he was oblivious of all but his own anger.

'You'll see —' he shouted. 'Oh, my God, but you'll see. Unless you show me a very different face tonight when I return, believe me, I'll —'

'And unless you show me a different face, Frank, one that is not drunken and disgusting, you won't see me at all,' Tilly said loudly. 'For I shall lock the doors against you, so there! You go to your office and give some thought to the way you behave to me before you return tonight. You have been unconscionably unkind this morning, speaking to me as though I were less than your servant and then abusing the breakfast table as you did. I deserve an apology and if you do not return sober at a decent hour to deliver it to me, then —'

'Oh, Christ!' Frank said and whirled on his father-in-law. 'I will have no more of this. Set her to rights, or I tell you, I shall not be answerable for what will happen. Take a warning, man. I was beguiled into this marriage with your daughter and by God I'll beguile myself right out of it unless you set this hellcat to rights. And don't think you'll get rid of my right to her dowry if you fail. I've suffered enough misery already — I've earned that pittance — when I get it —' And he was gone, slamming out of the room and then out of the house as Austen stared after him in speechless rage and Mrs Leander stood by the breakfast-room door looking at Tilly with a calculating expression on her face.

Chapter Five

TILLY WAS ACTUALLY standing with her hand on the green baize door, on her way down to the housekeeper's room and the kitchen, when she realized what a mistake she was making. It would be much easier to be stern and impose her will on Mrs Leander in her own morning room, rather than on the older woman's territory, and she turned to go back there to ring her bell and summon her.

And then she stopped again. Perhaps it would be better to make her stand under the eyes of Mrs Cashman and Eliza and even the slattern who came in to do the scrubbing and the extra dirty work by the day, and so display to them as well as to Mrs Leander the fact that Tilly was the mistress of this house. It was a difficult decision; but then any urgency to make it was taken out of her hands, for her father came stomping down the stairs on his way to the front door.

She stood very still, hoping, absurdly, that he wouldn't see her standing there and would just go on his way, but of course he did see her, and stood for a moment at the foot of the stairs gazing at her. And then jerked his head towards the morning room and said gruffly, 'In there. I have to speak to you.'

She followed him meekly. Strong as her new bravery and intentions of standing up to the people who usually oppressed her might be, they were not up to defying her father. His authority was, after all, unassailable; and she went to her chair beside the fire, which was at last burning properly and warming the cold room and sat there with what equanimity she could muster.

'Now, Madam,' he said and faced her across the table. And then a little surprisingly he said no more. She looked back at him, her face as smoothly free as she could make it of any expression apart from the politely receptive, and waited.

After a moment he moved sharply and sat himself down in the armchair on the opposite side of the fireplace, flicking up his coat tails behind and then leaning forwards with one hand on each of his podgy knees and his legs spread wide. There was something about the posture that she found alarming and she had to try hard to prevent herself from shrinking back in her chair.

'The thing of it is, it's high time you learned the truth of your situation,' he said and shook his head like an irritable horse. 'Yes. The truth.'

'And what is that, Papa?' she said warily, still sitting very erect.

'Why, that you aren't quite the lady of ease you may think yourself, Madam.'

She was started. 'Lady of ease? Me? But I go nowhere and do nothing apart from –'

'Aye, I know, I know. You do nothing. As for going nowhere – well, that is up to you.'

'I would run this house if I were allowed to,' she said with sudden spirit. 'And I intend to tell Mrs Leander so this very morning. She has prevented me from dealing as I should with domestic matters and –'

'I'll hear no words against her,' Austen said with a spurt of his familiar harshness. 'Don't you go thinking you can take over where your mother left off.'

'I had no intention of saying anything to you except that it is my wish to take the housekeeping into my own hands. The dinners you have been getting lately have been execrable –'

'By God, they are too!' Austen was very much his old self

for a moment and sounded it too. 'I've told her the same thing. I tell you, if you can get a better cook to work down there and send up decent victuals you'll hear no complaints from me. All I ask is that the house runs right and I have no part in any female fights and flurries over it. I'll not have you upsetting Mrs Leander, for she is my good friend and you as a married woman yourself – well, let be –' He looked away, and she thought, amazed, he's ashamed. He saw from my face how disgusted I am by the way he uses that woman. The feeling that came to her then, almost of warmth for him, was a strange one indeed. She could not remember ever having felt so before. 'Anyway, it is not of that I have to speak to you. It is of your – um – situation.'

'My situation?' she said carefully.

'That display this morning – you must understand that it cannot happen again. You hear me? You must treat your husband with respect and obedience.'

'And he should treat me with politeness and concern,' she said hotly. 'I will not be ordered about and sworn at like some kitchen maid. He shall say his pleases and his thank yous as any gentleman should, and mind his language, and not bring taproom talk to my breakfast table. And it would help, Papa, if you –' Did she dare? She did. '– if you set him an example.'

He stared at her and she was terrified. She'd gone too far, she must have done. But then, amazingly, he laughed, a short bark of sound that had little mirth in it, but which was a laugh none the less.

'You'll not change me after all these years, when that milk-and-water mother of yours failed! Though I must say there's more to you than I once thought. I never imagined you'd boo a goose, but you did this morning and I cannot deny –' He shook his head. 'Well, I like to see some spirit in a woman, and you've never had an atom. Till this morning. But it's ill-directed, that's the thing of it. You cannot afford to anger your husband and so I tell you shortly –'

'Cannot afford to?' she said and frowned, unable to see

what it was he was trying to say. He produced an impatient snort.

'Aye, Madam, aye. Afford! These past two years have been a disaster for me and my affairs and so I tell you. That is just for your ears, mind, and no one else's. But there it is. I invest high and take good chances and often times they pay me well, but the last two have not paid as I hoped. For all the growth that is happening in the town, those of us who deal in bricks and cement and suchlike are being hard squeezed. Mr Elgar and his houses –' His face darkened. '– He spends more than any man need on his properties and cuts away at the profit till it is a waste of time for such as I. And that means –' He got to his feet and started to prowl about the room and she watched him, still puzzled '– that your life is not so secure as you might suppose. The dowry I paid over to Quentin for you – well, clearly he has had no cause yet to use it, but when he does he will find it less rich than he supposed. I promised more than I was able to provide and there's an end to it.'

He turned on her then, his face its old and much too familiar sneering self. 'I had thought when I saw you together before you were wed that he had a tendresse for you and would take you and be happy enough without a dowry. Of course he asked, as any sensible man would. But I thought – when he tries to use it, after they are wed, well, by then he will be so enamoured of his married life he will settle for what there is, hate me though he might, and I care little for any man's hate.'

'I don't understand,' she said in a tight voice. 'Or at least – are you telling me that you have cheated Frank of my dowry?'

'I am,' he said after a moment and stood still and glared at her. 'What do you say to that, Madam? What do you say to that?'

'I say it is – it is very wrong of you, Papa.' She held his gaze as steadily as she could, very aware of the fact that her face had reddened unbecomingly.

'Wrong? Wrong you say? Pah! It was all I could do! I can

raise no money on this house, with that hellhound Elgar producing new properties so fast they all want 'em and old ones like this having small chance of changing hands, and my own business so sore beset. I did what best I could, Madam, to get you a husband. Who would have you, after all? A meagre drooping object such as you were! You have a little more spirit now, when it is too late, of course – when all the good it will do you is lose you the husband you have. You treat him shabbily again as you did this morning and you will be abandoned and so I warn you. You will have nothing but this house to call home, for I will not stand about here to take care of you. Why should I? You're married now. You continue here and make the best of it. And that means treating your husband better.'

He stopped then and looked at her with his head tilted to one side. 'Is all well between you in other ways?' he said after a long pause.

She was still trying to take in what he had said, and responded only with a frown and, 'I'm sorry? How do you mean?'

'Between the sheets, my girl! What else do you suppose I mean? A man needs his oats, not to put too fine a point on it, and it's a wise wife that tries to feed him well. Certainly in the early days. Establish a good connubial habit and he will come to your bed long after less happy men have sought comfort elsewhere. It was a lesson your mother never learned.' He scowled. 'She was all prettiness and gasps and smiles and sweet kisses, but when it came to any real victuals for a hungry man all she could do was weep and wail and shrink away like some half-witted sea anemone. Be sure you learn from her mistakes – don't let the light die out of these early days. It's good, I take it? He's happy with his – victuals?'

She felt the colour drain from her face and pool in her belly to make her feel sick, and now all she could do was sit and stare at him. He stared back and then came round the table to stand above her. She could not look up; only directly ahead at the way his watch chain strained over his rotund belly between the edges of his coat, breathing in the smell of him, of tobacco and brandy and some other indefinable scent that she knew all too well as part of him and hated deeply. Her heart was beating hard and thick in her throat and she wanted to get up, to hit him and then to run from him. But all she could do was sit and stare at his watch chain.

'Listen to me, girl. You may not think me much of a father, but I care enough for you in my own way. I did all I could to get you a husband, knowing you'd never snare one for the sake of your eyes, and now I'll do all I can to help you keep the one I got you. Treat him better. Don't be shrewish at him and make silly scenes over whether or not he says please, and don't complain if he behaves like a man and likes his claret. Above all make sure your bed is the best one he can come to. If you don't listen to me, then you're three times the fool you always were and deserve no better than you'll get. Which will be a life no better than your mother's, though at least you don't pickle yourself the way she does – or do you?' He bent down and peered into her face. 'Take a drop of gin do you, from time to time?'

'No!' she cried and leapt to her feet and ran. She must have pushed him aside though she had no awareness of doing so, and he called after her, but she had no idea what it was he said. All she could do was run and not stop until she was in her bedroom and the door shut safely behind her.

She stayed there for the next hour, trying to collect herself. She didn't know what had upset her most; her father's blunt admission that he had no money available, or his prying questions about her life with Frank, and decided eventually that it was neither and both, and anyway, what did it matter? She had never had any sort of happiness in her dealings with her father, so why should she expect any now? All she could do was go her own way, and do her best.

She had started the day determined to change things in this house, she told herself, and she would hold to that determina-

60

tion. She would face up to Mrs Leander, take the reins into her own hands, be a real grown-up person, she would, indeed she *would*. That conversation with her father had been just that, a conversation, no more. Nothing to concern herself about. She would push it out of her mind and get on with what she had planned.

On an impulse she changed her gown. She had put on her usual morning dark brown without any hoop, but now she pulled out the green foulard trimmed with black braid down the skirt, and with the bodice fastening to match, and set it over a small hoop, but a definite one none the less. She pulled her waist stays in as tightly as she could without aid, and then after a moment's thought added a black silk apron embroidered with red and yellow flowers; it symbolized her role as mistress of the household in a clear way while showing, in its obvious uselessness as a protection, that she expected to be tended by good servants. Her hair carefully draped about her ears and pulled back into a neat bun looked remarkably fine. She had been forced to do it herself in Dorcas's absence, and it was a great comfort to find it was nothing like as difficult as she had feared it would be. Now she put on a neat fanchon-style cap in white broderie, setting it well back over her bun so that the black satin ribbons with which it was trimmed could settle nicely at the back of her neck, pinched her cheeks with hard fingers, added a little eau-de-cologne to the handkerchief she had tucked into her waistband, took a deep breath and went downstairs.

'Yes, Mrs Leander,' Tilly said. 'I am indeed accusing you of stealing from us.'

Mrs Leander stared back nonplussed. She had put the direct question to Tilly, expecting her to climb down, to find some way to crawl around the matter, but she had responded so strongly that Mrs Leander was clearly put about. She stared at Tilly with her black eyes almost invisible behind narrowed lids, clearly thinking hard.

'Well,' she said at length. 'If I am, I have fair cause to.'

'No one ever has any cause to steal,' Tilly said flatly.

'Oh, piffle!' Mrs Leander said and she moved towards a chair as though about to sit down, caught Tilly's eye and clearly thought better of it. 'In a word, Missy, you have to make the best shift for yourself you can.'

'I am Mrs Quentin,' Tilly said steadily, never taking her eyes from Mrs Leander's face. 'Address me so. Or as Madam.' It really was much less difficult than she had thought it would be to face Mrs Leander. When she had first rung the bell in the morning room and sat waiting for it to be answered, she had been shaking. Her hands had been slippery with sweat and she felt it trickling down between her breasts, too, chilly though the room was, for the fire had burned down and no one had come to tend it. It was that which had helped, in fact. She had told Mrs Leander sharply to see to it when she came in response to the bell, and had stared her down when the woman looked as though she intended to refuse and to send for a lesser servant to do it. But Tilly had won and Mrs Leander had put some coals on, and stood beside the fireplace and waited for more.

She had got it in greater measure than she might have expected from the hitherto quiet Tilly. She sat with her back very straight, reminding herself she was not Miss Kingsley but Mrs Quentin, an altogether more important person, and said it all baldly.

'You took money from the girl Eliza's family to train her in an apprenticeship when there is no such possibility here, as well you know. The parson in the village where the mother lives has discovered it and complained to me.' She lied unblushingly, putting Eliza's pleas for protection in place of honesty and finding no difficulty in doing so. 'That is quite wicked. What happens to the girl's wages? Do you keep those as well?'

When Mrs Leander did not answer but stared insolently back at her, Tilly took a deep breath. 'In that case you had better leave at once,' she said clearly. 'There can be no room in this house for a self-confessed thief. You may pack your bags and be gone. At once, do you hear me?'

She caught her breath at her own audacity; what would her father say if he came home and found Mrs Leander gone? What would Mrs Leander herself say? Tilly's heart quickened as she readied herself for Mrs Leander's reaction. When it came, it was a surprising one. She laughed and, when she saw Tilly's expression of amazement, laughed even louder.

'Oh dear, oh deary me! And what am I supposed to do now? Run away with my tail between my legs? There's been no money coming into this house for servants' pay since — well, Christmas. He keeps saying he'll find the necessary and never does. Why else do you think we have such disgusting cookery? Why else is this house so cold? I do all I can to scrimp and save and what do I get from you but high and mighty sermonizing? It's stolen food you've been eating this past two months, if not paying your grocer's bills is stealing and I imagine you'll say it is.'

Tilly caught her breath and tried to understand. Her anger had melted away in the flood of Mrs Leander's words. 'But Papa —' she managed. And again Mrs Leander laughed.

'Your father is in debt, Missy — oh, I'm so sorry! *Missus* Quentin.' And she dropped an insultingly deep curtsey. 'He don't know where his next sov's coming from. He's got plans all right — talks about them all the time. But as for money — well, I have to make what shift I can. Including your precious Eliza's apprenticeship. I thought it an excellent scheme and so it's proved, for we've lived on it these many weeks past. So, do as you wish about your country parson and his complaints. You've had as much of the woman's money in your belly as I have. Much good may it do you.'

She turned to go and Tilly said quickly, 'You are not to beat Eliza over this. I won't have it —'

Mrs Leander shrugged. 'I care not what she does. I am past caring. You no longer want me to work here? That is a decision that suits me well, and glad I am to tell you so. But if you want me out, you must think again, for only your father can send me away. But for my part I'll deal no longer. I shall take to my room and give up all efforts on your behalf or your misery of a mother, who'd be better off dead. I shall tell your father you want no more of me about the house and you can manage as best you can. And good luck to you.'

She stopped at the door and looked back. 'And the same goes for my girl, too. Not another hand's turn will she do for you and yours. I'll see to that – she's got better things to do than act the scullion for you lot –'

'Is she back?' Tilly said quickly and for the first time Mrs Leander looked startled by Tilly's words.

'What do you mean? Back? She's gone nowhere.'

'Hasn't she?' Tilly smiled sweetly, caring nothing for any promise she might have made to Dorcas, caring only for the chance to strip the self-satisfaction from this hateful woman. 'As I understand it, she went off yesterday evening to get herself wed. To a *soldier*. She wants no part of your Mr Hearne, whoever he may be. I thought she might be back and showing off her wedding ring by now. But there, maybe she's no intention of ever seeing you again! I certainly wouldn't wish to were I in her shoes. Whatever else my mother may be, she is not a liar and a thief and a bawd. So, there!'

With which childish expletive she at last lost control and burst into tears. But it didn't matter. Mrs Leander had already slammed out of the room and rushed upstairs.

Chapter Six

IT WAS AMAZING to Tilly that her life could change so much in just one week. As April burgeoned in the new gardens in the streets beyond Brompton Grove, and the young plane trees lifted their heads to softer blue skies, she had set about putting her house in order.

Mrs Leander, true to her word, vanished to her room on the top floor of the house and was seen only rarely, as she made her way down the stairs to go out — using always the front staircase and never the back one, a piece of insolence Tilly found wiser to ignore than to comment upon — dressed in all her finery and looking very scornful. Mrs Cashman, the cook, departed in a flurry of anger when Tilly told her bluntly that she had to improve her efforts. Much to Tilly's relief, she relinquished any claim for wages by dint of marching akimbo into the dining-room and being thoroughly rude to Austen Kingsley, who almost attacked her physically as a result of her words. Tilly had to hold him back, but it was worth the hateful fuss for, without Mrs Cashman, and the tweeny and the housemaids who took deep umbrage at being told by Tilly that they would have to work much harder from now on, she felt she had a better chance of making the house run smoothly, even though she had only Eliza to help her do it.

Not that it would be easy. She spent a long morning in Mrs Leander's old sitting room beside the kitchen poring over the ill-kept household books and saw that the housekeeper had spoken the truth. They were in deep debt to every tradesman around: the grocer's bill alone had been running high for almost two years, and only the butcher, Mr Spurgeon, seemed to be paid regularly. Probably, Tilly thought shrewdly, because he made more fuss than the others. But everyone else was owed a lot of money – an aggregate of over six pounds, she discovered, when she totalled it, and her heart sank. She would have to deal with it all, somehow, and she sat thinking and gnawing the end of her pen until, eventually, she came to a decision.

If it had been good enough for Dorcas, it would be good enough for Tilly herself, she decided. It was clear that Dorcas had no intention of returning to Brompton Grove. She had vanished as surely as if she had jumped into the River Thames, without, as far as Tilly could tell, sending so much as a note to anyone in the house. On the occasions when she did get a glimpse of Mrs Leander it was obvious, from her tight lips and hard face, that she was less than happy, and it could not have been the change in her social situation that made her so – far from it; for Mrs Leander, Tilly decided, the changes were all to the good. She no longer had to rise early, or make any move about the house. She lived the life of a lady in many ways, for Tilly, brave though she had now become, still did not have the courage to forbid Eliza to keep Mrs Leander's room clean and cared for and her fire fed. In spite of all the extra work Eliza had to do, both in the house and in assisting Tilly to care for her mother, changing Henrietta's bedding whenever necessary (which was sometimes two or three times a day) and feeding and washing her, the girl also had to wait on Mrs Leander. She would scurry up and down stairs with trays of tea and assorted little dishes and scuttles of coal in a way that made Tilly furious, but she could do nothing about the situation, for she was only too well aware of what her father would do if his comfort was obstructed in any way. And obstructing Mrs Leander would definitely obstruct him, for he had now thrown any hint of caution to the wind and had moved his accoutrements into Mrs Leander's room, and spent what free time he had in the house in there with her. Yet still Mrs Leander looked angry and abstracted and Tilly was certain it was Dorcas's disappearance and subsequent silence which had that effect on her. She felt very warm towards Dorcas in consequence. She even forgave her for the loss of her spoons.

It was down the same road she went to relieve her own present financial difficulties. Dressed in her green pelisse with the coney trimming and her good black straw bonnet, she went to the dining-room and chose her items judiciously. Nothing that was too big or showy, for her father might notice the gaps; he could hardly complain too much at what she was doing, not if he wanted to eat, but all the same there was no need to draw his attention to what was happening. So she collected just half a dozen small items, vases and bon-bon dishes and a handsome set of little jugs made in the reign of Queen Anne, and put them into the capacious carpet bag she had with her. It threatened to be a most embarrassing experience, but she steeled herself to it, pretending it was not she who was doing it at all. She was someone quite other, a girl who wanted to be married, perhaps, and needed money to pay for the wedding breakfast.

She had thought carefully about where she would take her silver for sale and decided against the immediate neighbourhood. To go to insalubrious Knightsbridge would not be agreeable. It was true that with all the massive rebuilding going on the district was changing and a nicer class of person was moving in, but there were still streets that no respectable woman would risk entering and, anyway, she did not wish to be seen selling items in places where she might owe money. She could not, for example, go to the small jeweller and pawnbroker in Middle Queen's Buildings, the nearest group of shops to the Brompton Grove house, for fear of being seen by Mr Burdon of the grocery shop where the household owed a large sum of money for tea, soap and candles. She decided to go to Kensington High Street. She would walk there through the newly cut Montpelier Square and Rutland Gate, and thence past the big houses along Kensington Gore. It would take her but twenty or thirty minutes if she stepped out briskly and would be agreeable on a bright morning like this. And, if she had no success in Kensington she could take Mr Chancellor's omnibus, which ran from Chelsea to Mile End, as far as Bond Street or Piccadilly. So she told herself as she stepped bravely out of the house and on to the street.

There was mud everywhere and Tilly thought wryly of her good Balmoral boots and wished she had worn pattens, unfashionable and clumsy though they were considered to be for town life. She nearly went back for them, but then changed her mind. It had taken all her courage to get this far; if she returned to the haven of the house there was every likelihood she would not leave it again. So she steeled herself to the fact that her boots and indeed the skirts of her gown would need a good deal of attention after her return, and went purposefully on her way.

The noise of hammers and saws and shouting was everywhere, and she marvelled at how the district was changing. Before the Exhibition, just four years ago, these had been largely quiet lanes, with just a few houses and many trees and bushes; now everywhere she looked there was activity and bustle and people, people, people. It was as though a city was growing around her like an organic thing, and she felt a sudden lift of exhilaration. This was an exciting time in an exciting world; things might be difficult in her own home, but she could set them to rights there and after that, why, anything was possible. She felt uplifted and full of hope for the future.

She did not have to take Mr Chancellor's omnibus into town, after all, for the second shop she went to welcomed her cheerfully. It was a small but neat establishment, with several handsome pieces of silver displayed behind a careful lattice-work of small panes and woodwork in a shop window which was set well back to frustrate the hopes of any would-be thief.

'My wedding presents were so numerous and so generous,' she lied shamelessly, 'that I find myself with an excess of silver. There are other items I wish to purchase but cannot in all conscience do so until I have made space by disposing of these.'

She couldn't be sure whether or not the proprietor, a brisk and businesslike young man with his hair parted in the middle in the fashionable style and with most elegant bushy side whiskers, believed her, but did not really care for she was carried along by the novelty of what she was doing, and reckless about others' opinions in a way that was really quite remarkable for one who was usually so shy. She watched breathlessly as he took her items and turned them in his hands, and peered at the hallmarks and chewed his lower lip. When he shook his head and said dubiously, 'Well, I'm not sure I've much of a call for such as these —' Tilly, emboldened by his readiness to look, was ready with her protests.

'Oh, come Sir. Business must be good with so many new people coming to live in the neighbourhood and they will need new items for their dining-rooms, I am sure.'

'Well, that's as may be, Madam. But they're nice enough pieces and it's a pleasure to oblige a lady as might be a customer herself in due course.'

'Indeed. *And* my friends.' Tilly smiled up at him sweetly. 'I will tell them all of how well you treat me. I dare say they too will have needs they must bring to you.'

'No doubt,' he said a little drily. 'Now, as to a price —'

They settled down to haggle, a protracted business at which Tilly was amazed to find she was rather good, insisting on dealing with the goods piece by piece when the shopkeeper tried to suggest a price for the lot, and ending up well satisfied. She walked out of the shop into the bustle of Kensington High Street with nine sovereigns and seventeen shillings and sixpence tucked into her skirt pocket, highly pleased with herself.

She felt so good about it all that she decided to indulge

69

herself in a ride back to Brompton and duly waited by Breeze and James' at Number thirty-two (stifling a longing to go into that elegant emporium for ribbons) for one of Mr Chancellor's two-horse omnibuses. She squeezed herself in between a large lady in a fur pelisse, who was sweating heavily in consequence, and a small child who looked decidedly queasy as it bounced on its mother's lap, so that she feared for a while he would be sick on her; but arrived without mishap fifteen minutes later and a half-penny poorer at the corner of Brompton Grove. And set about what she expected to be the more agreeable side of her morning's plan.

It had been some time since she had come to Middle Queen's Buildings to do any shopping; Mrs Leander did not need anyone apart from herself to buy for the household and there were few linen drapers' or haberdashery shops there to attract a young girl, but she knew the shops well enough. They had supplied the household for as long as she could remember, and now she moved along the small row, peering at the windows with great interest. They were very small shops, since they had been built as single storey edifices over the front gardens of the row of two storey houses that gave the street its name, and each had clear indications of its wares displayed, though the shop owners were not content with that advertisement. Each of them had a man who stood at the door of his business and shouted its wares, so the din was considerable.

'Best candles, fourpence a package, light your 'ouse for a week. Best candles,' bawled a thin young man with drooping moustaches outside Perkins the chandlers, while further along John Barnes, the grocer, shouted lustily of the 'best Ceylon tips tea and coffee from Brazil' in an effort to outdo his neighbour. The brush shop contented itself with having great tangles of brooms and feather dusters in its portals which a diminutive shop-boy waved under the noses of passers-by, while Jobbins the second grocer had a boy at his door offering small portions of cheese to be tasted by any passers-by who wished to avail themselves. Tilly was enchanted with it all, and wished that it was Mr Jobbins who was the grocer to whom she owed money. He looked a jollier man altogether than his neighbour across the passage, Mr Burdon. And then she stopped and looked again, for the name had been painted out over Burdon's shop front and a new one put in its place.

She thought for a moment and then went in to stand beside the high central counter on the sawdust strewn floor, looking about her in the dimness. There were big japanned tins with black and orange and red dragons painted on them lining the shelves. They produced the rich smell of tea that overlay every other smell in the shop, though she could identify carbolic soap and candles as well and the hint of dried coconut and prunes and, oddly, boot blacking, and she took a deep breath as the lady at the counter who was being served tucked her hands into her pelisse and turned to go, leaving the boy behind the counter to look at Tilly and say, 'Yes, Miss?'

Tilly was deflated. She had been feeling so very much the woman in charge all morning and now this boy, who looked himself to be only about fifteen or so, had brought her smartly down to earth. She tried to overcome her sudden lack of confidence by being particularly lofty.

'I am Mrs Quentin,' she said loudly, 'of Brompton Grove. Number seventeen. I have come to deal with my account.'

There was a little flurry at the back of the dim shop and another figure appeared, a much older one, but clearly the parent of the boy behind the counter, for the likeness was strong. He had a high forehead, for his hair had receded considerably, where the boy had a short curly mop, and a tight rat-trap of a mouth which the boy would clearly have one day. But his eyes were friendly enough and he pushed his son aside and said smoothly, 'Mrs Quentin? Your account, you say?'

'Yes, Mr – ah – I thought this was Burdon's, but –'

'No, Madam. It was Mr Burdon's shop until recently – but he – he had difficulties. I have taken over this establishment

71

since I had long been supplying him with his highly superior goods. I am Charles Harrod, Ma'am, at your service.'

'Well, good morning, Mr Harrod. I suppose then my account is with you.'

'If you say so, Ma'am, though I have to say the name is not familiar.' He was being very careful and for a moment she was tempted to turn and run. He did not know her name, so perhaps when Mr Burdon left he tore up the accounts outstanding? But that was a ridiculous idea and she bit her lip, realizing just in time why Mr Harrod did not know her name.

'It will be in the name of my father, I dare say, with whom I and my husband reside,' she said. 'Mr Austen Kingsley.'

'Ah!' said Mr Harrod, and his mouth seemed tighter than ever. 'Mr Kingsley, yes. I know that name.' And he reached beneath his counter and pulled up a large ledger.

'I know,' Tilly said, trying not to sound apologetic, 'there is a large sum outstanding. We have just discovered the peccadilloes of our servant and I am here to put matters right. If I might have a chair, if you please, Mr Harrod.'

He was all punctiliousness at once. 'Charlie! What are you thinking of? Get the lady a chair. Now, Mrs – ah – Quentin.'

Once again she settled to bickering over a bill, only this time she was trying to cut the sums involved rather than increase them. It took a long time and much discussion of the quality of the tea, in particular, which had been supplied, but eventually they achieved agreement. She reached into her reticule and counted out four of her precious sovereigns and Mr Harrod, looking decidedly pleased with himself, went away to fetch change for her. *And*, Tilly thought privately, to check on the weight of the sovereigns to make sure he was not being cheated in any way.

The boy Charlie, who had been serving other customers in between putting orders together in neat piles on the counter, came and lounged near her and looked at her with wide bright eyes.

'You really Mrs Quentin, then?'

'Of course I am,' she said with great dignity. 'I would hardly say so if I were not.'

'You don't look to be no older than me,' the boy said. 'Fifteen – too young to be wed.'

She bridled. 'You're very impertinent!'

'Ain't I though? It's what boys is supposed to be.'

'You are also very vulgar.' Tilly glared at him. 'To speak in so common a manner.'

'Oh, such humbug!' the boy replied and laughed. 'I only do it to annoy the old man. I can speak as well as any gentleman, Ma'am, I do assure you, when it suits me so to do.' And his accent was indeed a perfectly respectable one now.

'Then why do you speak badly otherwise?'

'I told you. To annoy m' father.'

'That is not an agreeable trait in a young person,' she said reprovingly.

'I know.' He grinned widely. 'But it's good for him. Keeps him on his toes. I keep telling him what I'll do when I run the business and he goes mad at me – says I'll find out the hard way.'

She was shocked. 'It is most improper to speak about inheriting your father's business, for it is like speaking of the time when he will be dead. It is quite –'

'Oh, pooh. I've said nothing about him dying. I hope for a good long life for he and my revered Mamma! I just think he should let me have this business to run while he spends his time in Eastcheap. He has a City place, you see. He only has this because old Burdon couldn't pay his debts to the old man, who was his supplier, do you see, and Burdon ran up debts as a mouse runs up a clock. When he was in well over his head the old man took over this shop to put him out of his misery. And it's high time he gave it to me to put me out of mine. He is so old-fashioned, and I have so many better ideas than he has. But he won't.' He glowered over his shoulder at the darkness into which Mr Harrod had vanished. 'Says I have to earn it.'

'And quite right too!' Tilly said, positively scandalized at the boy's casual chatter of such intimate family matters. 'It is the outside of enough to speak as you have to a total stranger.'

'Oh, well, as to that,' the boy said, looking for the first time a little shamefaced. 'I've had a bad morning with him. His eyes are everywhere and I get no peace to do ought myself. And you look a friendly person – I thought you no more than my own age, to tell the truth. I still think –'

'I am fully eighteen!' Tilly said hotly and the boy lifted his brows at her.

'So much?' he said and laughed loudly, and she crimsoned with embarrassment and anger. But had no chance to retaliate.

'Charlie! Are those orders ready to go yet? Here's young Arthur more than ready to go and no work for him to be doing! Be about it now.'

The boy Charlie grimaced and then threw a wide smile at Tilly and in spite of her anger she found herself smiling back. He was a very beguiling young ruffian, she thought as she took the silver and pence Mr Harrod was carefully counting into her gloved palm. His father could do worse than let him spend more time with customers, after all.

She stopped as she was stowing away her change and then said with an air of casualness, 'Now, as to the future, Mr Harrod.'

'We shall of course be glad to continue to serve you to the best of our ability, Madam,' Mr Harrod said smoothly, and came out from behind the counter to lead the way to the door of the shop. 'Just see to it that your cook or butler, or whoever it may be, sends your order in in the usual way.'

'I shall not be sending a servant with the orders in future, Mr Harrod,' she said. 'I am not happy to allow so important a duty to be taken from my hands. I know it is common practice for shops to – ah – allow certain leeway to those who bring in the order. If this is to be done I do not see that it is only servants who should benefit. I shall myself decide all we need.'

74

Mr Harrod lifted his brows at her, and was clearly not impressed. His expression said that in *his* considerable experience, no lady of class would ever so demean herself as to do her own domestic shopping, but Tilly was not at all affected by the unspoken disapproval.

'I intend to pay my way as I go, Mr Harrod. I wish not to run up such huge bills again. I do not regard this as good practice.'

'Very commendable, Ma'am, though I do assure you that it is of no consequence to us if you —'

'Ah! No doubt it isn't,' Tilly said. 'I dare say you arrange in the pricing of your goods an allowance for any delay in paying.' Tilly had not grown up in her father's house without learning something of the way business was conducted. She had heard about discounts in his rantings at her mother from a very early age, and had discovered about interest and payment-at-a-premium from the same source. Now she had every intention of putting her knowledge to work. 'It seems to me, Mr Harrod, that if that is indeed so, I should be charged a lower price for goods for which I pay immediately. Don't you?'

He looked quite horrified at the idea and opened his eyes wide at her, and behind him Charlie laughed and said, 'Now, there's a new way to do business, Pa! What do you say to that?'

'I say hold your tongue,' the older man snapped and then turned back to Tilly. 'Well, Ma'am, it's a different way of doing business, I do grant you. But if you'll forgive me for knowing my own business best, I have to say — no. I don't think that would be a good plan at all.'

'Very well, Mr Harrod,' she said serenely. 'I shall go then. I dare say Mr Jobbins across the way will be interested in my suggestion. Good morning, Mr Harrod. And good morning to you, Master Harrod.'

And she went, feeling the older man's eyes on her back as she crossed the adjoining passageway and went straight into

Mr Jobbins's shop. Tilly was pleased at the way she had handled what might have been an awkward situation and she enjoyed the sudden hoot of laughter she heard coming from the back of Mr Harrod's shop almost as much as she enjoyed the almost equally sudden sound of a hard hand landing on human flesh that silenced it. That impertinent boy, she thought, has a lot to learn, indeed he has. And so has his father.

Chapter Seven

TILLY MOVED AROUND the table as quickly as she could, setting plates and knives and cups just so, taking a real pleasure in making it all look agreeable, though she wasn't feeling too agreeable herself. She had woken with a dry mouth which was filled with a metallic taste, hot puffy eyes and a head which ached in a dull heavy fashion, all of which made her feel queasy. Not surprising, she thought miserably, remembering all too vividly what had happened last night.

Frank had come in late, and she had woken suddenly as he set his lamp on her bedside table and blinked to see him grinning at her. He was dishevelled, with his cravat untied and his shirt crumpled, but he had clearly made some effort to look pleasing to her, for his hair was smoothed down with pomade, and he had anointed himself with bay-rum; she could smell it, mixing queasily with the reek of brandy which was always a part of him these days.

'Hello, little wife,' he said thickly. 'Time we were friendly, ain't it? Can't go on always arguin', can we? Got to be friends. The fellows all say it – got to make friends with the little lady or she won't play nice games. Le's be friendly, Tilly, eh? Nice 'n' friendly.'

He lurched forwards a step and still she stared up at him, wide-eyed and mesmerized, as thoughts jostled and flashed in her head: he's been talking to his friends about me. He's told other people about what happens in our bed. He's only being nice to me because he wants to use me, and his friends have told him this is the best way to beguile me. We might as well couple in the street for all to see, for that is how it would feel, knowing he has discussed me with others.

It had been extraordinary. She had not stopped to think, had not attempted to control her response at all. She just opened her mouth and screamed, and he had looked startled and then angry and had leaned over and clumsily put one hand over her mouth. No doubt, she thought drearily now as she polished each spoon before setting it in its place, he'd meant only to stop my noise, but all he'd done of course had been to increase the great wave of fear that had come up and which had prompted the scream in the first place.

She had started to fight then, too, kicking and flailing, and had caught him a sharp blow over one cheek-bone. Her wrist still ached a little at the point of impact, and she imagined he'd found it quite uncomfortable too. He'd gone on trying to control her, but he'd failed, pulling back at last from the bedside, and she'd been out of it like a bullet, pushing him and shouting at him until she had him out of the bedroom and into his dressing-room with the door locked against him.

He had thumped on the door several times, shouting at her to unlock it at once, but she had leaned on the panels, catching her breath and doing nothing, and at last he had thrown himself down on his couch and gone to sleep, and she had crept back to her bed, shaking and feeling sick and miserable.

She'd slept at last, of course, but was it any wonder she'd woken feeling poorly? None at all, she decided, and went on setting the breakfast table. Eliza would be in soon with the coffee and toast and the hot dishes, and the least she could do was be ready for her.

The girl was really a wonder, the best help she could possibly be, and deserved all the consideration Tilly could give her. She had been completely open with Eliza about the situation in which she found herself; she had told her baldly of the deception that had been used on her and her mother: 'For we cannot provide an apprenticeship here and indeed I know of no system of paid apprenticeship for domestic service. If a girl is hard-working and thoughtful of her employer, she may rise by her own efforts and ultimately indeed become an upper servant in an important house, but we cannot provide more than employment as a general maid of all work,' she had told the girl, 'for which you should be properly paid. The common rate at present for those in your position is some ten pounds per annum, but I tell you frankly, Eliza, I am not able to pay you so much. So, you had best go home to your mother and tell her I bitterly regret the way she was cheated but that it was none of my family that are to blame.'

She had bitten her lip, aware of being mendacious, for surely her father was very much to blame for keeping Mrs Leander on such short commons, for though she felt no respect for Mrs Leander she could not deny she had been put in a most difficult position by Austen Kingsley.

Eliza had responded without a moment's hesitation, smoothing her chapped red hands over her grubby apron and bobbing at the knees. 'Please, Missus, it don't matter none to me. I dare say it was wrong of that Mrs Leander to tell my Ma such lies, but bless you, Missus, my Ma was no better givin' of the money than Mrs Leander was for taken' of it, for wasn't I her own child? It was no way to treat me, Missus, and so I say to any as asks me, no matter what respect's due to a mother. I know she's got all the little ones to think of, but all the same she didn't have to send me to such misery as she did. But I ain't miserable now, M'm, with you to answer to and that Mrs Leander gone, so to speak, so I'm suited well enough. I get my victuals and I've no doubt you'll find me what I need if I comes and tells you. So I'll stay as I am for the present, please, Missus.' And she had smiled and bobbed and gone back to cleaning the kitchen, a task which was badly needed and which Mrs Cashman had totally ignored while she had been part of the household.

Tilly had wept a little in the privacy of the morning room, for the girl's trust and honesty had been very touching. Then she had gone and told her she would try somehow to find wages for her, though she could not at present say how much, and that she was glad to have her help and would teach her all she could '— or rather,' she added candidly, 'as much as I am able to learn myself. I have not been reared to the proper way of running a house, for my own Mamma has been — well, ill, for so long that she could not. But I am able to discover ways to do things and I am learning fast. All I learn you shall learn too, I promise you. Together, no doubt, we can become a good enough plain cook. If that will please you.'

Eliza had gone pink with pleasure and said eagerly, 'Oh, yes Missus. I've always wanted to know how to cook proper. Not the pot herbs and bones my Ma does, for it's all she can get, but real cooking. I've seen in the village at home, you know, the dishes they send down to the old and the sick from the big house, and some of them looks very good and the taste — well, you'd never guess how good, Missus. So if you can learn me to cook I'll be very set up with myself —' And she had gone on with her scrubbing in a positively light-hearted manner.

Now, therefore, it was important to be ready for Eliza, for she had learned already how to fry the bacon so that the rashers were cooked through, and the fat properly melted and crisped, and how to make sure the toast was evenly brown, none of it easy on an old-fashioned open fire. Tilly and Eliza agreed that a proper iron range would be a treasure in the kitchen, but Tilly had to shake her head regretfully and say that there was no possibility of such modern gewgaws in Brompton Grove. So Eliza had set to work learning how to handle a frying pan over open coals, and had learned it very well indeed. There were no eggs to be cooked this morning, for Tilly had decided that it was wasteful to provide the whole range of breakfast hot dishes in the usual way; her budget could not permit it. Eggs could be offered, she had told Eliza, on alternate days, and if the gentlemen object, 'Well,' Tilly said with rather more courage than she actually felt, 'We shall have to explain to them.'

The door was pushed open and she looked up, ready to go to help Eliza, but it was her father who stood there glowering at her.

'And what was all that noise about last night, Madam?' he said. 'I heard you at the top of the house beyond two pairs of closed doors! Caterwauling fit for a guttersnipe – did I not tell you to mind your manners with your husband?'

'I was dreaming, Papa,' she said quickly. 'I cried out in my sleep. I am sorry if you heard me.'

'Hmmph,' Austen said. 'I should think they could hear you as far as Kensington. Where's m' breakfast?'

'It is coming, Papa.' She swallowed. 'There is bacon and toast and coffee –'

'Eh?' He peered up at her over the newspaper which he had fetched with him from the hall. 'Of course there is, woman!'

'– but no eggs. Or sausages. Or cold dishes,' Tilly went on. 'I am afraid I am not able on the present level of money in my purse to provide that –'

'Eh?' he said again and stared at her nonplussed. 'What are you talking about?'

'You told me there was no money, Papa,' she said steadily. 'So I must manage on very short commons. I must know, however, what allowance I shall have for the running of the house.'

He glared at her and then behind him the door opened again and Eliza appeared, flushed, untidy and with her apron a little smeared with splashed bacon fat, bearing a heavy tray with a covered dish and several pots and a toast rack on it. Tilly hurried to help her unload it and fetched the coffee pot to her father and filled a cup for him as quickly as she could.

'I am trying a new kind of coffee, Papa,' she said hastily. 'I think you will like it. It is best Arabica –' The coffee steamed hot and fragrant in the cup and he seized it greedily and began to drink. She watched him anxiously.

81

'It seems good enough,' he muttered after half the cup had vanished. 'Now, as to money –' He stopped and drank again and then sniffed unappetizingly. 'Well, it is perhaps not quite so bad as you might have thought – I am able to give you *somewhat* towards the household bills. As long as you manage thriftily of course. And I may get better dinners –' He looked up at her then and said with an oddly gruff air, 'I would be as good a homebody as any were I to be fed properly.'

She stood looking down at him, puzzled at first, and then realized what was happening. He was holding out an olive branch to her. He knew she had been ill-treated, that he had let her down in his management of her marriage, and in his own way was trying to make some sort of amends. It would be easy, she thought with a sort of longing, really very easy to accept his offering, to respond warmly with assurances that she would see to it that he got the best dinners she could arrange, but something held her back. It was as though that familiar hateful dream had started unwinding at the base of her mind, the dream in which she hid under Mamma's lace tablecloth until he came and found her and then –

She stepped back and said carefully, 'I will do my best, Papa.'

'Well, see to it that you do,' he snapped and put his head down to his coffee cup. 'Now, fetch me what victuals you have there for me, and be about your business.'

'You told me there would be money for the household, Papa,' she said, not moving. 'It would be easier if I had it now, if you please.'

He stared up at her, his expression rather still for him, and for a moment she thought he was going to refuse her. But he nodded and reached into his pocket for his sovereign case.

He took out two sovereigns and slapped them on the table. 'That's the best I can do.'

'And when shall I come again for more, Papa?' she said as she picked them up with fingers that were a great deal steadier than she thought they would be, for inside she was shaking.

'How – is there no end to your pestering, woman? When I have it, that is when!'

'I need to know precisely what I may expect to run the house,' she said steadily. 'Week by week. I will need this much at least each week and would prefer it if I could have more –'

'No doubt you would,' he said and snapped his paper in front of his face. 'But you can't. You shall have two sovereigns each week to run your kitchen, and that is that. I expect value for that, mind you. It is a large enough sum in all conscience. Where's my breakfast, damn your eyes?'

Eliza, who had been silently serving a plate at the sideboard all this time slipped it in front of him and he looked down at the bacon – and she had given him a good deal of it – surrounded by sippets of fried bread, and made a derisive snorting sound. But he picked up his knife and fork and set to with obvious appetite and they watched him anxiously.

He said nothing, eating all there was and seizing toast with which to wipe the remains of the bacon fat from his plate and Eliza and Tilly exchanged glances and knew that each had thought the same thing. 'That's all right, then . . .'

Eliza had cleared the breakfast table and tended the fire in the morning room, and gone away to clean the rest of the house, and still Tilly sat on at the table with her head down over her computations.

It was agreeable in the morning room; the fire crackled in a cheerful fashion and outside the garden had filled with morning sunshine which showed up with great clarity the blush of new green vegetation and the clumps of daffodils and primroses, for at this time of the day the morning room received the best of the available light. She could hear birdsong and more distantly the sound of hammers and saws as the building all around the Grove went on, while from inside the house there came the comfortable clatter of Eliza's buckets and mops, and she looked about the small room and thought, almost in surprise, 'I'm happy.'

83

This room had always been a favourite of hers, with its old-fashioned light fruitwood furniture, not at all like the heavy modern mahogany of the dining-room and the drawing-room, and the rather faded but still handsome red Turkey carpet. It had been her mother's favourite room too, she remembered, when Tilly had been very small, back in the days when she had gone about her house like any other lady, rather than spent all her time immured in her own room. Poor Mamma, Tilly thought and tried to conjure up some sort of feeling for her apart from pity; but she could not. Henrietta Kingsley had become such a cipher in the house, so insignificant, so ignored, that no one, with the best will in the world, could really care about her. But Tilly cared about the house and about Eliza and about herself, and to a lesser degree about her Papa and her husband.

Papa was right, she told herself as she looked down at the columns of figures she had made. I must treat Frank better. I dare say it is not easy for him to have to live here rather than in a house of his own, and Papa has cheated him, after all. I must be kinder and less critical. I dare say last night he meant well enough. At least he was trying to be kind in his own way. How could he know how to behave to a lady, after all? Orphans sent away to school from their sixth year, as Frank had been by his guardian, to spend all their time with boys and men, must always be uneasy with women. Though speaking of our private affairs to strangers was unforgiveable. But at least he *tried*. So, I must too. I must make myself forgive the unforgiveable. I dare say if I had drunk as much as he had I would have been as stupid too. I dare say if I could go out and drink at a club, I would. She drifted into a sort of daydream, seeing herself dressed as a man, swaggering out of the house and away to the town to sit in a club and drink a lot, but it was very difficult to sustain the image. Try as she might she could not imagine herself dressed in trousers and coats and cravats; any more than she could imagine having the freedom to go where she wanted; it was an impossibility

84

for any woman. And as for the pleasures of drinking – she could not understand them at all. She rarely took anything stronger than a little sherry and even that she did not particularly like. Dorcas had often tried to make her drink daffy, but unless there was a great deal more water than gin in it she had found it unpalatable. So, entering into Frank's pleasure in drink was something she found very difficult.

But all the same, she told herself as she looked down at her columns of numbers again, I must try to please him better. Perhaps Papa is right, after all. And I don't want to be like poor Mamma, ignored and forgotten.

She did the additions again and was reasonably satisfied. If she followed the most frugal of plans for the kitchen and learned to cook as much as she could herself, it should be possible to live well enough on the money her father had allowed her. There were people who had to be paid, of course; the washerwoman, for a start. She was not very costly, being paid in pence rather than shillings, but she came every day, after all, to collect her work, and her father would make a dreadful fuss if his linen was not well ironed. There was a certain amount Tilly could do herself but laundry was out of the question. No lady could be supposed to understand how to deal with that.

There would have to be more help in the house. With Mrs Cashman gone and Mrs Leander retired to the top floor, it all fell on Eliza's shoulders and that was too much. A cleaner who could do the heavy work, that was what was needed; and she wondered what the rate would be for such a person, could she but find one. Respectable houses, after all, always had their staff living in; would not only ragamuffins consent to take a position that did not give them their keep and their victuals as well as firing and all the other hidden expenses of life? Tilly had to admit she did not know. But I can find out, she told herself, remembering the slattern who used to work in the kitchen. She had been used only as a scullery cleaner, but could she be used for other work? It seemed unlikely to Tilly,

85

but I can find out, she thought, and turned her attention to the lists she had made of costs of food.

She had worked largely from memory, of course, but she thought she had it pretty clear. Mr Burdon's prices – or rather Mr Harrod's, she reminded herself – were fresh in her mind from her visit to the shop to pay her bill as were, of course, Mr Jobbins's, from whom she now bought her groceries. The prices of other items such as Mr Spurgeon's meat bill and the money spent on fresh fish when the man came to the door, and the price of vegetables from the market gardener over towards Shepherd's Bush who came calling every other day, were also becoming familiar to her, as were the costs of their other supplies, since she had now paid all the bills. Yes, she thought, as long as I can find a better dairy – for the price of milk and butter and cheese and eggs seemed to her to be unconscionable – they would do well enough. There was little margin for such things as wine and brandy but, she told herself bravely, Papa must buy his own, for it was not precisely needed in the house. Except for Mamma – but she would not think that.

She became aware then of the way the sounds around her had changed, and lifted her head. Someone was shouting above stairs and she took a sharp little breath in through tightened nostrils. Papa again? She had thought he had gone out.

She listened again, more carefully, and realized with a plunge of spirits that it was Frank. They would have to mend fences at some point after last night's fracas, and now was as good as any other; at least she had unlocked his door before coming downstairs. She stood up and smoothed her gown over her hips and moved towards the door to go out and find him and speak to him.

He had reached the hall by the time she got there, and was shrugging himself into his top-coat and she went to help him.

'Good morning, Frank,' she said quietly as she lifted his coat collar, which had become crumpled, and set it in place. 'Did you not wish for breakfast this morning? We have cleared the morning room, but I can arrange –'

'No,' he said loudly. 'I want nothing at all. Not a damned thing.'

Her shoulders tightened. She had come out of the morning room intending to make friends again and to be sworn at in such a fashion melted some of her resolve. But she took a deep breath and persisted.

'Perhaps just come coffee?' she said and he whirled on her, his face tight with anger.

'Oh! Now you are trying to be all sweet and good to me, is that it? Treated me last night as though I were — as though I were a footpad set to cut your throat and now you think fit to offer me coffee in this mawkish fashion. What do you think I am, God damn your eyes?'

She couldn't help it. 'There is no need to swear at me, Frank. I did not mean to scream so last night, but you frightened me. I did not know who it was.'

'Who it *was*? You stupid bitch, who should it be but me — or are you such a bawd that a dozen come marching into your bedroom when I am not here?'

'Frank!' She had gone white. 'Don't you dare speak to me so.'

'I shall speak to you in any way I choose,' he shouted. 'You're my wife, God help my pathetic soul, and the least I can do is treat you as you deserve, you wretched —'

'Stop it!' she cried and then, unthinkingly, for the smell of his breath made her head reel, she shouted, 'You're still drunk! How much did you take last night, for pity's sake? You cannot treat your constitution so and expect —'

'All I expect is to be allowed to live my life as any man would, and that includes having a wife who obeys the demands I put on her and does not scream her stupid head off and lock me in my dressing-room rather than submit as she should. All I expect is that I shall drink as much as I choose. You hear me? And I shall use you as I choose, too. I have the right — I've had little enough out of this wedding I was pushed to, God knows. I'll have what's due to me — just you see.'

He marched to the front door, opened it and stood strad-
dling the threshold, swaying a little and glaring at her. She
could just see his face, for the light behind him threw his
features into shadow. 'You hear me?'

'I hear you,' she said steadily. 'And you hear me. If you
return to this house tonight in your drunken state, I shall lock
the doors against you. Not just your dressing-room, but the
front door and the back door too. I will not be abused so in
my own home.'

'You will, and you may as well get used to it! I shan't again
put up with what I put up with last night —' He stopped and
seemed to gather his wits about him. 'I shall be back late
tonight, and I shall be drunk if I choose to be. And you will
submit to me, and that's the end of it. So get yourself ready,
Madam. For that is how it shall be from now on.'

And he went out and slammed the door behind him so hard
that the glass in the windows rattled.

Chapter Eight

IT TOOK HER the greater part of the morning to feel calm again. She stood in the hall hearing the echo of the slam of the front door, looking dumbly at the patches of colour thrown on to the black-and-white floor tiles by the light shining through the decorative glass panels in the door, red and blue and green and a vibrant purple, and waited till she felt better. It had not just been anger he displayed, she thought. It had been plain hatred and she closed her eyes for a moment against the way that thought made her stomach tighten and heave a little. To be hated, when so short a time ago he had seemed as loving a man as any girl could hope for in a husband, was a bitter pill. She tried to remember that glorious year of being engaged; it was less than a year now that she had been a married woman, but the days when she had been Miss Matilda Kingsley seemed an eternity ago. She couldn't even be sure she was the same person.

She opened her eyes and took a deep breath and went down to the kitchen, putting on as collected and serene an appearance as she could. Eliza was scrubbing the kitchen table and smiled at her briefly as she came in, and Tilly glanced at her and then away. She was relaxed enough; perhaps she had not heard the altercation above stairs? But she must have done, she thought drearily; they must have heard in the street outside, and she was suddenly so grateful to the girl for her kind tact that she went across and in a moment of sheer affection hugged her. Eliza looked startled and then deeply embarrassed and bobbed her head and went on with her scrubbing with great vigour, but Tilly could see she was pleased. She went to sit in the chair beside the fire, which was burning sweetly now, next to the old iron kettle which Eliza had balanced on the coals. It was whispering a little, working itself up to full steam, and Tilly nodded at it and said easily, 'When it boils, Eliza, you and I shall sit here and share a dish of tea and discuss our plans for the rest of today and indeed for the rest of this week.'

Eliza finished the table and took her bucket and brush and rags out to the scullery beyond the kitchen, and called back over her shoulder. 'Thank you, Missus. I won't say no. And there's a bit of teacake here in the larder left after the baker went yesterday as'll only go to waste if we don't have it. You had nothing to eat at breakfast, and that can't be good for you. I'll set that to the toasting fork and you shall have it. I'll not be above a few moments.'

Tilly leaned back in her seat, which was the most comfortable in the kitchen, being a high backed armchair with a handsome rag cushion on its seat, made to match the rug that lay beneath her feet on the hearth, and looked about her. It was a pleasant kitchen, she thought, concentrating her mind on what she was looking at as a way of not thinking about the dreadful scene with Frank. And it's looking better all the time. Eliza had clearly worked hard to clean everything since Mrs Cashman had left. Not only the table had been scrubbed to within an inch of its life (and now it was drying to a soft creamy gold in which she could clearly see the deep grain in the wood) but so had the stone floor. The wide flags in various shades of brown and grey were hollowed with the action of many feet over many years, but had a pleasing gloss to them now that Eliza had dug out from the cracks between the flags the grime that had been embedded there. The wide dark varnished dresser, with its rows of blue and white plates and cups and arrangements of great copper pans of all sizes and shapes, was neat and pretty, and sent the firelight winking back at her most cheerfully. There was also a glass jam jar into which Eliza had set some primroses, freshly pulled from the garden. She had set primroses on the broad window sill, too, and cleaned the previously grimy windows so that now, looking outwards and upwards, Tilly could see the feet and legs of passers-by as they hurried on their way in the Grove. The railings, she could see, were a little rusty. A coat of paint, perhaps, she thought and then smiled almost against her will. I'm beginning to be quite overtaken with this business of being a housewife. At one time I would never have noticed such a thing as a little rust on the area railings.

Eliza came back in from the scullery with a tray on which the teacakes were set on a thick blue and white plate, and a square of butter had been put on a wooden dish. 'If you allow, Missus, I'll just set this to the embers and mash a pot of tea and then we can be comfortable, like.'

'I'll do the toasting,' Tilly said and took up the toasting fork from the hook beside the fire and impaled the teacake on it and held it to the bars of the fire as Eliza set to work making her tea in the big brown kitchen pot, and silence slipped back into the room, apart from the faint song of the kettle and the hiss of the coals. The scent of toast drifted to Tilly's nose and she thought almost with surprise, 'Oh! I am hungry after all,' and when both teacakes were ready and well buttered and her tea was set on the table within her reach, she ate with real appetite. The queasiness has quite gone, she thought a little wryly, now that both Papa and Frank are out of the house. It makes all the difference.

'That's better, Missus,' Eliza said when she'd finished eating. She was sitting on the three-legged stool that usually lived under the table, her round red arms folded on her knees and her back a little bent. She looked comfortable and cheerful, and Tilly smiled at her with real pleasure. 'You looked right peaky before. Got a bit of colour to you now, you 'ave.'

'It's been a difficult morning,' Tilly said. She was indeed

feeling better by the moment. The tea and toast filled her most comfortably.

'Ain't it always for women, Mum!' Eliza said cheerfully. 'My Ma's a right old harridan and no messing, but it ain't all her fault. Like she always says, God wasn't very pleased with Eve, one way and another, and we bin payin' for it ever since, us women, on account of God being a man, and them notably unfair.'

'I'm not sure that isn't blasphemous talk, Eliza,' Tilly said reprovingly. 'Perhaps I should not listen to you when —'

'Blasphemous, Missus? Why, bless you, you should 'ear the things Ma says about God when her time comes with the little 'uns! Curses the men hard enough but God even more for makin' 'em, and doing it the hard way, usin' us women. But there it is, Missus. We get over it, they say. I dare say we must. My Ma's makin' new little ones often enough, after all.' And she gave a coarse laugh that wasn't in the least offensive, Tilly thought. Just honest.

'Your father —' she began and then stopped. It was not her business, after all, to enquire what Eliza's home life was like, and she had problems enough of her own without becoming too embroiled in her housemaid's, but Eliza didn't seem to notice the hesitation.

'Father, Missus? We never 'ad one. A lot o' men around, you understand, but none of what you'd call a father what looked out for us. That's why my Ma was so eager to sell me to your Mrs Leander.'

'Oh, Eliza! I told you how sorry —'

'Oh, I'm not complaining, Missus! Just explaining like. I'll deal with these dishes, then, and you can tell me what you meant to tell me, hmm?' And she took the tray out to the scullery and rattled around there for a few minutes before returning to replace the washed cups and saucers on the dresser and to come and stand beside Tilly, waiting respectfully.

'Well,' Tilly said and smoothed her household books on her knee, all of them neatly piled with the week's page opened.

'I've been working out our budget Eliza, and I must tell you that though I must be exceedingly careful it is not so bad as I had feared, I am able to give you some money for yourself. It isn't much, I'm afraid. I can manage only one shilling and sixpence a week, which adds up in the year as three pounds eighteen shillings and sixpence. I shall make this to a round sum of four pounds, of course, but it is only a fraction of what you might have elsewhere, yet it is all I can manage.'

'And enough for me, Missus. I have my bed and roof – and me in a room all of my own, Mum, me what slept under the table in my Ma's house for want of room in any of the beds – why that's worth ten pound a year to me! And here I am in print dresses and aprons as you gave me, and I get my victuals same as you do. I got no complaints, Missus, like I said. You don't need to worry about money for me.'

'Well,' Tilly said firmly. 'I must pay the rate that is the fairest I can. I will also seek to find a woman who will clean for us. It is not easy to get good women to come by the day, of course.'

'Slatterns, Mum,' Eliza said with relish. 'Dirty and disgustin' as they come. I saw the sort they took from our village for such work at the big house, and it was something to make you 'eave, really it was. I don't need no slattern under foot, Missus, I can manage well enough.'

'But this is a big house, Eliza. There are the big rooms –'

'Dinin' room what we only uses of an evenin' and then not always, so cleaning it twice a week'll do well enough, once I get it right. Drawing-room – well, it's only you what sits there, Missus, ain't it? So that's no never mind. Once a week'll see me nicely there. Which leaves just the mornin' room and the kitchen what needs daily care, like, and the bedrooms and then not all of them. There's your Ma's boudoir, o' course, and her needs, but she's no trouble, poor soul, and your room and the Master's.'

'And Mrs Leander,' Tilly said. She kept her head down, not wanting to look at Eliza. 'I would prefer she was not here, and

93

also prefer you did not have to fetch and carry meals to her, but —'

'Well, Missus,' Eliza said comfortably. 'It's the Master what wants it, and like I said, men! It's no trouble to me as long as she keeps a civil tongue in 'er 'ead, and she does, you know.' A slow smile stretched her cheeks. 'I'll tell you what, Missus, she don't like her situation no better'n what you do. Sits up there aping the lady, while you're down 'ere bein' the house-keeper, but she knows and I know which one's the real lady, and which one's the jumped up fancy woman, and she don't like it one bit. She'd be away out of here like a ferret out of an 'ole, she would, if she had the chance. Only she don't, for she has no money neither, do she? So there it is, Missus. It's no trouble to me, none of it. The bedrooms what ain't bein' used I can turn out once a month or thereabouts, just to air 'em like. There're only the four of 'em, after all. As for the attics, where's the trouble there? My room I keep spick 'n' span without a moment's trouble and the other four, well, I'll tell you, Missus, until you're ready to put more servants in, and I won't deny I ain't in any hurry to see you do it, we can keep the rooms shut up like a tomb. No need for no slattern, Missus. You just leave it to me.'

'Heavens, Eliza, how you've grown this past few days!' Tilly couldn't help it. She looked up at the confident young face above the arms that were folded comfortably across her sizeable bust, at the wide smile and the clear green eyes under the rather untidy mass of reddish curly hair and tried to see the cowed child who had first come to the house. But she couldn't. Eliza might be little more than fourteen, but she was fit and strong, now she was eating so much better than she had in her village home and she had a naturally ebullient nature that ensured she was happy in circumstances that others might have found anything but agreeable. 'It seems to me you quite thrive on difficulties.'

'Bless you, Missus, you don't know what difficulties is compared to some I've known!' Eliza said. 'Now, what are we cooking for tonight's dinner? Will the gentlemen be here for it?'

Tilly came back to reality with a jolt.

'Oh dear,' she said. 'I – well, I cannot be sure who will be here. Papa, I have no doubt. My husband –' She hesitated. 'Well –'

'Suppose we make somethin' what'll not be wasted if it don't all get ate,' Eliza said. 'I've been reading of this magazine –'

Tilly didn't stop to think. 'You can read, Eliza!' And then blushed. But Eliza was unworried.

'I know it seems a bit strange for a village girl, Missus, but the parson, he took an interest in us, like. When we went for our Confirmation classes, he said as many of us as wanted could go to him to learn reading and he'd lend us books. So I did and I was quick.' She looked richly pleased with herself. 'Parson said I was the quickest what he ever taught, so I can read real good, Missus.'

Eliza darted to the kitchen table and tugged out the big drawer at the far end, and pulled out a magazine.

'I got it off the girl who works down the other end of the Grove,' she said and set it in front of Tilly. 'She wanted only a ha'penny for it and seein' as it cost tuppence to her, I thought it a fair buy. And it's got cookery in it.'

She turned the pages eagerly, riffling past fashion (unbelievably elegant plates stared up at Tilly, making her feel most dowdy) and gardening hints and what seemed to be a most enthralling tale of a duke on his travels, and finally stopped when she came to the page headed HOUSEHOLD MANAGEMENT. ECONOMIC DINNERS FOR DAINTY HOUSEHOLDS.

'Dainty households,' Tilly murmured. 'What do they mean by that?'

'Why, that you send the food to table dressed pretty,' Eliza said. 'But there's one dish here what I thought looked good and I could go over to Mr Spurgeon and get the necessary from him in no time. And the vegetable garden man comes this afternoon.'

'Stewed shin of beef,' read Tilly. 'Required to prepare: a shin of good beef, a head of celery, an onion, a faggot of savoury herbs and half a teaspoon of allspice, eight whole black peppercorns, carrots, small onions, turnips, butter and flour, mushroom ketchup, port wine and pepper and salt.'

'We have some mushroom ketchup in the larder, for I looked,' Eliza said. 'And the spices. I thought I could do that easy. It takes above four hours to cook, but that won't be no bother to me, and the instructions are here, nice as you like, see? Cut the meat up into five pieces or thereabouts − well, Mr Spurgeon will do that for me, I dare say − and boil it for four hours with herbs and spices and so forth. And then the vegetables all cut fancy − why, I'd be proud to work at that. It reads really tasty, don't it? And with a nice bit of mashed 'taters and a soup made of the gravy and p'raps some bread-and-butter pudding to follow − and there's the receipt for making of that here, and we've got some bread left from yesterday and there's two eggs from the last time the dairy man come, and I might even find a few raisins like what it says here. Well, Missus, it will be as good a dinner as you could have and not too much out of your purse, for see here what it says. "The shin of beef will serve seven." So it will leave some for tomorrow, *and* it keeps well, and costs but fourpence a serving. And the pudding can be made for ninepence and more than enough for twice. As for the soup, well, we can make that from the gravy we get from the beef, and there you are. I would say the Master would be well pleased. It won't be a lot o' courses, like what 'e's used to, but I'd ha' thought one dish cooked proper beat six as was cooked lazy and made bad eating, any time.'

'It looks very difficult,' Tilly said dubiously, staring at the page. 'There seems to be so much to do − cut the vegetables fancifully as it pleases you, it says here. I have never considered ways to cut vegetables fancifully, I must say.'

'That's where the dainty comes in,' Eliza said. 'If you cut 'em all into strips that's fancy enough, ain't it? And it can't be hard. The Master don't strike me as a man as'll fret over the shapes of his vegetables. It's the quality of his meat as'll worry him.'

'Oh, Eliza, you are as good as a tonic!' Tilly smiled broadly. 'You make me feel anything is possible!'

'Well, so it is, Missus! I'm going to be the best cook as ever stepped, you see if I don't. Betwixt and between us, we'll deal very well, you'll see.'

'I'm sure we shall,' Tilly said. 'Only, please, Eliza, stop calling me Missus. It sounds so − old.'

Eliza grinned. 'Well, I dare say it does, Mis − Mum. But I got to say summat, ain't I? I'll call you Madam if you like it better.'

'No,' Tilly said firmly. 'Mrs Quentin will do well enough.'

'I'll try to remember, Mum − er, Mrs Quentin. Bit of a mouthful, mind. I'll just say Mum, shall I, Missus? That'll be easy enough.'

She lifted her chin suddenly. 'Is that your Ma's bell? She had her breakfast and kept it down, what's more, and I thought she was asleep. I'll go and see.'

Tilly looked over her shoulder at the bell panel and shook her head. 'It's the front door, Eliza,' she said. 'Oh dear. You need − um − um −' and bit her lip, not wanting to hurt the girl's feelings, but she was quick and understood at once.

'I'll change my pinny fast as a bird goes up in front of the scythe,' she said and disappeared into the scullery as Tilly, a little flurried, got to her feet and smoothed her own gown. Could it be Frank coming back to beg her forgiveness for his unkindness? It was a pleasant thought but of course quite ridiculous. If he had come back it would be to shout at her, no doubt, and anyway, he would not ring the doorbell but use his key and come stamping in and −

She pulled her thoughts away and went hurriedly upstairs, with Eliza galloping a little heavily behind her. As they reached the hall she nodded at Eliza and then towards the

97

front door, where a shape could be seen against the glass. A woman's shape judging by the size of it.

'I shall be in the morning room, since we have a fire there,' she hissed. 'Bring her to me, whoever it is. And you look very neat.' For Eliza had not just changed her apron but had slicked back her hair and set her cap straight, and had even removed the smuts from her round cheeks.

Tilly had no sooner settled herself in her chair beside the morning-room fire and picked up her needlework, in an attempt to pretend she had been sitting there all morning, when Eliza appeared at the door.

'If you please, Mum, it's a lady payin' you a mornin' call. It's Mrs —' she peered at the card on the small silver salver she held in her hand and shook her head. 'Can't say, I'm sure, Mum.'

Behind her there was a rustle of silk taffeta and a high voice cried, 'Oh, Tilly, imagine — it is I! I have come back! Do say you remember me!' And Eliza was set aside unceremoniously and replaced by a rotund figure in the brightest of green silk pelisses over a very frilled and braided and remarkably large crinoline, considering the time of the day. The whole was set off by quite the most heavily trimmed of round hats Tilly had ever seen, and beneath its heavily bedecked brim and the lace curtain all around it, a roguish face peered smilingly at her. It had dimples that threatened to split the cheeks and wide dark eyes and lips that had clearly been rouged or at least well bitten to make them glow. And Tilly couldn't think for the life of her who this woman was who now bore down upon her and almost stifled her in a most ecstatic embrace.

Chapter Nine

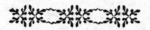

'ALICE, YOU SAY?' Tilly said in a somewhat muffled voice, as she extricated herself from another voluminous embrace. 'Ah – well, I am sure, though I cannot say precisely – ah – when do you say it was?'

'Oh, wretched, wretched perfidy,' cried the vision in the hat, dimpling alarmingly. 'To have forgotten me! Do not deny it! You have forgotten me completely!' She held Tilly at arms' length and gazed at her, her head on one side, and her smile wider than ever, if that were possible. 'Let me look at you. I would never have forgotten *you*, not in a million years. That sweet little face and so anxious an expression, like a dear little bird watching to see that the bigger ones do not steal its breadcrumbs – you dear sweet darling!' And had Tilly not managed by dint of some fast movements to sit herself down again, while indicating a chair to her visitor, she would have been hugged yet again. She already felt overwhelmed by the scent of Parma violets that her visitor had clearly used with abandon just before her arrival, and much more of it would, she feared, make her feel quite faint.

'Alice, you say? Er – if you could perhaps tell me your last name, it might jog what I must confess is an odiously bad memory.'

'Oh, I am Alice Compton now. It is spelled with an O, of course, but said with a U – Cumpton, like that. It is a very old family, you understand. My Freddy is collaterally related to a duke – but we do not consider that at all important! I was, as you will recall, always an honest person with no trace of the toad-eater about me.'

'But you were not Alice Compton when I knew you last?' Tilly tried again, floundering badly. Try as she might she could see no hint of any recognizable feature in this extra-ordinary person; had she ever been a friend of hers, surely she could not have forgotten her?

Alice Compton was unpinning her hat and Tilly's heart sank a little. It meant she was settling down for a very long prose indeed and although Tilly's life was generally dull and the few polite calls paid on her by her neighbours added a small interest to it, she did not feel that she could talk for long to Alice Compton, related to a duke by marriage. Quite apart from anything else, the chances of Tilly herself saying much at all in the company of this ebullient and very talkative person were slender. Alice was now chattering again.

'Now, if I were to be *really* cruel I would make you rehearse the names of every person you ever knew in all your life, but I will not do so, for cruelty is not in my nature. No, I shall tell you, if you are quite sure you cannot recollect?' She patted her hair with some complacency. It was extremely bright hair, quite golden in hue, and for a brief moment Tilly marvelled at it; she could not remember ever seeing such a colour on any head and surely would not have forgotten it if she had. It looked not unlike the sort of hair that was affixed to the heads of wax dolls and she wondered whether this hair had been dyed, and then dismissed the thought as unworthy. It was dressed most elaborately, particularly when compared with Tilly's own simple centre parting and ear-covering sweeps pulled back into a bun. It was frizzed and puffed and curled to an amazing degree, with ringlets at the ears and the back of the neck and the most amazing sweeps and curls in the fringe. How she could have borne to set a hat over it, Tilly could not imagine.

'I am afraid that you do indeed have the better of me,' Tilly said at last. 'For try as I might I cannot – I am sorry. I do hope you will forgive me.'

'Oh, of course I shall!' Alice smiled roguishly and then leaned forwards in a wash of Parma violet to pat Tilly's knee. 'My name before I married dear Freddy was Spender. *Now* do you remember?'

'Spender –' Tilly said and then it did come back, in a great rush. This was the child who had lived in the house next door and who had jeered at her over the garden wall and pinched her till she cried when she came to play in the garden at Mrs Leander's invitation, and then blamed Tilly for hurting her. The child who had sat on Austen Kingsley's knee as he bounced her up and down to make her squeal in utter delight, which had made Austen stare scornfully at Tilly, for when he did it to her – or tried to – she wept bitterly and would climb down quickly. The child Alice Spender who had had dull brown hair, she now recalled, as well as the sharpest of knees and elbows, for she had been a skinny little creature; could this be the same Alice, this plump person who beamed at her so happily and who clearly had such different childhood memories? It did not seem possible.

But it was. Alice rattled on, words bouncing round Tilly's ears till her head ached a little. How the Spender family had moved away to live in the country '– for Papa's business, you know, was so successful and he wanted a country place so that I should meet suitable people and be well turned off when the time came, and it did indeed pay him handsomely, I must say, for my Freddy is all a man should be and most charming as well as exceedingly well connected. And now, here we are, returned to the old family house, not that I was sure at first I wished to do so, but after all it is getting so fashionable around here now, is it not? Not at all as it was when we were little children and knew no better than to regard home as perfect, but I knew when I was a grown young lady that it would never do to remain here, for what chances does a girl have in such a neighbourhood? But now that I am wed, and the district is coming up with so many new properties after the Great Exhibition and so forth, why, when the old house appeared in Papa's will as my own and *not* part of the marriage agreement in any way, Freddy said it would be a sin and a crime not to come and live in it for a while, though we will not of course remain here, oh no, for we have such plans for the future, wishing to live nearer to some of his connections in Belgravia, don't you know.'

'I am sorry to hear of your father's death,' Tilly said, seizing on the one fact that she could use to join in. She was feeling quite stunned by the impact of Alice's conversation.

'Oh, yes, poor Papa. But he had been ill for many years, you know, and it would be quite improper of me to continue to mourn too long, as though I were making a show of it, you understand, though you see I am still in half mourning.' She patted her gown which indeed did have as its basic colour a deep purple, though its trimmings in emerald braid to match the pelisse quite overshadowed any hint of gloom that might have been in it. 'And it depresses Freddy so to see me in black, and one must always, of course, put one's husband first, is it not so?'

She settled even more comfortably in her chair. 'Now, my dear, *do* tell me all about you. I am positively agog to hear. I understand you are married! I was told so by our neighbours on the other side – the Selbies, you know? Now, do tell me all about him! Is he wonderfully rich and handsome?'

She cast a quick look about the morning room and as though she could read her mind, Tilly knew what Alice was thinking. He could hardly be rich, since he was living with her in her father's house – and her father's house though pleasant and comfortable enough was far from fashionable in its appearance or appurtenances.

Alice again cast her gaze around the morning room, taking in in one raking glance its old fruitwood table and chairs, the rather faded tapestry curtains and the undoubtedly worn blue carpet together with the absence of any heavily ornamented occasional tables of the sort currently so fashionable, and said with great brightness, 'Oh, it is such bliss to be in this dear old room again! Not a thing changed, so cosy and delightful!' She looked back at Tilly. 'Now, *do* go on. His name for a start!'

Unwillingly but unable to avoid doing so, Tilly told her about Frank. That he was indeed a most agreeable person (she gazed at her very directly as she said it) and much involved in his business which was in some way linked with her Papa's, though she did not know much about it.

'And nor should you!' Alice said warmly. 'It is none of a lady's affair, after all! But it is a pity if a man is so set in his business that he has scant time for his wife.'

'Oh, well, as to that,' Tilly said, holding her direct gaze. 'I am happy to accommodate myself to his needs. It is right and proper that I should, after all, for his welfare is my welfare.' So there, Miss Alice. Now tell me *your* husband is so rich he needs no business! she thought triumphantly.

Alice proceeded to do just that, extolling her Freddy's concern for her, his unwillingness ever to be absent from her side and her insistence that he went to his club and concerned himself with his own interests. 'It is healthier for a man to be kept away from his pleasures for some of the time, if only to sharpen his appetite when he returns.' At which the dimples became positively eloquent as the roguish knowing smiles chased each other around Alice's face.

By listening carefully to all this chatter – and it continued in the same vein quite unabated – Tilly was able to pick out some facts, and it seemed to her that the much praised Freddy had no occupation in particular, being in search of some sort of activity – 'In the City,' according to his adoring wife – and that the couple lived comfortably and indeed in some affluence on Alice's inheritance. Tilly now remembered her father as a rather noisy man with a long lugubrious face who owned a goodly number of acres of land in the fields between Knightsbridge and Kensington. Tilly had heard him talk to her father

103

on occasions about the plans he had for building on the land, and clearly he had done just that, and left his only daughter well provided for; but not so well provided that she and Freddy could make their hoped-for leap to the elegancies of Belgravia life before he had his berth in the City.

The more Tilly listened the more she remembered and the more she relaxed. Alice had been often tiresome, sometimes spiteful, and always silly, but she had been useful. When she was around Dorcas had less opportunity to be unkind and for that alone Tilly regarded her with affection. There was no doubt in Tilly's mind, however, that keeping household secrets from such a neighbour would be difficult, but why, after all, should she wish to? There was no shame in being kept on short commons, she told herself stoutly as Alice chattered happily on, and maybe it will make Alice feel superior and so even more warmly disposed towards me. It could be agreeable to have a friend of my own age about me, she told herself, watching the lively face and fluttering hands before her. The Selbie sisters, while pleasant, were all well over the age of fifty, being the four surviving daughters of the apothecary and his wife who had lived there for many years, and the other neighbours in Brompton Grove were all much of the same age. Tilly pictured a few more calls from Alice and further tides of her chatter and did not feel as put out by the prospect as she once might have been. A friend. Yes, a friend. That could brighten her life considerably.

The talk went on and, despite herself, Tilly listened and was amused. Alice loved balls and theatres and routs and parties of all kinds, and clearly had a great gift for getting herself invited to some rather spirited ones. Perhaps her Freddy's ducal connections helped (though Tilly rather suspected from the way Alice slid over the subject, for once not going into any details, that the connections were tenuous in the extreme) or perhaps it was Alice herself who was the attraction. She was overdressed and over-exuberant, and might even be a touch fast – for Tilly suspected a hint of rouge on her cheeks as well as that extremely golden hair – but for all that she was vital and exciting and set off sparks like a firework, which had the effect of making Tilly feel quite elevated herself. She could well imagine hostesses wanting Alice Compton at their parties as a form of entertainment for the other guests. And if her Freddy was half as amusing, the couple would indeed be entitled to their social popularity.

In the event, Freddy turned out to be quite a different creature. Almost three quarters of an hour after Alice had arrived (and that was an unconscionable time to extend a morning call, which should not have been made until after luncheon anyway, if one was to observe all the rules of polite society) the doorbell rang again. By now Tilly was ready to consider ways to persuade Alice the time had come to leave and, becoming ever more aware of the need to provide Eliza with the necessary authority to set about beginning to cook the dinner for tonight, lifted her head sharply.

She heard Eliza's shoes go clacking across the tiled hall and then a faint burst of voices, and she waited in some tension. Alice appeared to be quite unaware of any pending arrival, and was now talking with great excitement and in some considerable detail about the latest thing in the fashion warehouses of Oxford Street, and when the door opened and Eliza appeared in the doorway, seemed surprised when Tilly stood up to see what was required of her.

'Please, Missus – er – Mum – if you please, here's the lady's gentleman,' and almost pushed a man into the room and with an expressive look at Tilly, went away and closed the door behind her.

'Ooh!' squealed Alice. 'You wretched man, checking up on me so! Come and be kissed at once.' And she ran across the room and threw herself into his arms in a pretty flurry of skirts and curls.

He was, Tilly saw, when he had gently removed himself from his wife's arms, and had her instead hanging fondly on one elbow, a tall, indeed gangling, man of some thirty years.

He had hair as fair as his wife's, but without its gleam, and eyelashes and brows that were equally pale, which gave his rather prominent pale blue eyes a startled look. He made Tilly think of a newborn kitten as he stood and blinked at her over the knob of the cane he was carrying and which he had pushed into his mouth.

'This is my darling Freddy, Tilly, as I am sure you have guessed,' Alice trilled excitedly. 'Now, do admit, is he not the most charming man you ever set eyes on? After your own husband, of course! I will permit my women friends that much partiality, but no more. Quite divine, is he not?' And she surveyed him with proud adoration for all the world, Tilly thought, as though he were a pet dog newly bedecked in ribbons. First a kitten, now a dog. I must be careful or I shall start to giggle as much as Alice and make a complete cake of myself.'

'How do you do, Mr Compton,' she said gravely and held out her hand.

He stared at it for a moment, a touch nonplussed, for Alice was still clinging to his elbow, but he managed at last to pull himself free and held out his hand for Tilly's. It was a cold and rather limp hand, and Tilly looked at him a little more closely. This was not the person she had expected from Alice's detailed description of him; that had been a positive Adonis of a man, tall and fair and handsome, whereas this one was lean and drooping. Alice's word picture of her husband led one to expect a great wit and raconteur. This one seemed at a loss for words.

'How de do,' he said. 'Glad to make your acquaintance indeed, Ma'am. M'wife has spoken of you with great warmth. Yes indeed, great warmth. I am glad to know her dear friend.'

Tilly blinked at this description of herself, but did no more than smile. There seemed little else she could do. She indicated chairs and resettled herself in her own, very aware of the clock on the mantelpiece over her head. It really was getting very close to the luncheon hour. Were they hoping to be invited to

106

stay? Was that why they had come here before the usual hour for the paying of morning calls? She had intended to eat some toast and jam in the kitchen with Eliza, and had ordered nothing at all for the dining table. It would be embarrassing in the extreme if they were expecting an invitation for food that was not forthcoming.

'Well,' she said brightly, aware of her other duties as hostess, even if she had no intention of fulfilling the luncheon possibility. 'It is agreeable to meet you, Mr Compton.'

'Oh, do call him Freddy,' Alice cried. 'It is so horridly formal and unfriendly to address him so, when we are to be friends together and not merely neighbours. Are we not, Tilly?'

Tilly managed a smile. 'Oh, indeed, yes.'

'I shall look forward to that,' Freddy said and smiled and suddenly looked quite different. He seemed far less the lank weed and much more a man, Tilly thought with surprise. His voice was deep and pleasant, but she had noticed that when he had first spoken and paid small attention to it. Tilly blinked and tried to work out what had changed, and then thought – he's genuinely friendly. A genuinely nice man; how very agreeable. And smiled back.

'I shall too,' she said and he bent his head a little solemnly but still with that pleasant smile that had so warmed Tilly, and said nothing.

He didn't have to. Alice chattered again, guessing why he should be home at so early an hour and then surmising that there was no further business he could prosecute in town. Perhaps he had remembered that this afternoon workers would be coming for their instructions about the house ('For it dreadfully needs refurbishing, Tilly. You can't imagine!' Alice cried blithely, very obviously not looking at the shabbiness of the room in which they sat) and had come home to help his wife deal with them.

'You are exactly right, Alice,' Freddy said, interrupting with the ease of long practice, 'I recall what happened when I last allowed you to instruct workmen yourself; the result was mayhem. They believed, I think, that they had died and gone to heaven, for they demanded such rates for their work that only an Indian Nabob could have paid them, or would have, for they were ridiculous, yet my dear Alice agreed it. And then they did such scapegrace work it is amazing it did not fall on their heads. I felt I was much needed here this afternoon.'

Alice dimpled, grimaced and pouted all at the same time. 'Oh, you wretch! You make me sound quite useless. And I am not, surely?'

'No,' he said, 'you are not. Just my Alice, quite, ridiculous, but Alice all the same.'

He adores her! Tilly thought in amazement and then was ashamed of herself. Why should he not love his wife? She might seem a little noisy and fussed to me but who am I to know? Dull ordinary me who does nothing and goes nowhere? Clearly this is the sort of woman that men do love, for it is there in every movement he makes that he admires her, silly as she is. Perhaps if I were a little less dull and more like Alice, Frank would look so at me – but that was a thought not to be borne and so she pushed it away.

'Tell him it was not my fault the workmen tried to cheat me, Tilly. Tell him it is the way of all men and workmen in particular.'

'It cannot speak of all men, of course, nor even of all workmen,' Tilly said. 'But I do know that there are some who are, as you say, quite unscrupulous and ever ready to cheat a trusting person.'

'And Alice is very trusting,' Freddy said. 'So it is better, I think, that I deal with them this afternoon. And now –' He glanced at the clock so swiftly that it was as though he hadn't, but Tilly knew he had noticed the time and had the same thought as her '– Alice, my dear, we really must leave Mrs Quentin – I beg your pardon! (for Alice had started to protest shrilly at his formality) Tilly – to be about her day. We must see to our workmen, must we not?'

'Oh, but Freddy!' Alice began ingenuously. 'I thought perhaps we would stay for –'

'I think not, my dear.' Freddy was inexorable and with just one hand set beneath her elbow, lifted his wife to her feet. 'Now, here is your hat. No, no need to put it on. We are but to go home next door! Good afternoon, Mrs – ah – Tilly. I am sure I will become accustomed in time to this informality. I have had to learn many new ways since Alice entered my life.' He seemed again to be the rather drooping young man he had first appeared, but Tilly knew better now, and took his proffered hand with real warmth.

'I am sure we shall become good friends as well as good neighbours, Freddy,' she said. 'I too am happy to see you. And,' she turned to Alice, 'it is delightful to see you again, Alice. Forgive me for not remembering our childish days but you have grown up to be so much more interesting a person than you ever were as a child.'

'Oh, such stuff!' cried Alice, clearly delighted. 'And you have not changed a bit, my dear!' And she bestowed loud smacking kisses on each of Tilly's cheeks, seeming oblivious to the implied insult in her words, but Tilly was sure she genuinely meant no harm and took no umbrage.

She bade them farewell on the doorstep, and watched them go down to the road and then up the adjoining flight of steps to their own front door before one final wave. Then she returned to her own kitchen where Eliza awaited her impatiently, clearly wanting to be about the afternoon's cookery she had been promised.

Perhaps, Tilly thought as she pushed open the green baize door and went down to the warm kitchen below, perhaps things are not so bad after all. I am sure Frank will come home in a better mood, once he has got over his sore head from last night, and we shall make friends again. Perhaps if he meets our new neighbour and sees how kind he is to his wife, who is rather silly, he will find it in him to be kinder to me. I may not be perfect, but am not, I think, silly. Or at least I hope I'm not.

After which she had nothing more to think about than beef and fancily cut vegetables, which was a comfort. It was hard to concern herself with problems when struggling to make a dish fit for Austen Kingsley's table with an assistant who knew even less of cookery than she did herself. So she did not think of them at all.

Chapter Ten

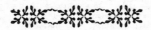

THE PREPARATION OF the meal went amazingly well. Eliza came panting back from Mr Spurgeon bearing a massive piece of meat weighing, as she put it, 'the same as a baby, Mum — good thing I got used to carryin' my little sisters around!' She slapped it down on the kitchen table in its wrapping of bloodied *Morning Post* pages, after which they stood and stared at it with some doubt.

It was a very bloody object indeed, and though it had been cut up, each piece remained partially attached to its neighbour so that the original shape of the cow's limb could be clearly seen. Tilly felt herself pale; although she had eaten meat all her life she had never had occasion to see it looking quite so much a part of the animal from which it came, and she shuddered slightly.

Eliza, however, had no qualms. 'First off, we got to get the meat into a pot and boil it up, shall we, Mum?'

Her enthusiasm was a spur to Tilly. She poked the fire to a good glow as Eliza fetched the big cast iron pot from the scullery, put in the meat and then topped it up with water from the huge enamelled jug of freshly pumped water. Then, with her muscles bulging over the rolled-up sleeves of her pink print dress, she hauled the pot to the fire and set it on the trivet over the coals.

'There,' she said with satisfaction. 'I got my skimmer all ready, see? I read about that in the book 'n' all.' She nodded at the magazine which was spread open on the dresser. 'It says as how you got to stand a bit to the side or you get your face burned, and have a nice cloth ready to hold over your hand in case it sort of splashes —'

Tilly felt far from useful as she watched the small solid figure bustle about, still chattering. Then, as the pot on the fire began to bubble and splash, she stood well back, alarmed by the spitting of the coals, as Eliza skimmed off the greasy unpleasant scum which had risen to the surface.

It was a dreadful job, Tilly decided, after she had insisted, albeit nervously, on taking a turn at it. No sooner did she remove a large skimmer full of the thick scum, plunging it into the jug of warm water Eliza had set ready at the side to receive it all, than another layer of the fat oily bubbles formed. It didn't just look disgusting either; it smelled revolting, and Tilly had to concentrate hard to stop her gorge rising. She skimmed and dipped and skimmed again, feeling her face get redder and the sweat trickling its way down inside her gown, and grew even more wretched.

Eliza seemed to have an awareness of just the right time to take over so that Tilly was saved from a nasty job but not made to feel useless and helpless. Coming to slip her freckled bare arm over Tilly's shoulder, she took the skimmer from her and Tilly, too hot to argue and grateful for her escape, released the spoon and went to the table.

The next part of their task, she found with relief, was less disagreeable. She peeled potatoes, rather clumsily at first but then finding a way to do it so that less potato remained attached to the peel she removed, and then turned her attention to carrots. By this time the pot of beef was boiling happily and the scum had virtually vanished. 'What's left won't do no one no harm when it gets all mixed up with the gravy,' Eliza said cheerfully. She was clearly enjoying herself hugely, and her delight was infectious.

'Now it's the celery head to go in and the faggot of herbs — oh, and the onion, and the allspice and the peppercorns,' Eliza read carefully from her magazine, counted out the allspice, and then tipped it all into the big pot and set the lid on it, at which it immediately hissed and overboiled and made her jump back like a scalded cat.

'I think I should set it to one side,' Tilly ventured. 'So that it does not boil so fast perhaps? And set the lid so that it can bounce a little. Then there will be less danger, I think. I have seen Mrs Cashman set it so.'

'Much she knew,' snorted Eliza, but she did as she was bid and it worked; and the pan settled to a steady bubbling as the two of them sat at the table and devoted themselves to the rest of the vegetables.

'You got to put them in a bowl under water with salt and a bit of lemon juice,' reported Eliza after another session with her *Gentlewoman's Magazine*. 'Otherwise, they goes all black like. It smells good, don't it?'

It did. The evil smell of the skimming stage gave way to the faint scent of the allspice which began to drift through the kitchen, and Tilly sighed deeply and actually enjoyed it.

'It's a very comforting smell,' she murmured and Eliza looked at her sharply and nodded with a knowing, 'Yes, Mum. And I shall make you some tea now, for there's little else we can do to this dinner till the meat be cooked and that'll be a good three hours yet, it says here. But we'll be ready for six o'clock when the Master's home, and won't he be delighted to have a proper dinner what's not burned to nothing?'

'Don't count chickens,' Tilly said and went to sit in the hearthside chair as Eliza packed the carefully cut vegetables into saucepans ready to be boiled nearer dinner time. 'Many a slip and so forth.'

Eliza was humming a soft melodic sound in the scullery and Tilly sat with her head back against the chair, felt the warmth of the fire come through her skirts and let the scent of the spiced beef fill her nostrils. There was much to be said for kitchen life, she told herself a little drowsily. It might not be elegant or precisely what well-brought-up ladies should be doing, but she could see the charm of it. Perhaps being born into that station of life that would have allowed her to be a housewife would have suited her better, she thought, instead of being a lady and having so many other things to worry about. Like morning calls from chatterboxes, and angry husbands, and jumped up housekeepers, and lost spoons . . .

She woke with a start as Eliza touched her shoulder. 'You'd be better off sleepin' on your bed, Mum,' she said kindly. 'Really you would. I'll make you some fresh tea, seeing as you let this one go cold, and I'll fetch it up to you in your room, shall I? Then you'll feel better by this evening and fit to come down and see to the Master's dinner proper. I'll be all right here for a bit. I got the magazine to tell me what to do, and you needs your rest in your condition.'

'In my condition?' Tilly said a little stupidly, staring up at the concerned face. 'What are you talking about, Eliza? I'm perfectly well —'

'Of course you are, Mum,' Eliza said comfortably. 'Couldn't be better, I've no doubt. But it's hard in the early days. I seen my Ma often enough to know that. She gets took this way too — don't eat, and goes all sickly like and sleeps — well, you'd never credit it! Takes naps just like a lady, she does, and says she got to in the first weeks.'

Tilly stood up. 'I'm sorry I dozed off. It was the heat of the fire, Eliza. I'm sorry to have ignored your tea. Don't bother to make more — it will do later.'

'It's no trouble, Missus, really it ain't. And like I said, you really oughtn't to push yourself so hard. You got to get used to the way you are, and the baby, you see, it —'

'I don't know what you're talking about.' Her lips felt stiff as they formed the words, because somewhere deep inside herself she was quite certain she did understand. Her knees began to tremble and she sat down again abruptly.

'I'm not wrong, Mum am I?' Eliza said. 'I mean, it's not my place to pry, I know that, but I seen my Ma often enough and she's just like you, sickly and that, and her hands all sort of knotty —'

'What?' Tilly said and spread her hands and looked at them. They were a little reddened from the time they had spent in the water peeling vegetables. The veins on the backs were thick and blue and tortuous and she looked at them and frowned. Had she always had such big ones?

'It happens to us, Mum,' Eliza was saying. 'My Ma always told me you could tell if a woman was increasin' by the state of her hands. And by the way she walks, o' course.'

'Walks?' Tilly said, a little bemused.

'Oh yes, Mum!' Eliza laughed, happily raucous. 'Just like a cow! All sort of slipping sideways, d'you know what I mean?'

'No —' Tilly said. 'No, I don't think I do.'

'My Ma says that it's 'cause your joints go all soggy like, so as to make room for the baby to grow and then to get out. So your hips sort of wobble. I saw you walking down the 'all in your wrapper the other day, and what with you bein' sickly and off your food, and your hands — well, I thought that's it, we're goin to 'ave a baby in the 'ouse and very nice too. That's something I really knows about. I may 'ave to learn cookin' only off a magazine but babies — ah, Mum, that's another thing entirely.'

'I think I will lie down, Eliza,' Tilly said and made for the door. 'And the tea might be rather nice at that,' and she escaped. Eliza was turning out to be a dear girl, a tower of strength if not quite the perfect servant, for her earthy humour was sometimes rather more than Tilly could handle. She would not wish to reprimand her for it, when her intentions were so good, but she would have to be told to modify it at some point.

But not now. Now Tilly needed time to herself and she tried to think.

Could it be true? Was all this a nonsense dream from which she would soon wake? She had been aware that her usual courses had been delayed this month, but had not thought about it unduly. She was not a person who suffered greatly at this time of the month, unlike some she knew who regularly took to their couches and lay there for a week at a time, looking wan. Most of the time she was unaffected, apart from the tiresomeness of having to deal with certain laundry for herself and of finding ways to dry her cloths discreetly. She did of course know why her courses had been delayed. How could she not, when Dorcas had told her so much and so coarsely all that time ago, when it happened for the first time and left her so terrified and ashamed?

And it was not, after all, surprising. She was a married woman now and having babies is what married women did. But it seemed wrong to Tilly for all that, for the women she knew who started increasing were attended by caring and concerned husbands. She had seen them all her life about the streets when she went shopping and to church on Sundays, wives who walked with their heads a little turned away from strangers, wearing large shawls and voluminous cloaks, even when the weather was quite sultry, and always accompanied by solicitous people, husbands or mothers or ladies' maids.

She hadn't realized that she had slipped off the bed and left her room until she was standing with her hand on the knob of her mother's door, gently easing it open. Her mother always slept in the afternoon, indeed, for most of the day now, and there was no need for discretion. But Tilly used it just the same, opening the door silently and slipping into the room as softly as she could.

Her mother lay on her bed, for nowadays she didn't even let anyone dress her and take her to her *chaise-longue* and it was easier to let her stay there anyway. Her head was lolling sideways on her pillow and her mouth hung open. She was flushed and there was a line of spittle marking her chin, and her breathing was thick and noisy.

Tilly sank to her knees beside the bed to bring her face close to Henrietta's and reached forward and with her forefinger gently raised the sagging chin. The breathing quietened for a moment and then Henrietta turned her head on the pillow fretfully and snorted and again her mouth opened and the snoring recommenced.

'Oh, Mamma,' Tilly whispered, 'come back and talk to me! I do need to talk to you, truly I do.'

There was no response, and she looked at the blotchy face with the tangled network of red veins across the cheeks and at the lax mouth and tried to remember the mother of her infancy. Had she ever been young and pretty? Tilly couldn't precisely recall. She had been active, of course. Tilly had memories of her mother sitting in the morning room and even walking down Brompton Grove with her hand holding firmly on to Tilly's small gloved fist, but they did not seem real. It was as though it was some other person she was seeing in her mind's eye, not this wreck of balding, smelly and ugly humanity sprawled on the bed in front of her.

She closed her eyes and rested her forehead against the bedclothes, not allowing herself to think or feel or do anything. Just resting there and making her mind a blank.

The sound of a door creaking made her realize that she had yet again dozed off. She remained unmoving, still lying against the side of the bed, listening, and then slowly raised her head and looked about her.

Mrs Leander was standing at the open doors of the double wardrobe. She was riffling through the gowns which hung in rows, quite oblivious to the fact that she was being watched.

Tilly took a deep breath, trying to clear her head and then moved, turning her body round so that she was sitting on the rug with her back to her mother and her skirts spread about her. She should have got to her feet to give herself authority; she knew that, but she still felt dreamy and not quite all together, as though part of her mind was away somewhere quite other.

Mrs Leander heard her slight movement and whirled round. There was a long silence and then Mrs Leander said in a high tight voice, 'I see. Spying on me, are we?'

'Spying? I think not,' Tilly said with a calmness she did not feel. 'I was sitting here with my mother. I have a right to do so, I believe. You do not, however, have a right to be looking in my mother's wardrobe.'

Mrs Leander had collected her wits by now. She turned back to the wardrobe to run her hand along the garments there in a dismissively insulting gesture. 'There is nothing here that is worth even considering,' she said. 'And so I shall tell your father.' And she pushed the wardrobe closed and went across the room to the dressing-table to seat herself at it.

Now Tilly did get to her feet in a flurry of skirts and stood furiously staring at the older woman.

'Leave this room at once! You have no —'

'Don't tell me again I have no right to be here.' Mrs Leander sounded bored. 'Your father *told* me to help myself to anything I fancied, seeing that she —' and she jerked her head dismissively at the figure in the bed '— is clearly never going to have any use for it.'

'I don't believe you,' Tilly said flatly. 'He said nothing to me.'

'Does he ever?' Mrs Leander said sweetly.

Tilly stood silently, and then took a deep breath. 'I will speak to him of this tonight. Now, if you please, I wish you to leave this room.'

Mrs Leander sat and stared at her and Tilly stared back, holding the gaze as bravely as she could, and at last Mrs Leander gave in. Her direct stare faltered and she looked away.

'Well, as I said, there's nothing here anyone with any taste would want. It's all absurdly out of mode, and shows no judgement of style at all.'

She got to her feet and turned and went, leaving Tilly standing shaking beside the bed, and still Henrietta Kingsley lay and snored, totally unaware of what had gone on around her. Now as Tilly looked at her, the spark of need and pity and even affection that had brought her to the room in the first place spluttered and died. All she could feel was a deep boredom, a sort of uncaringness for the wreck that lay in the bed. Whatever or whoever her mother had been, she certainly wasn't this creature here. There was no need to feel any regret or anything else for her. It would be wasted.

She went over to the wardrobe and looked in it, and as the skirts of the gowns stirred beneath her fingers the faintest hint of orange flower water rose from them. She tried to remember the first time she had smelled that, but even with so potent a prodder, there was no effect. There was no warming memory of her mother to be found, no tears to be shed for her, and she looked at the gowns and thought – that woman's right. These are not at all worth wearing again. They were insipid and dull when they were new and they are still. And she shut the door and went to the dressing-table, just as Mrs Leander had done.

She set to work purposefully on the drawers, turning them out one by one. There was little enough there. Some chemises and handkerchiefs and one drawer of nightgowns, but Henrietta still needed those. When Eliza washed her, which she did every day, she put a clean one on her. So Tilly folded them neatly and set them back in their place.

The top drawer on the right she left to the last because it was a problem. It was locked, and she had no idea where the key might be. Not even Mrs Leander had dared to break it open, and that was one comfort, and now Tilly sat and tugged at the drawer ineffectually. Then, on an impulse, she reached for the tortoiseshell-handled manicure file which lay on the dressing-table, between the tortoiseshell-backed mirror and brush and the ivory glove stretchers with her mother's entwined initials on them. Why should she not do it? Someone else would eventually if she didn't, of that she was sure. Her father, probably, after Mrs Leander complained to him of Tilly's interference, and Tilly was quite sure that was how she would be reporting the afternoon's events. So Tilly herself might as well do it.

The lock which, though strong, was simply made, clicked under the probings of the fine tip of the file and the drawer slid open. Tilly sat and stared at its contents. Little enough, after all. A tangle of coloured glass beads and crystal drops, in greens and blues and translucent reds; a scatter of hatpins and dress pins stuck into a fat dusty cushion; old dance programmes which she set aside, not wanting to look at any evidence of Henrietta's girlhood, for that would be too painful altogether; letters and bits of ribbon and scraps of lace. And then at the very back a familiar blue velvet box, which Tilly pulled forwards and took out. She sat and looked at it, and then with careful fingers opened it.

The pearls lay in their opalescent heap, gleaming softly in the afternoon light and she caught her breath again at their beauty. She picked them up and shook them out and held them against her throat as she looked in the mirror. And almost as though the woman were there in the room with her, she heard Mrs Leander talking to Dorcas on her, Tilly's, wedding day: *I can't see what the woman's thinking of — seeing as pearls means tears, as anyone of any sense knows.*

And holding the pearls to her throat, she let the tears run down her cheeks unhindered. So short a time ago, just seven months; yet now her mother lay in a sodden heap, and Frank treated her as though he hated her, and her father lived in open sinfulness with an insolent servant woman, and on what should have been a glorious day, the day she first realized she was to bear a child, she had to spend her time skimming greasy scum from a pot of boiling beef. It was all too horrible and she had every reason to weep. And she did, on and on and on.

Chapter Eleven

ELIZA FOUND HER there, and, clucking anxiously, herded her back to her room and made her take off her gown and go to bed. Tilly did not argue with her, but did not let go of the blue velvet box until Eliza took it from her hand when they reached her room and put it away in her own dressing-table.

'Whatever it is it can wait till later, Mum,' she said. 'Now you lie down, do. The dinner's comin' on lovely, and after an hour or so, when you've 'ad some sleep, you can come down and see for yourself. But you drink this tea this time, and stop your fretting. You'll be all right, Mum, just you wait and see.'

Her calm acceptance of Tilly's behaviour as completely normal had the desired effect. Tilly obediently drank her tea and fell into a dreamless sleep from which she woke an hour and a half later, feeling much restored and not a little ashamed of herself.

To have behaved in such a way was absurd. Mrs Leander had acted disgracefully in prying into her ailing mistress's wardrobe but, after all, servants did that sort of thing all the time. Whenever Tilly visited with neighbouring families, the talk of servants' peccadilloes was the most enthralling of subjects people could choose. It was ridiculous to have made such a fuss, she told herself, and began to dress for dinner.

She chose one of her prettier modes to wear; a pink silk double-skirted gown with a bodice trimmed with a deep lace bertha which matched the flounces on the skirt. The crinoline was a modest one, not at all of the size and shape that some of the more fashionable women affected now, and she managed to put it on without any difficulty. Usually Eliza came and helped her with her corsets, but tonight she had decided she did not wish to be too constrained, pretending to herself that it was because she felt less than perfectly set up in her health, but knowing at a deep level that it was because she was afraid to do so. She knew little enough about the processes of childbearing, but had a hazy notion that it would not be right to constrict herself excessively. This was something to discuss with one who knew more. Alice perhaps? After all, they had been childhood friends, and women were expected to discuss these matters with their friends. And in the absence of a mother, who else could she consult?

But that was an uncomfortable thought, so she banished it and instead concentrated on her toilette. She brushed her hair and pulled her usually modest ear puffs into a couple of ringlets on each side and fluffed up her fringe a little so that she looked, she felt, quite fetching. Then, after a moment's thought, she reached into the drawer of the dressing-table where Eliza had set the blue velvet box and drew out the pearls. Should she? Did she dare?

She did. Whatever her father said and whatever Mrs Leander thought, they were not going to be taken from her. It was bad enough that she had lost her spoons. She fastened the clasp with steady fingers and, lifting her chin with some pride, looked at herself again. She might not be a great beauty. She might not have the fire or the dimples or the excitement of the Alices of this world; she might be a small ordinary-looking person; but tonight she looked as well as any woman. And why should she not? She was the mistress of her household, a respectable married lady with an interesting secret, and as such was a person worthy of regard, and she left her room with her head up and a firm step to see how matters were progressing below stairs.

She stopped first at the dining-room door and looked in.

The table had been set for dinner and Eliza had done her best, but clearly it was far from right. The knives and forks and spoons had all been polished cleanly enough and the cloth was freshly laundered and the china and glass polished, but everything was in the wrong place and most oddly set, and she went round the table swiftly, rearranging it.

Eliza had set three places, and she nodded at that. Frank, of course, must be home for dinner. Even after this morning's scene — it seemed like aeons ago, so much had happened since — he could not dare stay out. After all, she had special news for him, and though it was foolish to think he could have any awareness of this and would therefore hurry home, surely, she thought, he might have some consideration of the possibility?

Tilly went down to the kitchen, her nose leading the way. The smells were really delectable once she was through the green baize door, and she went down holding her crinoline well out of the way to find a sweating rumpled Eliza leaning over the fire with a large ladle in her hand.

'Well, don't you look set up, Mum!' she said as she turned and saw Tilly. 'Such a difference in you, it does me good to see it. I told you as a cup o' tea and a bit of a nap'd set you up, now didn't I?'

'Indeed you did, Eliza,' she said, a little stiffly, aware that the girl was becoming a great deal too familiar in some ways. It would not be sensible to allow it to go too far. 'But that is enough about me. Tell me, if you please, the state of the dinner?'

Eliza shot a sharp glance at her, but seemed to understand, for she straightened her back and with her other hand smoothed back her untidy hair.

'Well, Mum, I done the meat like it said, adding the extra vegetables like, and turned it out into its dish, the way it said in the magazine. Shall I show you, Mum?'

'If you please, Eliza.' Tilly stood by the table with her hands folded on her crinoline and waited.

Eliza, moving with great care, took a large cloth and with it opened the oven door, the one to the right of the open fire, where the heat was generally supposed to be a little lower than the one on the left which was closer and burned up hotter. She lifted out, with an occasional grunt of effort, one of the largest of the serving dishes the kitchen possessed and set it on the table.

There was a tense moment as she turned to close the oven door and then returned to her dish and stood there with her hand poised above the polished steel cover, looking anxiously at Tilly as she did so.

'Well, Eliza, take it off and let me see!' Tilly said.

Eliza removed the steel cover as she was told. The meat was tumbled in large chunks all over the plate, and piled high. The vegetables, which indeed looked fanciful in shape, had been piled equally higgledy-piggledy wherever there was a space. The effect was of great quantity, so great that it was almost repellent.

'Oh dear,' Tilly said without stopping to think and Eliza's face crumpled.

'But it's cooked exactly like it says in the book, Mum! Take a taster and see if it don't taste real good.' And she seized a knife from the drawer and hacked off a piece of meat and held it out to Tilly on the point.

'But I cannot –' Tilly began and then stopped. She could not serve her father this food until she had made sure it was right, and tasting it was the only way to know. So she took the knife and, nibbling with uneasy delicacy, bit off some of the meat.

It was tender and rich and the spiciness was very pleasant. She nodded slowly as she swallowed and said, 'It tastes excellent, Eliza.'

The girl lit up with pleased self-satisfaction and at once lifted up the steel cover ready to set it in place again and return the dish to the oven, but Tilly stopped her.

'It must be made to look as good as it tastes, Eliza. Fetch me another dish. Not so large, I think –'

Eliza gawped at her, puzzled, opened her mouth to protest, saw the set of Tilly's jaw and closed it again. She went to fetch the plate.

'I shall need a fork and spoon too,' Tilly said. 'And an apron to cover my gown, if you please.'

Suitably protected against splashes she set to work, slicing the meat into more elegant pieces, though they were still a little ragged, and arranging them neatly in the centre of the clean plate. The vegetables she rescued from their disorder and set them prettily on each side, heaps of carrots, then small onions and then potatoes, so that there was some symmetry to it. At first Eliza watched with a scowl on her round face and then with a little more interest.

'It is not necessary to send all of it to table,' Tilly said. 'This will be enough for the three of us, I am sure, and the rest may be set in a pie tomorrow, perhaps. We must think about that. But do you not agree that this looks more pleasant?'

'It don't look as good as a hungry man might want it to, Mum, and so I tell you,' Eliza said with a return of her old bluntness. 'But I suppose seein' as you and the Master is gentry —'

'Well, yes, Eliza. Now take your own dinner from this remainder, and set the plate in the larder. If you eat yours now you will be better able to wait at table afterwards.' She stopped then and smiled widely at the girl.

'You have done so very well, Eliza. Indeed you have. I could never have managed alone as you have done. I am sure you will soon be a very fine cook and will want to be leaving me for that Duke's kitchen.'

Eliza lit up as though a lamp had been set behind her eyes. 'Oh, no, Mum, I'll never leave you, not till you send me away. You've been that kind to me, Mum, why I'd do anything for you. I do love you, Mum.' Her face suddenly went bright red and her eyes filled with tears.

Tilly was aghast. To receive so strong an avowal from a servant was not something she would ever have expected and she had no idea how to deal with it, so she bit her lip and shook her head and then said a little brusquely, 'Well, that's as may be, Eliza. But we really cannot waste time here talking — the Master will be home soon, I imagine.' She glanced at the kitchen clock. 'It is now gone six. So what else is ready?'

'The soup's in the pan to the back, Mum.' Eliza covered her own confusion with a rush of busyness. 'Taste that, if you please.'

Obediently Tilly tasted it and although it bore a strong similarity to the meat she did not think that this mattered too much. Indeed it could not, for there was no time to replace it with another dish.

'If there is time, make some sippets of toast to go with it,' she said. 'That will help. Now, the pudding . . .'

'It's still in the hot oven,' Eliza said and reached for her cloth again. 'We can take a peek like. It'll need a bit of time yet, though.'

Tilly duly peeked over her shoulder into the oven and saw the big brown dish with its heaped contents, which were just beginning to develop a golden glow on the crust, and nodded. 'I am sure that will do well enough,' she said and looked again at the clock. 'Do hurry along now, Eliza. It would never do to keep him waiting.'

She was getting nervous now, trying to imagine how her father would react to the dinner that would be set before him. For all her faults Mrs Cashman had known the right sort of victuals for a gentleman's table. There would usually be an entrée as well as the soup, perhaps some devilled kidneys or chicken rissoles, and roast meat as well as stewed for a second course, after some fish. To be offered a bare three dishes could be enough to send Austen Kingsley into a frenzy of anger. Unless of course he liked them. She took a deep breath and thought of the gravy soup and prayed a little. It tasted well enough to her, but how would it taste to him?

Eliza had already disappeared into the scullery and was washing. Tilly could hear the splash of the water from the pump and the sound of vigorous scrubbing and wondered whether the child had a clean apron; but she need not have concerned herself, for when Eliza reappeared her apron was as fresh as a daisy and her cap was set just so on her head. She looked what she was, a maid of all work, but not a slatternly one.

There was a sudden noise outside the kitchen, and Tilly turned, startled, as the door burst open and Austen Kingsley stood there. She felt her face whiten, for he was glaring at her in the way he used to do when she was a child and had been discovered in some crime or other.

'What are you doing here, Madam?' he demanded. 'Is this whole house run mad? I come home and discover my daughter sitting about in the kitchen, like some scullery maid!'

'Not sitting, Papa,' she said as levelly as she could and moved towards the door, desperate to get him out of Eliza's hearing before he said more than Tilly thought a servant should hear. 'I was supervising the preparation of your dinner, that is all. Shall we go upstairs? I would be glad of the keys to the wine cupboard so that we may choose a suitable wine for dinner. If you please, Papa.'

She was at his side now, moving past him, hoping he would follow her, but he remained still.

'Wine? For you? You don't want wine!' he shouted and she shook her head.

'Indeed I don't, Papa. But you and Frank, perhaps.'

'Your husband? D'you think I'll waste my good wine on that idiot who knows no better than to pickle himself in whatever comes out of a bottle and no notion of what quality is? I shall fry in hell first. Now, Madam —'

'If you please, Papa!' she said loudly, as Eliza gawped at Austen over Tilly's shoulder. 'I wish you would come upstairs so that we may discuss — well, whatever it is, there.'

'There is naught to discuss. I am here to tell you to set another place at table. Madam, I insist that Mrs Leander sits with us tonight. She is much put about at some sort of flimflam here this afternoon. I tell you I have no interest in what it was about so don't you try to tell me —' for Tilly had opened her mouth to protest. 'But see to it. I will not have any more fusses when I am at home. The woman wishes to sit at table and sit at table she shall. It will be better than having to wait on her, surely. Even you must agree on that. We shall have dinner at half of the clock, whether your precious husband be here or no.'

He turned to look at the fireplace. 'What is there to bring to the table? Good victuals, I trust. I'm as hungry as may be, and I have had enough of the sort of rubbish that —'

'Excellent victuals, Papa,' Tilly said, though her lips had dried in the surge of anger that followed her father's announcement about Mrs Leander. 'Not a number of dishes, but a good plain family dinner. You will have ample, I do assure you. But as to Mrs Leander —'

'I will brook no refusal,' Austen roared. 'You hear me? No refusal at all. She was waiting to pounce on me as I walked through the door and I have had enough of it to last me till next week, and there's an end of it. She shall eat with me, and so shall you and that is that. And the food smells good enough. Indeed, it smells quite — hmm —'

He moved across the kitchen to peer down at the pots on the fire and Eliza moved forwards and bobbed a little curtsey.

'Please Sir, would you like to taste, Sir? It's good soup and if there's aught you need different, why then —'

'Aye, I'll taste it,' Austen said and Eliza reached for her ladle and with great care filled it. Both women watched, breaths held, as he sipped it.

'Who made this?' He gave the ladle back to Eliza and nodded sharply to tell her to refill it. 'That cook woman come back?'

'Indeed no, Papa,' Tilly said. 'Eliza —'

'The Mistress,' Eliza said at the same time and handed the ladle back to him, brimming this time, and he looked from one to the other sharply.

'So, you're making a cook of yourself, are you?' he said to Tilly and laughed and supped up the ladleful with loud relish. 'Not bad. Not bad at all. I've tasted worse at the club, let alone here with that hellcat woman cooking it. Well, if you can do as well as this, I shall see no reason to waste my cash on expensive cooks in future. Now, away with you, girl.' And he leaned down and slapped Eliza's rump playfully, but with a sharp power behind it. 'Lay that extra place at table. And you, Madam — come and get that wine. Since there will be four of us, we might as well.'

And he went out of the kitchen at last, leaving the two women to follow him, Eliza clearly pleased as Punch because he had liked her soup, and Tilly even more clearly dismayed by the prospect of sharing her dining table with Mrs Leander. But at least her father seemed content now, and no longer in a temper, so she just sighed and pushed open the green baize door to enter her own side of the house, longing for Frank to come home. Perhaps, now that he would be over his anger of the morning, once he knew her special news, he would stand up to Papa for her in the matter of Mrs Leander? It was a pleasant thought, and she cherished it.

Chapter Twelve

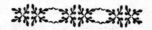

TILLY SAT BESIDE the morning-room fire, or rather the almost dead embers of it, and forced herself not to look at the clock. What was the point? Every time she did, it seemed the hands had not moved one iota, so why torment herself?

Almost midnight. Around her the house had settled to silence, with just the occasional creak of a settling floorboard to highlight it. The creaking would increase, she knew, if she let the fire go out completely, for it was chilly outside and would soon become so within doors unless she fed coals to the embers. But still she did not move. It did not matter that she was cold. It would not matter if the house froze and fell down. Nothing mattered —

She stirred then, and got to her feet and reached for the coal scuttle. This was silly. To sit here and be chilled to the marrow would not punish Frank for his defection. Only she would suffer. So she threw a shovelful of coal on and the embers took them greedily and smoke rose again to the chimney as she settled herself back in her chair.

The evening had been perfectly dreadful. Her father had decided that the best action, when faced with sharing a table with two women who patently hated each other, was to eat and drink a great deal and ignore them both. He had set himself on the wine with great concentration and then eaten two vast platefuls of the beef. Mrs Leander had picked at her plate, all delicacy and would-be aristocratic sensitivity and

Tilly had made not the slightest effort to eat any of the food Eliza set before her. All she could do was sit in frozen silence, wishing she were anywhere but where she was.

The only good thing was that neither Mrs Leander nor, more importantly, her father, said anything about the pearls still clasped about Tilly's neck. He looked at them sharply, opened his mouth to speak, glanced at Mrs Leander and then closed it again. At least he'd decided that discretion was wiser than confrontation, Tilly told herself drearily. I shall hear no more about these, at any rate. He cannot give them to her, not now. Oh, Frank, please come soon so that I can tell you about that as well as about – well, everything else.

But Frank clearly had no intention of coming in time for dinner. The clock had crept round to half past seven and then to eight by which time her father had wolfed a great deal of the bread-and-butter pudding too, and had started on the second bottle of wine, and she knew herself to be defeated. She had consented to sit at table with Mrs Leander only because she was sure that Frank would arrive at any moment and put an end to her humiliation. Now, because he hadn't, Mrs Leander had won. When she rose from the table at a quarter past eight and left the room, following Austen who had demanded that coffee be brought up to them in the drawing-room, she had thrown a triumphant glance at Tilly that said all that and more. From now on Mrs Leander was an established member of the family – pearls or no pearls – and that was that. Tilly could do nothing.

Sitting now gazing at the strengthening flames, she brooded. It was all Frank's fault. Had he returned for dinner he could have dealt with the matter, but he hadn't and now suddenly, at last, she was angry. Not miserable, not crushed beneath the weight of her unhappiness, but hotly, indeed incandescently, angry, and that made her feel a great deal better.

She got briskly to her feet and went down to the kitchen. She had eaten nothing and that was not wise at any time and particularly not now, in her condition, as Eliza had put it. She spooned a large plateful of the now cold bread-and-butter pudding into a porridge bowl and gobbled it greedily, standing in the middle of the kitchen under the watchful eye of the large brindled cat which Eliza had adopted and permitted to sleep the night away in the hearthside chair. Once she'd eaten it all – and it was quite delicious, she had to admit – she would lock up and go to bed.

Lock up. That was definitely what she would do, she thought grimly, and she went first to the back door, which led out to the area steps, and checked the key in the big old lock, and then to doubly assure herself that she was being careful, pushed home the bolts at the top and bottom. She checked the larder window too, the one which Eliza usually left open 'to keep it airy, like, Mum.' Well, the larder would have to do without its air for this night, she told Eliza inside her head, pulling it to and fastening it. No one would enter number seventeen Brompton Grove that way. And then went upstairs.

Methodically she poked down the fire in the morning room so that the new coals were pushed to one side where they would die and could then be used to relight the fire in the morning, and put the screen in front of it. She checked the dining-room windows and pushed the locks home on them, and finally went to the hall.

Here she became even more thorough. She lifted up the oil lamp she had been carrying with her from room to room so that she could more clearly inspect the small windows that flanked the front door. Both were firmly locked and indeed almost immovable because of the many layers of paint that had been applied to them and she nodded in satisfaction and then turned the big brass key in the front door and, instead of removing it and leaving it on the table as usual, left it in the lock, half-turned. Finally, she stood on tiptoe to reach the top bolt which was stiff for want of use, and dealt with that, and ended by shooting the bottom bolt.

The house has not been so firmly secured for many years, she told herself with great satisfaction. There had been a time long ago when her father became alarmed at the possibility of robbery, for there had been a flurry of such crimes in the neighbourhood. Since the building of the new terraces in the open land between Brompton and Knightsbridge, however, fewer lawless men lurked in the area now and the need for domestic security had lessened; but the bolts had stayed in place, even though they were unused, and tonight Tilly was glad of them.

She went upstairs slowly, letting the scene play out in her imagination. Frank arriving, drunken, on the doorstep. Frank trying to set his key in the lock and finding it impossible because of the key being left in place on the inside. Frank trying to open the dining-room windows in order to climb in and finding them locked too. Frank turning his attention instead to the steps that led down to the area and the kitchen door and larder window, only to find that they too were barred against him. Oh, but he'd be miserable! And, oh, but he'd be cold! And she saw him sit huddling unhappily against the back door to sleep the night away in great discomfort before being permitted to enter the house again, a sadder and much wiser man who was full of remorse, a man who had learned his lesson. A man who knew that when his wife said she would bar the door against him if he returned drunk and late, she meant every word.

She took her time undressing and washing in the now lukewarm water, listening all the time and pretending she wasn't. If she heard him arrive now would she go down and let him in? No, she told herself strongly. No, I would not, and then slid into a sort of frantic prayer. Don't let me give in if he comes now, make me strong, he has to learn, make me strong enough to teach him.

But he did not come and at last she knew that immediate revenge would be denied her. He was sleeping at his club tonight, clearly, and all her elaborate barricading had been a waste of time. As he had done before Frank would come when he was ready and carry on as he always had, and would never know how strong her resolve had been.

And she wept into her pillow and yearned for sleep to take her away from her misery and the cold and emptiness that was left behind now that her hot anger had cooled.

It did not come. All day and indeed for some weeks now (and could it be because she was with child, as Eliza had suggested?) she had fallen asleep on the slightest pretext. Sitting at table, over her breakfast, resting in a chair, almost all the time weariness hovered over her, but now it was banished completely. Her bed felt hot and heavy so she pushed back the covers and stretched her legs to the cool air, and then was chilled through and needed to tug the blankets and sheets back into position. The result was a tangle of such discomfort she had to get up and remake her bed altogether, never an easy task at the best of times and almost impossible in the dark.

And still he did not come. She lay first on one side and then on the other as the clock on the distant Trinity Church chimed the quarters and the halves and the hours. Two a.m., a quarter past two, half past.

At last her control of her thoughts began to slip. Images slid past her mind's eye and she began to drift, gratefully. Then, suddenly, she was sitting bolt upright and staring out into the darkness of her room.

The noise from below had started at a low level, but it got louder very quickly. There was a voice shouting and loud banging on the knocker and on the panels of the door and then a loud crashing and tinkling sound and she knew a window had been broken.

She did not stop to think. She leapt out of bed and felt for the box of matches that lay on her bedside table and cried aloud as her fumbling hand sent them spinning to the floor. She fell to her knees, sweeping her arms wide from side to side in order to find them and at last did, and got to her feet again and with shaking fingers struck one to light her bedside candle.

By this time the noise below was quite horrendous. She

pulled on her wrapper and wasting no time in seeking her slippers, picked up her candle and, shaking so much that some of the hot wax spilled on her hand and made her wince, opened her door.

From the floor above she could hear her father's voice and loud thuds as feet landed on the bedside rug, and she could almost see him scrambling out of bed in a rage and wanted to weep with terror. Hurrying to the top of the stairs she almost tumbled down them in her eagerness to reach the bottom and stop the din.

The light of her now leaping candle flame showed her for a split moment that there was a shower of broken glass glittering on the floor beside the front door and then the candle blew out, as the cold wind rattled the door and came curling into the house through the broken pane. She cried out in distress and turned and threw herself into the darkness on her way back to her room and the box of matches she had left on her bedside table.

When she got there she had enough presence of mind this time to light her oil lamp rather than the candle, though it took a couple of tries, for her hands were shaking so much she kept dousing the match before it could ignite the wick. At last the flame took hold and she could put the glass chimney in place and go downstairs once more.

The din had gone on, though not in the same way. The banging on the front door had stopped, but then there was a great metallic rattling and she realized that the railings beside the area were being battered with some sort of implement. She ran down the stairs, her wrapper flying behind her, to find her father and Mrs Leander, he in just his nightshirt and she in a somewhat heavily frilled peignoir in lavender muslin and her hair tied up in curl papers beneath a matching cap. Austen was shouting at the top of his voice as Mrs Leander tried to hush him and behind them Eliza hovered, her eyes wide and her white nightgown flapping around her rather red bare legs and feet.

As Tilly reached the hallway and set down her lamp on the table her father turned on her furiously. 'What's going on here? Why is he making such a noise?'

'I – is it Frank?' she managed and his eyes seemed to bulge in his head as he loomed over her.

'Who else would it be, God damn your stupid soul? The man's been shouting his head off this past God knows how long and you bleat, "is it Frank?" at me? Don't you know your own husband's voice? And who the devil else would it be, anyway?'

'I –' she tried and could say no more.

'Who locked the door on him? Where's the front door key? Has he forgotten his own key? What's going on?' Austen cried and still she could say nothing, straining her ears to discover what was going on outside.

Mrs Leander had been feeling about on the table for the key and now she said in a loud voice, 'It isn't here. Austen. The key – it isn't here.'

'It's in the lock,' Tilly managed and they both stared at her.

'In the lock? Why?' her father roared, as from outside there came a loud thudding sound and a crash as of falling bins, and somewhere at the back of her mind Tilly thought – he's fallen and landed against the ash cans by the kitchen door. He was trying to go down to the kitchen door and he fell on the steps, and she could almost see him doing it, as though she were inside his head and not her own. She could see the grey stone steps, worn and old with bitten edges from the frost damage of many winters, peeling away in front of her as she – he – went . . .

'Yes,' she raised her voice to be heard above the din. 'I left it there so that he could not use his key –'

But she need not have shouted, for the noise had stopped, quite suddenly. Her voice seemed to echo through the hall, and her father looked at her and said in a normal tone of voice but with an air of amazement, 'You left it there on purpose? To keep him out?'

'Yes,' Tilly said dully. 'I told him if he came home to me drunken again I would do so. I could not bear that, but he would not listen and I wanted him to learn.'

'You locked him *out*?' Mrs Leander said with a shrill note in her voice. 'Good God, the creature's got some spunk at that, Austen! She locked him out!'

'Aye, and now he's made enough noise to wake up the whole of Kensington, let alone Brompton!' Her father whirled round. 'Well, he shall have to pay the glazier for the damage he has done and pay him soon, for I shall not freeze in my own house, you may be sure. Go and fetch him and tell him so.'

''E's gone ever so quiet,' Eliza said, and they all turned to look at her. They had forgotten she was there, and the girl went bright red and swallowed.

'I mean, 'e made a noise like anythin' and now all of a sudden 'e's as quiet as the grave. It don't seem right, do it?'

Tilly felt it rising like a cold tide. Fear. She had hurt him. He had fallen and was now lying in pain, insensible at the foot of the area steps, and it was all her fault.

'Oh, God,' she whispered and turned and ran to the front door, quite oblivious of the glass shards beneath her feet, reaching for the key, turning it in the lock, pulling on the bolts at top and bottom.

'Oh, you stupid creature,' her father bawled. 'You cannot go out of the house unshod!' But she ignored him and at last managed to pull open the door.

Before she could run out, the entry was blocked by the tall figure of a man in an ulster coat, worn over a nightgown which showed incongruously below the heavy fabric. His bare hairy legs were stuck into large untied boots.

'Is there something amiss?' he said. 'We heard it, and were somewhat alarmed —'

'Oh, Freddy, do tell me what is happening!' a voice squealed behind him and there was Alice, in a peignoir even more frilled than Mrs Leander's and a most enormous nightcap, her eyes wide and scared so that she looked rather like a distraught baby.

'What the blazes –' Austen began and Tilly shook her head almost in a rage of impatience.

'It is Mr and Mrs Compton from next door – Alice Spender – oh, please do let me pass. I'm so afraid – it's Frank – my husband, I think he must have fallen. I must go and see.'

Freddy put out a hand and set it on her shoulder. 'No,' he said and his voice had a ring of authority that made Tilly stop pushing to get past him. She looked up at him and shook her head, trying to convey to him the degree of her anxiety, but still he held her back, and he went on more gently, 'It is better I or your father should look, my dear. If he is hurt it will not help at all if you swoon – you remain here with Alice and your people, and I shall go and see. Sir? How do. Frederick Pomfret Compton at your service. From number sixteen. Shall we go?'

Amazingly Austen Kingsley nodded and followed the younger man, looking very much in control despite his somewhat undignified costume, down the steps and along the railings to the area gate.

Tilly was able to remain where she was only for a matter of moments. Alice was exclaiming at a great rate about the amount of noise she had heard, how alarmed she had been and how terrifying it was when there were accidents and how she did hope dear Tilly's husband was all right, until Tilly wanted to scream at her to be silent. Instead she darted out of the door and down the steps, only now becoming aware that her feet hurt, and were wet and slippery. She looked down and saw they were bleeding and shook her head almost in irritation. Such a silly thing to notice at such a time; and she ran along the pavement to the area steps to peer down.

'Oh, Papa!' she cried. 'Papa! Is it Frank? Do tell me, is he all right?'

'All right?' Her father's voice boomed up at her. 'The man's

138

as dead as bleeding mutton and you ask if he is all right? What possessed you to lock him out, hey? Now see what you've done!'

Chapter Thirteen

BEING ILL, THOUGHT Tilly, was agreeable. She lay staring up at the ceiling, her nostrils filled with the scent of the lavender pastilles that were burning in a saucer on her bedside table and her limbs feeling wonderfully languorous. I wonder what disease I've got? Is it a fever? And she managed to move her head enough to look at her bedroom window. But there were no rolled cloths set on the sills against the cracks to keep out any noxious night airs, as there would surely have been had she a fever; and anyway she was not hot. Nor was she particularly cool, she discovered as she thought about it. She was not anything, really. Just sleepy. And she closed her eyes with a deep sense of luxury and dozed once more.

When she opened them again it was in response to the sound of voices. The sun lay long on her counterpane, and the light had the deep hue of late afternoon. She blinked up at the ceiling and then turned her head towards the murmur.

That man, she thought, I don't know at all. Who is he? And what is he doing here? The woman — ah! That is Eliza! Looking surprisingly neat, with her hair pulled back very tightly under her cap, and an almost shiningly clean apron. Tilly wanted to say out loud that she approved and tried to, but no sound came out of her lips when she opened them but an odd croak which startled her. It startled the two murmuring people even more for they hurried from the window where they had been standing, and came to each side of her bed.

'Well, Mrs Quentin, and how are we feeling now?' the man said and took her wrist in his hand and she thought — Mrs *Quentin*? Who is — is he talking to me? Oh, yes, of course he is. How strange to have forgotten that she was no longer Miss Kingsley. There was something else I should remember, she thought, and blinked at him a little owlishly. Something else —

He nodded at her, a serious little bobbing of the head, for all the world like a greedy bird which has just seen a worm, and she thought with a rush of gratitude, for her memory was coming back — oh, of course I know who this is. It is Mr Fildes, the apothecary from Kensington High Street. I must indeed be ill for him to he here. Papa would not have him in the house otherwise.

Again memory stirred and the delicious languorous feeling began to retreat. Papa. Papa angry. Papa telling her it was all her fault. Papa —

'I did not mean to be ill,' she said, needing to tell Papa that, but it came out in a low whisper and Mr Fildes bent his head and said, 'Eh, m'dear? What's that?'

She tried again, 'I did not mean to be ill. I am so sorry.' This too came out as a low croak and Mr Fildes patted her hand kindly.

'Don't you stretch yourself, m'dear. You have had a nasty turn and need all the time you can to get yourself fit again. Your voice will indeed be bad for a while, for the disease was deep. Very deep.' He nodded in the same serious manner and set her hand back on the bed. 'But you are mending nicely, indeed you are. With my medicines and the good Lord's help, of course.' He smiled with satisfaction and Tilly knew at once that he meant her to understand that it had been his medicine that was responsible for her recovery. She frowned again and tried once more to speak.

'What's the matter with me?' It came out more easily this time.

It was Eliza who heard and she leaned close. 'You've 'ad a

very nasty turn, Missus,' she said earnestly. 'Got the pneumony, you did, from being all chilled through that dreadful night, going out in your bare feet and cutting them up so terrible, and then it all goin' to your chest and throat like it did.'

'Hush, girl!' Mr Fildes said loudly. 'You must not alarm your mistress so.'

Tilly managed to get one hand from beneath the covers to clutch on to Eliza's wrist. She ignored Mr Fildes and said urgently, 'Tell me again —'

Eliza looked over her shoulder at Mr Fildes and then, clearly making a choice as to which person to obey, returned to Tilly.

'You've had the pneumony, Mum.'

'The baby —' whispered Tilly, and Eliza closed one rough red hand over Tilly's clutching one.

'I done all your personal care, Mum, and it's all right. Nothing ain't gone wrong that I could see,' she whispered back. 'And no one knows but you an' me —' and Mr Fildes came closer, leaning over fussily, clearly wanting to join in.

'Now, what's all this, what's all this?' he demanded. 'Mrs Quentin needs her rest, not a lot of chit-chat from you, my girl. If you are determined to nurse her, then you must do it under my instruction.'

'Yes, Sir,' Eliza said demurely and very deliberately using the eye that was out of Mr Fildes's view, winked at Tilly, and Tilly's own eyes filled with tears of gratitude and she fell asleep again, as suddenly as if she were a baby herself.

The next time she woke it was dark and there was a fire burning brightly in her grate and oil lamps to warm the ceiling above her to an amber glow. There was also the smell of something savoury and she turned her head almost eagerly, aware of being very hungry.

Eliza was beside the bed and reached for her the moment she moved. 'That's it, Mum! Let's see if we can't make you feel a bit more comfy, like.'

She lifted Tilly up the bed as easily as if she had been a child and plumped her pillows behind her and pulled her bedsheet smooth beneath her. Then she fetched a wet cloth and a towel and cleaned her face and hands so that Tilly felt a great deal more alert and, finally, placed a white cloth over the sheet in front of her.

'I hotted up for you some of this here soup sent from next door, Missus,' she said. 'It's safe enough — Mrs Compton's cook is a bad-tempered piece and no friend o' mine, but she makes good enough chicken broth, I'll grant 'er that. You try this, Mum.'

Tilly let Eliza feed her, swallowing the soup gratefully. The sharp saltiness of it honed her appetite for more and she emptied the bowl before leaning back on her pillow, almost exhausted by her efforts at swallowing.

'There,' said Eliza, highly gratified. 'Don't you feel better, Mum?'

Tilly had closed her eyes, and she did not open them to speak. 'Tell me what happened, Eliza,' she said. Her voice was stronger now, lubricated by the heat of the soup. 'I think — have I been dreaming? Bad things —'

There was a silence and now Tilly did open her eyes. Eliza was still sitting on the stool she had brought to the bedside to enable her to feed Tilly her supper, and her face was a study of confusion, distress and excitement at having portentous news to impart.

'It all depends on what you dreamed, Mum,' Eliza said cautiously and flushed when Tilly made a derisive sound deep in her throat. 'You tell me what it was, Mum, and I'll see if I can —'

'Frank,' Tilly said after a long moment. 'Frank . . .'

There was a long silence broken only by the cheerful crackle of the fire and then Eliza said gently, 'Yes, Mum. It was what you thought.'

'I didn't dream it then. Outside. The steps and the noise —'

'No, Mum,' Eliza said shortly and after a moment Tilly stirred.

143

'Well, thank you for that,' she said. 'For not lying to me.'

Fatigue was creeping into her again. She had to fight the urgent desire to sleep, because there was more to know. 'How – when – how long have I been ill?'

Eliza became expansive now. 'It's been nine days, Mum! We was in despair over you, we really was. You was in such a taking over it all that night, and then your fever started and the Master had to send for Mr Fildes, though he didn't want to, but Mr Freddy made him.'

'Freddy?' Tilly said, opening her eyes which had closed in spite of her struggle to remain alert.

'Oh, he's been wonderful, Mum, him and Mrs Compton. In and out of here like – well, family, you might say. It was Mr Freddy as made the Master see he had to have someone to you, on account he didn't want no one here. And it was Mr Freddy sorted it all with the Crowner and all that.'

'Coroner –' Tilly shuddered and closed her eyes deliberately this time. 'Of course. There had to be –'

'That's right, Mum. An inquest.' Eliza said it with huge relish, her excitement about all that had happened no longer controllable. 'We 'ad the police 'ere an 'all! A sergeant it was *and* a constable. Oh, it was a real carry on, Mum, and no error. The Master goin' mad and you not fit for nothin', you was in such a takin', and where we'd ha' been without Mr Freddy I just don't know.'

'What did the inquest –' Tilly managed and got no further. But she need not have said that much. Eliza was well on her way now.

'The Crowner said as 'ow it was accidental death and regretted it for the family, and the police said there was no mysterious circumstances and gentlemen will be gentlemen and there was no 'old on the funeral so the Master got it all arranged.'

Tilly dragged herself out of the depths of her weariness and managed to focus on Eliza's face.

'It's over then?'

'Oh, yes, Mum. The day before yesterday. At Old Trinity.'

'Oh –' Tilly said and sighed deeply and let the sleep engulf her. There seemed no need to keep herself awake now.

Three days later she felt a good deal stronger and had managed to eat most of Alice Compton's cook's soup, together with some of Eliza's own culinary efforts (which consisted mainly of eggs beaten up in hot milk with sugar and brandy, a concoction Tilly found rather sickly but which did fill her up with a minimum of eating effort). Mr Fildes even allowed her to get out of bed.

'In a chair by the window is all I will permit, Mrs Quentin,' he said importantly. 'It is vital that we do not drain away your strength with unnecessary activity, you see.'

'I will feel better, I am sure, if I might get up and stay up,' Tilly said a little peevishly. 'It is very dispiriting to lie in bed when you are not ill.'

'Ah, but you have *been* ill. Very ill,' Mr Fildes said as though that settled it. 'You had pneumonia, you know! The left lung was quite consolidated. The crisis was a severe one and lysis has only just completed.'

'I'm all right now, though,' Tilly snapped. 'Aren't I? Just a little weak for want of exercise.'

'Later you may enjoy a little carriage exercise,' Mr Fildes said firmly. 'When I permit it and not before. Now, you may stay in your chair for an hour and Eliza will then put you back to bed. Eliza – remember, I am quite adamant about this.'

'Oh, yes, Sir, Mr Fildes.' Eliza bobbed a curtsey, and Tilly could have smacked her for being so co-operative with him. Altogether she was feeling very bad tempered indeed. And suddenly, from nowhere, a memory seeped into her head. Herself very small, crying out, and her mother's voice saying, 'It is not her fault, Austen. Do not be angry please! It is now she is recovering that she is fretful.'

She turned her head suddenly to Mr Fildes. 'Sir, since you are here, would it be possible for you to examine my mother?'

145

He had been at the door, fussing with his watch to show how busy a man he was, and now he looked at her sharply.

'Your mother, Mrs Quentin?'

'Yes. She has been — bedridden for some time now. I — er — I know that there are things — well, not to make too fine a point of it, she does take too much daffy.'

He shook his head and came back to her chair, his eyes bright and somehow avid. 'I did not know that your mother was — well, that — I thought that, I mean to say, the lady I met — Mrs Leander —'

'A friend of my father,' Tilly said shortly. 'My mother is confined to her room, I am afraid.'

He looked even more eager, his eyes taking on an almost salacious glint. 'I see! Well, these matters are — they are not my concern, of course.'

'Indeed,' Tilly said a little frostily. 'I ask you only to look at my mother and see if there is more that could be done for her. It would be foolish to deny the root cause of her trouble, but all the same —'

'I quite understand,' Mr Fildes said smoothly. 'So I have your authority to visit Mrs — ah — Kingsley?' He put a slight emphasis on the 'your' but not so slight that she did not fully understand what he was saying.

'Eliza,' she said. 'Fetch me my reticule, if you please.'

Eliza did and Tilly opened it and hunted around inside. 'I imagine your charge would be —'

'Two shillings and sixpence,' Mr Fildes said promptly.

'But since you are here at the house anyway for me, and my father of course will pay that bill, it is not so much, I suppose, to see another person?'

Mr Fildes hesitated, clearly torn between curiosity and cupidity. Curiosity won.

'One shilling will be the fee to attend on Mrs Kingsley,' he said with all the dignity he could muster and held out his hand. But Tilly returned the money to her reticule.

'I shall pay when you return and tell me of her health, Mr

Fildes,' she said. 'Eliza, will you see that my mother is – ah – ready to be seen?' And she fixed Eliza with a sharp eye and knew that the girl understood as she nodded and went away. It would never do for the man to find Henrietta in a bed that was wet or worse.

Eliza came back in five minutes, by which time Tilly was heartily sick of Mr Fildes's rather too bright small talk, and took him away, and Tilly waited with some anxiety for his return. Quite why she had asked him to see Henrietta she did not really know: Eliza had assured her, when asked, that her mother remained much the same. Perhaps, she thought, it is because I am ashamed that no medical man has examined her in all these years. She cannot be well, in her state. We have allowed her her daffy because it is so much easier than dealing with her when she does not have it, but perhaps it is different care she needs.

Mr Fildes returned in half an hour with Eliza at his heels.

'Well?' Tilly demanded and stared at him closely. She had the light behind her and his face was well lit by the afternoon sun, bright and invasive on this April day, and she could see that he looked grave.

'Well, Mrs Quentin, she is not a well lady –'

'That,' said Tilly with some acerbity, 'is something we have known for some time.'

'– and it is a matter of regret that she should have been – ahem – permitted to develop a dipsomaniac habit.'

'That is a very harsh term,' Tilly protested but he shook his head.

'I have questioned your maid here, Mrs Quentin, and it is clear that it is a just term. She has a steady intake of gin and becomes very agitated without it. There are other signs that her intemperance has caused permanent damage. But that is not the only thing.' He shook his head again lugubriously.

'Then tell me what is,' Tilly said sharply and blinked back sudden tears, hating the weakness of her illness that made her so vulnerable and so childishly prone to weeping.

147

'She has had a stroke, Madam. An apoplectic stroke. This is why her face is misshapen and why she has lost the use of her right hand. There is weakness and lack of movement in the right leg and foot also. Her – um – absence of spirit is not due entirely to the gin. It is due as much to the effects of this cataclysmic event.'

'Oh?' was all Tilly could say, and he lifted his brows at her.

'This surprises you?'

'I – I cannot say. I mean, I was not aware of any particular –'

'That fall she 'ad, Mum.' Eliza pushed forward eagerly. 'Do you remember? Not long after I came 'ere it was, when you was first wed. I remember, she fell down in 'er room and couldn't walk proper. That there Dorcas used to push 'er out in a Bath chair.'

'Yes,' Tilly said, and felt guilt fill her in a sickening wave. She did indeed remember. It had happened just the week after she and Frank returned from their wedding trip to Brighton. Tilly had been so anxious about their disastrous honeymoon that she had no eyes for anyone; she had dismissed her mother's fall as just another manifestation of daffy, and been quite unconcerned. To discover now that it had been due to an apoplectic stroke rather than gin was shaming indeed.

Mr Fildes nodded at her in some sympathy. 'It is understandable, Ma'am, that you and your esteemed father were not aware of the reality of her situation. It takes considerable diagnostic skill, after all.' He preened. 'Now, I am afraid that I must give you more bad news. I have to tell you that she can never be other than she is.'

'I did not think otherwise,' Tilly managed and bent her head, unable to hide her tears any longer and Mr Fildes patted her hand kindly, clearly approving strongly of such daughterly piety.

'It is no one's fault, Madam. I venture to say that this would have happened had she been a model of sobriety. In some ways it will have helped her to be – er – as she is. At least she has no awareness of her condition. It is a dreadful thing when

148

a hale and active person is struck down by such a disease. For them the loss of mobility or their senses is a case for much grieving. For your mother, well, I do not hesitate to aver that she probably had no awareness at all of what happened to her. She has been entirely sheltered from any distress.'

Tilly nodded, still tearful and then reached for her handkerchief and blew her nose, struggling to find her composure again. She succeeded tolerably well.

'Is there anything we can do for her?' she asked.

He shook his head. 'I would continue as you are, Mrs Quentin. Seeing she is fed as much as possible and kept reasonably sweet about her person and allowed her gin. If it were withdrawn now it would cause her misery and would be of small value. She cannot be restored to normal life, so sobriety would be of no advantage to her.'

Suddenly Tilly liked this fussy man; he was greedy, possibly, self-important certainly, and deeply inquisitive undoubtedly, but he had a genuine concern for sick people, and a real awareness of what life might be like for such a person as her mother. She lifted her chin and smiled at him warmly and he looked quite confused and then pleased.

'You are most kind, Mr Fildes. I thank you for your efforts.' She reached into her reticule and took out her money. 'One shilling and sixpence, I think we agreed.'

He opened his mouth, looked at the money she had put into his palm and then closed it again, beaming widely.

'And I would appreciate it if this matter were not – um – discussed with my father. It is between ourselves.'

'Indeed,' Mr Fildes said fervently. 'I can fully understand the painful business it would be for Mr Kingsley to have to discuss the health of his beloved wife. It is a good thing he has so dutiful and caring a daughter.'

'Exactly so,' she said and smiled again. He was trying so very hard. 'You are a kindly man, are you not, Mr Fildes. I appreciate it, indeed I do.'

He went a little pink and bobbed his head. 'Well, I try to

prosecute the welfare of my patients as best I can. It is the task of the apothecary, you understand.'

'Completely,' Tilly said.

He became very brisk then. 'And you are also under my care, Ma'am, and I am concerned that you are agitating yourself too much. You are still weak and I have had to be the bearer of unhappy tidings. It is time, I think, that you returned to bed. Eliza —'

Tilly didn't argue. She had been a longer time in the chair than she had imagined, and her back was aching and so were her legs. To lie in bed again would be agreeable, and she let Eliza almost carry her there and set her against the pillows.

'I am sure I shall recover swiftly now,' she said as she relaxed gratefully. 'Each day must surely get easier. Unlike those of my mother. For her, each day must be a deterioration.'

'I fear so,' Mr Fildes said. 'But she can remain with us for many years yet if she is well cared for. Good food, you know — beef juice and eggs and milk if she will take no solid food. And ensure she has plenty of bland liquids in addition to her — to her other fluids. She will be at some risk of dyspepsia and that can make her fretful and may indeed lead to a haemorrhage which would be very worrying.'

Despite his concern for his weary patient he seemed inclined to linger, and Tilly closed her eyes and settled herself more deeply into her pillows as though she were about to sleep. 'Yes, indeed, Mr Fildes,' she murmured drowsily. 'Thank you so much.' She listened as Eliza took him away and closed the door behind them. And then opened her eyes and stared at the ceiling, thinking of her mother as tears slid down her thin cheeks.

Chapter Fourteen

'NO MONEY AT ALL?' Tilly said, and stared at him. The solicitor said nothing, just looking back at her with his bland expression. 'There must surely be some.'

'All there is, Mrs Quentin, is the – um – promised settlement on the occasion of your marriage. That has not been paid into Mr Quentin's account by your father yet. However, I have no doubt that – um –'

'Yes,' Tilly said dully and looked down at her hands on her lap. They were frail, like a bag of bird's bones, and very white against the black merino of her gown. It felt strange to be wearing such deep mourning and yet not to be grief-stricken. She wasn't. She was numb, as far as Frank was concerned. Sometimes she felt she had never been married at all, really; and then she remembered the baby and moved her hands so that they were clasped across her front, wanting to hold the secret safe, wanting no one to know, least of all this smooth watchful man who sat facing her across his desk.

She had decided to visit him, arduous though a journey into the City was in her still weak state, rather than ask him to wait upon her at home, because she needed to know all there was to know about her situation and she felt, for reasons she could not have explained, that he was more likely to be truthful here than in Brompton Grove. Also, although he had been her husband's solicitor, he was the partner of Mr Cobbold, her father's man of law, and that should make it easier, she had thought, to ask questions. In the event it was not.

'Ah – Mr Conroy,' she began, and looked at that smooth face again and lost her nerve. He was so guarded, so very unapproachable, that coming out bluntly with her question was almost impossible. Involuntarily she tightened her hands across her belly and that made her able to try again. She was not, after all, asking only for herself.

'I take it, Mr Conroy, that you would be willing to continue as my man of business, even though my husband has died?'

'Indeed, Ma'am, if that is your wish, although I must say that I see little business that is required. The will your husband left is clear – he had no other family but yourself and you are his sole legatee. But as I say, there is nothing there to be –'

'Quite so, Mr Conroy,' she said as steadily as she could. It wasn't easy to ignore the supercilious look that had come over the solicitor's face. 'But I am, I imagine, an heiress in my own right.'

He was very still then. 'Mrs Quentin?' he said at length.

'I mean, of course, that my father –' She swallowed. 'Your partner is his man of business, Mr Conroy. I am asking you to tell me, from the knowledge of my father's affairs that I dare say you may have gleaned from Mr Cobbold, precisely what my situation is. I am a widow, after all, and have no further means of support. I need to know what provisions for my future may have been made.'

He stirred in his chair and set his hands together and looked over them at her. 'My dear Mrs Quentin, I realize of course that these are early days and you are still quite *bouleversé* with grief, but I must point out to you that you are but eighteen years of age, and quite – um – unencumbered. I have no doubt that there will be other suitors. It is sure that you will wed again within a short space of time. Especially if –' he looked at her consideringly '– you do not go out of your way to tell people your husband left you so ill provided for.'

She flushed. 'I do not see myself as goods in a marriage market, Sir,' she said sharply. 'And anyway –' But she would not tell him. Why should she? He was not the sort of man who would regard the fact that she was expecting Frank's child as good news in any way. She could not bear that her coming child should be described as an 'encumbrance'. She was too frightened already about the state of her affairs.

'Yes, Mrs Quentin?'

'And anyway,' she went on, 'one thing has nothing to do with another. I wish to know what my situation is if — what my situation is.'

'Is there any reason for you to doubt your father's good intentions towards you, Mrs Quentin?'

She was disliking this man more by the second. Prying and showing clearly that he didn't care at all that she was aware of his doing so.

'That is beside the point, Mr Conroy. I am asking for facts. I cannot consider my future on the basis of — of mere feelings and surmises. Is it possible for you to give me this information? Answer me yes or no and I will go away.'

He smiled, and she thought that he looked even more unlikeable than when his face was still. 'You are asking me to break confidence, Mrs Quentin, with a client of this house.'

'If it is so difficult, then I will ask no more,' she said, her patience giving out as suddenly as her composure. Another moment with this man, she told herself, and I shall weep again. This hateful illness! It has made me weak in every possible way.

'It is not so much difficult, Mrs Quentin, as not possible. We may be partners, Mr Cobbold and I, but we still guard most jealously the confidence of our individual clients.'

'Is that so?' she snapped, using temper as a way of control-ling shameful tears. 'Perhaps if you had been more concerned about the welfare of your clients, Mr Conroy, you would have told me long since that my marriage settlement had not been paid.'

'But you were not my client until now, Mrs Quentin,' he said smoothly. 'Your late husband was. Had he wished you to

153

know, I dare say he would have told you. No doubt he wished to protect you from pain.'

'No doubt,' she said sharply and went to the door. 'Well, Mr Conroy, I must thank you for your time. Good morning.'

'It is my pleasure, Mrs Quentin,' he said and smiled, but did not get up from his desk. 'If I can be of any help in the future please do not hesitate to call upon me.'

Tilly reached Leadenhall Street with her knees shaking and not entirely from fatigue. How dare he be so condescending? She was not, of course, a rich woman. Had she been, she was sure he would have been bowing and scraping at her like some –

She suddenly stopped in the middle of the crowded pavement, as people rushed by, eddying round her as water eddies round rocks in streams. Mr Conroy had, in his behaviour, given her the answer to her questions. Her father had no intention of making her his heiress. He was planning, as she had begun to suspect, to leave his wealth to Mrs Leander.

However much he might plead poverty and bad investments, there was no doubt in her mind that her father had a comfortable sum of money tucked away somewhere and of course there was the house, which had considerable real worth. It would make a tidy inheritance and until Frank's death she had never thought about it. But now she had to; indeed it had been one of Eliza's casual remarks that made her aware of the need to do so.

'Lucky ain't it, Mum, that you ain't in a situation like my Ma was when my Pa went and died – or the one I was told was my Pa. Got throwed out of 'er 'ouse she did, on account it was tied to 'im working on Mr Lumley's farm. But you're all right, God be thanked. You got your father's house to live in and no problems.'

But had she? And if she had, for how long? Since Frank's death Mrs Leander had become more and more outrageous in her behaviour, treating the house as though it were hers entirely, and being exceedingly haughty with Tilly; indeed,

154

almost as much as she was with Eliza. It was becoming quite unbearable and Tilly smarted under it painfully. Perhaps she was in no better a state than Eliza's unsupported mother, thrown out of her village hovel. Could not the same thing happen to a widowed Tilly should her father die?

She had never thought much about death before. There had been no real need to do so. Now, however, Frank was dead. He had been but five and twenty, yet he was dead. Night after night as she made the slow progression back to health, Tilly struggled with the guilt that filled her about Frank's death. If she had not locked him out he would not have fallen down the area steps. If he had listened to me he would not have come home drunk again, a part of her mind would retort. But perhaps if I had not threatened to lock him out, he would not have been driven to drinking too much, just to assert his authority.

So the arguments went on and on inside her head until they were displaced by fears for her father. Was it not reasonable to suppose that her father, at the age of fifty-six (as she suspected he was, from something he had once said about the year of his birth being in the last year of the old century), might soon die? He also drank heavily, and often came home much the worse for wear because of it. It was hard to love someone of whom you were so very afraid, but he was her father and, anyway, all she had. There were no other relations that she knew of. Both her parents had been only children, and neither had ever spoken of any connections of their own, so who else did she have? What shall I do if he dies and Mrs Leander throws me out of the house . . .?

Such fears had driven her, on this sultry July afternoon, into the City to see what she could discover from Frank's solicitor. No one had come to tell her of her situation after his death and in many ways life in the Brompton Grove house continued as though he had never been there, had never existed at all. Tilly's father went on in his normal way, totally absorbed in his business affairs and coming home only occasionally to eat his dinners and spend time with Mrs Leander. He and Tilly had little contact, although he did at least continue to pay her the agreed money to run the house and she was grateful for that. Eliza had, by dint of working her way through *The English Gentlewoman's Magazine*, managed to provide him with tolerable enough victuals so that he complained less than he once had. The house was certainly cleaner under Eliza's devoted care and Tilly often marvelled at how energetic the girl was. She not only did all the cleaning and the cooking, but also looked after Henrietta and Tilly herself. And that was something else for Tilly to feel bad about, for Eliza earned so little for all she did and yet was so very contented.

Altogether, as she stood there in the middle of the pavement in Leadenhall Street, Tilly felt very confused and unhappy. She tried again to marshall her thoughts logically, but she could not rid herself of the notion that had fixed itself in her mind. Mr Conroy had, in refusing to answer her questions, made it clear that he knew Austin Kingsley had no intention of leaving his house or his money to his daughter.

And his daughter's child. Tilly set one hand on her belly, feeling the small bump she knew was there, so small that no one could yet see it but which was very apparent to her when she ran her hands over herself in bed at night. My child, she thought. Left with nothing. No home. No support. Nothing.

This cannot happen, she told herself. I must find a way to prevent it. My father must be told – her thoughts baulked then. Tell her father what he should do with his own property? It was unthinkable. No, she must think again.

Mrs Leander must forfeit her right to the house and the money. Again Tilly had to stop that line of thought. It was as impossible to imagine speaking to Mrs Leander of such a matter as it was to imagine the sun rising in the west tomorrow. There had to be another way. Quite what, she could not see, but there had to be another way.

'Tilly,' a voice said and she whirled, startled at hearing her own name said so warmly. She was suddenly aware of all the surrounding noise as horses plunged and jangled their harnesses in the shafts of vans and omnibuses, costers shouted and passers-by chattered and van drivers swore in the maelstrom that was Leadenhall Street.

Freddy Compton was standing with his head on one side so that his top hat seemed most precariously perched on it, with the knob of his cane held in his mouth, watching her quizzically through those pallid lashes that made him look so startled and kitten-like.

'Good morning,' he said cheerfully and smiled, once again making the transformation of himself that had so surprised her the first time she met him, from a weedy young man to a very reassuring presence indeed. 'How are you, my dear?'

She stared at him, quite nonplussed. 'Imagine seeing you here!' was all she could say. 'So far from home and in the middle of such a crowded street!'

He went a little pink and then reached out, took her elbow and steered her to the side of the pavement, out of the way of an irritable passer-by who almost pushed her as he hurried past. 'Well, that's as may be,' he said and smiled down at her again.

'But it is most strange!' she persisted, quite open-eyed at the coincidence of it all and he sighed, clearly embarrassed.

'You quite undo me, Tilly,' he said. 'It is not perhaps such a coincidence after all. I was told by Eliza that you had insisted on coming up to town to see your man of business. She was most disapproving, I must tell you.'

Tilly smiled at that. 'I know. She told me so often! Such a very watchful child she is! I am fortunate to have her to take care of me so kindly.'

'You are indeed. But she is also a chatterbox of course and when she told me where you had gone, I thought — well I must be in that part of town myself. I too have business to prosecute. After I have done it, why then perhaps I shall see Mrs Tilly and be able to take care of her and fetch her home. Just to please her housemaid, you understand.'

'I understand well enough!' Tilly said with mock reproof. 'You and she were in a conspiracy over me! She tried to prevent my going out on the grounds that it was too much for me – and I have been better these many weeks now – and failing to persuade me, goes complaining to you.'

'It's not quite so bad. I did in truth come to call. Alice is in the country, visiting an old friend in Staffordshire and I am quite alone. I needed to flee from the rest of the workmen – they will never be done, they are so dreadfully slow – and you were not there, but here. Now I am here too.' He looked at her a little more closely. 'And not before time, I suspect. I think you are more tired than you know. You are quite white about the mouth.'

She bit her lip and looked away. 'Such nonsense –'

'Not at all. Now, the time is past twelve. Time for a small luncheon, I believe. You will permit me, I am sure, to arrange this for you. Come along.' And he made an elbow and tucked her hand into it and moved through the crowds to the kerbside again, waving his stick in the air with his other hand to summon a cab.

She tried to protest but not very loudly. She was, to tell the truth, more tired than she had expected to be. She was still far from restored to her full health, and the thought of sitting down and drinking some hot tea, perhaps, was very attractive.

He was quite masterful, putting her in the cab and talking easily of commonplaces as the driver whipped up his horse and plunged into the traffic; and she relaxed and allowed it.

After a while she became aware that he had stopped talking and was regarding her anxiously.

'Forgive me for my distracted state,' she said quickly. 'I have much to think about.'

'Indeed,' he said at once and then added sympathetically, 'I hope your man of business did not have bad news for you?'

She could not help it. She knew it was not right to burden a man who was little more than a stranger, however long ago she might have known his wife, with such matters, but it would be such a luxury to let out some of her anxiety, and so she indulged herself.

'It was not good news,' she said. 'My husband left me nothing, and my father —' She hesitated. 'I am of the impression that he is less interested in my welfare than I would like.'

'I see.' He was grave and said little more as the cab arrived at the destination he had given to the driver, and they were decanted on to the pavement.

'I have chosen this hotel,' he said, as he helped her up a pair of handsome wide steps into a broad marble-clad hallway, 'as one that is luxurious and yet totally respectable. The Hotel Cecil has an excellent reputation. They will provide a small luncheon that you will not find unpalatable. And,' he added as she looked about her at the richly carpeted and clearly very expensive establishment, 'we will be able to talk quietly of your situation. I am sure we will think of something that you can do to ease matters for yourself.'

She looked up at him and surrendered the last of her doubts. It would indeed be comforting to have some help with her dilemma, and talking about it would be the greatest comfort. She followed him as he led the way to the hotel dining-room with more spring in her step than she would have thought possible half an hour ago.

Chapter Fifteen

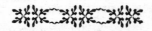

BY THE TIME she reached home again she felt both rested and a great deal happier. She also felt that Freddy and she had been friends for many years and was at such ease with him that she was able to sit in the cab and kick off her boots, which had become tight and uncomfortable with the passage of time.

She leaned back on the dusty leather squabs of the cab and said a little sleepily, 'That was indeed a perfect luncheon. I do thank you for it.'

'It was my pleasure to see you enjoying it so well,' he said. 'It is always delightful to introduce a friend to a dish they have not tried before.'

'That one was most interesting.' She stifled a yawn. 'I wonder if they really do eat eggs so in Florence? Or is it perhaps an invention of an English cook?'

'I am assured at the Hotel Cecil that their chef is Italian and his dishes are quite authentic. Have you not eaten eggs served with spinach and so rich a sauce anywhere else?'

'Indeed not —' She lapsed into silence and then could not make polite talk any longer. 'Will it work, do you think, Freddy?'

'I am sure it will. Just leave it to me.' He leaned forwards and patted her hand in an avuncular sort of way. 'You must not worry, my dear. Just go to your room and rest and when you come down, it is my belief that Mrs Leander will have gone.'

'But how can you be so sure that what you have to say will be enough to make her — I mean, will you not tell me what you are planning to say to her? What can there possibly be that —'

'Now, you promised me! When I said I had an idea that would serve but that I must be left alone to apply it, you agreed. Yet you question me like a Bishop at a catechism!'

'I am sorry, Freddy — it's just that I can't imagine what you could say to such a woman to alarm her enough to send her packing. Nothing,' she added with great feeling, '*nothing* at all ever alarms Mrs Leander!'

He sighed, pretending to be exasperated. 'My dear girl, I told you! If you tell persons like Mrs Leander that All is Discovered and that you hold information about their past lives, they will believe you. Such people always have past histories of which they are ashamed. They are also very well accustomed to making the best of their situations and regard caution as the wisest way. She will be no different, I am quite sure of it.'

'But how do you *know* this, Freddy?' She was wide awake now and looked at him thoughtfully as she sat with one hand tucked into the leather strap at the side of the cab to maintain her balance, for they were now out of the City and well on their way to Brompton village, and the cab was fairly rattling along and swaying severely in consequence. 'You are after all a person I do not know well. Perhaps there are things about your past — perhaps I could tell *you* to flee because All is Known.'

'Oh, pooh,' he smiled. 'Are we not old friends?'

'Well,' she said candidly, 'not really. Are we? I knew your wife, of course, when we were children, though even then —'

He chuckled. 'I am well aware of that. She has a great gift for elevating memory to a higher status than it warrants. Dear Alice. I have no doubt that you hardly remembered her.'

'Not at first,' Tilly allowed.

'But that does not matter. Now we are neighbours we must be closer. It is better for both our families.'

'You have not answered my question. How is it you know how to deal with such persons as Mrs Leander? What in *your* past makes that possible?'

'Put it down to worldly wisdom,' he said easily. 'I am, after all, rather older than you – almost twice as old, I believe – and I have travelled a good deal. France and Italy . . .'

She could hear the invitation to quiz him about his adventures, but she ignored it, sticking firmly to her point.

'You are so sure that your trick on Mrs Leander will rid me of her, yet I cannot help but –'

'We are almost home now,' he said. 'Why not leave it to me? You are tired, I know, and will rest gladly. Do so, while I speak to Mrs Leander. If I am proved wrong, by all means quiz me. But if I am right you must accept the way of it, and ask no more questions. Is that fair?'

She considered carefully. 'I'm not sure –'

He laughed. 'I am,' he said as the cab stopped. He opened the door and jumped out. 'Come along now.'

'My boots,' she said, and reached for them, but he was too quick for her.

'I will see to them,' and he stretched out and took them in his hand, scooped her up before she could protest and carried her up the steps to the front door of number seventeen as she protested, her face crimson with embarrassment.

'It is indeed high time you strengthened yourself with a little more good food,' he said reprovingly as he set her on her feet. 'You are as delicate and light as a bird. Here are your boots. Now, away to your room while I see off the cab. And –' again he laughed '– see off Mrs Leander.'

Eliza had heard their arrival from the kitchen below and came hurrying up to open the front door. She gaped at the sight of her mistress holding her boots in her hand.

'Eliza,' Tilly said hurriedly. 'Where is Mrs Leander?'

Eliza made a grimace. 'Sittin' in the drawin' room as cool as

162

you please,' she said. 'Made me light the fire an' everythin',
like I didn't have enough to do, and the weather so sultry.
Well, it was just her bein' awkward. She'd rather sit there and
sweat than let me be free of doin' the fire for her —'

'Hush, Eliza,' Tilly said and looked a little nervously up the
stairs. 'I would prefer there should be no — um — arguments
between you and her at present.' Preventing Eliza from saying
more than she should to Mrs Leander was a constant problem
for Tilly. 'Now, listen, I am going to my room to rest. When
Mr Compton comes in, take him up to the drawing-room and
leave him there. Do not interrupt, even if Mrs Leander rings
for tea. Do you understand? Just leave him there with her.'

'Yes, Mum,' Eliza said, staring as Tilly went hurrying
upstairs, silent in her stocking feet, and then looked back over
her shoulder as Freddy came up the front steps.

The last Tilly saw, as she paused at the top of the stairs,
was his face turned towards her with a reassuring grin on it as
he handed his hat to Eliza. And then she fled to throw herself
on her bed and wait.

To her amazement, she dozed off. She had imagined that
after the anxiety of her visit to Mr Conroy, let alone her
luncheon and extraordinary conversation with Freddy, she
would have been too tense to sleep. But sleep she did, and
only woke suddenly when Eliza came into her room bearing a
jug of cool lemonade and a glass.

'Hmm?' She struggled to sit up, so Eliza set down the tray
and helped her.

'Oh, Missus,' she said, radiant. 'Oh, Missus, such a to-do!'
And stood there with her hands folded on her apron, her face
shining like a new apple and clearly bursting with news.

'What has happened, Eliza?' Tilly peered at her and then
rubbed her eyes. 'Bless my soul, what has happened?'

'She's gone, Mum,' Eliza burst out as though she could hold
it in no longer. 'Bin and packed her bags and *gone*! Ain't that
something? Mr Freddy, he said she would, he come down to
the kitchen to tell me to leave you restin' and on no account

to see her – Mrs Leander – and left you this note, Mum, and then he went.' She pulled a folded sheet of paper from her apron pocket. 'And then not half an hour after that, yon Madam sets to pealing the bell like a crazy thing and makes me go all the way up to the top, and tells me to carry down 'er bags and fetch 'er a cab on account she's bin called away urgent like. And then she went and, well Mum, I was that turned about, I 'ardly knew what I was doin'. But it's true, Mum, it really is, and I'm that happy I could cry!' And she did, catching her breath as the tears ran down her face.

Tilly calmed her down as best she could and sent her back to the kitchen. When Eliza had gone, Tilly unfolded Freddy's letter.

> All is well, Tilly. I explained to Mrs Leander why it would be better if she left. She did not argue too much. I do not think you will have further problems. I trust you are quite recovered from the exertions of the morning.
>> Your friend, F.

She refolded the letter slowly and put it in her reticule and then went down to the kitchen, bearing the tray of untasted lemonade.

'Thank you, Eliza,' she said absently. 'That lemonade was very good.'

'Yes, Mum,' Eliza said joyously, not noticing the lie. 'Oh Mum, everythin's good, ain't it?' Tilly nodded and went back upstairs to the morning room to sit and collect her thoughts.

Mrs Leander had worked in this house for – she had to work it out – thirteen years. Tilly had only been a child of five when she and Dorcas arrived. What could Freddy Compton possibly have found out about her to make Mrs Leander depart in such a hugger-mugger fashion? Tilly could bear it no longer: she had to ask him, and she got to her feet and hurried to the door. She did not even stop to tell Eliza where she was going. She just hurried out of the house and up the steps of the adjoining house, her skirts flying and bouncing as she went.

The door was answered by their housemaid, a woman of some forty summers Tilly judged, and not one with whom Eliza had struck up any sort of friendship, nor was likely to. She stood looking disapprovingly at Tilly, clearly scandalized by the fact that she had come out in a house gown and with no hat or pelisse of the sort that was required for street wear. But Tilly was past noticing any such matter and said breathlessly, 'Mr Compton, where is he?'

The housemaid became positively wooden with disapproval and opened her mouth to speak, but Tilly could not wait. She ran past her and up the stairs, holding her skirts high to avoid the wet paint at the sides, and dodging past the workman who was crouching halfway up with a paint brush in his hand, and burst straight into the drawing-room.

Freddy was standing in his shirt sleeves, his head bent over a sheaf of papers, and he looked up at her, startled, as the housemaid came thumping along behind.

'I could not prevent —' the housemaid began but Freddy waved an irritably dismissive hand at her and the woman sniffed and went away.

'Tell me what has happened!' he commanded and she clapped her hands together and shook her head at him.

'It is quite amazing! It is exactly as you said! She *went*. I did not even wake to hear her. I did fall asleep, and when I woke Eliza told me — she wasted no time at all. Freddy, you *must* tell me! What was it you said to her?'

He shook his head, laughing, clearly delighted to hear her news, but not unduly surprised. 'We made a bargain, my dear Tilly, did we not? If she obliged and did as I told her, why then, you would ask no more questions.'

'I made no such bargain!' she protested. 'You said it was to be so but I made no promises. Now, you must tell me, or I shall sit here until you do.'

'No chairs,' he pointed out. 'The paper hangers have only just finished. The carpet is laid in place, I grant you, but the furniture does not arrive from the repository until tomorrow.'

'I don't care!' she said. 'I shall just sit on the floor!' And she did, in a soft ballooning of her black skirt. She settled her crinoline around her as neatly as she could, and gazed up at him with her expression as quizzical as she could make it. She was, she realized with some surprise, happier than she could ever remember being. Freddy had made her happy; it was wonderful and delightful and such a relief after so long a period of unhappiness that she laughed aloud at the sheer joy of it. Then she folded her hands on her lap very neatly and firmly to make it clear to him that she would not budge until he answered her questions.

He laughed too and at once sat down beside her, cross-legged, and then they were both laughing, quite immoderately. The door opened again, and the housemaid came in, bearing a small table before her.

'I took it upon myself to arrange tea, Sir,' she said with the same wooden expression on her face. 'I thought Madam might like some.' Without seeming to show any awareness of the highly unusual manner in which her master was conversing with his guest, she fetched the tray of tea and set the plates and cups on the table with all the neatness that was possible and then, bobbing her head, went away. And all the time the two of them sat, unable to look at each other and bursting with laughter. The maid was barely out of the door before they both collapsed with it. Freddy threw himself back on the carpet and lay there quite abandoned to his merriment.

'This is quite a shocking way to behave!' Tilly said reprovingly. 'What would Alice say if she were here?'

'She would laugh loudest of all,' Freddy said and Tilly nodded, for she was sure he was right.

'She would also,' she said, 'make you tell us both what it was you said to Mrs Leander that had the effect that it did.'

He was sitting up again now and looking at her and the laughter had vanished from his face.

'Ah – Alice,' he said. 'I had not thought –'

'Yes?' She too stopped laughing and looked at him and

166

somewhere at the back of her mind she thought how different he looked when he smiled. Now he looks rather – well, foolish again. He should smile or laugh all the time.

'It would be better not to tell Alice about all this, I think,' he said after a moment. 'She would give me no peace until she knew all about – well, it is, after all, not a matter to be bruited abroad. I promised Mrs Leander that if she went I would say nothing about her to any one. That I would keep her secret as if it were my own.' He made a little face then, and it acted the way a smile did in that it took away the air of foolishness from his countenance. 'That was the arrangement I made. I told her fairly that she was not welcome by you, however comfortable Mr Kingsley might be, and that as your friend I had charged myself with the task of persuading her to leave the house as you wished her to. I assured her that I would never make any mention of the matters I knew about, that not a whisper about them would pass my lips and the least I can do is be honourable. You would not wish me to be otherwise, I think.'

Tilly was silent for a long moment and then nodded. 'I see. Then there *was* really something that you knew about her.'

'Truly, Tilly, you are unkind to press me.' He looked serious again and with it his normal, rather uninteresting self, and she did not feel comfortable with that, and anyway she knew he was right. She must ask no more.

'Well,' she said. 'I must go home. I thank you, more than you can imagine.' She put out her hand and he at once clambered to his feet and held out his and pulled her up.

'Now Mary has fetched the tea, I think we must drink it,' he said. 'Permit me to give you some. Cream? Sugar?'

'If you please,' she said gravely and took the cup from him and they stood there, side by side, drinking their tea, as he told her of the changes that had been made in the room and the plans they had to redecorate the dining- and breakfast-rooms on the floor below.

'It is better for dear Alice to be away while all this is going on,' he said. 'It is so dispiriting for a woman to have to see her home in such disarray – I was glad when she was invited into Staffordshire.'

They continued to make small talk until he at last took her cup from her and saw her to the front door and she went home, marvelling at the way the man could change so. It was very odd the way they had laughed and he had seemed so charming, and how rapidly all that had vanished when he started to speak seriously; and she thought – he is quite the opposite of most people, who seem foolish when they laugh. I am so glad he is my neighbour. Even if Alice is sometimes tiresome.

She had to talk to Eliza about the dinner and make what plans she could for her father's return, because she knew that however elated she might be at Mrs Leander's departure, he would be quite the reverse. She had to decide what to say to him and she had not thought at all about that yet; she had hardly had time, and she stood for a moment in the quiet hall, looking about her, trying to arrange her thoughts.

It felt different now, knowing that that woman was no longer there; more like her own true home, and she took a deep breath and hurried to the stairs. She would have to go to Mrs Leander's room and check that all was well. The fact that the room was also her father's was something that she did not care to think about; it still seemed necessary to her to check that the woman had really gone. After all, she only had Eliza's word for it. It might be as well to be certain she had left no possessions behind, thus showing perhaps that she intended to return.

But it was clear that Eliza had reported no more than the truth. The wardrobes that had been filled with Mrs Leander's clothes, and still smelled of the Chypre perfume she always used, were quite empty. The drawers of the tallboy had been tugged out and emptied and now hung drunkenly in their frames, and she pushed them back into position carefully, her heart lifting with each one. The woman had gone, she really had, and she did not intend to return; and Tilly went down to the kitchen to talk to Eliza about dinner in an almost bemused state.

By the time she had settled Eliza, who was so excited and happy that she seemed ready to float to the ceiling and fly around it, and put her to mincing yesterday's cold beef to be made into a cottage pie — which, fortunately, Austen Kingsley liked a great deal — some of Tilly's fatigue was returning. She would have liked nothing better than an early night and a cup of hot milk for supper, but that could not be. Not tonight. So she dressed as carefully as she could, pulling on her black silk gown with the jet beads and dressing her hair as carefully as she could. Then, at the last moment, she turned back to her dressing-table to get her mother's pearls. It would help her, she felt, to have them clasped about her neck. She would feel more like the mistress of the house as she now undoubtedly was, and that would strengthen her in her dealings with her father, which were not going to be at all easy.

She found the blue velvet box where she had hidden it, behind her handkerchiefs in her top right-hand drawer. When she opened it, it was empty.

Chapter Sixteen

'YOU'RE LYING,' Austen Kingsley said flatly. 'She would not have dared.'

Tilly took a sharp little breath in through her nose. She had known he would be angry, had expected shouting and rage, but she had not thought he would behave like this. To deny so flatly the truth that was before his eyes, that Mrs Leander had gone and had no intention of returning, and had taken from Tilly's dressing-table her mother's pearls; that she had not expected. She tried again.

'I assure you, Papa, that it is so. She sent for Eliza, bade her carry her bags down and call a cab. And she went. You may speak to Eliza yourself. She was quite clear in every detail.'

'She would not dare,' he said again. 'She could not.'

He sat at the table, his shoulders hunched and his head down, like a bull about to charge, staring at her from beneath brows that looked rough and ugly from the angle at which she saw them. It was an odd posture for him and despite his similarity to a dangerous animal, she suddenly realized that there was no danger in him at all, and thought – he's frightened. This is not anger, nor is it disbelief. He's frightened. What is there for him to be afraid of? I don't understand.

'And to steal your mother's pearls? Why should she do that?'

'Because they are valuable, I imagine,' Tilly said with a touch of acerbity. 'I never noticed Mrs Leander not to be interested in money.'

'And what sensible person is not interested in money?' he roared and she winced but was oddly glad to see the rage again. This was the familiar father she understood. 'Don't talk stupid rubbish to me, Madam, or by God I'll —' But the fire seemed to die down as fast as it had burned up. 'She had only to ask,' he mumbled. 'Only to ask.'

Tilly said nothing, just sat and watched him. The remains of their dinner lay congealing on the table, and a cabinet pudding carefully made by Eliza and well garnished with jam to hide its imperfections stood untouched on the sideboard. It clearly would not be eaten tonight.

She tried, genuinely tried, to enter his feelings. Was he fond of Mrs Leander? Had she been more to him than just a harlot, kept conveniently at home to save him the trouble of venturing out to a house of assignation? Tilly had always believed that to be the case, if she had thought of the matter at all. She certainly could not imagine her father caring for any person other than himself. All her life he had been a presence that was noise and bombast and coldness.

To perceive him now, as she was trying to do, as a person like herself inasmuch as he had emotions that were soft and vulnerable to pain, was difficult if not impossible. And imperceptibly she shook her head in an act of denial of her own. He could not feel as she had in the long weeks after Frank's death, could not know the guilt, the emptiness, the loneliness of it all. Not until this afternoon with Freddy had she known any lighter feelings at all. Was her father now thrown into the self-same state of misery and loss because of Mrs Leander? The shake of her head became more definite. It was not possible. Not her father. Not Mrs *Leander*.

She leaned forwards and tried again. 'Papa, I am afraid that it is true. If you doubt it, simply look in your room. The wardrobes she used are quite empty.'

He lifted his chin and stared at her. 'I care not,' he said with an attempt at insouciance, a sort of sketch of the way he usually was, and she felt again a pang for him and it amazed her. To feel sorry for her father? Everything was getting stranger and stranger this evening.

'I care not a whit for her, nor for anyone else,' he shouted suddenly. He pulled himself to his feet, holding on to the table so tightly that he pulled the cloth askew and threatened to send plates and glasses tumbling to the floor. 'Whatever I do, it makes no nevermind, does it? God damn all you women and all of your souls to hellfire. I hope you rot!' And he turned, lumbering and awkward, and pushed his way out of the room. She stood there staring after him and listened to the thud of the front door as he slammed out of the house.

He did not return that night, nor on any of the following nights. At first all she felt was relief. Her father was not there, and that could be nothing but good. She spent her time seeing to the house, continuing with Eliza's cookery education – and, of course, her own – as they pored over the sizeable collection of magazines Eliza had now amassed, and generally feeling stronger and better with each day that passed. Her father, she assured herself, would get over his sulk and come home from his club eventually, and she would deal with him. For the present the peace and quiet and the sheer joy of having the house free of Mrs Leander was enough for her.

But after five days she became uneasy. The weather had remained hot and heavy and there were occasional thunderstorms. She tried to convince herself that that was what made her feel so restless and anxious.

She stood at the drawing-room window staring out at Brompton Grove, watching the horses plodding by with sweaty flanks and drooping heads as they pulled their heavy loads of carriages and laden carts, and the languorous way passers-by moved along the pavements, stirring up little spurts of dust with each step, and felt again the queasiness she had thought no longer bothered her, now that she was into the fifth month of her pregnancy.

She set her hand to her round belly and caught her breath

172

as she felt a sudden odd sensation. She knew little about the processes of pregnancy, for she had no mother to talk to of what was happening to her, nor friends with whom to discuss it, but Eliza knew, and had regaled her with much information. It was Eliza who had patted her hand reassuringly and told her that she was 'quickening' when, a few weeks ago, she had felt as though she had swallowed a butterfly which was leaping around within her, deep in her belly. Now there was a definite little kick and her heart almost rose into her mouth at the excitement of it; and then sank as she thought: poor baby. Poor fatherless baby.

And what of your grandfather? she thought then. Do you not even have him to care for you? And that notion was so strange she felt more uneasy than ever. He who was always so noisy and frightening and difficult, was she missing him? She had to admit she was. She was alone, without a husband and, she reminded herself with another lift of fear, precious little money. In spite of her careful shopping and most abstemious housekeeping she had barely seven shillings in her reticule. It would pay for food for the next week for Eliza and herself, but what would happen after that?

'Come home, Papa,' she whispered into the failing evening light. 'That woman is not worth abandoning all for, surely?' And on impulse she seized the black silk shawl that she had left lying on the sofa and went downstairs.

'Eliza.' She put her head around the kitchen door to see Eliza sitting in her rocking chair by the hearth, the brindled cat on her lap and her head down over one of her magazines. 'I am going to visit next door. Don't worry about me, and of course don't lock the house until I return. I doubt I shall be long.'

She had not seen Freddy since the day Mrs Leander had left. He had called in one afternoon while she was resting but had forbidden Eliza to disturb her – not that she would have done so willingly anyway – and Tilly had thought he might come the next day and had remained in the drawing-room all afternoon, waiting. But he had not, so she would have to go to him with her worries now. Not that she wished to burden him, but who else did she have to talk to? He had proved a good friend so far – or, at least, she *thought* he had.

The street smelled of dust and horses and, faintly, of dying roses, for the gardens behind the houses here had many rose bushes, drooping in the still air, and she stopped for a moment to take a deep breath. The outside air made a change after the stuffiness of the house and she looked up at the sky, which was a deep opalescent blue shading to a rich pink where the sun touched the western horizon, and let the moment wash over her. There will never be a time like this again, she thought, this moment when there is just me and my baby and this perfect sky. Live this moment, know it in all its specialness; if only it could be like this for always and always.

Along the road wheels rattled and harnesses jingled and she came to herself with a little start as a horse pulling a cab came alongside her and then stopped at the house which she was going to visit. The animal stamped and steamed as the cabby shouted at it, and the door of the cab opened and Freddy stepped down.

He paid the driver and turned to go up his front steps but stopped as he caught sight of her. He had been wearing his usual expression, but now his face broke into its familiar transforming smile.

'Tilly! How agreeable to see you! Are you taking a constitutional?'

'Ah – no, not precisely,' she said and pulled her shawl away from her shoulders, suddenly feeling rather warm. 'I was in fact coming to see you.'

He lifted his brows. 'A little late for a morning call!'

'I know. I'm sorry. If it isn't convenient, I shall –'

'Oh, pooh! Of course you must visit. Come in now, do! I am sure Alice will be delighted to see you.'

'Alice is home again? I had thought she was still away since she had not been to visit me.'

'Oh?' He had stopped on the step, his key in his hand, and

looked down at her in some surprise. 'I would have expected – oh, well. Perhaps she has been busy getting the house put to rights now the workmen are gone. It has no doubt kept her fully occupied.'

He reached towards the keyhole but before he could insert his key, the door opened and the forbidding housemaid stood in the entrance.

'Oh, it's you, Sir,' she said heavily.

'Of course it is! Who else should it be, Mary?' Freddy stood back to allow Tilly to enter before him. 'I have fetched a guest as well. Where is Mrs Compton?'

'Madam is in the drawing-room, Sir,' the maid said and there was a flatness about her voice that made Tilly glance at her.

'We shall go up at once,' Freddy said and tossed his hat and stick to Mary and ushered Tilly upstairs, chattering all the way of the work that had been done.

It did indeed look very good. There was pristine white paint and crimson carpet and gleaming brass everywhere, as well as the most elegant of flowered wallpapers and handsome dark mahogany furniture in the latest taste, which was richer and more embellished than the rather more delicate, older furniture in Tilly's house.

The drawing-room, which contained many sofas and chairs as well as plenty of occasional tables well laden with pictures in frames, knick-knacks and kickshaws of all sorts, was as handsome as the staircase and hall. Alice, resplendent in a gown of lemon silk with green braid, was sitting in a large armchair beside the fireplace which was hidden behind a very grand arrangement of ferns. She leapt up as the door opened and cried, 'Freddy,' in a high happy note and ran towards him, arms prettily outstretched. And then stopped short as she caught sight of Tilly.

'Oh,' she said blankly and stood very still.

Tilly was nonplussed. This was not at all as Alice had been the last time they met. 'I was coming to see you, Alice,' Tilly said. 'And met Freddy on the doorstep. I was about to return home for fear of discommoding you, for I had not thought how late it is, but he insisted that —'

'Of course I did!' Freddy said. 'It does not discommode us in the least, does it, Alice? It is a pleasure to see you. Now sit down, and we shall deal cosily.' He moved towards the fireplace and indicated a chair for Tilly.

She followed him and sat down, spreading her black silk skirts neatly and letting her shawl fall from her shoulders and looked across at Alice, who had come to take her chair again and pick up her embroidery.

'I am sorry to be a nuisance, Alice,' she said. 'But I am in a — well — I have a dilemma and I don't quite know what to do about it. And I hoped that you would advise me. I can think of no one better to guide me.'

Quite why she lied she did not know. It was Freddy's advice she wanted, not Alice's. She knew perfectly that only a fool would seek the counsel of such a flibberty-gibbet as Alice Compton, but it seemed politic to let her think otherwise.

Alice showed no sign of being mollified. She sat with her face still and her head bent. 'Oh?' was all she said.

'It is my father,' Tilly said and then stopped, ashamed to realize that her voice had tightened as though she were about to weep.

Alice looked up sharply and tilted her head to one side. 'Your father? What of him?'

'He —' Tilly shook her head. 'It is hard to explain. I feel I am bothering you when I should not. I did not mean to intrude. I —' She stood up, sure now that Alice was angry with her for some reason and feeling unable to cope with that. She could imagine no reason why Alice should be, except for the possibility that she wanted to be alone with Freddy and resented Tilly's intrusion. If so, that was natural enough, she supposed, and ached with a sense of deep loneliness. She had never felt that close to her Frank. Alice was indeed fortunate. 'I will leave you now. Perhaps another time —'

'Oh no, now, my dear,' Freddy said warmly. 'If you are so anxious we are glad to help, are we not, Alice? Clearly you have a cause for some anxiety? Tell us what it is and we will see what we can do to help you.'

'Yes, indeed,' Alice said, but there was no matching warmth in her tone.

'I –' Tilly sat down again with a small thump. 'He has not been home for five days. Ever since I told him of Mrs Leander's departure, when he was as I feared he would be, most put about. And now I have hardly any money left and I do not know what to do.'

Alice was staring at her, round-eyed. Clearly whatever had annoyed her had been set aside in the rush of intense curiosity that now filled her. 'Your father has vanished? Oh, goodness me, what can have happened? Do you think he has been set upon and murdered? Or that – and what is this about Mrs Leander? Is she, too, vanished?'

'Yes,' Tilly said. 'I was so glad of that, for she was – well – I will tell you all about it one day. She went as soon as Freddy told her to go and I was so grateful. But now Papa has gone and I dare say he is at his club. But I expected he would have returned by now. It has been five days and I – it is not like him, you see. Although he is – I cannot pretend he is – well, I cannot speak unkindly of him, of course, but oh dear, I am running on and I should not. I am so worried, you see.' And she folded her hands on her lap, bit her lower lip hard and bent her head in an effort to prevent the rush of tears that threatened to overwhelm her. She did now know why she was so distressed. It was not love of her father surely, just fear, just uncertainty, just ... She stopped trying to think and concentrated instead on not weeping. It was easier.

Freddy was on his feet. 'Five days? That is the outside of enough! He is quite wrong to leave you alone in your house, and you a widow and in your condition! I shall –'

'Condition?' Alice cried and looked sharply from one to the other. 'You are increasing?'

177

Tilly allowed herself only a nod.

'Oh!' Alice said again in that rather odd hard voice and this time Tilly stole a glance at her, and saw the cold, closed expression had returned to her face. But she did not have time to consider it further, for Freddy was now at the door.

'I shall find him, never fear,' he said. 'Alice, I shall return as soon as may be. Stay here with Tilly, will you? Look after her. I shall let you know as soon as I am able what is happening.' And he was gone, leaping down the stairs to the hall below, calling loudly to Mary to give him his hat, leaving the two women sitting staring at each other.

'Well,' Alice said, and her voice was tight with anger. 'Well now, what a situation this is to be sure! There is much we must talk about, Madam Tilly, you and I! Just what have you been doing with my husband while my back has been turned, hey? What have you been doing? Tell me now and all of it, or I swear to you I shall scratch your wicked eyes out of your nasty scheming little head!'

Chapter Seventeen

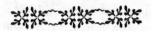

'BUT I DO assure you Alice, I have done nothing wrong! I cannot think why you should even consider it possible.' Tilly said again and put one hand up to her head, for it was aching now. Alice's attack had been so unexpected and so altogether repugnant that it had made her ears sing and her eyes become hot and sandy. She yearned to get to her feet and run back to the security of her own home, but she knew she could not do that, not while Alice still remained so incensed and so determined not to believe her.

'Oh, do not pretend to be ailing, just to get out of it,' Alice cried. 'I have no doubt you were cheerful enough when you set out to come here, not knowing I was here.'

'I do not deny that I was not certain whether you were here or not,' Tilly said. 'I am glad you were, however. I needed advice and I could think of no one better to give it than —'

'My husband,' snapped Alice. 'No sooner was my back turned and I was away on a necessary visit to sick friends, than you are in here, weaselling your way into —'

'Alice!' Tilly cried, bewildered. 'Where did you get such a foolish notion? My husband has just died under dreadful circumstances and I am quite bereft — How can you think I would — who would make you believe such a nonsense?'

'Nonsense, is it?' Alice leapt to her feet and was marching about her elegant drawing-room at such a rate that her skirts threatened to sweep the occasional tables clear of all their ornaments at every turn. 'I wish it were, indeed I do. But how can it be a nonsense when all those about me assure me they have seen you with their own eyes, positively flirting with him, sitting on the *floor* with him! That you are but recently widowed makes such behaviour the more reprehensible.'

'All those about you?' Tilly said, and shook her head. 'Talking about me? But how can – who can – Oh!' She stopped as the thought came to her.

'Oh, indeed,' snapped Alice, whipping up her wrath even more. 'Well may you say, "Oh!"'

'Have you been listening to servants' surmises?' Tilly said and managed to put such withering scorn into her voice that even the thoroughly agitated Alice was made to stop short in her perambulations. 'There is no other about you, as you say it, who could have observed me sitting on your drawing-room floor! We did so because your furniture had not yet been delivered and for no other reason. My call that day was a perfectly normal neighbourly one, yet you allow a servant's assumptions and gossip to convert it into something disagreeable! To listen to such talk should be beneath you!' Tilly warmed to her theme as her anger grew. 'And to listen to it from such a one as that *Mary* – I have never seen so sour a countenance nor so unpleasant a stare! There has been nothing between Freddy and me that has not been totally innocent. Had we been flirting, do you suppose we would have done so in the view of a woman as disagreeable as your servant? That you should believe such malice is a poor reflection on the quality of your judgement, Alice, and so I tell you. Flirting, indeed! How could anyone think such a thing of so kind and generous a person as your good husband? How could *you* think it? I am a widow. I am, as you now know, increasing. I have great problems at home and I am in need of true caring friendship, not attacks from those who profess friendship for me!' She jumped to her feet and stood there, her fists clenched at each side. 'I see that I am in the wrong entirely in believing that you meant kindly when you first called on me again after all the years of separation between our first acquaintance and this, and will no longer bother you. I greatly regret that your husband has used his time on my behalf, and beg you to assure him that I will manage very well indeed, thank you, without his or your further aid. I leave you to your *servant-woman*, Ma'am, and wish you well of her company and her poisonous conversation!' And she swept to the door, turned and dropped a curtsey and went, rushing down the stairs, to see Mary the maid gawping up at her from the hall below.

She stopped and stared her straight in the eyes, and let every atom of her now flaming anger show in her face and her voice.

'As for you – you *object* you, allow me to advise you to mind your manners and bite your evil tongue. You should be ashamed of yourself to fill your foolish mistress's ears with the sort of venom you have been dripping into them, and you should fall on your knees and pray for forgiveness from your Maker. I assure you, you will never have mine for the way you have gossiped and lied! Now, get out of my way.' And with that she marched to the front door and slammed it behind her, and ran up the steps to her own house and leaned on the bell for Eliza to let her in. She was weeping copiously now and felt very shaky indeed, and was so glad when the door opened that she nearly tumbled in.

Eliza gawped, protested and then reached for her and with strong young arms bore her as far as the chair in the hall beside the foot of the stairs. She turned back to the front door just as Alice came running up the steps.

'Close the door, close it!' Tilly cried and Eliza promptly did so, so firmly that it amounted to slamming the door in Alice's face; and that made Tilly feel a little better for a moment. But not for long; the memory of the things Alice had said to her and of her own tirade – and she could still see Alice's slack-jawed amazement as the words had flooded out of her – made her feel quite sick. She wept more bitterly than ever.

'Oh, lawks, Mum, this'll do you no good,' Eliza said, and

without any hindrance from Tilly and with a constant stream of scolding chatter, she swept her upstairs, undressed her and put her into her bed.

'There,' she said when at last Tilly lay exhausted against her pillows. 'That's better! No need to fret yourself the way you do – you'll make your baby come with a frown already set on its poor little face. If you want a nice baby that sleeps a lot and cries but little, why then you must be the same while you carry him.'

'Oh, Eliza, what will become of us?' Tilly cried. 'My father gone God knows where, perhaps abandoning us and –'

'Oh, pooh!' said Eliza. 'Men like him don't go far from their mangers, and never you think it. He'll be back when he's over his skinful. I've no doubt he's been drinkin' hisself stupid and that's all there is to it. He'll be back, you mark my words.'

'Oh, Eliza, I don't know – and now this, with Alice and Freddy – that hateful woman! How dare she tell Alice such stuff.'

'If you mean that there Mary Prescott, then you're right,' Eliza said warmly. 'I've had fair cause to tell her a thing or two 'n' all, prying around the way she does! I know her type, you believe me I do – she's the spit image of the woman what lived next door to my Ma, in the village, knows more about everyone else's business than her own, not that she's got any of her own for she's so pryin' and hateful no one'll call her friend. I sent that Mary off with a right blow on her ear, that I did.' She nodded with great satisfaction. 'Nothing ever surprises me about that one. She been makin' trouble, has she?'

'Oh, yes, so much! Telling Alice that – well never mind!'

'Oh, I can imagine well enough!' Eliza said cheerfully. 'I know how she was when she came round here, askin' questions about the way you and Mr Freddy was when he was visitin' here and all! I told her stuff to make her hair curl, that I did, filled her with such rubbish and her believed it. Wicked old besom!'

'You told her – what did you tell her?' Tilly said, aghast. 'Surely, you did not let her think that –'

182

'I told her that he sat and stared at you like you was an angel and that you paid him no mind at all and never even noticed, that's what I told her. If she wants to puff up her Madam the way she does, carryin' on as though she were a very angel, she needn't think I won't defend mine and defend you I did, Mum, you believe me. I told her, straight out I did, as how you was above noticin' how her precious master watched you and liked you.' She giggled. 'You should ha' seen her face, Mum! Fair put out she was. Never come back, anyway. Now, I'm agoin' down to fetch you some tea and then you sleep, Mum. You'll feel better then.'

Tilly closed her eyes. She couldn't believe what had happened: that Alice should attack her so was amazing. That Eliza had been so partisan as to lead Alice's maid to think that — oh, what was the point of rehearsing it all in her mind like this? Both she and Alice had been the victims of servants' gossip, and though the talk in Eliza's case was meant to be kind and was based on fierce loyalty, and in Mary's had been malicious, the result was the same. Tilly and her only immediate friends, such as they were, were parted for ever. She could never rely on them again for any aid; and she closed her eyes and thought of Freddy. He had been so kind and so reliable. Who shall I turn to now in trouble? There is no one. I am alone.

Her eyes snapped open then. Her father. Freddy had gone to seek her father and that meant when he came back he would wish to speak to her. He would return to his own house, expecting to find her there, and would find only Alice who would regale him at once with all that had occurred.

She shook her head. It was impossible to know what to do or how to plan and she turned on to her side, curled up into a ball and slept. It was almost as though she had deliberately backed away from all conscious thought, taking refuge from the world and from reality in her sleep. I hope I never wake up, she thought as she slid over the barrier into emptiness. Never wake up.

*

But of course she did. When Eliza came and touched her shoulder she emerged from the depths of a painful dream that left her feeling sick and frightened and unable to say why, for she had no recollection of its content and could only stare up at Eliza in the light of the candle she was holding, blinking and fearful.

'I had to call you, Mum, though I'd have rather left it till mornin',' she said. 'It's just that – it's Mr Freddy, Mum. He's downstairs and says he has to talk to you.'

'No!' Tilly and strongly, and pulled herself up against her pillows and held the bedclothes against her as though they were some sort of bulwark. 'I cannot see him ever again.'

'He says he knows you will be unwilling but it is important he speaks to you of your Papa. I think you'd better, Mum, on account that I think he'll come up here if you don't.'

That got Tilly out of bed and she pulled on her wrapper and smoothed her rumpled hair over her ears and set her cap straight. She put a shawl about her shoulders to make herself more respectable and went down to her drawing-room, Eliza hovering at her elbow. Tilly didn't need that sort of support, she told herself, but was glad to have it all the same.

Freddy was standing on the hearth, staring down at the folded paper fan that hid the empty grate, and he turned his head as she came in and she saw that he was quite unsmiling.

'I have to say first how much I regret the – um – disagreement between you and Alice about which I have been told in full. She now sees the error of her ways and is most distressed that you exchanged words you might have preferred to leave unsaid.'

'I prefer not to speak of the matter,' Tilly said.

'I can understand that, and I must respect it. I shall speak only of – I am afraid I have bad news for you, Tilly. Please sit down.'

She did, with a little thump and looked up at Eliza. 'I shall be all right, Eliza,' she said steadily. 'You may leave me now.'

'Oh, but Mum –, Eliza protested, but Tilly was adamant. She

184

had allowed Eliza far too much leeway already. Her loneliness and uncertainty had led her into what she knew was a dangerous trap — making a friend of a servant. Doing so had already led her into problems with her social equals; she could not allow such a situation to persist. So she looked very steadily at Eliza and shook her head.

'I shall be perfectly all right, Eliza. This is a matter that I wish to discuss with Mr Compton in private. Please leave us.'

Eliza looked puzzled, then her face crumpled and she bobbed and went away and Freddy took a deep breath.

'That was wise,' he said. 'One forgets how much harm —'

'Yes,' Tilly said and folded her hands, which were trembling now, on her lap. 'If you will tell me about my father, please?'

He turned away and looked down at the fireplace again. 'I checked at his club,' he said. 'They told me they had not seen him at all this past week.'

'Not seen — but where else could he be?' She felt terror rising in her. 'It is not possible that he was not there. Perhaps the person you asked happened not to see him or —'

'No, it is quite true.' Now he looked at her. 'I have found him, you see. He may have set out to go to his club but he did not reach it.'

'What happened? Oh, Freddy, please do tell me! What happened?'

'I went to the hospitals all around London, and I found him in one of them. In the Charing Cross Hospital, in fact, hard by the railway station, you know? At the end of the Strand.'

'In hospital? Oh, Freddy how — what for? Was he injured in some way? Such a terrible place to be.'

'He was, it seemed, caught by an apoplexy. He is in a pauper's ward. They did not know who he was, you see. He was found lying in the gutter just off Endell Street. They cannot say why he was there.'

'But not to know who he was! That is absurd — why, he carries so many papers and so forth about him, he always has. They had but to look in his pockets and —'

'They did. He was found by a night watchman who said he had been turned over completely.'

'Turned over?'

'Robbed. They thought at first he had been set upon by some sort of cut-purse or street hooligan, but when they examined him it was clear he had been struck down by an apoplectic attack and that probably some passer-by had seized the opportunity to steal all he had. Indeed, he was fortunate they did not strip all his clothes from his back. It has been known – there are bad people in Seven Dials and thereabouts. It is understandable enough, I am afraid, for they are very poor there. I cannot imagine why he was in such a district.' His tone was careful and delicate but there was a question in it.

'He may have been looking for her,' Tilly said, her head down and her voice a little muffled. 'Mrs Leander. He was very distressed at her departure.' She lifted her head and looked directly at Freddy. 'I think he truly cared for her. And we sent her away.'

There was a silence then and Freddy looked back at her with that flat look on his face in which she could read nothing, and she bit her lip and looked away.

'I just wanted life to be better,' she said. 'Mrs Leander made it all so – I thought that without her it could be different – and now this. Oh God, when will I do something *right*? First Frank and now this – I must be the wickedest person in the whole world.'

'That,' said Freddy vehemently, 'is pernicious nonsense. I will not hear you speak so. You have been tragically unfortunate, but you are not to blame for what has happened! Frank was the one who drank so much he lost all sense of himself and fell to his death. Your father's misfortune can hardly be laid at your door, since apoplexy is an act of God. Nor indeed, can I be blamed. That woman was truly a bad person, and it was right and proper that she should be told there were those who knew of her past and who – well, let it be. I shall not

186

discuss it. But I do insist that you must not blame yourself for what has happened.'

'How can I not blame myself?' she said. 'Does not everything I touch turn to misery? There is even you and Alice. You were so happy and now because of me you are disagreeing and —'

'What can you know of what happens with Alice and me?' he said in a low voice. 'You have no knowledge at all. Our marriage is a matter for ourselves alone. You can't be blamed because Alice was foolish enough to listen to a jealous servant. The woman has a deep attachment to my wife and is as jealous of me as she is of anyone who comes near Alice. She has been with her many years now — since long before our marriage in fact — and that is why she is so, well, it is she who is my problem, not you. I will not have you blaming yourself, you understand me? I will not.'

She glanced at him and was startled. He was not smiling but he did not have that heavy look she was accustomed to seeing when he was serious. He was slightly flushed about the nose and cheeks, and could have looked a little ridiculous, his expression was so intense. But instead he looked concerned and comforting in his distress for her, and she ached to be able to relax and be as they had been before, friendly and cheerful together. It would have helped so much.

She looked away, silent for a moment, and then shook her head. 'It is kind of you to be so concerned,' she said. 'But I must be permitted to know what is best for myself, I believe. Now, tell me,' and she stiffened her shoulders with resolve, 'about my father. His condition is —'

'Parlous,' he said after a moment. 'He is quite unconscious and has some signs, the surgeon told me, of pneumonia. This is not surprising, considering he was lying in the street for some time before he was fetched into the Charing Cross Hospital.'

'I see.' She stood up. 'I must go to him then.' She moved towards the door. 'Thank you for your care of me, Mr Compton. I appreciate it. I shall not disturb you again, I

187

promise. Do tell Ali– your wife – that I greatly regret any disturbance to her peace of mind and can assure her that there will be no further cause for concern for her from any action of mine. Good-night, Mr Compton.'

'Mr Compton?' he protested. 'But we have been on better terms than this.'

'Mr Compton,' she said firmly. 'Good-night. And goodbye.' She walked out of the room, leaving him standing on her hearthrug looking as heavy of expression as she had ever seen him.

Chapter Eighteen

THE NEXT FEW DAYS were perfectly dreadful. The sight of her father with his face twisted to one side and his sunken cheeks, looking a great deal worse than her mother even though they had both been stricken with the same disease, was quite horrifying. She stood at the foot of the bed in the huge malodorous room at Charing Cross Hospital, where men lay in serried ranks of beds and cried and whimpered in a way that made the back of her neck creep with horror, and tried to recognize in the wreck of humanity that lay beneath the rough sheets the man who had so dominated her life. But it was impossible. All that lay there was the shell of Austen Kingsley. She looked at him more closely and the nurse, a rather slatternly woman standing beside her, said sharply, 'Well, Ma'am? Is this man known to you?'

She nodded dumbly, for although he looked so altered there was no doubt in her mind that this was her father; and the nurse said, 'Well, Ma'am, I must tell you that his state is poor. Yes, very poor. Moribund, in fact. You hear the way he is breathing?'

Tilly was indeed very aware of the way he was breathing; short, shallow little breaths and then a few deep intakes accompanied by the most unpleasant rattling sound in the throat and she knew perfectly well what it was before the nurse told her.

'That is the death rattle, Ma'am, I regret to tell you. It is sad it should be so, but we must commit ourselves to the ways of the Lord. He will be dead by dawn, I have no doubt — and I've seen a dunnamany cases of this sort.' She went away and left Tilly to stand and stare at what was left of Austen Kingsley, without so much as a chair to sit upon.

Another nurse eventually fetched her a stool and again left her alone, and there she sat not just till dawn, but for two more days, waiting for her father to die. He did not move or show any awareness of where he was, but lay there making that dreadful sound in his throat for hour after hour, until she thought she would scream. At which point she would get to her feet and take a turn around the corridors outside the big ward. One of the nurses of a kinder disposition had fetched her a cup of chocolate from time to time, which helped her greatly, and someone who was visiting another patient, a pleasant old woman, took pity and shared her small collation of bread and jam with her. But for the rest she just sat and waited.

It came so quietly and in so casual a manner that she hardly realized it. She was sitting there, her hands in her lap, trying to arrange her back and shoulders in such a way that she could relax, and not be at risk of falling off the stool if she became sleepy — as she often did — when she became aware, as one is aware of a slowly developing toothache, of a nagging something that was bothering her and could not think what it was. She lifted her head and looked at her father on his rough grey linen pillow beneath the coarse red blanket and was about to glance away again when she realized what it was. The noisy breathing had not restarted the last time it stopped.

She had become used to that, the way the breaths came in little runs and then seemed to cease altogether before starting up again with a deep noisy intake. But this time the restart had simply not happened and Austen Kingsley lay there, quite dead. And she hadn't noticed it happen. She had no idea at all at what time his soul had passed from the shell that lay before her, and that realization made her shake with horror.

Not so the surgeon. The nurse whom Tilly ran to fetch showed not an atom of emotion; and the surgeon who came to look at Austen made a most perfunctory examination.

'Dead,' he said. 'You can deal with him now.' He nodded at Tilly and walked away, leaving her feeling quite useless and also numb. She had no feeling left at all, she realized. Only fatigue.

Mechanically, Tilly made the arrangements with the hospital, and with the undertaker who was fetched by the mortuary attendant (and how he was to be paid, heaven only knew!) and left for home at last, determined to send Eliza away so that she had at least one mouth less to feed.

But she found Eliza far from her usual obliging self.

'If I didn't leave you before, Mum, I don't see no reason why I should now,' she said mulishly. 'I don't want no money nor nothin'. I'll be happy enough to work like I always did and wait till it's all sorted out with your Pa's will and all.'

'Eliza, you must understand!' Tilly leaned across the kitchen table to stare up at Eliza, who was standing on the other side with her arms folded across her chest in a most intransigent posture. 'I have no money at all. I have looked, since my father's death, in every part of his study, but there seems to be none there that I can see. There was none on his person.'

She swallowed, aware of a sudden return of the distress she had been battling with these past three days. 'So there it is. I cannot feed us, for I used all the money I had to go to the hospital to see my father and to — I had to pay something to the mortuary attendant.' She swallowed again. 'It was so little that I was ashamed, to tell the truth. But I have nothing left at all. I have sent a message to the lawyers to tell them of all that has befallen and they will no doubt be in touch with me to set matters straight. But until then I cannot possibly employ a servant.'

'But Mum, ain't I your friend now?' Eliza burst out. 'Ain't I bin with you through terrible times and helped all I could? Ain't I showed you every way I know 'ow as I likes it here

191

and cares about you?' Suddenly she was sniffing and gulping, as her eyes brimmed with tears.

'Oh Eliza, don't weep please, or you will set me off,' Tilly cried and Eliza at once took a deep breath and wiped the back of one hand ferociously across her face as if to punish herself.

'Well, Mum, don't you go sayin' that you'll send me away then!' she said. 'Where can I go anyway? My Ma, she won't want me back even if I wants to go, for she's got the little 'uns to feed an' all. And though I've learned a lot I still couldn't get no place anywhere else except as a scullery maid and I'd sooner stop here and be the maid of all work an' take care of you than that.'

'Oh, Eliza, this really won't do, you know!' Tilly sat back in her chair again and surveyed the girl helplessly.

'What won't do, Mum? I'm happy to do it, truly. And anyway, Mum, you can't manage, not on your own! Not with your Ma and all. 'Oo else but me knows how to turn her and clean her up like? Eh, Mum? I been doing it ever since I come here. That Mrs Leander, she never did much of that, you can be bound, and Mrs Cashman, well, you couldn't get her out o' the kitchen! You couldn't manage her alone, Mum, so I got to stay — it don't matter about the money.'

Tilly gave in. There seemed no choice and she could not deny that though Eliza's transparent adoration of her made her feel a little uncomfortable in one sense, in another it gave her great comfort. To have someone so young and of such a class of society so concerned for her well-being was agreeable, to say the least.

'Well, let it be! I must make some arrangements to feed us in the meantime. I need eggs and milk for Mamma, too, of course. Have we enough for today for her?'

'Oh, yes, Mum!' Eliza said, incandescent with relief. 'I told the egg man when he came, and the dairy man, as we'd settle up later, like all the ladies and gentlemen, and they went off without a murmur. You don't have to pay on the nail, you know, Mum! *I* know that. None of the people round here do.

Charlie told me, last time I went to get some coffee and candles and that.'

Tilly's brows snapped down. 'You have not been going to Mr Harrod's shop, have you, Eliza? I told you, I have an arrangement with Mr Jobbins that I pay cash and he charges me the keenest prices.'

'No, Mum, course I didn't! But he's in the shop alongside after all, and if he's there in the alley you know, asweepin' of the front, well, we 'as a bit of a laugh and that. And he told me as all the other ladies in these parts think nothing of running up huge great bills and paying when it suits 'em. Well, Mum, why can't you?'

'Because I have made an arrangement with Mr Jobbins.'

'Yes, Mum, but not with Mr Harrod! I bet if you went along he'd be glad to have your trade. He don't know as how you ain't got much of the ready at present, and by the time he does, why, you'll be well set up on account of the lawyers'll have sorted it all out.'

'I hope so,' Tilly said, remembering all too painfully how unwilling her lawyer had been to tell her anything of her prospects. Well, he would have to now, she thought; and soon.

'Well,' she said in as dampening a tone as she could. 'I will think about that. Meanwhile, I would prefer you to leave the shopping to me.' And she took herself to the morning room to sit and think about what to do next.

Now Tilly could hold it back no longer. Her fatigue and the numbness and sheer busyness that had involved her this past few days of her father's illness and death had had one highly beneficial effect. She had been able to stop herself from thinking about her real fear. Now, sitting in her morning room on this hot day in early August, she had to face the truth.

She did not expect to get anything from her father's will. Her visit to Mr Conroy had filled her with doubts about her future, but since that day there had been little time or reason to think about what he had told her or, rather, not told her in the matter of her father's intentions.

There was every possibility that her father had left all his possessions to Mrs Leander. There! She had allowed the thought to escape her control and to stare at her, and she stared back at it.

It might not be true, she told herself. Perhaps he had done the thing expected of him and left his entire fortune – such as it was in these difficult times – to his only child? But she knew her father had always done what he considered right for him and gave not a moment's consideration to others' opinions. She now also knew, all too painfully, just how much her father had been attached to Mrs Leander. Tilly had feared the loss of her home to the woman even when she thought she was just his paramour. Now she knew he had actually cared for her, how much more likely was it that he would have given her all his worldly goods?

Tilly began to shiver. She had to deal now with the harshest reality of her life. She was a pauper, an orphan without any means of support, and she was carrying a baby. How on earth was she going to manage?

The day after the funeral, which was carried out by the curate at Holy Trinity, for the vicar had long ago had a great argument with Austen Kingsley and could not be prevailed upon to bury him, Tilly went back to the church and told the curate all about her situation. He sat steepling his hands in quite the accepted priestly manner, even though he was not above five and twenty years old, and listened to her gravely.

'The Lord will provide,' he said at last when she had finished pouring out her tale of woe. Tilly stiffened her jaw at that.

'Not necessarily, Mr Lincoln,' she said sharply. 'I have seen people in the streets of London who have no homes at all to go to. Does the Lord provide for them?'

He looked disapproving. 'That is a somewhat impious way

for a lady of delicacy to speak,' he said. 'I mean only that "Sufficient unto the day is the evil thereof", and you have at present the comfort of a home. So I see no point in discussing this matter with me – ahem – at present.'

'But surely if I wait until I am sent out of my home I will be neglecting to take sensible care of myself? That would be reprehensible, would it not? I have heard the vicar preach often enough about the need for hard work and foresight in order to make the world a goodly place.'

Mr Lincoln coughed. 'In a parish like this, Mrs Quentin, it is important to remember that the people to whom one preaches are – ahem – people who have an understanding of the world as it is. We cannot ignore their – um – tastes or their inclinations but must preach in the manner they will find easiest to understand.'

She felt hopeless listening to him and with that loss of hope anger began to grow. 'You are saying that the vicar here at Holy Trinity is concerned only with the welfare of the rich parishioners who are building houses here, and who make fortunes for themselves in so doing? That you are not concerned with the problems of one of your parishioners who has fallen on hard times?'

'But you do not know that you have,' Mr Lincoln pointed out with what seemed to be sweet reason. 'You are assuming that your father – ahem – has left his property away from you. I am sure you will find that, when the will is read, common sense will have prevailed and an awareness of what is right and proper will have –'

'I wish I could be so sanguine,' snapped Tilly. 'I do not so believe. I fear that I will have no home in the next few weeks because the property has been left to – to another, and that I and my coming infant and my ailing mother will be penniless. I came to ask you if you knew of any respectable Christian charity that would be of aid to me, as a widow in a parlous situation.'

He had gone very pink, and she realized it was her indelicacy in referring to her condition that had so shocked him, and didn't mind at all. In fact she leaned back in her chair and smoothed her gown over her front so that the growing bump was clearly apparent. Her fear and her anger, she realized were making her positively unwomanly.

The redness on his face was joined by a moistness about the upper lip and forehead as he looked away from her.

'I really cannot see, Mrs Quentin, what we here at Holy Trinity can do for you. This is a well-to-do neighbourhood and we have little experience of — ahem — the sort of situation you describe.'

'And so are uninterested in me despite the fact that I am your parishioner,' she retorted and got to her feet. 'Then I must make other arrangements for myself. I will find someone somewhere who will aid me, I hope. In the meantime, Mr Lincoln, you may rest assured that whatever church I might attend in future — if I do — it will not be Holy Trinity. Clearly you are far too busy here for one such as I.' And she swept out, her face burning. Quite what she had expected the church to be able to do for her, she was not sure. She had assumed that there were people here who would care about her predicament, but now she knew better. She was alone and would remain so. And she set out to return to Brompton Grove in a deep study.

This was broken as she reached the corner of the Grove and saw one of the omnibuses, brave and bright in its green paint, go spanking by behind a pair of very large black horses. She stared at the boards on the side where the destinations were painted and bit her lip, thinking hard. Then she turned and began to walk along the road down which the omnibus was now disappearing. She would go home the long way round, she decided. First there were visits she might usefully make.

Chapter Nineteen

SHE KNEW SHE WAS being less than honest, yet it did not matter. All that was important was that her mother and Eliza and of course she herself should eat. Mr Harrod, it was clear, was not a man who lacked the wherewithal to keep body and soul together, whereas she and those for whom she was responsible undoubtedly did. And although she did not think directly about the importance of making sure her baby above all others was protected from any hunger the household might suffer, her awareness of her child was never far from her mind.

And there was another reason why she was able to be so insouciant about what she was doing; the curate's dismissal of her from Holy Trinity Church had made her deeply, coldly angry, had convinced her that if she had been abandoned by God as well as by her father, then she had every right to do what she had to do without any respect for God's rules. Not that she thought this in so many words, but it was there at the back of her mind and made it remarkably easy for her to give Mr Harrod a wide and innocent smile.

'There, Mr Harrod, I think that is all – unless you can think of something I might have forgotten? I am open to any suggestions you might have to make since you know your stock as you do.'

Mr Harrod looked down at his order book and positively smirked. 'Well now, Mrs Quentin, it would be hard, indeed it would, to fault your thoroughness, though I could add some new tins of fruit, an excellent line we have just added? Very modern, very good – shall I?'

She nodded, and happily he wrote it into the list with a flourish.

'You won't be sorry, Mrs Quentin. Quite delectable these plums are. I must say that it really does my heart good to see so young a lady, if I might be permitted to so put it, show such a keen grasp of kitchen needs and economy. Your husband is indeed a fortunate man to have so careful yet sensible a wife.'

'I am sadly, now a widow, Mr Harrod,' she said and cast her eyes down. He reddened, hurrumphed, rubbed his hands together and begged her pardon for his clumsiness all at once, and she thought almost gleefully – another point in my favour. It would be a long time before he would harry her now, however large the bill became.

'You must forgive me, Ma'am. Deepest regrets, Ma'am. The thing of it is, we haven't seen you at the shop of recent time, and –'

'Ah, yes,' she said, as smoothly as she was able. 'I did take my custom elsewhere in order to pay lower prices for ready money. I decided I – er – that the saving involved was not so great that – um –'

He beamed, pleased with himself again. 'If you'll forgive me, Madam, I must say that I could have told you as much! We carry far superior goods to Mr Jobbins.'

'Well, no doubt,' she said hurriedly, not wishing to enter into any denigration of Mr Jobbins, who had been an excellent supplier of goods so far. 'Let us just say I am happy to be dealing with you now.'

'I too, Madam, am more than happy,' Mr Harrod said fervently as she got to her feet and collected her gloves and her reticule. 'Very happy.'

'Well then, Mr Harrod,' she said. 'I look forward to receiving the order as soon as may be. As I told you, the kitchen is quite painted and restored now and we are ready to take delivery at any moment.'

'This afternoon, Ma'am,' Mr Harrod beamed. 'No later than three p.m.'

'Thank you,' she said serenely and went to the door. 'I shall of course see you again in due course. Good morning, Mr Harrod!' And she let him show her out to the street, bobbing politely all the way.

She stood outside for a moment, pulling on her gloves, and smiling to herself in satisfaction. All that tea, a full double tin, would last them at least two months, and the coffee likewise. The flour, the rice, the oats and lentils together with the jams, the pots of honey and the sugar would go almost as long as the rest of it – the paraffin oil, the candles, the soap, knife powder and all the other kitchen goods would last even longer. Not that such items mattered as much as comestibles but she had thought it politic to include them. Mr Harrod after all had swallowed whole her tale of a newly overhauled and redecorated kitchen; to neglect to purchase cleaning materials and lighting would surely have made him suspicious.

She turned and began to walk briskly along past Middle Queen's Buildings, but lifted her head at the sound of a hail behind her.

'Mrs Quentin!' someone called and her heart sank. Had Mr Harrod looked again at the size of the order and decided that after all he wished to be paid for it in advance or at least on delivery? If he did, then her plan was quite ruined. There was no other grocer she could go to to run up such a bill. Mr Jobbins and she had been dealing on a cash-only basis for so long that he would naturally be highly suspicious if she suddenly demanded credit, and none of the other grocers in the row were well enough known to her to permit her even to consider approaching them in her present state of insolvency.

It was not Mr Harrod who was running after her but Charlie, his son, and she bit her lip as tears of disappointment, and perhaps anger and even, to an extent, shame rose in her. It was all to easy to cry these days, she found herself thinking. Too easy; and steeled herself to control the weeping as best she could until young Charlie had told her the order could not be filled. Then she'd be free to escape.

'Mrs Quentin, I must say you've left my Pa looking like the original pup with two tails! You must have given him a very big order!'

She felt her nostrils narrow as she put all her efforts into controlling herself. 'You clearly know perfectly well that I did,' she said. 'And I am sorry indeed that you should object.'

He gaped at her. 'Object? Bless my soul, why would any tradesman object to the order of so excellent a customer as yourself? We would be strange indeed if we did business that way!' He laughed heartily. 'I know my old father's a bit of a stick in the mud, Mrs Quentin, but he ain't a fool!'

She looked at him thoughtfully. 'Then the order will arrive this afternoon as promised?'

'You may be sure of it!' He beamed at her. 'I'll be abringin' of it myself.'

'Good,' she said and turned to go. 'Then that's splendid.'

'Uh, Mrs Quentin,' he said and she turned back. He was looking a little uncomfortable and much younger. Quite a boy, in fact. 'I was just wondering – could I – I just wanted a word.' He looked back over his shoulder along the row of shops. The usual shopmen were out in front of each one, crying their wares, and he bit his lip. 'If my Pa discovers I ain't there, he'll set about me when I do get back – I am very sorry to detain you but – well the thing of it is, I wanted to ask you for some help.'

'Ask me for – how could I possibly be of help to you?' She stared at him, genuinely puzzled. Whatever she had expected from this boy it wasn't this. 'I am in no position to –'

'Well, yes you are, Mrs Quentin. Thing is,' he swallowed, 'it's my Pa. He carries on amazing at me sometimes, really he does. I tell him it's high time I got the chance to run the shop on my own, and I could, you know. I'm as smart a tradesman as he is. Just give me my chance and watch me go! But he won't give me my chance, that's the thing – every time I ask, it turns into a right up-and-downer and my Ma gets very angry too, and – well, I think it's time I set up on my own. Not precisely on my own, you understand. I mean, I can't get my own business, not yet. But I could live away from them, couldn't I? It'd make life a deal more peaceful all round and like I said to him, I'd be near enough if I went into the right lodgings.'

'Lodgings.' She was bemused but he seemed not to notice and ran on.

'If he thought I was in a decent household, well, maybe he'd consider letting me do it. And I talked to your Eliza.' He went crimson and she set her head on one side as she began to understand for the first time.

'Ah,' she said, 'Eliza.'

'I've seen her when she comes to buy at that Jobbins's. And I said to her once as how I was looking for good lodgings and she happened to say as the house was a big one and I thought maybe – so I asked her to ask you, but she said she'd do no such thing. So I had to come and talk to you myself. There I was thinking of it, and there you are in the shop. It was like it was meant, you know? I thought – oh, lawks!'

From along the row of shops a stentorian roar had gone up, and even Tilly recognized it. Mr Harrod had noticed his son's absence and like some primaeval animal concerned for its young, was bellowing for him.

'I can't stop, Ma'am,' he said quickly. 'But will you think about it? I'd pay a fair rent and all, and I'd be no trouble. I know you've got no servants in all those rooms now, Eliza said, and if you –'

'I shall be speaking to Eliza,' Tilly said firmly. 'In the meantime, I have to tell you that she's misled you. I cannot –'

'Charlie!' The roar came again and the boy fled, throwing her a comical glance that was an amalgam of regret and irritation at his father and hopefulness and a sort of pleading.

'Don't get me in trouble with Eliza, Mrs Quentin,' he called back. 'Even if you say no I'd hate that above all things.' And he was gone, haring back down the street with his white apron flapping in the breeze, and Tilly watched him go, a faint frown between her eyes.

'I never said he could come here, Mum, indeed I never did!' Eliza's eyes were wide with protest. 'I wouldn't take it upon myself to say any such thing! He was bein' a deal cheekier than a boy should.' She reddened. 'He said he'd like to share a roof with me and I told him that even though there wasn't that many rooms used for servants now, I wouldn't share a roof with him not for anything, and him so pushful. And that was all I did say, Mum, as God is my witness, on my little sisters' lives.'

'Well, that will do, Eliza.' Tilly was weary of it now, wishing she'd left matters alone. 'Just let me say that you must really guard your tongue. People hear things you didn't say if you give them half the chance and you have to be careful. I have enough problems as it is.'

Eliza looked at her with brimming eyes. 'I wouldn't do anything to upset you, Mum, you knows that.'

'Yes, yes, I know,' Tilly said hurriedly. 'Now, let's set about some work. There will be an order of goods delivered this afternoon. Charlie Harrod will bring it, but don't let that be an excuse for chattering! Just see to it that it's all put away as carefully as may be. And we must use it all very economically, for I tell you flatly I have no notion whence the next is coming. And for heaven's sake, Eliza, don't mention that fact to a soul.'

'I promise,' Eliza said with all the fervour she could muster. 'Not a word shall ever pass my lips.'

'Yes, well, let be.' Tilly got to her feet. 'Now, I must ready myself for a most disagreeable task.' She stood in the middle of the kitchen staring at the hearthrug which, with its bright colours and cheerful pattern, seemed so incongruous in her present state of mind, and Eliza looked over her shoulder at her as she made for the larder which she would scrub and tidy ready for the afternoon's delivery.

'I wager it won't be as bad as you think, Mum,' she said encouragingly. 'Old vicar, him what taught me to read, he always said it's much worse when you think about what's comin' than when it comes. Or something like that.'

Tilly managed a smile. 'I imagine it was rather different.'

Eliza grinned cheerfully. 'Well, I never listened as much as I might, I don't deny, not when he took to preachin' like. But I took it to mean that the more you think about a thing one day, the worse it looks. And then, when the real thing happens next day, why it's not half the trouble you'd expected.'

'I think he was probably saying, "Sufficient unto the day is the evil thereof,"' Tilly said and Eliza looked amazed.

'Well, fancy that! You got it exactly right, Mum. That was it.'

'Yes,' Tilly murmured, remembering her encounter with Charlie and her conviction that he was about to expose her to his father as a liar and a would-be cheat. 'Well, Eliza, as I say, I must go and deal with my task. I am going to visit the City. I shall, I hope, return before too late. Certainly before dark. But I must hurry. It's almost two now and it will take me some time to reach him on the omnibus.'

'Him?' Eliza could not hide her curiosity.

'Mr Conroy,' Tilly said. 'My lawyer.'

It was in fact past four when she reached the City. The omnibuses had been full of people, even in this middle part of the day in a month when so many had left London for the country or the seaside to escape the heat and the smells. When at last it had been possible for her to secure a place, the horses had been slow and sweating and quite impervious to their driver's shouts and whippings.

She left the equipage at the top of Leadenhall Street, quite convinced that her journey would prove to have been a wasted one. It was entirely possible that by this time on a hot August afternoon, Mr Conroy would have left his office for the day.

But at last her good fortune returned for his clerk, although he looked thoroughly disapproving at being disturbed, allowed that indeed Mr Conroy was in attendance and that Mr Cobbold was there also. He agreed to go and find out if they would see Mrs – ah – Quentin, was it?, and went away, looking like a bad-tempered crane with his long black-trousered legs and shiny shabby frock-coat flapping above them.

He came back looking just as sour and indicated with a mere tilt of his head that she was to follow him, and she did, to Mr Cobbold's office where she found both men waiting for her, and she thought – there is bad news for me. If it were not, they would not have seen me so quickly. She then realized how silly she was being, for surely the reverse could have been just as true. 'Sufficient unto the day,' she whispered beneath her breath and moved forwards with what dignity she could muster.

'It is good of you to see me at such short notice, gentlemen,' she said. 'I dare say you have much work to prosecute and I will not long detain you.'

Mr Cobbold, as round and cheerful as his partner was tall and remote, got to his feet and came hurrying round the desk towards her.

'My dear Mrs Quentin! So good to see you – I would have waited on you tomorrow, you know, no later, to offer you my sincere condolences and regret. Sad loss, very sad loss, a man of – um – an excellent gentleman, your father. Excellent. I regret we were not able to attend his funeral – pressure of business, you understand.'

'I understand perfectly,' Tilly said as she took the chair which he showed her, and indeed she did. Her father and this man had had many altercations over the years. She had heard Austen ranting about things Mr Cobbold had warned him over and, 'the way the old buzzard sits on a man's tail and stops him from doing all he might with his own money,' often enough to be aware of the difficulties that had lain between them. She smiled at Mr Cobbold, grateful for the way he was not letting her father's past behaviour affect his attitude towards her. In which, she thought, shooting a glance at Conroy, he was a much more agreeable person than his partner, who looked as miserable as she remembered.

'I dare say I should have waited,' she said. 'But I must speak frankly, Mr Cobbold, and tell you that my situation *vis-à-vis* money is such that I cannot indulge myself with patience. I must think carefully of my predicament, and also of my mother. And —' she looked directly at Mr Cobbold '— also of my coming infant. It will be born, I estimate, at about Christmas time.'

Mr Cobbold looked not in the least embarrassed, but pleasantly avuncular. He almost beamed.

'I am glad indeed to hear you have some joy in your life and some pleasure to which you can look forward, dear Mrs Quentin,' he said. 'To have lost both husband and father in so short a space of time is indeed a cruel blow for one so young, and dare I say it, so delicate and sensitive in nature.' He sketched a little bow. 'I am happy for you.'

She felt a wave of warmth towards this man, and thought: he is right. The baby *is* a joy to look forward to. Not just a problem and a fear and a responsibility. But then she remembered her situation and shook her head.

'It will be easier to look forward with pleasure once I know where I stand with the world, Mr Cobbold,' she said steadily. 'I must tell you frankly that I am so beset with anxiety I cannot find any source of pleasure in anything at all.'

'Oh dear!' Mr Cobbold's face was creased with concern. 'Your medical man will be most put out, I am sure, if he thinks that —'

'I am not under the care of any medical man,' Tilly said. 'To tell you truly, Sir, I cannot be, for I cannot pay the necessary fees. At present I am taking care of myself.'

Mr Cobbold looked distressed. 'That is not wise, my dear lady. Why, when my daughter was in a delicate state, my wife was most concerned that —'

'But I cannot pay for medical care,' Tilly said again as patiently as she was able. 'And that is why I am here. I need to know whether or not I am to lose my home, Mr Cobbold. I am aware that my father's financial situation was perilous to say the least. He told me that some time ago. But the house, Sir. Is that left to me? Or to −' She swallowed. 'Mrs Leander? I have to know as soon as may be. For if he has left it to her, then I have no roof to my head, and that is far more of a problem, I do assure you, than not being able to pay an apothecary.'

Chapter Twenty

'BUT IT COULD have been much worse!' Tilly said and positively beamed at Mr Cobbold, who still had the creased and worried look on his face that she found so endearing; so much so that she felt she had to comfort him. 'You must understand I was quite terrified that I was to be thrown out of the house! To be told that there is no money is of small consequence compared with the prospect of having no home.'

'Of small consequence?' It was Mr Conroy who let the words burst from him. He looked as shocked as if she had suddenly jumped up on his side of the vast partners' desk they shared and started to dance in the libidinous French manner, kicking her heels in the air. 'How can you say it is of small consequence to lose a fortune?'

'But you must understand that I did not *know* there was any fortune,' she said reasonably. 'I expected no money, so I cannot grieve over its loss. I am simply happy that the roof over my head, and that of my mother and coming child, is safe. It is all I had hoped for. I was quite terrified that he would leave the house to Mrs Leander.'

'But he could not!' Mr Cobbold said, almost wonderingly. 'It is entailed to your mother and thus held in trust for you — it is an unusual arrangement, of course, since as a married woman her property is her husband's. However, it is clear an ancestor was concerned to protect the security of his daughters and granddaughters, and so made this trust. It is a scheme I have used for several other clients, I must confess.'

'I did not know that. No one told me that.' She lifted her chin. 'No one ever told me anything, in fact. My mother –' she hesitated '– is unable to speak now, and as for my father –'

'You said that he told you he was unable to give you money to run the house?' Mr Cobbold said grimly. 'Oh, if he were but here today! Well, I know it is wrong of me to question the work of the good Lord, but had He left your father here long enough I would have dealt with him in no uncertain terms. He had made bad investments indeed, as I warned him. I knew he was involved in a ridiculous get-rich-quick bubble of a scheme of precisely the sort he most loved and which was most pernicious, and so I told him. But he would not listen, and burned his fingers smartly in consequence, and serve him right, say I. But that did not mean he was quite penniless. Impulsive the man might have been, completely mad he was not! To have kept you on short commons was outrageous.'

'Hardly mad,' Mr Conroy said dryly. 'Seeing he left some fifteen thousand pounds.'

Mr Cobbold sighed. 'Indeed he did. And all to go to a Mrs Leander.'

'And none of *my* client's money paid to him as it should have been, as promised on his marriage,' Mr Conroy said sharply.

Mr Cobbold spread his hands. 'What can I do, Conroy? It was written into the contract as carefully as you please. Should Mr Quentin predecease Mr Kingsley no marriage settlement was to stand. He did so predecease –'

'If you agreed to pay the sum out of the estate, Mrs Quentin here would at least have some money,' Mr Conroy said and Tilly looked at him, amazed. Was the man fighting for her? It seemed an odd notion, especially as kind Mr Cobbold of the anxiety-creased face was the opponent. But then she realized he was not fighting for her at all; only for a

208

dry-as-dust principle, and though she might benefit from such a battle she found she had small appetite for it.

'I could not, I think, do it,' Mr Cobbold said, almost wringing his hands in his distress. 'It is so clearly written in the will that not a penny of his money is to go – anywhere except to Mrs Leander. In the event of her death it is to go to her further issue or other relations – he was clearly determined that you should have none of it, my dear.' He looked apologetically at her. 'Though it may comfort you a little to know that it is his wife, your esteemed mother, the former Miss Henrietta Speakman Cox, against whom he – ahem – expressed opprobrium. He made mention of her in most disagreeable terms.'

'I should know what they are, I think,' Tilly said. 'Should I not?'

'I would prefer not to –' Mr Cobbold began, but she shook her head.

'Perhaps so, Mr Cobbold, but since I am involved in this will, I have a right to know what he said.'

'It is a disagreeable task to be a lawyer on occasion,' Mr Cobbold said and got to his feet and went to the door. 'Fetch me the Kingsley will,' he called to his clerk, who gracelessly obliged. Mr Cobbold spread it on the desk before him.

'Here it is. Oh dear, oh dear, I would really rather –'

'Read it,' Tilly said and he glanced at her and sighed and read it.

'"To my wife, God help me, one Henrietta Speakman Cox, I leave nothing but my curses for the life of hell she has given me. Not a penny shall she or her issue have of me. She has enough possessions of her own –" That's all that is germane.' He rolled up the will quickly. 'Truly, it is.'

'I see,' Tilly said and managed a sort of smile. 'I suspected he had scant regard for me. Now I know.'

'I am sorry,' Mr Cobbold said and shook his head. 'He was a most difficult man – I would have preferred you not to know all this.'

'I am happy enough,' Tilly said stolidly and got to her feet, showing a courage she did not really have. 'I have my house, my *mother's* house, and I bless her for it. I shall contrive well enough with that.'

'It is not enough to own a house,' Mr Conroy said and she thought – he is not as unpleasant as I thought him. There was an expression on his face that showed anger and she knew it was directed at the dead Austen Kingsley. 'What will you do for cash?'

'I am not entirely sure,' she said and buttoned her gloves with steady fingers. 'I need to think a little.' She smoothed her gloves over her fingers and said slowly, 'I believe I have the answer.' She tilted her chin and smiled. 'I believe I actually do.'

'Indeed?' Mr Cobbold and Mr Conroy looked at her curiously, but she didn't care what either of them were thinking. She had matters of her own on her mind.

'Oh, I shall not discuss it now!' she said cheerfully. 'This is just a notion I have derived from an earlier conversation. I have further thought to put to it. Thank you for your help, gentlemen. You will see to it that the necessary documents relating to my house are sent to me?' And she put a gentle but unmistakable emphasis on the 'my'.

Mr Cobbold shook his head regretfully. 'They will be sent to your mother, Mrs Quentin,' he murmured. 'But I shall see the envelope is marked in care of you.'

'That will do well enough. Good afternoon, gentlemen.' She was at the door before the thought came to her and she turned to them. 'Mrs Leander's legacy, gentlemen. How will she receive it?'

The two men looked at each other. 'When she claims it,' Mr Cobbold said. 'She may choose the form in which it will be paid.' And Tilly lifted her brows at him.

'But she has vanished,' she said. 'Gone from my house, and left no address behind her. She could be anywhere.'

'Ah,' said Mr Cobbold, and he looked at Mr Conroy who said nothing.

Tilly persisted. 'Is it not incumbent upon you to make searches for her?'

'I must legally advertise where I consider it possible she might see such an advertisement,' Mr Cobbold said after a moment. 'A line in the *London Gazette* perhaps. But I cannot in all conscience fritter away the money in fruitless expense on searches.'

A smile curved Tilly's mouth. 'Thank you, Mr Cobbold,' she said simply. 'That does help a little. I wish the woman no harm, but I would not be human if I did not admit I don't wish her well. Good afternoon, gentlemen.' And she went, to catch the omnibus to Brompton Grove and the house into which at last she knew it was safe for her baby to be born.

'Oh, Mum!' Eliza said. And could say no more.

'Perhaps I should not have told you.' Tilly was uneasy. When would she learn not to be too familiar with Eliza? It was very difficult to remember to treat her as a servant now that she was so much part of her life. It was even more difficult when she so needed to have someone to talk to, to relieve her of the pent-up feelings that often consumed her. It was impossible not to run down to the kitchen on her return home to assure Eliza excitedly that the house was safe, and that they were not about to be turned out on to the street.

'All we have to worry about now is getting the money we need to eat and to pay the other bills that are inevitable to a house,' Tilly said. 'And I have a notion regarding that.' She looked closely at Eliza and gave up her struggle to be a distant employer. 'I must talk of it with you. I think some tea would be delightful, what do you say? Has my Mamma had her evening meal?'

'Oh, yes, Mum. I did all that an hour gone. Sleeping happy, she is, and took only half the usual daffy and made no fuss at all!' Eliza darted to the scullery to fetch the tea things. 'Now sit yourself down, Mum, an' I'll be about it.'

Tilly threw her pelisse on to the table and sat down in the

211

big rocker, easing off her boots as she did so. They were not tight precisely, but her ankles ached. She put her feet up on the low fender and relaxed as Eliza came back with the tray and fussed over the kettle.

The evening was slowly drawing in; the last light of the August day was dying in the window panes and she looked at it languorously, enjoying the moment and relishing it for what it was. The fears that had consumed her for, it seemed, so long a time had been vanquished. She had but to make arrangements of the sort that had buzzed through her head all the way back on the omnibus, and all would be well. It will be easy, truly it will. Live the moment, she thought, before more problems come.

She opened her eyes at Eliza's touch and took the tea gratefully and with it the slice of seed cake she was offered.

'I made it, Mum, this afternoon,' Eliza said. 'I've tried it and I must say I ain't ashamed of it.'

It was excellent cake, if a little heavy in the middle, and Tilly praised her warmly for it. Eliza was glowing with pleasure as she pulled up her stool beside Tilly, her face turned trustingly up at her.

'Our problem, Eliza,' she said at length, when the tea and cake were finished, 'is to obtain sufficient income for us all. I have an idea of how to do it, though at first I could not imagine myself undertaking such a thing. But the more I considered it, the more sensible it seemed to me. It will, however, mean extra work for you.'

'Oh, that don't matter none, Mum,' Eliza cried. 'Why, I —'

'Hear me out,' Tilly said. 'And think before you speak. It is a serious matter. Now, this is my plan. You may recall your friend Charlie Harrod suggested he come here as a lodger —'

Eliza looked embarrassed and excited all at the same time. 'That limb o' Satan!' she said virtuously. 'Suggesting such things!'

'It was an excellent idea. And I shall follow it,' Tilly said firmly. 'But not with him.'

Eliza stared, puzzled. 'Not with – oh!' And her disappoint-ment was clear to see.

'It would not be wise, I think, to allow a young man who clearly holds you in some regard to live under the same roof,' Tilly said. 'He is a young man rather than a boy, and at sixteen, which age he is I believe, not entirely to be trusted.' She looked severe, or as severe as she could, considering she was speaking of a person only a year or so her junior. 'I fear he might seek to – shall I say, take advantage of you.'

'He'd not get far,' Eliza said stoutly.

'Would he not, Eliza?' Tilly said gently. 'You know you like the lad.'

Eliza was still for a moment and then went pink. 'I sup-pose I do,' she said and frowned. 'That's the way my Ma talks, sometimes. It makes me feel all – I don't know. Uncomfortable.'

'Well I dare say,' Tilly said. 'But sometimes such talk has to be endured. Now, as I was saying, he put the notion of lodgers into my head and it is that which will be our answer. But they cannot be male lodgers. Oh, no. That would never do.'

Eliza looked doubtful. 'Do ladies lodge, Mum? I mean, I know young men does. In the village the blacksmith's appren-tice, he lodges, and the man what works at the inn, in the taproom, when there's no space for him in the tavern itself he lodges with my Ma's friend, Mrs Gentle, but I never knew no ladies. Do ladies go into lodgings here in London?'

'Some of them must,' Tilly said. 'Surely? I have been thinking all the way home – what about ladies who are milliners or dressmakers or apprenticed to similar trades?'

'They live in their workshops,' Eliza said. 'There's some down in Middle Queen's Buildings. I knows about them from Mr Jobbins. That's different, Mum. This is a gentleman's house, here in Brompton Grove. You can't have milliner's apprentices here.'

'My father may have been a gentleman, and I may be a

lady,' Tilly said with some grimness, 'but that doesn't mean we don't need to pay our way like anyone else. There have to be some ladies somewhere who need lodgings. Find them I shall. However, it will mean more work for you, especially once I'm —' And she put her hand to her belly.

'Once the baby comes, Mum, you'll be busy enough,' Eliza said. 'But that's no trouble to me, Mum. So I makes breakfast for a few more and dinner too, and make a couple of extra beds and clean the rooms — it won't be that hard.' She hesitated. 'And then I suppose I might get some wages. Not that it matters, you understand, but —'

'I knew the moment would come,' Tilly leaned over and patted Eliza's shoulder. 'Have you seen a gown you like?'

'I saw some stuff, Mum. A lovely bit of taffeta, all shot like in blue and green and it'd make a lovely afternoon gown for when I walk out.' She reddened again. 'I mean, young men mightn't come here to lodge but they might want to walk out with me, mightn't they, Mum?'

'Indeed they might,' Tilly said. 'Yes, there would of course be wages for you. More work means wages for us all.'

Eliza nodded. 'Then that's settled.' She looked over her shoulder to where the sun was slanting, in its last efforts of the day, to light the small sitting room that had been Mrs Leander's. 'I dare say you'll want them to have a sitting room, Mum?'

'I beg your pardon?' Tilly was feeling sleepy suddenly. It had been a long hard day.

'I was thinking — they could have a sitting room. How many lodgers? If you does up the top rooms then you could have three. But if you do two of them and let them have a sitting room as well, you could get more pay for them, couldn't you? And you could do up the attic rooms, make 'em not so servantlike but more for gentry, and maybe let them too, I don't mind coming down here, to this room.' She jerked her head towards Mrs Leander's room. 'It would make a nice enough bedroom for me, and it'd be handy, like.'

Tilly roused herself. 'You're right. Of course that would be an excellent idea. I will see to it that we rearrange the furniture.'

'Not you, Mum,' Eliza said. 'I'll get Char– young Mr Harrod to give me a hand.' She got to her feet. 'The fact that you won't have him as a lodger don't mean I can't speak to him.'

Tilly, sighed. 'Be sensible then, Eliza.'

'As if I'd be anything else!' Eliza said. 'I've got more respect for you and myself, Mum, than to be otherwise!'

It was amazingly easy, once they put their minds to it, to rearrange the house. Charlie Harrod came cheerfully enough to help, announcing that since Tilly had refused him he had found a very nice house to lodge in a bit nearer the shop, which was better than being at Brompton Grove (a dig that did not escape Tilly's awareness, but to which she prudently said nothing). He buckled to generously with the shifting of beds and tables and small sofas, while Eliza worked herself to a shadow, though clearly enjoying every minute of the preparations. She made the two spare servants' rooms on the top floor as charming as she could, as well as the attic rooms. The third room on the third floor made a tolerable sitting room and when it was all finished, Tilly surveyed their handiwork with pride.

'All I have to do now,' she said, 'is find the tenants.'

It took her less time than she had feared. She started by putting a discreet notice on the doors of all the dressmaking and millinery establishments in the area, as far as Knightsbridge and well down into Kensington. However, that drew only one disagreeable female applicant to whom Tilly took such an instant dislike because she was so inquisitive and asked such personal questions in a high squeaking voice, that she told her on an impulse that the rooms were promised.

After that, afraid that all dressmakers and milliners would be horrid, she sent her notice to the three or four dame schools in the area, and this time drew a successful covert.

215

The two ladies who came together to call upon her were as like each other as peas in a pod, so much so that Tilly thought them sisters.

'No, Mrs Quentin,' the older one said. 'We are not sisters except in our aspirations. We are close friends who are interested in education.' She made the word sound like the blast of a trumpet and looked sternly at Tilly, who shrank back a little in her chair.

'I see,' she said. 'Education.'

'It is our wish,' said the younger lady, who seemed as stern as her friend, 'to start a school for older girls. We already teach small boys, of course, and prepare them for their first days in the harsh reality of a boys' school –' she almost shuddered as she said it, '– but our interests lie elsewhere.'

The other leaned forwards and said earnestly, 'We wish to teach girls, for as a general rule their education is sorely neglected. Mrs Quentin, did you go to school?'

'Er – no,' Tilly said, wondering if she should be ashamed and then straightening her back again, for once more she had shrunk back from the impact of these strong ladies. 'But none of my friends did either. We had lessons together, with a governess, as I recall.'

'Precisely,' said the older woman triumphantly. 'It is always so for girls. Well, we wish to teach girls *in school* to fit them for university.'

Tilly stared, amazed. 'Girls at university? Are you sure – I mean –'

'Oh, everyone is surprised,' the other said severely, clearly pleased with her reaction. 'But that is how it is to be. We shall start a school for females, a school of the highest academic standard. Meanwhile, we run our dame school and excellent it is.' She frowned with some ferocity as though Tilly had said something slighting about it, and she nodded quickly in response.

'I'm sure it is,' she said. 'And that is why –'

'Indeed yes. That is why we are seeking accommodation for

ourselves. The school has only just started but we are doing very well. We have fully twelve small pupils and hope to double that soon. There are many young families in this district.' She looked quickly at Tilly and said, 'Ladies like yourself who will soon be interested in schools for small children.'

Tilly went pink. She had not thought herself obvious in her crinoline, though of course she had to wear her stays very loose these days.

'Perhaps you would like to see the accommodation,' she said hastily and got to her feet. 'We are able to offer you two bedrooms with service, and a sitting room. Breakfast will be served there and you are free of course to use it in total privacy.'

'It was that aspect of your notice we most liked,' the younger woman said approvingly. 'Privacy matters greatly to us. We would dine here as well?'

'Oh,' Tilly caught her breath. 'I am not sure that will be —'

'I would prefer we did not,' the older woman said firmly. 'We must devote our evenings to hard work, Sophia. Formal dining is not the way to be sure that we will do all the school work that is necessary. I prefer that we eat a good breakfast and share luncheon at school with the children. Then in the evenings we shall manage perfectly well on a little soup and perhaps some toast which we can contrive for ourselves in the school kitchens. Your charges, of course, will reflect the fact that we do not dine.'

'Oh, yes, of course,' Tilly said and led the way to the upper floor, quite nervously, for they seemed such a strong-willed pair.

But they clearly liked the rooms and agreed to her rates at once with no argument. 'I particularly liked the quietness of your house,' said the older woman who had by now introduced herself as Miss Priscilla Knapp. 'It will ensure that we are able to rest when we need to. No good work is done without adequate rest.'

Tilly caught her breath and said carefully, 'Of course, I do understand that. But you may recollect that you noticed yourself that there will be an infant here in due course.'

The younger lady, Miss Sophia Fleetwood, looked a little scornful at that. 'We are not concerned with the sound that children make, Mrs Quentin! We are accustomed to the bawling of the young, and hardly hear it when it happens. No, it is the noise of *men* when they sit at table and drink too much that we find objectionable. It fills the house with din. As does the smell of their cigars which creeps everywhere. The lack of men in this house is something we find *most* agreeable.'

'Yes indeed,' said Miss Knapp, and the two of them went away leaving Tilly a little startled, and somewhat uncertain as to whether these two formidable ladies would be agreeable to have in her home. But she told herself, I am now assured of a steady income of three pounds every week. There should be more than enough to feed them all and to give the Misses Knapp and Fleetwood excellent breakfasts; it would be sufficient for Eliza's wages and even something to put aside against a bad time. Altogether, Tilly had found peace of mind at last.

And she revelled in it, spending the next four months in a comfortable domesticity, helping Eliza to improve her cooking skills — which she did very successfully, with only a few disasters — and feeling her baby grow within her. The ladies upstairs proved to be almost invisible, rising early, leaving immediately after eating their large breakfasts ('Appetites like my Ma's billy-goats they've got,' Eliza said admiringly. 'Eat anything they will, *and* come back for more'), and returning late. The memory of the early part of the year slid away into the past, and Tilly was happy. Totally and completely happy.

Until the evening, late in November, when the pains began.

Chapter Twenty-one

IT HAD BEEN a busy but pleasant day. Eliza had set her heart on making Christmas puddings, and although Tilly had small appetite for any sort of year's end celebration, she allowed that a small Christmas dinner shared by the two of them might be agreeable, with perhaps an invitation extended to the Misses Knapp and Fleetwood. She ended the day rather more tired than she had expected to be (for helping Eliza in the kitchen was often hard work) but happy enough.

She went, as usual, to her Mamma's room after dinner to see how she was, even though of course Henrietta was quite unaware of her. Tilly sat beside her for ten minutes or so, looking at the sagging old face and listening to her heavy breathing as she settled into the night, before going wearily to her own room to go to bed. Her back had been aching all day and she rubbed it as she stepped out of her wrapper — for she had long since given up wearing a day gown — and stretched herself on her bed. She would undress properly later, she told herself drowsily. To lie here in her chemise and drawers was no great crime, after all.

She woke suddenly, aware of the dragging pain inside her, deep in her belly, and stared up at the darkness overhead. She was a little befuddled for she had been dreaming, and a confused *mélange* of images still slid around inside her head. Alice, shouting at her and kicking her with sharp little shoes, and Freddy trying to stop her and Alice kicking even harder whenever he said anything, hitting Tilly's middle over and over again, until at last Freddy had picked her up and hurled her into the air, like a great kite. In her dream Tilly had stood and watched Alice slowly turning and turning in the sky, silhouetted against a big moon; and as she fell towards earth again, trying to shriek at Freddy to catch her while he only smiled back at her.

Why should I dream of Freddy and Alice? she wondered as she rolled over on to her side before sitting up. It was the only way she could get upright now that her belly was so huge, and she sat there for a moment on the edge of the bed, catching her breath and with both hands resting high on the bump, feeling the hardness beneath her fingers. Freddy and Alice; they had not spoken to each other these past four months. Tilly had seen Freddy go by number seventeen, on his way into town she assumed, but there had been no sign of Alice; and she had come to the conclusion that Alice was deliberately avoiding her. Well, that was probably the best answer to their situation, she thought sadly; the close neighbours who might have been friends were completely out of her life now. Yet she had dreamed about them, and she shook her head to rid it of the last rags of unease that the dream had left there. Then she caught her breath, for the pain had returned, a deep creaking sort of pain and she thought for a moment that she was asleep again and Alice was kicking her. But it was real, very real, and she lifted her head in exultation. It had started. Her baby was about to be born, and she sat still as the pain heightened, then eased, and went away.

Well, she thought – that wasn't so bad! She remembered Dorcas's vivid and terrifying descriptions of what it was like to have a baby and shook her head at her own foolishness in believing her all that time ago and then thought – that's someone else I haven't thought about for a long time: Dorcas. I wonder whether she married her soldier? She must have had her baby by now. Perhaps she's regretting the lies she told me?

But it was impossible to imagine Dorcas regretting anything, and she laughed softly under her breath at her own absurdity and slid off the bed to make her way to her fireplace, there to kneel down — for she could not bend — and stir the embers and feed them with a little coal. She was wide awake now, and it was a cold night; she would need the room warm for the baby when he was born. He? She? How exciting it all was, she thought, and then sat back on her heels as another of the pains struck her.

It seemed a little deeper this time, more creaking than the one before and she thought — I wonder how long this must go on before the baby is ready to come out of me? But she didn't want to think about something that seemed so indelicate, and climbed awkwardly to her feet and took off the rest of her underwear and pulled on her nightdress.

The odd thing was that she felt so comfortable. She had thought often about this moment and how it would be, and had expected herself to be anxious, calling for Eliza to come and help her. It had been agreed with a Mrs Elphinstone, who lived on the other side of Brompton Grove and who acted as a midwife and monthly nurse for the ladies of the area, that she would take care of young Mrs Quentin when her time came, and that Eliza would fetch her when she was needed.

Standing now on her hearthrug before her bedroom fire Tilly thought dreamily — I should send Eliza now. But she didn't want to. She wanted to be alone, just herself and her baby in this special quiet time, before they were parted and then reunited when she took her infant into her arms, and she smiled at the strangeness of that notion. There was no hurry to send for Mrs Elphinstone. Surely Dorcas had told her long ago — and Eliza had confirmed it — that several hours of the pains had to go by before the baby could actually be born? Tilly had only the haziest notion of why that should be, but imagined she had to stretch somewhat to make it possible for the baby to emerge; and moving gingerly and aware of the improper nature of what she was doing, she touched herself where the baby would emerge to see how stretched she was. As far as she could tell nothing there had changed at all, and she relaxed. Clearly she had a long time to wait yet.

She pulled her armchair closer to the fire, which was beginning to burn up now, and then added more coal to the flames. She was about to sit down but became anxious about the state of her room. She would be mortified if Mrs Elphinstone should find it untidy, and she set to work to tidy her bed and rearrange her dressing-table.

It was odd. She felt so alive and so active, yet every little while she had to stand quite still and wait for the pain to flood its way through her body. She would stop whatever she was doing and put her hands on to her belly again, finding the hardening of it very peculiar, and concentrate her mind on the part of her body she imagined was stretching. But it didn't seem to be stretching at all when she checked, and that puzzled her.

Eventually she sat in her armchair again in front of the now vigorous fire and watched the way the light flickered on the ceiling, and made shadows and patterns which leapt and died and warmed her imagination so that she saw babies dancing among them and small four-legged creatures too, and it was so very pretty.

She dozed between the pains and listened as the clock on Holy Trinity Church struck the hours. Three o'clock came and went and then four o'clock and then it was five and the pinging of the quarters seemed to her to be further and further apart, until she realized that it was the pains that had speeded up. She estimated they were now coming nine or ten times each quarter hour. Surely by now she should be able to detect some of the necessary stretching? Again with shrinking fingers she touched herself; and suddenly she was alarmed. Her body felt the same as it usually did there; there seemed to her to be no space through which her baby could emerge and she had a sudden vision of herself never being able to give birth. At the same time as this realization another pain came, and this one seemed so much deeper and harder and tighter and somehow noisier that she cried aloud, a great wail of sound that startled her; and she got to her feet and made for the door, holding her belly with both hands beneath the bump. If she didn't, she thought, something dreadful would happen, and she felt the fear roll over her and could do nothing to control it.

From then on it all seemed to change. She managed somehow to reach Eliza's door downstairs beside the kitchen, and at her hesitant touch Eliza leapt from her bed and pulled on her print gown and shoes and then, muttering and exclaiming continuously, helped Tilly back up to her room.

'Don't you fret none now, Mum, it's all right – the pains'll go on a while yet – how often did you say? My Ma always says it takes longer with a first baby and it's not till they're every minute or so you need to fret, and even then not till the pushing starts.'

'Pushing?' Tilly clung to her and wailed again as yet another pain moved round her belly. Oh God, she thought. Dorcas, Dorcas, you said it would be so and it is: 'What pushing?'

'To get the baby out, Mum. You has to push it out – my Ma says it's like passin' a cannon ball – you got plenty of time now, Mum – just you be easy.'

But she could not be easy. For the first time she began to understand how the actual birth would be. The pains had nothing to do with stretching her. She had to do that herself, and she felt the bump again and the smooth hugeness of it and tried to imagine pushing that out of her body and cried aloud.

'Oh, please Mum, be easy,' Eliza implored. 'You'll get that tired you won't be able to do nothing. Be easy, and I'll fetch you a posset.'

'Fetch Mrs Elphinstone,' shrieked Tilly. 'I want to do this now and get it done with.'

Eliza peered at her and shook her head. 'It'll come when it's ready to, Mum, and not before. It's no use a-fetching Mrs

223

Elphinstone yet. You didn't start the pains till after you'd gone to bed, did you? No — so there's not above seven or so hours gone. It'll be a while yet — you won't want Mrs E here before you got to have 'er. She'll cost you if you keep 'er 'ere too long.'

From then on it was a blur. The pains seemed to come less swiftly, but they were bigger and noisier and infinitely worse than they had been, and she wept and shouted at Eliza, who seemed to grow in age and stature as the morning wore on. She was firm in all she did and paid small attention to Tilly's rantings.

'I'll fetch Mrs Elphinstone for a look-see about nine o'clock,' she promised, as she rubbed Tilly's back in an effort to comfort her through one of the pains. 'That'll be soon enough, mark my words. I seen all this, many's the time, so I ain't fidgeting yet.'

The Misses Knapp and Fleetwood tapped on her bedroom door as they came down, seeking their breakfasts, and Eliza told Tilly firmly that she had to go and see to them, but would be back directly, and for the next hour Tilly coped as best she might, alone.

But it helped her, for she realized that Eliza was in fact right; nothing much seemed to be happening except the string of pains, and once she stopped shouting at Eliza, and demanding she do something, somehow, they seemed less unbearable. Certainly she was able to doze a little between each one and that helped a lot.

It was fully daylight when at last Eliza returned and this time Mrs Elphinstone was with her. She was a tall thin woman, with a wide smile and a tendency to hiss through her teeth as she spoke, which was disconcerting, but oddly helpful. In trying to understand what she said, Tilly found herself able to ride the pain in her belly and back rather better.

'Oh, this is all very nice, yessss — very nice,' Mrs Elphinstone smiled widely and hissed at the same time. 'Very nice-sss.'

'Is it?' Tilly managed for another pain had started. 'It does

224

not seem to me –' And then she was stretching her face into a grimace to prevent herself crying out, for to do so in front of Mrs Elphinstone would be, she felt, a most shameful thing.

'Oh, yessss, fine and very nice,' said Mrs Elphinstone and then nodded at Eliza. 'A nice cup of tea, pleassse – that would be very nice too.'

She sat and drank her tea happily, watching Tilly as she tried to control her desire to cry out and then smiled again and said, 'Perhaps we'll do a little checking now – Yessssss –' She came to lean over Tilly and investigate her belly with large chilly hands. But they felt pleasant enough, pushing and prodding at her, and it gave her something else to think about other than the pain.

'Yesssss.' Mrs Elphinstone stood up. 'Well, no need for me for a while yet. Call me, Eliza, when she starts the pushing.' As she went Tilly reared up in the bed as best she could and shouted after her; but it was no use. Eliza and Mrs Elphinstone had disappeared and left her alone, and now she wept, angrily and childishly, hating all of them, hating the baby too, for making her feel so dreadful, and then hating herself most of all for being so hateful a person. Altogether, she felt horrid.

And so it went on, all afternoon and well into the evening; until at last Mrs Elphinstone came back and Eliza was leaning over her and begging her to hold on to her hand and to stop pushing, for there was a need to wait. Tilly peered up at her in the lamplight and wanted to argue with her, tell her that she was not pushing anything. How could she be, here on her bed? And then it started again and she knew what Eliza meant; the huge shrieking pain and with it a desperate urge to push down on her own body as though she could turn it inside out. She felt her face redden as she held her breath and made a vast effort; Eliza was shouting at her not to do it, to open her mouth and pant instead – and at last she heard and understood and tried to obey; and Mrs Elphinstone, who was far out of sight, somewhere at the other end of the world it seemed to

Tilly, cried, 'Yesssss, wait now – yesssssssss – ssss,' and Tilly could feel her fumbling at the other end of her body, so very far away and so foreign to her. But then the desire to push came back and she cried, 'I must – I must,' and at the same time Mrs Elphinstone cried, 'It's all right – it's free – it's free,' and Eliza leaned over and bawled in Tilly's ear, 'You may push all you like now – push hard – the harder the better.'

It was all over in a slither and a rush that took Tilly by surprise. The agony and the effort of the pushing all succeeded at the same moment, and Mrs Elphinstone was crying out in excitement and holding something aloft. All Tilly could see was a twirled greyish pink rope dangling and above it something large and also grey and strange held in Mrs Elphinstone's wide hands; and she lifted her head to peer down the bed at the extraordinary scene.

'Such a long cord!' Mrs Elphinstone was hissing. 'Sssso very long – no wonder it caught itself round itssss poor little neck – poor sssscrap – almost sssstrangled.'

'Oh, Eliza!' Tilly cried. Eliza was standing close to her and there were tears running down her cheeks as she looked down at Tilly and said huskily, 'There, Mum. You done it. Can you see? He's a fine big boy, Mum, a fine boy – oh Mum!'

It was more than Tilly could bear. She too began to weep, great sobs which sent tears streaming down her cheeks, but it was a wonderful feeling. The tears were enjoyable, even comforting, and she abandoned herself to the luxury of it all.

Mrs Elphinstone had been busy attending to matters at the other end of the bed, and now she came and leaned over Tilly and set a towel in her arms. Tilly frowned, puzzled at first, but then she looked more closely and saw the baby within it. Crumpled, angry red and streaked with yellowish grease of some sort, its mouth was wide open and as she closed her arms convulsively around the towel it shrieked in protest. They all laughed, Eliza and Mrs Elphinstone and even Tilly; and she lifted her head and looked at the other two women and then at the child again.

'I didn't know,' she said. 'I didn't know it was like this.' The baby lifted his creased eyelids and looked at her. The eyes were dark blue and looked weary in the wrinkled face, exceedingly old and exceedingly knowing, and he blinked once and then turned his head towards her, and she held him close in a sudden agony of adoration.

'Put him to your breast, Mrs Quentin — yessss — that'sss what he wants — it will sssettle the afterbirth nicely — yesssss. Let him sssssuckle now.'

Tilly did not quite understand, but Eliza did and with swift fingers she untied Tilly's nightgown and set the baby's cheek against one swollen breast. The baby opened his mouth widely, curling it towards Tilly's skin and Eliza lifted him a little in Tilly's arm so that the seeking greedy mouth was on a line with the nipple. He seemed to snuffle and to push his head even more urgently and seized the nipple and held on, hard; and Tilly gasped, for it sent a wave of sensation through her that was unlike any she had ever had before, exciting and wonderfully pleasurable. But it did not last, for the pain in her belly began again. Not as bad as it had been, but there all the same and Mrs Elphinstone said triumphantly, 'Oh, here it issss then,' and Eliza laughed.

'It was the goats that taught me about that,' she said loudly. 'When they drops their kids the sooner they sucks the sooner the afterbirth comes. There, Mum. Isn't that worth the trouble then? Isn't he the best baby you ever saw?'

Chapter Twenty-two

ON AN EARLY afternoon in April, Tilly decided to venture into the garden. It had been warm and dry for almost a week and the garden, though sadly neglected, was attractive, being full of daffodils and lilac and some early tulips. She set the crib beneath the old plane tree near the summer house, halfway down the long plot, in such a way that the baby's face was shaded by the branches but his body left out in the sunshine. She pulled the skirts of his baby gown back as far as his thighs, so that he could lie and kick, and hoped Eliza would not come out of the house and see, for she would be sure to scold. Eliza was very watchful of the baby, to the point of being possessive, and she was often scandalized by the way Tilly liked to break the rules of baby care with him. Like letting him lie on a rug in the bedroom before the fire, quite naked, so that he could kick to his heart's content. Eliza found that deeply suspect, an invitation to the most dreadful of disorders and diseases; she would be even more alarmed at seeing him with bare legs in the open air.

Tilly played with the baby for a while, cooing at him and repeating the new nickname she had devised for him. 'Duff,' she murmured. 'Duff, Duff, Duff!' He looked back at her with alert dark blue eyes and a wide toothless smile; but his only reply was a few excited squeals and burbles. But that didn't deter Tilly. It was never too soon to learn, she told him solemnly. 'Duff, Duff, Duff.'

She had decided only last week to call him so, for however hard she tried, she could not bring herself to use his given names. She had had him christened at St Peter's Church, a little further west along Brompton Grove towards the newly built Egertons – Gardens, Terrace and Crescent – having sworn never to set foot in Holy Trinity again. The vicar had been so determined, when he heard of the baby's orphan status, that he would have his father's name that she had been unable to resist him; he had managed to convince her that failure to give the boy his patronymic would be tantamount to orphaning him twice over, so she had succumbed and he had been christened Francis Xavier. But however hard she tried, Tilly could not manage to use either names; they would not pass her lips. That meant that for the first four months of his life her son had been called 'baby dear', or 'little darling', or some such; until last week when she had been bathing him and Eliza, on hand as ever to dote on him and coo at him and to hand over the necessary equipment, had said adoringly, 'See how plump he's got, Mum. Looks for all the world like one of my nice plum duffs, don't he? As round and as bursting with goodness as may be!'

'Duff he is and Duff he shall be!' Tilly had cried delightedly, much struck, and Eliza, though she had protested at first, had decided that after all it was a nice enough nickname for a round plump baby and had given it her approval. Which would make matters easier for Tilly, undoubtedly.

She had long ago given up any attempt to treat Eliza as a servant and to keep her distance. Ever since the baby's birth she had been more of a working housekeeper and companion than a servant, young as she was. It was difficult, after all, to be remote with a person who has given you the most intimate care a woman can have, as Eliza had for Tilly in the weeks following the baby's birth. So, pleasing Eliza was important.

'Duff,' Tilly said again but he was bored now and had closed his eyes and drifted into sleep and she stood above him a little longer, tracing with her eyes the line of his round jaw and his soft mouth, amazed at his perfection. There had never been so beautiful a baby and there never would be.

She turned to drift around the garden, looking at the state of it. It badly needed some attention and she would have to consider becoming something of a gardener herself, for she could not afford to pay one, unless she found herself another lodger or two. She thought about that possibility often, for the Misses Knapp and Fleetwood were of small trouble to anyone, and there were the attic rooms available, after all. But new lodgers would have to be most carefully chosen, for it would never do to upset the Misses K and F (as Eliza often called them, much to Tilly's disapproval) and anyway, would the attic rooms attract the Right Sort? When she had ventured to discuss the possibility with the lady teachers, they had made a good deal of fuss about the importance of 'Choosing the Right Sort' which Tilly had found dispiriting, and quite enough to put her off the whole idea. Again.

She sighed and decided to think no more about the matter at present. Concentrate on the garden, she told herself. Get a man in once a week or so to scythe the grass and root out the worst of the weeds. The rest she could perhaps deal with herself, tending to the plants and even growing a few vegetables. It could be an agreeable occupation if she had time left over after caring for Duff.

He cried suddenly and she hurried across to him. He was lying staring at the branches of the plane trees and chewing his fist, and she thought indulgently – Ah, he's hungry. He often was, seeming to have as vigorous an appetite as any baby possibly could have, and she bent and picked him up and held him close to her face, hating to hear him miserable.

At once his head turned into her cheek and he began to search urgently with his mouth and she chuckled softly. There was something very special about this trick of his; it was almost as though his eagerness added to her pleasure in satisfying him. Feeding him gave her great delight, so much so that sometimes she felt almost guilty about it; surely doing her duty as a mother should not make her feel quite so — well — aware of her body? She felt her breasts tighten and the nipples tingle as his hunger made him cry more loudly.

She should, she knew, take him into the house and feed him in privacy, but an imp of mischief seemed to have entered her, itself fed by her body's clamour to give Duff what he was demanding. There was the summer house, after all, dilapidated indeed, but nicely hidden from the windows of the house by an overgrown rose bush, and it was so set that the afternoon sun was pouring into it. The old basket chair at the back looked sturdy though, and surrendering to her impulsiveness, she stepped into the small building and pulled the chair forwards and settled herself in it. The baby whimpered as she unbuttoned the bodice of her gown.

It was as agreeable a feeding as she had ever known. The baby lay with his downy head against her skin, both of them warmed by the spring sunshine, and she rested her back against the comfy cushions of the chair, watching her baby with half-closed eyes. His own eyes were equally half-lidded as, with one hand starfished against the naked skin of her breast, she felt him drawing hard on her nipple, and her whole body crept with pleasure. Dear Duff. Dear sunshine. Dear everything.

Quite when she became aware that there was someone else present, she did not know. When she looked up and saw the tall figure standing there she was certainly not surprised, so she must have realized she was no longer alone. But she didn't care, even though the curve of her right breast was clearly visible and the baby's mouth clamped to her nipple was making the sort of sounds that told the entire world within hearing what was happening.

'I should have fled as soon as I realized what you were doing,' he said in a low voice. 'But I could not. I have never seen anything so wonderfully beautiful. I was rooted here. Please forgive me.'

She lifted her chin to squint at him against the sun and saw that indeed he was moved; there was a glitter of tears in his eyes and she bent her head, far from being embarrassed as she knew she ought to be, and lifted Duff's shawl. With a gentle movement she arranged it over herself and the baby so that he could continue to feed, but could not be seen.

'I am surprised to see you here,' she said at length. 'I told you, did I not, that we – that our friendship was at an end.'

'I know,' Freddy said. 'And I accepted my *congé*. Or I thought I had. But when it came to it, and I was leaving – I could not bear to go without seeing you. And then to intrude so upon you – I am devastated. I should go at once.'

But he did not move and she saw he was afraid to, and understood that he was having to use all his strength to remain where he was.

'Well, it has happened now,' she said, amazed at her own equanimity. 'So there is little sense in your running away. You had best to sit down. There is a bench there beside the tree.'

Now he did move and fetched the bench a little nearer, but set it discreetly so that he was sitting at a decent distance from her, and certainly not looking directly at her. She smiled and looked down at Duff, who had decided beneath his covering shawl that he had suckled enough and had drifted into surfeited sleep. With one unobtrusive hand she rebuttoned her bodice and then sat, decently covered, with Duff in her arms.

'I came to say goodbye,' he said after a long pause, and still did not look at her.

'I said goodbye to you the night you – some time ago,' she said steadily. 'I cannot see that it is necessary to say it again.'

'I am going away.' He said it abruptly. 'We have let the house, or rather Alice has.' There was a bitterness in his tone which was strange, for she had never heard such a note from him. 'I would not of course make any claim to her property. I regard men who do that as – well, I will not behave so. Her inheritance remains her own to handle as she wishes, whatever

232

may be the fate of the law. Now she has decided to go and live amongst some friends in Staffordshire, with Mary to look after her. I shall find other accommodation.'

'Mary?' Tilly said wonderingly. 'The maid who –'

'I told you she had a powerful attachment to my wife. Not an entirely healthy one, I believe. However, let that be. Sufficient to say I have been told she is to live in rural peace and wishes no longer to live under my roof, or to have me under hers. I shall of course not argue with her. She has to be free to live her own life as she wishes. I believe this most ardently.' He smiled a little crookedly. 'As you see, I am a supporter of the old politics, a follower of Thomas Paine.'

'Politics,' she said wonderingly. 'What has that to do with the ways of married people? She may say she wishes to live elsewhere, but – how can you permit this?'

'Permit it? How can I stop it?' He sounded angry but resigned. 'Politics is as much a matter of family life as public life, I do assure you. And the principles I hold dear for public expression I must, in all conscience, follow at home. If she wishes to leave me, therefore, she must be free to do so.'

'I do not understand. I know husbands and wives disagree –' She reddened suddenly, remembering with a painful vividness the way she and Frank had argued. 'But to live separately, how can that be possible?'

'Some people seek divorce,' he said and she blinked at him.

'That is shameful!' she said. 'I hear of such matters – of cases of crim. con. – isn't that what they say, the fast set? But it is not for people like us.'

'I am glad to hear it,' he said.

There was a silence and then she ventured, 'I trust, Fred– Mr Compton, that this – this schism between you – is not in any way due to – I mean, that I did not – oh dear!' She felt wretched, remembering the adoring way Alice had hung on this man's arm, and then the tigerish attack of misplaced wifely jealousy she had mounted on Tilly. Could that be the same woman who had abandoned him now? It seemed incredible.

He laughed, a short ugly sound. 'Oh please, do not take all the credit. She assures me I am quite hatefully boring after all, and she wishes no more of me.' He caught his breath. 'She may have a point. I have found myself in recent months thinking so much of other things that — well, perhaps I have not been the best of husbandly company.'

She said nothing, and he turned and looked directly at her for the first time. 'It cannot come as a surprise, Tilly, that I have developed a *tendresse* for you. You are — well, there it is. I believed myself to be fully attached to my wife and indeed I was. But after — after our disagreement — she displayed so unpleasant a side to her nature and tormented me so — and she *did*, I must tell you, indeed she did — that love died. But in its place —'

'Please, not another word.' She got to her feet and Duff stirred and whimpered in her arms but did not wake. 'I must go inside now. I wish you well, Mr Compton, indeed I do, but —'

'Please. Call me Freddy,' he tried to smile at her, 'in the old way? It would comfort me more than a little.'

She could have wept for him. The dull heaviness she had come to associate with his unsmiling face was quite gone. What she saw now was a man so deeply unhappy that he could barely lift his head; and she wanted to reach out to touch him, even hug him to restore him to the good-humoured, agreeable man he had been in the past. But of course that was not possible. All she could do was shake her head.

'You must see that however large is the debt I owe you for your past friendship towards me, I cannot possibly permit myself any familiarity now. Especially as you — as Alice has gone. You must see that.'

He sat silently for a while and then nodded. 'I suppose so.' He too stood up. 'I was of small service of course, but for what I was able to do, I am glad. I am particularly happy to see that your fears for your security here in this house were unfounded. Your father did after all leave you his house and fortune.'

'The house yes. It was in fact held in trust for my mother and so he could not have left it away from me. It was different with his personal fortune of course.'

She stopped and he looked at her sharply. 'Oh?'

She should not confide in him, she knew; he was after all going away and rightly so. But she let it come out all the same. 'He left what monies he had to Mrs Leander,' she said in a low voice. 'It is being held for her by the lawyer. They have not been able to find her to give it her, despite advertising.'

There was a silence and then he gave an odd sort of groan.

'Whatever is the matter?' He had gone quite white and she was alarmed. 'Are you ill? Is there anything —'

'No, I am not ill.' He seemed to recover himself. 'I have just —' He managed a sort of smile. 'I am once again *bouleversé* by my beliefs — those politics that you did not think affected our daily life.'

She frowned, and shook her head in mystification.

'I am sorry — it is just that you have presented me with a dilemma. I — I am sad indeed that your father left his money so. It is a shocking thing to have done to you.'

'Indeed,' she said. 'But I manage well enough. I have my lodgers. They pay the bills for me, and feed us. I can contrive —'

'I am sure you can. I simply wish it were not necessary. But now, as to Mrs Leander.'

'What about her?'

'I cannot — it is difficult to know what to do.' He seemed genuinely distressed, and sat down again and so did she, staring at him over Duff's sleeping head. He thought broodingly for a while and then lifted his chin.

'I am afraid that I may know where Mrs Leander is to be found. The question is, should I reveal the fact so that your lawyers might give to her her rightful inheritance? A painful question indeed.'

'Rightful?' Tilly cried wrathfully. 'You call it rightful?'

'It is not just and it is not kind of your father to have left his money so,' he said steadily. 'But having done so, it is her right to receive it, is it not?'

She was silent for a long moment and then said unwillingly, 'I suppose so.'

'So knowing, as I suspect I do, where she might be – is it not right I should say so? Or will the money come to you in due course if I do not? And even if that is the case, would it be right of me to – oh dear, it is so difficult to behave as an honourable man should!' His face was twisted with anxiety, and he looked at her almost piteously. 'I have indeed a problem to be solved here.'

'If she does not claim it, it does not come to me,' Tilly said after a pause. 'It is to go to her issue. That is her daughter Dorcas, wherever she may be. She ran away some time ago. I have not seen or heard from her since.'

'Then telling the laywers where they might find Mrs Leander will not harm you?' His face cleared and he looked almost his old beaming self. 'Oh, that helps me greatly! I am, I know, weak. I should do the right thing, painful or not, but it is so much easier if – well, never mind. I must go and see the laywers. I know where to find them from that day we spent in the City, you will remember.'

She remembered and preferred not to. 'I would rather you told me so that I might tell them,' she said.

He went a sudden deep red and she was puzzled. He looked as ashamed as a child caught stealing, and it seemed so odd a reaction that she stared at him, almost open-mouthed.

'I – it is a matter of some shame to me that I should know,' he said. 'I would prefer – and yet –' Again he seemed lost in thought, and then lifted his head and spoke with some energy. 'I have no right to hide my own sins behind another's – well, there it is. I must, I think, tell the truth. I was mendacious when we dealt with the woman before, Tilly. It is time to be honest now. Then we can part as good friends, I hope, with nothing disagreeable left for me to remember when I am alone.'

236

'I don't understand,' she said. 'You're speaking in riddles.'

'I think in riddles too, I sometimes believe.' He laughed oddly. 'Perhaps I think too much. Well, there it is. I trust your delicacy will not be too offended by what I must tell you.'

'Delicacy?' She managed to laugh herself. 'Mr Compton, I am a married lady – a widow – and a mother. Surely I don't need to be protected, as though I were an infant, from the truths of this world!'

'I would protect you for ever if I could,' he said fiercely and then looked away as she in her turn reddened. 'I am sorry if I offended you in any way at all. So,' he took a deep breath, 'I think – I believe Mrs Leander might be found –' He looked at her almost piteously. 'I would so much rather tell the lawyer.'

'And I would rather you told me,' she said firmly. 'If this is a matter affecting my father, as it is, then I have a right to know, surely.'

He seemed to make up his mind fully at last.

'Very well,' he said with a new crisp note in his voice. 'I must tell you then that when I told Mrs Leander I knew matters of her past which made her remaining in this house no longer permissible, I was not pretending. I did know she was. She used to live in a house of – a house of assignation. She had earned her living in this manner for some time, before she came here as a housekeeper. I told her that unless she left at once I would tell Mr Kingsley this fact. She chose to go.' He bent his head. 'I believed the means justified the ends, heaven help me. I was so concerned for your peace of mind that I resorted to what is a form of threat. It was not admirable in me.'

'Oh, but it was!' she cried. 'You made me so happy, sending her away, even though afterwards it all – well, you were kind to me. Don't punish yourself for that.'

'Thank you,' he said. 'I am grateful for that.'

There was a silence and then she said, as though the words were being pushed out of her, 'How did you know this?'

He smiled, a tight ugly grimace. 'I was waiting for the

237

question. Because, of course, I saw her there. Often.' He took a sharp breath. 'When I told the full story of our friendship and my actions on your behalf to Alice – feeling it the best way to reassure her – she asked the same question. It was my answer to it that made her so – that turned her against me, and that led to our parting. She could not understand that men some- times, that men have needs that – well, she had a point. If such places and the behaviour inside them is reprehensible for women, I suppose it should be so regarded for men. Though most sensible people do understand that we – well, let be. So, now you know it, and I hope indeed I have not offended you as I offended Alice. I feel so much better than I did. Confession indeed is a source of great release. I have burdened you with my guilt, however, and I beg your pardon for that.'

She shook her head, trying to get some order into her thoughts which were whirling and confused. 'You need not. You were good to me and I make no – I do not care how it was you were able to be of help to me. It was enough that you were. Anyway, we all know that gentlemen are different. They are able to behave in ways that would indeed be disgusting in women but which matter little to them. I see no reason to be angry with you.'

'Ah, but you are not my wife,' he said.

Again she was embarrassed. 'That is true. I suppose – I can understand Alice's anger.'

'Revulsion,' he said.

'Well, perhaps, if that is not too strong a word.'

'It was not for her,' he said.

Again there was a silence between them and then she got to her feet once more, this time with some determination. 'We must say goodbye, Mr Compton. I will ask you indeed to tell Mr Cobbold what you know of Mrs Leander. I have no pecuniary interest in the matter at all, but I agree with you. However bitterly I resent my father's action she has the right to her legal inheritance, I suppose.'

He too was on his feet. 'Thank you. You have saved my

conscience. And now – once again, may I ask you that we part as friends. Will you say, "Goodbye Freddy", to me in the old way? To send me on my way, if not happy, at least with peace of mind?'

She looked at him for a long moment and then nodded.

'Goodbye Freddy,' she said. 'And I do indeed wish you well. You've always been most kind to me, and I most bitterly regret the difficulties in which you find yourself. If I am able some time in the future to be – to be of friendly service to you –' She could say no more, but he understood and reached out and took her hand and half shook it, half patted it, and then turned and walked away across the sunny garden.

She stood and watched him go, past the back of the house, towards the way that led out to Brompton Grove, and went on looking long after he had disappeared and the sound of his footsteps were gone.

Chapter Twenty-three

'AFTER SO LONG a time,' Tilly said, to have located her after so many years only to discover she had died so recently? It is very strange.'

'Not at all strange,' Mr Cobbold said weightily. 'God will not be mocked, Mrs Quentin. It is clear to me that this was divine intention. He wished to destroy the woman in her wickedness and not permit her to benefit from it in any way.'

Tilly set her head on one side and looked at him consideringly. When the letter from the lawyer had arrived, asking for permission to wait upon her, her first reaction had been amazement, her second, fear. It had been, after all, more than four years since she had had any direct dealings with him; four busy, peaceful, happy years watching Duff grow from infancy to determined, sturdy noisy childhood; four years of peace during which she had not thought about Mrs Leander at all. And his letter had forced Tilly to think of her, which was not an agreeable experience.

But once she had listened to what he had to say, her fear vanished, for there was now no more to fear from the woman who had once had the power to make her so miserable. And she looked at Mr Cobbold and thought about him instead.

It was clear to her that he had in the past four years become caught up with the fervour of the currently fashionable evangelical movement, and she had at first found it incongruous in a man she remembered as being cheerful and comfortable.

Then, as a woman who could not share his pleasure in the frequent mention of the hellfire and damnation that seemed to preoccupy him, she became profoundly irritated and no longer responded to those of his comments which derived from his beliefs.

'It was just three months ago, you say?' she asked. 'Do you know no more about the circumstances of her death?'

'Only that she died of the most dreadful ravages of the pox. I hesitate even to name the disease under the roof of a respectable and delicate lady like yourself, but you asked me, and I must answer you.'

And enjoy having something on which to hang a sermon while you do it, Tilly thought, crossly, and cut in quickly, 'And she is buried where?'

'In Kensal Green. They drew on a special fund to enable her to escape a pauper's funeral. I told them that *I* would not have been so — well, I believe, as you know, that people must take the consequences of their own actions and hers were so evil, so devoted to Satan and all his wiles, that they led her to ignominy and death. They should have left her to the —'

'Who drew on a fund?' Tilly interrupted and he blinked.

'Who? The hospital. She was sent to St Mary's Hospital, in Highgate at the Archway, where they specialize in such horrid disorders. The — ahem — people at the house where she lived were concerned only with getting her off their premises so that she would not alarm the other drabsters, or their customers. She was, I am told, a dreadful sight. Covered in blisters and sores and —'

She shuddered at the relish with which he spoke and held up a hand to silence him. Clearly gratified to have affected her so, he at once apologized copiously for any indelicacy and again she stopped him, sickened at his hypocrisy.

'I cannot understand why it took so long to find the house where she lived,' she said with some sharpness. 'I know that Mr Compton told you five years ago that she would almost certainly be living in such a house of assignation — a brothel —'

241

Mr Cobbold winced at the word '— And there cannot be so many in London, after all.'

'I lack knowledge of the precise numbers,' Mr Cobbold said, with an air of great reasonableness. 'How could one like myself possess such disgraceful information? I had to send out investigators. And since it is always incumbent upon me to use the monies in any legacy carefully, I could not in all conscience disburse large sums on the search. So it took a long time.'

'While of course the money was invested?' Tilly said, and for the first time the old look of the shrewd man of affairs appeared in Mr Cobbold's eyes and she knew she had hit the target. They had been using Mrs Leander's legacy for their own purposes, and had not prosecuted the search for her with any diligence at all; and now she was angry. The woman might have cheated her of her rightful inheritance from her father, but that did not mean these sharp lawyers should be permitted to do the same.

'I can assure you that all of the money left to Mrs Leander is perfectly safe,' Mr Cobbold said smoothly. 'You need have no fears that the sum is not precisely as it was left.'

'I am sure it is. But I wonder if she would have enjoyed the full amount of interest in that — well, let it be. I have no power in this matter, except in that it was my father's money. I do, however, have some moral authority, I hope.'

'We all have that, Mrs Quentin,' Mr Cobbold murmured, once again his unctuous self, and she looked at him unsmilingly.

'I am glad to hear you agree with me. Then you will make vigorous searches for her daughter?'

'Her daughter?' Mr Cobbold frowned. Clearly he had not given much thought to the matter of Mrs Leander's issue. 'Indeed, yes. You know where she is to be found?'

'If I had known that, I would of course have told you,' Tilly said scathingly. 'Since I am clearly more anxious than you appear to be to see right done.'

242

'That is quite a disgraceful thing to say!' Mr Cobbold said, his cheeks shaking with anger. 'I hope I know my duty as a Christian gentleman and –'

'I am more concerned with what is right than what is merely dutiful.' Tilly was now very angry too. 'To have been so lax in making searches for Mrs Leander all these years while I believed you were being most industrious in your efforts – I believe *that* to be disgraceful! Now I trust you will repair the errors of omission you have committed and seek diligently for Mrs Leander's daughter.'

He got to his feet and dusted down his black coat with an air of rectitude that made the normally equable Tilly want to throw something at him. 'I will forgive you, Mrs Quentin, for your intemperate speech, as it is my duty to forgive,' he said. 'And put it down to the sad megrims with which so many of you of the gentler sex are afflicted. If you will tell me what you know of Mrs Leander's daughter I will see to it that advertisements are put in the usual organs and –'

'But that doesn't work,' Tilly cried. 'You first advertised for Mrs Leander five years ago and that brought no satisfaction! Now you are proposing to go down the same road again? It is really not good enough.'

He bent his head in a frosty little bow. 'It is as far as my duty goes, Ma'am. I will see to it at once. Good afternoon.'

He did not wait to be shown out but moved majestically across the drawing-room to the door, but she was after him at once, holding on to his sleeve.

'I must insist that you do more. It is not right that she should be kept in ignorance of either her mother's death or of her legacy.'

He looked down at her hand on his sleeve and then with an air of fastidiousness stepped back from her so that she had to let go. 'Madam, I acted in all good faith and I must say, in generosity, in coming here today. It is not incumbent upon me to tell you of these matters at all. The legacy is not yours. I told you only because I believed you would be interested to know what is happening to your father's money. I happened to be in the neighbourhood and, out of my sense of Christian benevolence, called upon you with this news. But that does not give you the right to harangue me. And I must say, Ma'am, that I find it most unseemly that any gentlewoman should behave in such an importunate manner. I understand that your need to occupy yourself making money will inevitably have coarsened your sensibilities, but –'

'Coarsened my –' Tilly could go no further and clapped her hands together in her rage. 'How dare you, Sir! I show a proper concern for the rights of a legatee of my father, and you put this down to my – you are the outside of enough, Sir, and I wish you to leave my house forthwith! Any future legal business I have to pursue will be taken elsewhere, you may be sure. I allowed you to deal with my affairs after Mr Conroy's death since I believed you to be an honourable man. I now know better!'

She ran across the room to the fireplace and tugged on the bell, and then stood there glowering at him as he brushed down his sleeves and coat front, and with what dignity he could muster opened the door. He was in time to meet Eliza who was about to open it from the other side.

'Eliza,' Tilly said loudly. 'Show this – person – to the street. And if he ever appears here again, I will not receive him!'

Mr Cobbold opened his mouth to speak, caught her glare and closed it again and without a word turned and went. Eliza, her face alive with interest, stepped back to show him the way, as the small figure who had been peering from behind her skirts darted out and ran into the drawing-room. Tilly held out one hand and the child ran to her. He was as excited and interested as Eliza, and stared with wide eyes at the man whose back was now receding down the stairs.

'Is that a bad man, Mamma?' he said and tugged on Tilly's arm as she did not reply. 'Shall I go after him with my stick? I will hit his legs and *hit* his legs till he skips and shouts and –'

'Now, Duff, hush,' Tilly said absently. 'You must do no such thing to the gentleman.'

'You said to Eliza he was a person, not a gentleman at all!' Duff protested, and tugged on her skirts instead of her arm. 'Do let me hit him with my stick, Mamma, for he has made you cross and you don't like being made cross.'

She managed a smile and reached down and picked him up, straining a little, for he was well filled out for a child not yet five. 'Darling Duff, you must not be so fierce! There are a lot of things that make Mamma cross, but they do not mean that you must come and hit people. This was a private grown-up matter and –'

'You always say that when things are interesting.' Duff wriggled and pushed her away. 'Put me down, Mamma! I'm too old to be carried like a baby!'

She put him down and sighed. 'Yes, indeed you are, my darling. Too heavy too – you have been eating too much of Eliza's cake.'

'You can't eat too much cake.' He ran to the window to look out into the street. 'There he goes – he walks like that great fat dog from the house on the corner, Mamma. So important and all side to side, like my boat on a windy day when I sail it on the Long Water in the park – who is he, Mamma?'

'He is a lawyer,' Tilly said. 'And you mustn't ask so many questions. Have you done your pothooks this morning as I told you?'

'Yes, Mamma,' he said sunnily and came back to join her on the sofa, where she was now sitting very straight staring into the fire, lost in thought. 'You won't think them good enough, I dare say, but I like them. I left my book in the kitchen. I shall get it later and show you – Mamma, why are you still so cross? He's gone now.'

She roused herself and put her arms about him and hugged him. 'You ask too many questions for a small person! Now, fetch your book and I shall look at your work. We must be sure it is right before Miss Knapp sees it.'

'I suppose I must go to school with the Misses K and F?' Duff said gloomily. 'It's so much easier to do pothooks and read here at home with you.'

'You must not call them so,' Tilly said. 'Miss Knapp and Miss Fleetwood, young man, and don't you forget it!'

'Eliza says —'

'What Eliza says has nothing to do with what you may say. You must not speak so of them,' Tilly said firmly, making a resolve to try yet again to put a curb on Eliza's tongue when she was with Duff, and knowing it to be a waste of time. 'You just mind your manners. And yes, of course you are to go to school. It will be great fun for you. Lots of other little boys to play with.'

'I have Archie and Tom from the house on the corner,' Duff said, and curled up closer to her. 'Though I'm not speaking to Tom at the present, for he broke my hoop and is quite quite hateful.

'It is wicked to hate people,' Tilly said reprovingly. 'You know that we must love our friends.'

'You hated that horrid man,' Duff said, all sweet reasonableness. 'And you aren't wicked. And anyway, Tom was wicked to break my hoop. If I go to school there'll be lots of other boys to break all my things. My whips and my tops and my cart.'

'Of course they won't. Miss Knapp and Miss Fleetwood would never let people break your toys at school!'

'I don't suppose they'll let me play at school at all,' Duff said with an air of misery. 'I shall have to work and work all day until I get thin and ill and have to go to bed with Dr Gregory's powder and you know how much I hate that. You won't send me to school to make me ill, Mamma, will you? You wouldn't do that to me, Mamma? Of course you wouldn't.'

She laughed and released him. 'Duff, you are a wretch, and very good at changing subjects. It is some time yet before you have to go to school but we must be sure you are ready when the time comes. So, to return to the subject, go and

246

fetch your book from the kitchen and we shall look at your pothooks. Off you go, now.'

He went and she was able to sit quietly and think at last. She put more coal on the fire and then curled herself up on the footstool close beside it, staring down into the flames, glad of the warmth on this chilly November day.

Mrs Leander dead. It seemed hard to believe. It was not merely the fact of her death that had shaken Tilly so when Mr Cobbold told her of it; it was the manner of her dying. Tilly had hated the woman cordially, had been delighted when she was driven from the house by Freddy's intervention; but to hear now that her life thereafter had been so — well, sordid was the only word that came to Tilly's mind — was dreadful. She felt wretched about it, and undoubtedly guilty. Had she been a little more tolerant Mrs Leander would have remained in the house and her father would not have gone in search of her and died so dreadfully.

Tears welled up in Tilly's eyes and she rubbed them away angrily. She had been through all this, many times, this past five years since her father's death. When her mother had died in her sleep three years ago, slipping out of life as quietly and unobtrusively as she had occupied it, Tilly had been quite devastated with distress; Mr Fildes had been most concerned for her well-being and dosed her heavily and put her to bed for several days. He and Eliza thought her grief was over the loss of her mother but it wasn't that at all; how could she begrudge her mother the peace of death when her last years had been so dreadful for her? No, it was guilt about her father and her husband that consumed her so during those painful days. If she had not behaved as she had, both of them, she had told her sodden pillow, would still be alive.

She had come to her senses eventually of course, realizing that she did not hold the entire world in her own hands and also that she had a duty to care for her baby son, which she could not do if she indulged her emotions to this degree. So, she had applied her common sense. Whatever she had done, her father would no doubt still have suffered his apoplexy. Mr Fildes had assured her of that: 'Too much port and too much hard living, Ma'am,' he had said to her. 'His constitution was sorely damaged.' And as for Frank's death — well, she had long ago taught herself not to think about that. It was the only way she could live with the situation.

Now, however, sitting on this cold November afternoon and staring into her fireplace, all the old guilt came flooding back, and she hugged her knees and let the tears run down her cheeks unchecked. Until she heard Duff's thudding steps on the staircase and rubbed them away and composed her face to turn a smile to him. He deserved only the best of everything, she had told herself fiercely the day he was born, and that included a mother who was sweet-tempered and kindly. She would never let her boy suffer the loneliness and fear that had been her own lot as a child.

'Here they are, Mamma,' he said a little heavily as he came in, plopped himself down on the hearthrug and put his exercise book on her lap. She looked down at it and then at him and she did not have to force her smile, for he looked so woebegone that his small face was adorable to her fond eyes.

'I don't suppose it is so very bad,' she said and kissed the top of his head.

'It is dreadful, Mamma. I looked again and now I know they are quite the worst pothooks I've ever done, and you will be so cross and make me do them ten times over and then I shan't have time to eat my supper and I shall be very miserable and —'

'We shall look,' Tilly said firmly, well accustomed to her son's flights of fancy, designed to distract her attention from the matter in hand, and she opened the book and looked down at its inky pages.

The rows of pothooks trailed across the pages, shaky at first and then a little more certain and then finally and quite clearly dashed off in a great rush; and she smiled even more widely.

'They are not perfect,' she allowed. 'But you tried hard. At *first*. This one and this one – why, they are really quite good!'

He looked brighter. 'Are they, Mamma? There, and I was sure you would be cross with all the blots!'

'Oh, indeed, I dislike the blots. I dislike, too, the way you rushed at the last ones. You must always be as careful with the last as with the first, you know.'

'Well, it gets so dull,' Duff said and jumped to his feet. 'Oh, Mamma, guess what I have in my pocket? I got it from Charlie, when he fetched the order.'

'Fetched the order?' Tilly lifted her head. 'He came himself, and did not send his boy?'

'He is very excited about something to do with the shop. He came to tell Eliza and he gave me this because of it, he said.' He held out a small red cardboard box and she took it and looked inside. It was filled with comfits made of boiled sugar and she smiled indulgently and gave it back to him.

'Not to be eaten till after supper,' she said firmly. 'Well, I wonder what his news is? I dare say Eliza will tell me in due course. Now, young man, those pothooks –'

'But you said they were splendid, Mamma! The best I ever did.'

'I said no such thing, naughty one. I said some of them were not too bad. Now, they must be done again – no, not today. I am not such a hard taskmistress as that. Tomorrow, you must try again and we shall show them to Miss Knapp. I am sure she will be very pleased because soon when you are five you will be ready to go to school with her. And it will be lovely for you, indeed it will.'

'Oh, Mamma, I *never* want to go to school, not ever. I'll have to leave Archie and Tom and –'

'But you're not speaking to Tom!'

'Oh, I am now. He came to play this afternoon and we did a hopscotch square in the garden and he fell and made his knee all bloody, it was lovely. Mamma –'

'Darling Duff,' she said and got to her feet. 'I cannot sit and talk now. I have something I must do. I have to go out.'

249

He stood with his legs set well apart and his arms akimbo, staring at her over his pouting lower lip. He looked decidedly mulish. 'Why must you go out? I get lonely when you go out.'

'Eliza is here —'

'Eliza is always here. It's you I want to be here.'

'Dearest, I'm sorry, but I must go out. I have to look for someone.'

'Who?'

'No one you know, darling. A — someone who was my friend, long ago.'

'What's his name?'

'*Her* name is Dorcas.'

'That's a funny name.'

'No it isn't. It's rather a pretty name.'

'Well, who is she?'

'I told you. An old friend.'

'Where are you going to look for her?'

She sighed and took his hand and led him to the door. 'That's the problem, darling. I don't know. But I have an idea where I might begin. It is still only just four o'clock, and if I hurry I think I might be able to — well, never mind. Off to the kitchen now, and tell Eliza I must speak to her to arrange things with her before I go out. Off you go, now.' She gave him a gentle slap on his small round rump, resplendent in dark green knickerbockers, and sent him from the room.

It was probably absurd not to wait till tomorrow, but she had to start now, she told herself firmly, she really had to. She could think of no other way to assuage her guilt than to do what she knew Mr Cobbold most certainly would not do; find Dorcas. She could never change what had happened in the past to Dorcas's mother, any more than she could change what had happened to her own father; but she could do something about making the future better. And do it she would.

Chapter Twenty-four

SHE STARTED WITH the Knightsbridge Barracks. The ugly, ramshackle building with its busy population of men and horses — some six hundred of the former and five hundred of the latter — had long been a malodorous blot on the landscape, as far as the more elegant new residents of the district were concerned. Looking about her she understood for the first time just why a petition to have them demolished had been got up and hawked around the streets as far away as her own modest home. The huge central square, even at this dark time of the late afternoon, was aflame with light from naked naphtha flares as well as great hissing gas jets and the reek of horses made her throat constrict and her eyes smart. She did not dare lift her gaze from her feet as she picked her way over the wet, greasy cobbles towards the doorway that seemed to lead into the main building.

When she found herself at length at the guard-house she was greeted with raucous jeers by some of the soldiers, and cold disapproval by the officer who saw her hesitating in the doorway and came bustling out to see what she wanted. She tried to explain, and had to be led into a private office before she could get the tale out completely.

'She is a distant cousin,' she extemporized a little wildly, 'who suffered so much from the power of her feelings as a girl that sadly she left the security of her home and went away. We knew only that she — er — that she intended to marry a soldier. Now we wish only to find her so that she may – um – return safely to the bosom of her family. Her mother is ailing, you see.'

Prudently she said nothing about any legacy. This young officer might be the soul of probity, but equally possibly he might be cut of the same cloth as Mr Cobbold. She had assumed *him* to be a man of virtue until she found out otherwise, so she would take no chances now.

He looked at her dubiously. 'I don't see what we can do here, Madam,' he said. 'There's a large number of – ahem – young lady cousins who find themselves more enamoured of a uniform than they might be.' He smirked slightly. 'No doubt your young relation has her own reasons for staying away from her family. Who are we, after all, to expose her shame unless –'

'Why assume there is shame to be exposed?' Tilly was now irritated and forgot to be demure. 'I assure you that when we last spoke all that time ago she had every intention of marrying. She told me his name.'

'That's different. Why didn't you say sooner? If you've got a name – and better still a regiment.'

'I have no details other than a name and even there –' She hesitated. 'I recall his first name perfectly. His second name was – another Christian name.' She shook her head. 'I have tried and tried to recall it, but it eludes me. However, I am sure that if I see it written down I will know it at once.'

He stared at her and then laughed. 'Oh, come, madam!' You cannot expect to be able to read the whole roster of men here and just pick one to accuse of running off with this cousin of yours!'

She was scarlet with embarrassment and anger now. 'It is not like that! I do most strongly assure you it is not. She was to marry her Walter – whatever his name was. I have tried so hard to recall it. It was a classical name, I am sure – perhaps it was in a poem I once read. I do assure you that I am not trying to do anything at all underhand! I seek only to help a distant relative. If I were your sister, would you expect a brother officer to treat me as unkindly as you are doing?'

He looked back at her in the soft light of the gas as it hissed and plopped overhead, and it was his turn to be embarrassed. 'Well, I suppose it can do no harm — though if the adjutant discovers — well, I will let you see some of the lists. Not all. There are hundreds of men here and we cannot allow you time to sit and read the entire roster of their names. But you may start when you choose. See how far you get.'

'Oh, thank you, Sir.' She was irradiated with gratitude and he seemed for the first time aware of the fact that, for all her dark respectable pelisse, she was a young and not uncomely woman.

He bobbed his head and said awkwardly, 'Well, Ma'am, that's well enough,' and hurried away to fetch the big ledger books which bore the names of the men at Knightsbridge Barracks, in row after row of spidery copperplate.

He allowed her to remain with the ledger until six o'clock, at which point he returned to tell her that he was now off duty and it was as much as his life was worth to permit her to remain until the next officer took over; but agreed a little unwillingly that she might return next morning when he would again be on duty. She had, she pointed out, got only as far as the Ds, having skimmed the surnames in search of those that might be similar to Christian names. 'I am sure I will be able to identify the man after a couple of hours with these ledgers,' she told him earnestly.

And so it turned out. She returned the next day at nine in the morning (much to Duff's noisy delight, for it meant she had to abandon his lessons for the day). This time she wore a gown of lilac sarsenet beneath her nicest pelisse in purple satin-trimmed velours with a chip bonnet decorated with matching ribbons. Prudently remembering the ordure-strewn barrack yard she added pattens to protect her feet, and after she had picked her way delicately to the guard-house, holding her crinoline well clear of her ankles, she was gratified to catch approving eye of the young lieutenant. Today, she promised herself, she would succeed. It would be much easier in daylight to beguile the officer into letting her check the names of every soldier here. She must find Dorcas's husband that way, surely?

And she did. It was well past the luncheon hour (and she had politely but firmly refused the lieutenant's offer of a little collation in his quarters) when she reached the Os. She was about to slide over them, not being able to imagine any classical male Christian name that began with that letter, but scolded herself for lacking diligence. She plodded through them and there it was. It leapt off the page at her so forcefully that she could almost hear Dorcas's voice whispering it down the long corridor of the years. 'Walter Oliver's a big man – a lot of substance there.'

She sat and stared at the name and tried to think. She had been so set on tracking Dorcas down that she had not thought much beyond this point, and it was high time she did. She was still struggling with her confusion when the lieutenant came back.

'I'm afraid I have to –' he began, and she shook her head and jumped to her feet.

'I have found him,' she said simply.

He looked startled and then dubious. 'Who?'

'Oliver. Walter Oliver. I told you it was a man's Christian name, and a classic one, did I not? Like in Roland and Oliver, you know. That was the man my cousin planned to marry. If you can arrange for me to see him then?'

He looked at the roster over her shoulder and shook his head, almost with relief. 'Oh, no. The star next to his name – you see? That indicates he is to be deleted from the roster when the next roll is made up. Got his discharge, he did. Or maybe –' He peered again at the page and looked a shade uncomfortable. 'Ah – maybe it wasn't quite – well, he's not here any more, that's the thing.'

'Not – but he is listed here! Surely if a man is enlisted that means he –'

'It means only that he was here,' the lieutenant said brusquely. 'Once they're discharged or dead, then we can't just scratch their names out. We star 'em like that, so we know the next time the page is rewritten it's got to be done without that name. That's all.'

She looked at him sharply. 'Are you saying he's been killed?' she said bluntly. 'Is that why you were so – you seemed uncomfortable when you looked at the entry.'

He looked more uncomfortable still. 'Well, it's not for me to say. Matter for the Commanding Officer, don't you know.'

'Oh, really, Captain!' she said, knowing perfectly well she was promoting him and hoping that would smooth her path. 'I am not a woman given to fits of the vapours at the mere mention of death! I did not know the man, remember, only Dor– my cousin. I will not weep to hear she is a widow. I am a widow myself, and it is after all not so bad a state.' She did her best to dimple at him, disgusted at her own duplicity but at a deeper level enjoying her new-found ability to get her own way by such means.

He took a deep breath and nodded at her, making a little grimace as he did so. 'You've got it pretty right, Ma'am,' he said candidly. 'According to the small cross by the name – not the star, see? – he is indeed dead. Could have been the Chinese Expedition.'

'Chinese?' She was startled.

'Oh, yes, we were there. Last year, you know – there was a force sent to Peking to put down those Chinese pagans who'd been causing so much trouble these past twenty years or more. They had it coming to them, of course, disgraceful carryings on. Boarded one of our ships, don't you know – the *Arrow* – arrested our men on a charge of piracy. Outrageous. We'd have put them down long since, I've no doubt, but that we were still sorting out the business in the Crimea. Last year –' He was clearly enjoying his reminiscences and she lifted her brows at him.

'You were in China too, then?'

255

'Me? Er, no — held the fort here, don't you know. But we sent detachments from this Barracks, indeed we did. Took a lot of work, servicing that little fracas. It would seem your Walter Oliver was one of 'em. Can't say I remember the fellow, you understand, but —'

'Have you any record of where his wife might be?' He reddened a little at the sharpness of her interruption.

'Well, as to that —'

'I'm sure you'll want to help a poor widow to re-establish her ties with her family,' Tilly said, making herself demure again with an effort. 'Since he gave up his life for his —'

'Yes, yes, quite so,' the lieutenant said hurriedly, clearly undecided as she gazed at him beseechingly. After a long pause he picked up the ledger and took it away to his inner office.

'Wait here,' he said and disappeared. Fifteen minutes later the lieutenant returned, and she jumped to her feet.

'It is against all the rules of the service of course,' he said in a low voice. 'And if you tell anyone whence you received this information I shall be forced to deny it. But here is the address of the person he gave as his next of kin. It is the only help I can give you. I truly have gone too far already. I'd be grateful, Ma'am, if you'd leave as soon as maybe. I fear the adjutant may be here soon.' He urged her towards the door and she went gladly, clutching the scrap of paper firmly in her hand, and made her way out of the office and across the barrack square, before escaping gratefully out on to the street beyond. Only then did she look at the paper.

'Mrs Walter Oliver,' she read, '17 Waterford Street, Fulham —' and took a sharp little breath in through her nose. Not far away at all; and she peered at the watch on her fob, fumbling inside her pelisse. Three in the afternoon. Still time to go there, if she could get a fast cab; she bit her lip, thinking of Duff waiting at home for her, and then decided. The sooner this was sorted out the better. Duff was in safe and happy hands with Eliza, and she would not fuss too much if Tilly was late returning. She had warned Eliza when she left this morning that she could not promise any time for her return, but would endeavour of course to be in before dark when there might be footpads about. Eliza was sure that the night streets were infested with persons who were hell-bent on murder and mayhem, even though Tilly often reminded her that Knightsbridge was a respectable area now and not at all the thieves' kitchen it had been before the Great Exhibition had brought prosperity to the district.

At last she saw in all the traffic a four-wheeler available for hire — a hansom would be cheaper, but a four-wheeler was more comfortable, and perhaps quicker — and for once her natural thrift was overcome.

Waterford Street proved to be a narrow thoroughfare of neat and tolerably well-kept artisan's cottages, and she stood on the pavement outside number seventeen looking at the front door beyond its tiny sliver of front garden tucked behind intricate railings. It looked spick and span indeed, and had window boxes on the lower sills in which a few late geraniums straggled, trying to look brave and bright in the fading light of the November afternoon. Behind her she heard the cab turn and the horse's hooves clop away and for a moment she wanted to run after it and climb in and go home; but she straightened her shoulders and tucked one hand into her pelisse and walked up the tiled front path, to knock on the door.

There was a long silence, and then a shuffling sound, and finally the door opened, but only enough to allow one suspicious eye to peer out at her.

'Yerss?' a cracked voice said. ''Oo is it?'

'I am looking for Mrs Walter Oliver,' Tilly said. 'Is she here?'

''Oo wants to know?'

'I am a — er — a distant connection,' Tilly said, hoping that Dorcas, if she were indeed in this little house, would not discover her lie. 'I am anxious to reach her.'

''Oo says she's 'ere?' The eye, Tilly realized, belonged to an elderly man, for it had that gummy, watery look of antiquity, and the voice, though thin and cracked, still had some depth to it. 'Eh? You tell me that. 'Oo says she's 'ere?'

'I got this address from Knightsbridge Barracks,' Tilly said. 'I assure you, Sir, that if I am at the wrong house and am incommoding you, I would be most —'

'The Barracks?' The door opened wider. 'You bin down the Barracks?'

'Why, yes,' Tilly said, puzzled, for now suddenly the manner of the speaker was all affability. 'I went there to seek the whereabouts of Mr Oliver and with some little persuasion they told me that he — he was killed in a recent battle in China and that his widow resides at this address.'

'Well, well, well!' The old man cackled with great glee and put out a grimy hand towards her. 'The Barracks sent you, did they? Told you it was my old Regiment, did they? Nineteenth Light Infantry Trooper, that was me. Show you me old shako I will, what got shot into when I was fighting the Afghans. Nasty 'eathens they was! Poor old General Whatsisname, oh 'e didn't know what to do with 'em! Our General — Lightower, 'e was, 'e should ha' bin the Commander-in-Chief.'

'No — er — they did not precisely tell me —' Tilly said awkwardly and then stopped. He was such a very odd looking old man, tall and thin, the wreck of what must once have been a magnificent body seeming to hang on the scaffolding of his bones like old rags. He was wrapped in a large tartan rug and his slippered feet peered out from beneath it, and on his clearly bald head he was wearing a very tattered and rather dirty nightcap.

'Then why did they send you 'ere, eh? Tell me that. Why should they?'

He was suspicious again, and peered at her with narrowed eyes as he began to shuffle backwards into the house, for he had come right out on to the doorstep.

'I told you. To find Mrs Oliver.'

258

'Well, you can't 'ave her. She ain't 'ere, see? There's only me, Trooper Adams, at your service.' And he essayed a shaky salute and she felt a sudden pang of deep pity and immediately reacted to it, impulsively holding out one hand.

'Oh, Sir, I am proud to meet you,' she said. 'I would not have disturbed an old soldier like you for the world, indeed I would not. I will go away and —'

There was a creaking behind her as the front gate opened and she was pushed aside, and almost lost her balance as something small but very firm and strong shot past her. She looked round and then down, and saw a small child standing there. She had dark red hair that her bonnet displayed quite clearly, for it hung by its ribbons halfway down her back, and the lavish curls spread over her shoulders in a most delectable fashion. Her eyes were wide and dark in a face that was small, pale and pointed and the mouth that was pursed a little in consideration as its owner stared up at Tilly was as pink and rosebud-like as any of those depicted in the sentimental pictures in Eliza's favourite domestic magazines. Her coat was a deep turquoise blue and trimmed with black fur and looked very costly; and the small matching muff that hung in front on twisted silk cords was of a most elegant design. The child's boots were polished so brightly that even in this uncertain light they shone, and her legs in their black stockings were slim and handsome above them.

'Who are you?' she demanded in a shrill and very self-confident voice for one so young — and Tilly estimated she could not be much different in age from her own Duff. 'What do you want?'

Tilly looked at her and then back at the man, puzzled. They seemed a very unlikely pair to inhabit the same house, yet the child was standing next to him now, with her legs firmly apart on the doorstep and her head up, every inch a person on her own territory. Tilly lifted her brows and said, 'And who are you? Is this your grandpapa?'

'Of course not!' the child said scathingly. 'This is Trooper A, the best man in the Regiment — you tell me who *you* are.'

'It's no matter, Sophie. I know who the lady is.'

The voice came from behind Tilly and she whirled, and stared and then took a deep and rather shaky breath. A woman was standing there, her face a little shadowed by her most elegant bonnet. Her hands were tucked into a handsome fur muff. She was wearing a pelisse of dark red and the gown beneath it was most tastefully trimmed with matching braid on its rich, darker crimson flounces. She looked every inch the modern lady of fashion, and she was Dorcas.

Chapter Twenty-five

'IT IS NOT SO much as I might have expected,' Dorcas said judiciously and stretched out one foot from beneath her silk flounces to admire her new kid boots and white silk stockings. They all looked very fine. 'Only fifteen thousand pounds.'

Tilly felt the familiar irritation Dorcas had always been able to arouse in her and firmly put it aside.

'I would find it a useful enough sum,' she said in a neutral tone, and Dorcas laughed.

'Oh, my dear, I am sure you would. But then you are so much more sensible than I, are you not? Oh, Tilly, do look at her! Isn't she quite delicious?' On the other side of the room Sophie behaved as though she had not heard a word and continued to build her bricks, but now with a somewhat studied air rather than the genuine absorption she had displayed hitherto and which had indeed looked charming. 'I get such delight from her when she is being good! Which is all too rarely, of course – dearest Sophie, you must let Duff play with the bricks a little if he chooses – they are his, after all!'

'I am far too old for bricks,' Duff said with a lofty air, though he had been watching Sophie for some time and clearly ached to be meddling with the building she was constructing. 'I stopped playing with them *years* ago! But I will help you if you like,' he added magnanimously and moved a little closer to Sophie, who at once glared at him fiercely and hissed, 'If you touch this I shall break it all to pieces, so there!'

'Well, if you do not wish to play, that is all right, Duff,' Dorcas said and beamed at Sophie. 'But do not spoil Sophie's sweet games, will you? That would never do.' She had clearly already lost interest in the children and returned her attention to her new boots. 'These are indeed most elegant, are they not, Tilly? I shall get some more I think.'

'They look very nice,' Tilly said, still managing to sound neutral.

'Oh, indeed they are,' Dorcas said with great satisfaction. 'Quite the best of quality.'

'So you had no problems with Mr Cobbold? He was – was he surprised to see you?'

Dorcas thought for a moment and then smiled slowly. 'Not too much, I think. He seemed to be more resigned than surprised. He said he expected that you had had some hand in letting me know of my good fortune.'

'Of your bereavement,' Tilly said a touch sharply. 'I thought telling you of your mother's death more important than speaking of any legacy.'

'Oh, yes, of course,' Dorcas said perfunctorily. 'Yes. And then of course we got down to business. I was sharp with him, I do promise you.' She laughed reminiscently. 'He expected me to say only, "Oh, thank you, Sir," and go away. But I did not. I insisted I see the books he had kept since the beginning.' She shook her head. 'I do not believe he told me the truth even so, but I did make it clear to him that I was not a stupid person to be gulled of my rights.'

'In what way gulled?' In spite of herself Tilly was interested and she looked across the drawing-room briefly to be sure the children were happy and then concentrated her attention on Dorcas again.

'Oh, I suspect he had been using the money to invest, thinking that my mother would never be found. I told him I did not believe he had not made some return on my money for himself and managed to make him agree, even though I could not prove the matter, that I should receive the entire sum your father left, without any deductions for advertising and so forth, which he claimed to have spent. So I have the full fifteen thousand. But for such a man of business as your father had been, it wasn't what I would have expected.'

'Perhaps not.' Tilly bent her head to her sewing again. She was making a shirt for Duff and she could concentrate on the collar without seeming too ill-mannered, but it was also an excellent way to disguise the anger she was feeling.

Not once had Dorcas thanked her for her efforts, not on old Trooper Adams's doorstep in Fulham when she had blurted everything out, about her mother's death and the inheritance and the search she, Tilly, had made to ensure Dorcas got it; not even when she had insisted on packing up and removing herself forthwith, bag and baggage, from the Waterford Street house (despite Trooper Adams's almost pitiful inability to understand what was going on) so that she could go to a hotel; and now sitting in Tilly's drawing-room, to celebrate Christmas-tide. She and Sophie had enjoyed an excellent dinner, in the company of the Misses K and F as well as Duff and Tilly, while Eliza bustled between them all in a seventh heaven of happiness at having so many people for whom to cook. But Dorcas had taken it all for granted and said nothing in appreciation.

Tilly's fingers moved swiftly and neatly as she turned the seam of the collar at the awkward corners. Dorcas was humming softly beneath her breath as she leafed through a magazine she had found, and everything was peaceful, though she was aware of Duff's rather sullen silence. Usually it was he who did all the chattering and made all the decisions about what was to happen in his favourite corner of the drawing-room; now it was Sophie who talked and pushed herself forwards, and suddenly Tilly was angry again.

'Well, now,' she said. 'What is to happen with Trooper Adams?'

'What?' Dorcas did not lift her eyes from her magazine.

'Trooper Adams. The man with whom you were living. Were you his lodger? As the Misses K and F are with me?'

'His lodger?' Dorcas laughed. She was looking very beautiful, Tilly realized suddenly. Her skin had the rich creaminess that Tilly had forgotten about and her eyes were dark and lively and seemed not to have changed in all the years Tilly had known her. She must be now – she worked it out quickly – twenty-eight years old. Well past the first flush of youth. Yet she looked as delicious as she had at eighteen when young Tilly had found her so terrifying and fascinating in equal measure. Such a contrast to Tilly's own appearance, she thought dolefully. I am muddy of complexion and have shadows of fatigue under my eyes and I am far too thin; Dorcas's rich ripeness made her feel quite dowdy. But she must not diminish herself, she decided, and instead repeated her question.

'Well, are you?'

'No, of course not. Do you not think that if I could afford lodgings I would have gone somewhere better than that? I would not pay to live in such a place – as it was, I took the post as his housekeeper only because I had no other choice. After Walter died –' Her face darkened suddenly and for a brief moment a glimpse of misery was there. But it was gone so fast, Tilly could not be sure she'd seen it at all. 'After he died I had so many debts, for I had expected him to return from Afghan – they had told me it was a most safe posting – and was awaiting his pay to settle my debts. But when he did not come and I received no money, for he was not due for any army pension, I had to take what I could and the Barracks told me of this old pensioner of theirs who needed care.' She shrugged. 'I went there because he did not object to a child. I could not have gone to other places where they certainly did. And no matter what –' she lifted her chin to look across to her daughter, 'Sophie and I remain together, do we not, my dearest one?'

Sophie did not look at her. She simply pushed her bricks into another pattern and sang out as though she had rehearsed it, 'Yes, Mamma! Always together, Mamma and Sophie, yes, Mamma!'

Dorcas laughed fondly. 'You see, Tilly? I have taught her well. No, we must always be together. I could not send her away to any other person, as I was so often advised, in order that I might be employed as a servent elsewhere. At least with the Trooper I was housekeeper and not kitchen maid.' Her mouth twisted with disgust suddenly. 'I will never again be kitchen maid to anyone.'

'How long had you been his housekeeper?' Tilly asked.

'Oh, perhaps six months or so, I cannot quite recall. Nor do I wish to. It is enough to be out of there.'

'But how will he manage? He seemed a pleasant enough old man, if a trifle confused.'

'A trifle? A disgusting randy old — well, let be! I will shock you if I speak my mind. Let it be enough that for the last many months I have been able to feed Sophie and me on his pension, and could do well enough for us all with small effort. He will have to manage alone now, and that is the end of it. I am not his keeper.'

'But he seemed fond of you,' Tilly said. 'He was fit to weep when you were ready to go.'

Dorcas shrugged. 'So be it. I cannot worry for others. I have enough problems of my own. Do you not quiz me, Tilly! It is, after all, not your concern. Anyway, I dare say the Barracks will discover soon enough he is in need of another housekeeper. They pay his pension, lucky creature, after all.'

With a private resolution to send a message — unsigned perhaps, she thought a little guiltily — about Trooper Adams to his old Barracks, Tilly changed the subject. There was, after all, plenty to speak about.

'Those clothes you were wearing,' she said, 'The day I found you — they looked —'

'Bought on tick,' Dorcas said pithily and then laughed as she saw Tilly's face. 'My dear, you do not think I paid ready cash for them, do you? Of course not. It was indeed strange for I had decided that very morning I had had enough of the misery and the general lowness of that house. I went out with

Sophie to some warehouses in Oxford Street and I opened an account. I did not lie precisely, but I was not entirely truthful either! But I am good at being believed, you know, and they let me take these items away with me and arranged that I should return for others soon. That is a shopkeeper's downfall, you know. He is greedy and open to flattery and believes a person who announces she will buy a great deal in future – so he lets her take what he regards as a little in advance. Do this in two or three shops or warehouses and in no time you have an excellent wardrobe at small personal expense. They are just the same in Oxford Street as anywhere else and very happy with so many large orders!' She laughed. 'Well, in future I shall be able to do even better. These clothes I found here in Knightsbridge. I will pay for these, I think, for I liked the emporium so well I wish to return to it.'

Tilly was quite horrified at such deviousness. 'So you mean that –'

'That I shan't pay the Oxford Street bills? My dear Tilly, you are such a good sweet soul.' And she leaned over and kissed Tilly's cheek soundly. And Tilly subsided, aware that her face was red with disapproval.

There was another silence between them though the children were noisy enough now with their heads close together and talking with great animation, and Tilly bit her lip and tried to find the right words for what she wanted to say. And then decided it was best just to blurt it out.

'You cannot afford to live in a hotel all the time, I imagine. Even so much as fifteen thousand pounds will vanish swiftly. Will you – what will you do?'

Dorcas leaned back in her chair and looked at Tilly thoughtfully and then smiled, a long slow smile that Tilly remembered very well. So well that her heart seemed to thump harder in her breast in agitation. Dorcas always looked so when she planned mischief.

'I too have been thinking about that. I think I should like to come home, dear Tilly.'

266

'Home?' Tilly said carefully. 'But you have no —'

'This house was home to me for many a long year.' Dorcas sounded quite dreamy. 'I was only twelve when I came here, after all, and you were just a tiny thing, not much above Sophie in size — though she is, you must agree, much livelier than you were!'

'As to that, I cannot say,' Tilly said with a touch of asperity. 'I do not remember what I looked like then. And I do believe that all children are beautiful, for they are God's innocents.'

'Well, yes,' Dorcas said, clearly dismissing such notions. 'But as I said, this is home to me. I shall take your upper rooms, Tilly. I have been looking about the house today and though I would prefer the rooms the Misses K and F have, I can see it would cause too much upheaval were I to fuss and demand them, so I shall not.' She was clearly pleased with her own magnanimity. 'The two rooms at the top of the house will do nicely enough for us. I shall take the one at the front and Sophie the small one next to Duff. They will need painting in the spring, of course, but this will not be a problem. The remaining room up there will make an excellent sitting room for us. We will take our meals in the dining-room, of course. We don't mind sharing with you and Duff and the Misses K and F.'

Tilly stared at her, bewildered. 'But you cannot be — Dorcas, this is not at all — no, Dorcas!'

Dorcas gazed at her with brows raised and a look of amazement on her face, but Tilly was not deceived. Dorcas had expected this reaction.

'What makes you protest, Tilly? You know it is necessary for you. You have let only one set of your rooms so far and you need more money; I have seen the way the house is. It is, to be honest, dreadfully shabby. This drawing-room sorely needs the attention of the painters and you should have new sheets and other household linen. I have been looking most closely. The kitchen — well, there is your precious Eliza, and I must say she really does not know her place, does she? That needs some attention, but you do not help her to be good at her work with so antiquated a set of cooking arrangements. She should have a proper stove, not that open fire. I have seen some excellent examples of good stoves that provide several ovens of different heats and quite remove the need for the open spit for roasting, which makes all in the kitchen so grimy with grease. When meat is roasted in a closed oven, then it cooks just as well with half the trouble.'

'But I cannot pay for such things! And anyway, none of this is your concern! This is my house and remains so. It was left to me in trust through my mother and my father could not touch it and nor can you. He was able to leave your mother only the cash and that is all you have. Now take it away and leave me be. I wished only to do the − the honourable thing by finding you so that you would have what is your entitlement, even though in all decency − well, if the world were run justly you know as well as I do that the money would be mine. Mine and Duff's −' and she looked across the room to the children. 'He will need more and more and −'

'And,' Dorcas said triumphantly, 'that is why I must come here to live. I do not wish to have the trouble of my own house. I should hate to do what you are doing, which I would have to if I spent my money on an establishment. After I had bought a house and set up the furniture and so forth − and indeed I did consider it − then I would need some income, would I not? You own this house, but without income − well, I prefer to be one of those who owns nothing but who is waited upon and cooked for rather than the reverse. And I prefer also to live where I am comfortable. It will be very comfortable to be here.'

Slowly her lips curved. 'To be a lady of leisure in a house where once I worked as a maid − can you not see the charm of it for me, Tilly? I am quite determined, you know. And you will be a fool if you do not agree. I am willing, you see, to spend some of my money − your father's money − to improve my comfort here in a manner that will benefit you and your son. He will not, as you said, always be a small child of small needs. One day he will be a large young man with large expenses. Surely to have money coming in from my rent in his growing years will be of use to you and him. You know I am right, Tilly. You cannot refuse me.'

Tilly stared at her, knowing that however much she argued, she was defeated. And not only because of money, and Duff's special needs. There was too much history between Dorcas and herself, too much shared memory. Dorcas had bullied the small Tilly, had frightened her half out of her wits, but she had also enchanted her and filled her life with drama. Tilly could never say she had affection for Dorcas, could never claim true friendship, yet there was something there, almost a sisterly link; not that Tilly had experience of having a sister, of course, but she imagined it would be something like the way she and Dorcas had been. And still were. So, once again Dorcas was absolutely right. It was not possible for Tilly to refuse her.

Dorcas and Sophie left at five thirty, by which time it was dark but the evening was not so far advanced that they did not feel safe to go out. Standing in the hall wrapped in her handsome blue coat, Sophie looked bewitching and Tilly smiled at the child almost against her will; it was such a pleasure to look at her. But Sophie stared back without a glimmer of response, and Tilly looked away to where Dorcas was standing before the mirror on the hatstand setting her bonnet precisely in place, and then caught sight of her small Duff. He was standing on the bottom step with his new Christmas hobby horse dangling from one hand and staring fixedly at Sophie. His eyes were wide and seemed a little anxious in his pale face and Tilly's heart contracted for a moment. Was he ill? But then he caught her eyes on him and smiled broadly at her, and at once he was her own Duff again. But now he was looking back at Sophie and she thought, almost wonderingly; why, he is as bewitched by her as I almost was; and frowned a little as she tried to understand how she felt about this. What was it about this child that had this effect on both adults and other children? She was just a pretty little thing with abundant red hair and very dark eyes, after all; but there was more to it than that, she felt at some deep level, and as she caught that unsmiling glance again she was a little chilled.

But then, just as Dorcas turned away from the mirror and announced that she was ready too, Sophie turned her head and looked at Duff and this time she smiled; and it was as though someone had lit a gas jet inside her. Her eyes crinkled into wicked little slits of merriment, and Tilly saw Duff redden and then smile back adoringly. And she thought – I have to let them live here. He needs someone to be his friend and clearly he loves this child already. I cannot part them.

'I shall send a message to you when I am ready to come,' Dorcas announced. 'In the meantime I would beg you to arrange for the decent furnishing of the rooms. I will perhaps come to see you in a day or so and we will make some choices together, shall we? We could perhaps go into London to Shoolbread's – Tottenham Court Road, you know. They have some excellent sofas and chairs and so forth. Don't worry about the cost, dear Tilly, I will see to that – you may pay me back later when you are ready.'

Tilly opened her mouth to say, 'When you return my spoons perhaps?' But the words did not come; although she was aware of a pang as she recalled, for the first time for some years now, her mother's adored possession. No, she could not speak of them now, though she knew one day she would. Instead, she contented herself by saying sharply, 'I will never enter into heavy debt.'

Dorcas laughed. 'Silly one! It will not be heavy. How can it be heavy when it is I you are dealing with? Anyway, money is for spending, so spend it we shall! Good-night, my dear. Come along, Sophie. Good-night Duff!' And they disappeared out into the street to find a cab to take them to the hotel in which they were staying in Kensington Gore.

Tilly watched her go with mixed feelings, as Duff came to stand beside her on the top step and slipped his warm, somewhat sticky little hand into hers.

'Is Sophie coming here to live, Mamma?' he said after a while and she looked at the way his eyes gleamed in the light thrown from the front door and at the faint tendrils of breath escaping from his lips.

'Why do you ask?'

He shook his head crossly. 'You must not think me silly, Mamma. I listened to all you said, you and Sophie's Mamma. Is she coming here to live, Mamma? Is she?'

'Would you like her to?'

'Oh, yes,' Duff said fervently. 'Oh, *yes*.' And then he thought for a while and added, 'I think —'

Tilly had already begun to take him inside the house again but now she stopped and looked at him sharply. 'You are not sure, my darling? You must tell me. I will listen, you know.'

'She does meddle in my games,' he said doubtfully, but then smiling widely at her. 'But she does so in such a funny way I don't really mind. Mamma, when will she come? Do tell me, Mamma. Will it be tomorrow? Will it?'

'Not quite tomorrow, darling, but soon, I expect. Now you must be away to bed. Eliza will be up soon to help you but you must start to get ready. No, no argument. I will speak to Eliza and then she will come up to you. Scoot now —' And she patted his rump affectionately and he went padding upstairs as she made her way to the green baize door that led to the kitchen.

There was much to do and much to think of, but first of all she had to speak to Eliza, for she would be more affected by these new plans than anyone else in the house. And anyway, she always did tell Eliza everything.

Chapter Twenty-six

'OH!' TILLY SAID and hesitated at the kitchen door, uncomfortable in a somewhat surprising way. There was no reason why Eliza should not be alone, yet seeing she had company startled her.

Eliza sprang to her feet immediately, beaming from ear to ear. 'Why, Mum, I never heard you comin' down! Was there something —'

'No, Eliza, it is quite all right. I can speak to you later. I did not know you had — um — visitors.'

'Oh, this isn't visitors, Mum! That is, well, you know Charlie, that I do know. Charlie, what are you thinking of, sitting there like a great lummox?'

The young man who had been sitting beside Eliza at a kitchen table spread with all manner of Christmas delicacies — mince pies, plum pudding and a jug of daffy — got to his feet at once. Tilly had been aware of two other people besides Eliza in the kitchen but it was hard to see them, for the oil lamp on the dresser had its wick turned low and the room was illuminated mainly by the leaping flames of the fire. Now she smiled as she recognized young Harrod.

'Good evening to you, Charlie, and Christmas wishes to you. I trust you and your father are well?'

'We are very well, Ma'am, and prospering, as I trust you are. And I do of course return your good wishes on behalf of my father as well as myself, and thank you for your custom in this past year, and we look forward to continuing it in 1862 as before. Now that I am in charge of the shop, I –'

'Indeed?' Tilly said hastily, not wishing to discuss Charlie Harrod's business affairs, and glanced at the other figure who was now also standing. He was a square young man with thick dark hair which was clearly meant to be exuberantly curly but had been cut brutally short in order to control it. He had a round face and surprisingly blue eyes, considering the darkness of his hair, and he looked decidely uncomfortable as he stood there.

'This is my friend James Leland from the linen draper's on the other side but three of us in Middle Queen's Buildings,' Charlie said, clearly enjoying his role as old friend of the establishment. 'I took the liberty of bringing him around to exchange the greetings of the season with Miss Horace.'

'Miss – oh, yes,' Tilly said. It was so rarely she heard Eliza's surname that it came as a small shock to her to remember she had one at all. 'How d'you do, Mr Leland.'

'Your servant, Madam,' the young man said. His voice was pleasant if rather choked with shyness and she smiled on him as kindly as she could.

'I give you the greetings of the season too,' she said. 'Eliza, I would wish to speak to you on a – a matter that has arisen, but it will wait till Master Duff is in bed.'

Eliza took the hint and at once was all bustle. 'I'll go and settle him right away,' she said. 'If he's gone up, Mum and the – the others have gone?' Tilly heard the note of disapproval in her tone and took no notice. That Eliza should be suspicious of Dorcas was natural enough; she had after all loathed her mother most cordially. That was why it was so important to explain carefully why Dorcas was to move into number seventeen. Tilly nodded briskly at Eliza.

'Yes, and he is getting ready now. I shall make his bread and milk and fetch it up directly.'

'We must go,' Charlie said regretfully. 'Back to our lodgings. Not such good ones as these, Mrs Quentin, but well enough for Jem and me.'

'I would have expected you to spend the holiday with your parents,' Tilly said a touch dampeningly as she made way for Eliza to go upstairs to Duff. 'Are they not expecting you?'

'Oh, we've been there,' Charlie said blithely. 'And glad enough to get away again, for my Pa gets stuffier with each day that passes, and now that it has been agreed I shall have the running of the shop he is stuffier than ever.' He grinned with self-satisfaction. 'We thought it politic to leave before too long and let him recover his peace of mind – for my Mamma's sake, if none other. So we came to see Eliza – Miss Horace.'

'Eliza sounds well enough to me,' Tilly said drily and moved across the kitchen to the scullery. 'Well, time to make my son's supper.'

'And we must leave,' Jem said and pushed his friend sharply in the ribs. 'I told you it was an imposition to go calling on Christmas Day.'

'It is no imposition,' Tilly said, as she fetched a pan from the scullery and went to the big stone bread crock to get some sweet white bread. 'I have told Eliza she is always more than welcome to have her friends to visit. I recall others being here – Caroline, was it? – er – a Miss Godsmark, as I remember.'

Charlie went a bright pink and Jem Leland produced a soft chuckle.

'That is his intended, Mrs Quentin,' he said. 'She is the real reason he is so restless. She is with her family today and he is not invited. And with me not encumbered by any relations, why, he attached himself to me. We are calling on all his friends.'

Tilly laughed and cocked an eye at the still blushing Charlie as she tipped cubes of bread into a saucepan and added a large knob of butter and half a jugful of rich milk together with a spoonful of honey from the comb. 'And I thought it was our Eliza who interested you!'

'She is my friend, Ma'am, and always has been. It's been six years now.' Charlie glared at Jem.

'Indeed it has,' Tilly said and set the pan on the fire, to stand and watch it carefully, aware of the pleasant heat of the flames on her face. 'A long time.' She felt old, suddenly; she was not so very long in the tooth herself, but she was a widow and had a son, and a great deal of responsibility. She would be twenty-four in the coming year, not a girl any more, but still hardly old; yet she felt it, reminiscing in this fashion with the young Charlie.

'Well,' she said. 'I am sure she will continue your good friend. She is a very loyal person, Eliza.'

'I told Jem that. That was why I fetched him here. It is high time she had a follower of her own, don't you think, Ma'am? She will be looking about her, I dare say — all girls wish to be wed, after all.'

She looked up at him, startled. She had not thought much about the possibility of Eliza wanting a husband, but of course the time would come. Eliza was no longer the child Tilly still sometimes thought her. She must be — she worked it out — twenty this year coming. Well old enough to be considering a husband, and she bent her head over the bread-and-milk, which was beginning to bubble in the pan. Life without Eliza in this house was an almost impossible thought after all these busy years.

'Well, I dare say,' she said and took the pan from the flames and tipped its contents into the blue and white striped bowl which was Duff's favourite. 'And are you interested, Mr Leland?' Again she felt old; to be discussing a young man's matchmaking plans was to be very senior indeed, positively haggish.

'No, Ma'am,' Jem Leland said so firmly that Tilly looked up at him startled.

'Oh? Has Eliza offended you in some way?'

'Not at all, Ma'am. It's just that I am not prepared to think of such matters. I am in a very small way of business yet, and though the shop is my own it will be some years before it is in any sort of situation to support a married man. Had I known that this was in Charlie's mind, I can assure you I would not be here.' He looked at his friend sharply. 'He did not speak of it to me.'

'Then I hope he did not speak to Eliza either.' Tilly smiled, her heart suddenly lightened. It was selfish of her, she knew, but it would be a great blow to lose Eliza's constant attentions to her and her household. If she were to become enamoured of a young man there was no knowing what might go wrong below stairs. Followers were a known source of much trouble with servants, Tilly knew perfectly well. She had heard too much comment on such matters from other ladies with household responsibilities to be in any doubt.

'So, we will leave, Ma'am,' Jem Leland said and bowed stiffly. 'Charlie —'

'Yes, well,' Charlie said a little sulkily. 'If you will give Miss — Eliza our good wishes and say good-night.'

'With pleasure, Charlie,' Tilly said gravely and watched them go and then smiled again. Well, he would get over it. When next she went to put in an order at the shop she would discuss with him his business plans, which he would enjoy, she knew, and that would comfort him. And she dismissed him and his friend from her mind and took herself off upstairs with the blue and white bowl and a big spoon, remembering just in time to sprinkle some crushed sugar and a little cinnamon on the top, to give it the taste Duff most liked.

The two women went through the bedtime ritual with their usual contented rhythm and Duff, particularly sleepy tonight and therefore more than usually co-operative, was soon tucked up in bed spooning up his bread-and-milk as Tilly read him his bedtime story about the doings of the three bears and Eliza tidied away the bath and folded his clothes neatly ready for the morning.

Duff was asleep almost before they left the room, and as Eliza took the tray and empty bowl down to the kitchen Tilly lingered in the doorway to look back at him. In the soft glow of the light, his face promised so much beauty to come that she felt the familiar rush of adoration. Love him dearly as she did when he was awake and rushing about the house like a small tornado, when he was asleep and vulnerable her very bones seemed to melt at the sight of him, and she went back and kissed his cheek; and he murmured and reached up one warm arm, fragrant with soap from his bath, and hugged her and then was asleep again. She tucked in his sheet, quite unnecessarily, and went downstairs to the kitchen.

'They said good-night,' Tilly said. 'I did not realize that Charlie was — he and your friend Caroline —'

'Oh, yes,' Eliza said cheerfully as she moved about the kitchen clearing away the dishes. 'They've been hand-fast these past eighteen months. As soon as he makes enough money from the shop they'll be wed, and I shall be her bridesmaid. It's all arranged. I think his father as mean a man as they come, but then rich men is mean, ain't they?' She nodded wisely. 'I mean he's got another shop, over in the City at Eastcheap, so why make Charlie buy this one from 'im? You'd think a good father'd give it to him like, wouldn't you, and not be so grasping?' She leaned on the broom she had fetched to sweep away the few crumbs that had fallen on to the stone flags. 'But then, I'm just a country girl, and a poor widder's daughter. I got no knowledge of such matters.'

'Perhaps you should have, Eliza,' Tilly said, trying to sound light. 'Maybe one day you will wed such a young man as Charlie.'

'Me, wed?' Eliza stared at her, scandalized. '*Wed*? I would not be so stupid, Mum! I like to have young men as friends — it does a girl good to be fussed over — but wed 'em and you gets no more fussin' and a great deal of trouble.' She began to sweep at the crumbs with some vigour. 'I seen too much of other girls to think otherwise, Mum. Besides, I got enough to do here.'

'I would not wish to hold you back, Eliza,' Tilly said and Eliza looked up at her sharply.

'Hold me back? You couldn't do that, Mum. You're — why, you brung me forwards better than anyone could ever imagine.

I'm housekeeper here, and proud to be it! How can you ever think —'

'Eliza!' Tilly said hastily, realizing she had gone too far and that another avowal of Eliza's adoration was trembling on the end of her tongue. 'There is a matter I must discuss with you. It is about Dorcas — sit down and we shall talk.'

'Dorcas?' Eliza propped her broom against the dresser and sat down. 'What about her, Mum?'

Tilly thought for a moment and then decided to go in directly with no devious softening of language. 'She wishes to live here with her little girl. At first I thought it an impossible scheme, but now — well, we must talk of it.'

Eliza looked down at her rough red hands, which were loosely folded on the table before her. Her head, its frilled cap askew as usual on her unruly hair, seemed to droop a little. 'Mrs Leander's daughter?'

'I thought about that,' Tilly said. 'But I do not think she is the same. Anyway the plan she has will not — let me explain.' And she did, as succinctly as she could, trying not to paint too glowing a picture of the benefits — the new cooking stove (at which Eliza glanced at the old-fashioned open fire and looked yearning for a moment) and the decorating and new furniture promised — and then added, 'You will not be able to manage single-handed. I will have to get you a housemaid, and even perhaps a tweeny to deal with the dirty work. You will have much organizing and cooking to do if they come. She will pay well enough, you see, for us to afford it.'

All through this discourse Eliza had sat with her head bent, except for that brief glance at the fire, and now she lifted her chin and stared at Tilly. She looked troubled.

'That there Dorcas was always the pushy sort,' she said bluntly. 'It's not for me to say, Mum, but I'm going to say it all the same. Was this your notion or hers?'

'Hers,' Tilly said steadily. 'I told you. At first I was not sure. Not at all. But then as she talked I saw the benefits. And there is also, of course, Duff.'

278

'Duff?' Eliza was at once alert, for her adoration of Duff couldn't have been more than a whisper less than his mother's. 'What of him?'

'He adores the child Sophie. If you had but seen them together, Eliza! He watched her and played with her – he was quite bewitched. He says he wishes her to live here, though there was a moment when he doubted. Just as I did. And just as I think you are. But then he was certain.'

Eliza was silent for a while and then she nodded. 'I can see the good of it clear enough. A bit o' money comin' into a house never does no harm. But she's a funny one, that Dorcas.'

'I know it well,' Tilly said with great feeling. 'I have known her since I was a small child, and in those days she by turns terrified and entranced me. It is so difficult – but I am fully grown now and if she misbehaves I will not be terrified again! Angry perhaps, but not terrified. I can and will always make it plain to her that if she upsets any of us in any way, then she will have to leave. This remains my house, after all, and always will.'

Eliza grinned suddenly. 'You sound like you're talking to her and not to me, Mum.'

Tilly grinned. 'I know. I am, perhaps, practising. But I would so speak to her if we agreed. Do we agree, Eliza?'

Again Eliza looked at the fire, and then sighed deeply. 'A new stove would be a grand thing,' she said longingly. 'I've got a dunnamany good receipts in my drawer here what I could cook if I had a modern stove. With proper rails in the front of the fire basket and a set o' close covers and no more spit to grease the room up so cruel.' She looked up at the ceiling. 'That was whitewashed not three months ago, wasn't it? And don't it scream for a new coat? If it lasts till we spring-clean in February I'll be as surprised as – well, there it is. No spit would be a delight. And if you tells her clear and strong that if she makes trouble out she goes – well, we'll have the stove then, won't we?' And she grinned widely.

Tilly shook her head in reproof. 'I should not let you be so — well, there it is. I shall agree then. But I wish you to understand that it is important the house runs as smoothly as it does now and that the Misses K and F are not discommoded. They are our old friends now, after all.'

'They won't be,' Eliza said sturdily. 'I'll not fuss unduly, you have my word on that. Have I ever —'

'No,' Tilly said and leaned over and patted the rough red hands. 'No, you have not. So it is settled. Now, let's have a little supper of our own. I cannot eat much after so splendid a dinner as you gave us, but perhaps a little cold collation would be agreeable.'

'I'll take some up to the Misses.' Eliza got to her feet. 'As soon as you've got yours up in the dining-room and then —'

'No need to run to the dining-room, just for me. I let the fire go out there anyway. I shall stay down here, Eliza, if you will have me.' And Eliza dimpled and beamed happily.

It was agreed that the Misses Knapp and Fleetwood would have their suppers first and while Eliza prepared them, Tilly went to her room to wash and tidy herself, for she felt gritty after a long day of entertaining people and playing with two children. She returned afresh to the kitchen to find the table neatly set for her own supper and no sign of Eliza. Clearly she was still upstairs with the Misses K and F, and while she waited Tilly looked at the table and discovered she did have an appetite after all.

Eliza had set a plate of newly cut ham and cold beef, and a bowl of winter salad made up largely of celery and the mustard and cress Eliza grew herself in the scullery on trays of old linen cloth. She had garnished the salad with beetroot and hard-boiled eggs in the manner of one of the illustrations in her newest and most favoured magazine, Mr Beeton's *Englishwoman's Domestic Magazine*. There was also a basket of fresh rolls which Eliza had baked that morning, and a piece of plum pudding and mince pies set under a cover. All this together with the kettle singing on the fire and the coffee pot standing ready in the hearth alongside, waiting for the water, made a very inviting scene indeed. Tilly sat down, enjoying it greatly and very conscious of Eliza's efficiency. She had even remembered to set on the table Tilly's favourite pickled walnuts which she had put up last year.

She almost jumped out of her bodice when the door to the area opened. She whirled, swallowing a mouthful of ham and holding her napkin to her mouth to stare with wide, terrified eyes over it.

'Oh, I am sorry! I had hoped there would be no one here and I could find them and be gone!' A head appeared round the door followed by a stocky body and she let out a sigh of relief.

'Really, Mr Leland! You positively alarmed me,' she said.

'I should have knocked,' the young man said wretchedly. 'Indeed, I stood outside for some time, not sure what to do, but I heard no sound from within so I — I did not wish to discommode anyone, but I was so anxious to obtain my gloves. They were a gift from Charlie, you see, and he would be most put out if he thought I had lost them even before Christmas was over.'

'Gloves?' Tilly said wonderingly and he looked around, turning his hat in his hands as he did so, his face a picture of misery. Then his expression lightened.

'There!' he said eagerly. 'On the dresser.' And he darted across the kitchen and picked up the gloves that were indeed lying there, and showed them to Tilly.

'You see! I put them down and since I have had them such a short time quite forgot to pick them up when I collected my hat. I do beg your pardon. I would not have distressed you for the world.'

'I am not distressed,' Tilly said goodnaturedly, now quite recovered from her surprise. 'Now you are here, perhaps you would care for some supper? I have far too much here for my needs and I am sure you are hungry. I never yet knew a young man who was not.'

He looked at the table and then at her. 'It is kind of you to ask me, Ma'am, but I think it would not be right of me to accept.'

'Not right?' She stared at him puzzled. 'How can that be?'

'I would like it too well,' he said simply. 'Not for the food, you understand, but for the chance to talk to you. You seem to me to be a — you are a very interesting — and — kind lady and talking to you would be a great — um — pleasure. But I must not.'

She shook her head, more mystified than ever. 'I do not understand.'

'I am a shopkeeper, Ma'am, in a very small line of business as yet. It will be better one day, but — well, a small business. And you are a lady of property and therefore it would not be right in me to consider spending time at your table even though you have asked me in so generous and — and kind a manner.'

'Oh, Mr Leland.' She understood now and was embarrassed. 'I am nobody special! Just a woman who —'

'You are a lady of property, Ma'am, a respectable widow and it would not be seemly of me to accept your kind invitation,' he said stubbornly, staring at a point somewhere above her head. 'But I take it kind in you to ask, indeed I do.'

'Mr Leland,' Tilly said and smiled. 'Mr Leland, I do believe you are a snob!'

'I, Ma'am?' He sounded scandalized. 'I am a person who knows the proprieties, I hope, but that does not mean I am so mean spirited as to be a snob.'

'You are too concerned with proprieties, Mr Leland, and sadly diminish your own most generous spirit if you think your so-called proprieties prevent us from sharing a meal in an agreeable manner with no harm to either. And anyway, I am no special lady of property! I may own this house, but I must earn my keep in it. I take in lodgers, Sir, to maintain myself and my child, and I cannot see that sets me any higher in station than you. You sell your goods in a shop. I sell my services in my house. We are much of a muchness, I think!'

'I fear you are too kind, Mrs Quentin.' He was looking doubtful now. 'I am so anxious never to intrude or to seem to be any sort of – of tuft-hunter and to know my place.'

'Mr Leland, your place is here at this table for the next little while,' she said firmly. 'And let us hear no more nonsense. Now, you will take some ham, won't you? And some of Eliza's excellent beef? Can you eat two slices? Here you are – and the salad.'

Chapter Twenty-seven

'WELL!' SAID DORCAS, and steepled her hands in front of her elegant bodice in a considering sort of pose. 'I think you will agree that we have wrought well here?'

Eliza, who had been bustling about her new stove with a cloth and pot of blacking ever since the last of the installing workmen had gone, looked up, her face flushed with effort and pleasure.

'Oh, yes!' she said fervently. 'It's quite the most – well, I tell you, I feel like the cow's dropped twin calves and all the hens are laying at home, I'm that pleased!' And she set to polishing again, before starting the fire in the brand new grate. 'I'll take a day or two to get the way of it, no doubt, but then just you see the sort of dinners I'll be making.'

'Except, of course, that Mrs Oliver will not see, since she does not dine with us,' Tilly said a little sharply. 'It is but breakfast we agreed –'

'Oh, pooh,' Dorcas said. 'I know that is what we agreed, but now we have been here a month it is clear to me that dining out so often is not as agreeable as I thought it would be. I prefer to dine at home more, and now you have your stove, Eliza, I imagine this will not be too big a task for you? Of course, if it is –'

She did not need to wait for Eliza's response. It was obvious from the glowing face she turned to Dorcas that dinner would be no trouble at all; and Dorcas smiled at Tilly.

'I had already decided, my dear, that you have made us so comfortable, Sophie and I, that we prefer to remain within doors more than we thought we would. I will add two guineas a week to my rent and that will, I know, cover our dinners. You cannot accuse me of being parsimonious, Tilly, can you? The rent I pay is generous.'

'Yes,' Tilly said a little heavily. Of course it was; she knew that perfectly well. She could easily have supplied dinner for Dorcas and her daughter each day for the rent they already paid and not been out of pocket. As it was, the extra two guineas was a handsome sum. It was just the inevitability of it all that rankled and she opened her mouth to say as much and then closed it again. Not here, in the kitchen, with Eliza listening. And Eliza, to boot, was now Dorcas's warm ally.

Dorcas had gone to a great deal of trouble in her first weeks at number seventeen to be charming to everyone; the Misses K and F already adored Sophie and had enrolled her at their school (where fortunately she was very happy) much to Duff's delight, who was now clamouring to start school himself, instead of being unwilling and anxious about it; to Eliza, who was eating out of her hand in no time; and to Charlie, who met her when she insisted on accompanying Tilly one morning to the grocer's shop to place her weekly order.

He had persuaded Tilly that the new arrangement with Dorcas was a successful one. Now that she had to buy rather more for an enlarged household, Charlie told her, she was eligible for even greater discounts.

'I learned a lot from you the first time you came to the shop and talked to Pa, Mrs Quentin,' he assured her. 'I run my business along your sensible lines now, cutting prices rather than supporting large debts, and that means I can offer sensible discounts to important customers, of which you are of course one. It's as well your friend has come to join you, is it not?'

And so it was, in financial terms, undoubtedly. Dorcas, by coming to live in her house, had found a way to ensure that

Tilly enjoyed some of the benefits of her father's money. She should feel grateful, not uneasy. It was not a good way to be, she told herself sternly. She should be a better person and not so grudging.

Standing beside Dorcas in the kitchen, watching Eliza so happy with all her new toys – for there were other items Dorcas had paid for, including several pots and pans and patent devices for chopping meat fine or for chipping loaf sugar and sifting flour, all of which were going to save much labour for the hardworked Eliza – she castigated herself for being so – well – suspicious. Tomorrow the new housemaid was to start, an event which Eliza was eagerly awaiting. To have someone to order about and lord it over would, she told Tilly ingenuously, make her feel like a real housekeeper; and that was another occasion for happiness due to Dorcas's arrival. Yet Tilly was still uncertain.

'I must go,' she said abruptly. 'I have a number of things to do.'

'Oh, but Tilly,' Dorcas followed her from the kitchen. 'I was hoping to persuade you to come with me to choose some new curtains for our bedrooms. I like what we have done so far very well. The new furniture is exceedingly handsome and the painters have made an excellent fist of the rooms. But I cannot be sure which curtains would look best, and I would so value your opinion.'

It had been precisely this task that Tilly had wanted to carry out herself. She too was aware that the present curtains in the newly furbished rooms occupied by Dorcas and Sophie left much to be desired, and had planned to go out this very morning to seek new ones. To be forced to take Dorcas along – she bit back her resentment and nodded. 'I was intending to deal with that today, in any case,' she said.

'Splendid!' cried Dorcas. 'There are two or three linen drapers' establishments, as I recall, in Knightsbridge and in the Kensington High Street. We could try Knightsbridge first and then if we must, take a cab to Kensington High Street?'

'Indeed we could,' Tilly said. 'But I would prefer to —'

'I am glad to hear that,' Dorcas said blithely. 'Wait a moment while I fetch my pelisse and tippet,' and she was gone, disappearing upstairs in a pretty flurry of magenta ruffles.

Tilly sighed and went to fetch her own outdoor garments of a new long paletot in purple plush trimmed with gimp cord and black Spanish lace. At least, she told herself defiantly as she put on her new spoon bonnet which showed her hair prettily and was adorned with a bunch of Parma violets, I can show her I can be as elegant as she is. This had been her first purchase of new clothes for some time, and indeed had only been made possible by Dorcas's arrival. But she did not wish to think about that.

But when at last Dorcas arrived downstairs, Tilly's heart sank. She was wearing a most elegant outfit in the first stare of fashion; the magazines had been full of excited chatter for some weeks about the new Garibaldi shirt, in blazing scarlet trimmed with black braid and buttons, a black silk cravat and very full sleeves, worn over black skirts with the whole surmounted for outdoor wear by a short square-cut Zouave jacket and a black Tudor hat with a scarlet feather. Dorcas was wearing all of this, with the addition of a broad band of scarlet silk let into her black silk skirt well above the hem, and scarlet shoes with a black ribbon rosette at the toe. She looked perfectly delectable and it was all Tilly could do not to gape at her like some bystander in the street when the Queen rode by.

'I knew you'd like it,' Dorcas said with satisfaction. 'I have purchased a fully matching costume for darling Sophie — she shall wear it to show you this very evening. I decided I really must take it all out this morning, even if only to buy curtains. Now, my dear, are you ready? I adore your bonnet. One of the new ones, is it? Too, too sweetly pretty. Come along now. I'm sure a walk will make us both feel in excellent spirits.' And she linked her arm in Tilly's and led her out of the house.

'It is just like when I was a child,' Tilly said abruptly when they reached the end of the Grove and were about to set out towards Knightsbridge. 'You always did what *you* wanted and made me feel quite set about, for you never did as I wanted.'

'Oh, my dear Tilly!' Dorcas opened her eyes wide and stopped walking. '*Am* I being a burden to you? I wouldn't wish that for the world – I wanted only to come home to live and – and to make life easier for you. It is all wrong that your Papa should have left you no money, and I thought when you had gone to such pains to find me that it would be good and proper to share with you the money your Papa left.'

'I have heard all that before,' Tilly said. 'And I agree it sounds – it sounds polite and kind in you. But when I was small you could beguile me, and I fear you still do.'

'But you are not small now, Tilly,' Dorcas said with what seemed a most sensible air. 'And I have no wish to beguile you. Tell me how I am beguiling you now and I will stop it at once. I only thought that it would be agreeable to share a shopping expedition as we did when we bought the furniture at Shoolbread's, and show off my new clothes – and indeed yours too. That paletot is new, after all! And so is your bonnet. And here we are prosing along agreeably and yet you are like the fretful porcupine and accuse me of – well, I don't know what. I do think you're being a little – well, captious. How am I beguiling you, tell me that?'

Tilly stared at her, nonplussed, knowing there was right in all she said and took a sharp little breath.

'Oh, I don't know! It is just the way you make me feel. You always did. You chose to go to Knightsbridge or to Kensington for curtains, when I might well have chosen to shop here in Brompton. There are excellent shops in Middle Queen's Buildings and –'

'Then that is where we shall go!' Dorcas said heartily. 'I would not for a moment wish you to think I was being *beguiling* simply by suggesting where we go. Of course we do not have to do as I suggest. I am all yours, my dear Tilly, to do as you wish. Lead and I shall follow.'

Tilly shook her head in a helpless gesture and set out walking again, now in the direction of the nearest shops, knowing she had been silly. The shops in Knightsbridge would have given them a much greater choice of curtains than the linen drapers' in Brompton; she knew that and she knew Dorcas did too.

And then, as they walked along the street, holding their skirts well clear of the slush – much to the delight of gentlemen passers-by who were greatly taken by the flash of Dorcas's scarlet stockings – for no apparent reason Tilly remembered and said, almost before she realized the words were in her mind, 'Dorcas – what happened to my spoons?'

'Your spoons?' Dorcas looked at her in complete bewilderment. 'What spoons?'

Tilly's face hardened. 'My mother's Russian enamel spoons. The day you ran away to marry Walter, you came to me in great distress for money. I had none but I gave you my mother's spoons – the ones she had promised me. What did you do with them?'

'Oh, those!' Dorcas's face cleared. 'I had quite forgotten, you know! They were enamel, were they? I had not recollected – I took them to – let me see now, if I can remember.'

She bent her head as they walked on, watching her red shoes flashing in and out under her black silk skirt, greatly pleased at the effect. 'I must see if I can remember – ah yes! I took them to a shop in Knightsbridge! I recall perfectly now. He gave me three sovereigns for them.'

'Three – but they were worth much more than that, I am sure!' Tilly stared at her companion. 'You could not have let them go for so little.'

'I did not think they were worth more,' Dorcas replied. 'He offered that and I was glad to get it. It was enough for my needs, I thought.'

'Enough for – you told me you needed five pounds. I remember perfectly.'

'Oh, you always ask for more than you need in such

circumstances!' Dorcas said. 'And I believed I could manage with three.' She dimpled. 'And I did. We *were* married, after all.'

'So you sold them cheaply for that reason?' Tilly cried. 'They were my mother's. And mine!'

'But you gave them to me. I didn't think you ever expected to have them back,' Dorcas said. 'You did not say.'

Tilly looked at her, lost for words. Could she ever understand the way Dorcas's mind worked? She did not believe she ever would and sighed deeply. 'I suppose not. Can you at least remember at which shop you sold them?'

'After all this time, I cannot be sure — but wait. Perhaps I can.' She frowned. 'It was a small jewellery shop, opposite that toyshop in Kensington High Street — is it still there? Joseph Toms, that was the one.'

'I think Toms's shop is there yet,' Tilly said and suddenly her spirits lifted. 'I wonder if we could get them back? I'd like that above all things!'

'He must have sold them on by now,' Dorcas said. 'I can't see why he would not, if they were in truth worth so much more as you say and he got them cheaply.'

'But perhaps not — can you recall the name of the shop?'

Dorcas shook her head. 'I remember only it was opposite Toms's establishment. Shall we go and see? Now?'

'Not now,' Tilly said after a moment. 'We said we were to buy curtains.'

'Indeed we did. It is entirely up to you, Tilly,' Dorcas said submissively. 'Which shop do you intend to visit, Tilly?'

'Elizabeth's,' Tilly said firmly. 'Elizabeth Harvey's. I have known her for many years. We went to church together when I used to go to Holy Trinity. When her father died she was left the shop and her husband, the Colonel, helps her run it. It bears both their names now. It is at the other end of the row.' She pointed out a shop front that bore in large letters the superscription, HARVEY NICHOLS.

Dorcas nodded. 'I remember when it was the old man's

hop, before the Great Exhibition, when we first came to Brompton, Mamma and I.'

There was a little silence and then Tilly said, 'I need some silks for finishing those shirts of Duff's. I will get them here.' She turned towards the small haberdashery they were passing. 'Elizabeth has silks too but I must say they are expensive, though very fine. Perhaps they will have the same, but not so costly. I will be very quick.'

'I am in no hurry,' Dorcas said sunnily and together they went into the shop, which was small and rather dark and cluttered, but smelled agreeably of new fabric and lavender.

'Can I help you?' a voice said and Tilly peered into the dimness as a man came forward.

'Oh! Good morning, Mr Leland,' she said.

'Good morning, Mrs Quentin,' he said and smiled, obviously pleased to see her. 'I thought you usually bought your haberdashery from Mrs Nichols.'

'I do,' Tilly said. 'I have known her these many years, but she has become very costly for silks lately and I thought I would see what your prices are. I had no notion this was your shop. It does not say Leland outside.'

'No, it does not. It was my uncle's shop. He is William Hatch and has started another shop in Gloucester Road which is doing very well, so he said I should have this one as my mother had died. She was his sister, you see.'

'You did not tell me this when last we talked,' Tilly said. 'I would have been most interested —' Tilly began, but Dorcas interrupted.

'You must introduce me, Tilly,' Dorcas said softly from somewhere behind Tilly's left ear. 'It is clear you have met an old friend.'

'What? Oh, no! I mean, not precisely. Mr Leland, this is Mrs Oliver who — she has rooms at my house. I am her landlady.' She lifted her chin and said with a hint of wickedness, 'I told you I was in trade as you are yourself. Mrs Oliver, of course, is not.'

291

Quite why she had made that sharp little comment she did not know; she had not meant it to sound as waspish as she suspected it had. But her companion seemed not to have heard anything untoward, for they were shaking hands in a friendly fashion and James Leland was saying, 'I am honoured, Ma'am,' and Dorcas was saying, 'It is a pleasure to make your acquaintance, Sir. You have a most charming establishment here,' – and neither was paying Tilly any attention at all.

'It will be better when I am able to expand a little,' James said. 'It is still very small, but Charlie Harrod and I – he owns the grocer's shop along the Buildings – we have ideas that may serve to enlarge our premises. In the meantime I am able to hold some stock of linens and other drapery, if I am careful about storage.'

'I am sure you have an excellent range,' Dorcas said. 'And excellent linens too. So, while Tilly matches her silks, will you show me your curtain stuffs, Mr Leland? It will save time Tilly, and leave us enough to visit Knightsbridge after all, will it not?'

'Oh – er – yes,' Tilly said, and again was swept along with Dorcas's plans whether she wanted to be or not. And how could she object? It would be well worth a visit to Knightsbridge if, as a result, she found her mother's spoons again. The chances of their still being at the jeweller's shop were slender; but it would be a great worry to her if she did not try; and Dorcas's plan for their shopping would provide time for that. So how could she argue?

Mr Leland seemed as swept along as she was. He fetched a tray of silks for her to match and sat her on a comfortable chair by the door so that she had the best of the light. Then he led Dorcas away to the back of the small shop where Tilly could hear them laughing and chattering over swatches of curtain fabric, as she set skein after skein of silk against the patterns of poplin she was using for Duff's shirts. She had planned to embroider the collars and cuffs with small designs, since he was still a small enough boy to be permitted such fancies in his clothes, and she sat there doggedly until she had the necessary skeins and then got to her feet and bore the tray of silks to the mahogany counter and set it down with a small thud.

But they did not seem to hear her above their own chatter and she went deeper into the shop to find them. The scene she saw when she turned a corner made by a pile of bolts of muslin window netting, was pretty in the extreme. Dorcas was sitting on a low stool with swathes of fabric of various colours and weaves spread on the floor in front of her. Her elegant red shoes peeped out from beneath her black silk skirt and her face glowed in the reflection of her scarlet shirt.

James Leland was crouching at her feet, talking earnestly to her about the fabrics as she sat there looking intently into his eyes; and Tilly stopped short at the sight of them. She felt as though intruding on them would be an embarrassment, and essayed a little cough.

James heard her and scrambled to his feet at once. 'Mrs Quentin? We have here some half dozen that Madam likes.'

'Oh, I am Mrs Oliver!' Dorcas said. 'You must not be so remote with me!'

'Mrs Oliver,' James said. 'And she wishes only that you choose which you like.'

'The price is not important, Tilly,' Dorcas called. 'I want only the best for our rooms. And for your house of course.' And she dimpled up at James Leland as if to say, see how generous I am? Tilly could have cuffed her.

But she just bit her lip and cast her eyes swiftly over the proffered lengths of fabric. 'I will take that and that,' she said, pointing. 'This lilac for the drapes, for that will go well with the blue of the carpet and the muslin for the close curtains. And for the other room, that yellow with the toning nets. The measures are here.' She reached into her reticule and pulled out the piece of paper on which she had written her careful calculations for the curtains. 'And if you will deliver them as soon as may be, Mr Leland, I will be grateful.'

'I would be happy to help with the cutting of these, if you wish, Mrs Quentin,' James said with some eagerness. 'I have learned this skill and I know how to cut them so that there is the greatest economy. The sewing then is very simple.'

'Oh, Mr Leland, will you do that?' Dorcas cried. 'That would be most kind. Now, let me see – I shall be ready to start the sewing tomorrow – no, do not look so anxious, Tilly. I am quite set on making these curtains myself. And if Mr Leland will cut them for us at home that will be splendid. Will you come tomorrow evening, Mr Leland? Eliza will show you up to my rooms, and I will be ready for you at – let me see, shall we say seven o'clock? Splendid. There, Tilly – have you chosen your silks? Good! Then we must be on our way to Knightsbridge. Goodbye for the present, Mr Leland. It has been a great pleasure to meet you.' And she led the way out into Brompton with a flash of scarlet ankles at such speed that Tilly had to run to follow her.

Chapter Twenty-eight

TILLY HAD FINISHED embroidering Duff's shirts long before Dorcas finished sewing the bedroom curtains.

February melted into March and Duff started school with great excitement and some trepidation but settled quickly enough in the familiar company of not only the Misses K and F, but also Sophie whose adoring shadow he had become. And still Dorcas needed to ask Jem Leland to call, to advise her and instruct her in the next stage of making the curtains.

He would arrive most evenings not long after they had dined and while Dorcas was still sitting at the table with Tilly, toying with one of Eliza's splendid puddings, for which she had developed a great gift now she had her new stove.

The door knocker would sound and Eliza would cast her gaze up to the ceiling in exasperation and go stomping across the hall to let him in. He would come to the dining-room — Dorcas had cried cheerfully on his first visit that there was no need for formality, surely — and stand silently as Dorcas chattered brightly at him for a while before taking him away upstairs to her sitting room, begging Eliza as she went to bring, if she would, a tray of madeira and ratafias. Eliza would do so willingly enough: she had no objection to pleasing Dorcas, but a good deal of reservation about Jem Leland.

'It don't seem right to me, Mum,' she said earnestly to Tilly on the first occasion she voiced her objections, 'him being in trade an' all. It's one thing to come to the kitchen to talk to me with Charlie, another entirely to take it on himself to come to the front door like any gentleman and expect to be treated according.'

'I see no reason why he should not, Eliza,' Tilly said. 'It is not as though we were not ourselves trade people, after all. I am but a lodging housekeeper. Any notions I may have had when I was younger of being a lady, above considerations of making my own living, have long since been pushed out of me!'

'You're a lady, Mum, and there's an end of it,' Eliza said sharply. 'I'll not have no one treating you except with the highest of respect at all times. And it ain't fully respectful for tradesmen to come callin' at the front door in this fashion for Mrs Oliver.'

'But she is —' Tilly was about to remind Eliza that Dorcas had started her career as a housemaid, but realized that this might seem as though she were making disparaging remarks about Eliza herself, and desisted. Instead she said mildly, 'Her husband was but a soldier.'

'An 'ero, Mum,' Eliza said. 'Mr Oliver was from all accounts a most brave soldier and of high reputation. That makes all the difference. She's your tenant, anyhow, like the Misses K and F, whatever she was when she started life, and that makes her a lady. But it don't make a gentleman of Jem Leland.' And she went marching down to the kitchen with her tray of dishes, looking far from happy.

Tilly was unhappy too but for a different reason. She could not, however, say what that reason was. Dorcas's choice of friends was no concern of hers; Tilly was but her landlady and as such had no right to an opinion about her behaviour. She did not feel that there was any lack of propriety in Jem's interest in Dorcas; as she told Eliza, she had quite accustomed herself to the idea that her present station in life was firmly amongst tradespeople.

Perhaps it was fear that the young man and Dorcas might make a match of it? It was very clear to Tilly that Dorcas's interest in Jem Leland went far beyond curtains; and why not? He was a well set up young man, and looked to be about thirty years old or thereabouts; an excellent age to be wed. He could make a good husband for Dorcas, Tilly told herself, and no doubt an excellent Papa for Sophie, who might learn to be a little less imperious if she experienced the restraining hand of a father.

Or am I fearful of losing her as a tenant? she asked herself and was able to be quite certain of her reply. She certainly was not; indeed, losing Dorcas could be from her own point of view quite agreeable, sisterly though their link might be, and however much it might distress Duff to lose Sophie. She would still, after all, have the items of furniture and kitchen equipment for which Dorcas had paid; she had made it very clear when she installed them that she regarded them now as part of the house rather than her own possessions, and there was no doubt in Tilly's mind that she had meant what she said. She was far too careless about money, being a positive spendthrift, in Tilly's estimation, to take such things away again. So losing Dorcas would mean only that she, Tilly would be left with excellent chambers to offer to a new tenant who, though she might not pay so well, would be less of a source of confusion and irritation to Tilly. Any sense of need for Dorcas's company, which was one of the reasons she allowed her to move into the house in the first place, had been firmly erased by the experience of living with her ever since: no, letting Dorcas go would not be painful.

Later, as she sat over her own sewing in the drawing-room, she reminded herself that the friendship between Dorcas and Jem Leland was none of her concern. None at all. But it was remarkably difficult to obey her own commands.

It was in April that the matter came to a head at last. The curtains were finished and had been hung in the rooms occupied by Dorcas and Sophie and duly admired. They were certainly of a very fancy style, being much swagged and draped and decorated with braid, and it was clear to Tilly that Jem Leland had taught his customer well, and she said as much to him as they stood and looked solemnly at the well-dressed windows.

'As to that, I had small choice,' he said in a low voice. Dorcas had been distracted by Sophie's wish to tug at the curtains to see how they drew at night, and was remonstrating with her. In the middle of the resulting fracas, it was possible for Tilly and Jem to speak without being overheard. 'I was under some pressure, Mrs Quentin, and found it difficult to —'

'Oh, Jem,' Dorcas called fretfully. 'See what this little wretch has done! She has pulled a thread. Will the damage spread, do you think, or is it possible to repair it at once?'

He glanced over at Tilly and then moved across to the window, as the now bawling Sophie, who had been soundly pinched by her irate Mamma for her naughtiness, was led away by Eliza followed by a worried Duff, who could not bear to see his beloved in any sort of scrape. Tilly remained where she was, by the door, watching.

He bent to look at the damage and Dorcas bent down in the same posture to look more closely also, and it seemed to Tilly was a deal nearer to him than she had any real need to be. Suddenly Tilly felt herself blushing hotly. There was a physical tension in the room that seemed to communicate itself to her, and she felt it crawl through her body in a way she found startling to say the least. It was just the sort of frisson she had sometimes experienced at the age of sixteen when she had been engaged to Frank, and she stepped back and said in a tight little voice, 'They are excellent curtains, Dorcas. I congratulate you on your needlework,' and escaped, running down the stairs as fast as she could.

As she passed the door to the bedroom next to the one that had been her own, long ago, and which was now occupied by Miss Knapp, she caught her breath and had to stand with one hand against the wall; for something had happened to shock her profoundly.

A vision appeared in her mind's eye, so vivid that it was as though she were looking at reality. She saw herself in her drawers and chemise on her wedding day, standing at the door of the same room looking at the brass bedstead and the piled up blankets and sheets; she saw Dorcas in a cascade of petticoat frills, lying on her back on the bed with her knees bent and spread wide, and kneeling on the floor in front of her, her bridegroom Frank, fiddling with his trouser buttons.

Her head swam and she took a deep breath and waited for the sensation of giddiness to pass. What had possessed her to permit such a vision to overwhelm her? Was she not a grown woman now, in control of all that happened to her? She should not let such foolishness intrude.

She had not heard his footsteps on the carpeted stairs, had not been aware that he was there until she felt his arm across her shoulders.

'Mrs Quentin! Are you ill? Permit me to take you to a sofa.'

'I am perfectly − I am all right,' she tried to say but her voice was pinched and tight and he did not seem to hear as he bent and picked her up. He was not a great deal taller than she was, but was certainly stockier and seemed to have no difficulty with her weight. She tried to protest, finding his proximity surprisingly powerful. Ignoring her pleas, he carried her to the drawing-room door, kicked it open and bore her inside and set her down with great care on the sofa near the fireplace. She let her head rest on the cushions gratefully and closed her eyes. Perhaps if she remained very quiet he would go away.

But he did not, and she was very aware of him standing there beside her. Her eyes snapped open as she heard Dorcas's voice, loud and crisp, at the door of the drawing-room.

'What's amiss? Is she ill?'

'I fear so. I found her almost swooning.' He bent his head to look at Tilly. 'Are you feeling a little better yet?'

'Smelling salts,' said Dorcas confidently and came across the room, reaching into the pocket in her skirt as she did so. She almost pushed Jem Leland aside and crouched beside the sofa.

'Now, Tilly, what is it? You must not get into your old ways of sickness, you know!'

Tilly opened her mouth to protest; she had not been all that sickly as a child, she was sure; but Dorcas thrust a bottle of smelling salts beneath her nose and the reek of the ammonia made her cough and choke, and her eyes ran painfully.

Dorcas took the bottle away at last and said with some satisfaction, 'There! I am sure she will be very well now. Best to come away, Jem. I will take care of her now.'

'I do not need taking care of,' Tilly managed and sat up gingerly, reaching for her handkerchief which was tucked into her waistband. She mopped her streaming eyes and looked up at them both. 'I would be grateful please, if you would leave me be. I am perfectly well. It was but a temporary matter.'

'I will not go until you have your maid with you,' Jem said firmly and Dorcas turned her head to stare at him.

'Oh, come Jem, you must not make too much of female megrims, you know!'

'I do not need my maid!' Tilly said crossly. She was feeling better by the moment and now swung her legs from the sofa and set them on the floor, finding the movement of air agreeable as her skirts settled softly around them. 'Please leave me, both of you. I am perfectly well, I do insist.'

'Oh, well then, we had better go!' Dorcas said brightly and with a swish of her own skirts went over to the door. 'Come along, Jem!'

'I will wait on you later to ensure you are all right,' he said in a low voice, and at last the door closed and she was able to relax again. And now she did lie back on the sofa, for in truth her head was still a touch giddy and she needed time to think.

Why in the name of all that was sensible had she behaved so absurdly? Why had such memories come to her after all this time? She had not been at all disturbed by the lack of a man in her life since Frank died. There had been so much to do and think about; the matter of her property and of course beloved Duff. She thought about him as she lay there, remembering

300

him as a greedy baby at her breast and later as he learned to sit and then crawl and at last to walk, and how much joy he had given her: he had filled many gaps in her life that she had not even known were there. Now he was at school all day, of course it was different. He returned home with Sophie at two in the afternoon, by which time they both needed a nap, so it was not until the late afternoon that she could spend much time with him. In the three hours between waking him from his nap at four and his bedtime at seven she spent as much time with him as she could, or rather that he could spare from his play with Sophie, and that had to suffice for her. Was that why she had been so overwhelmed this morning? Had seeing love burgeoning between two people, as it clearly was between Dorcas and Jem, aroused jealousy in her? If so, she hated herself. It was an ugly emotion and one that shamed her.

She slept for a little while and woke only when an anxious Eliza came to seek her. She was amazed to discover that Tilly had had a disagreeable experience. She had not been told of it by Dorcas until just before luncheon time, when Eliza enquired if she had seen her mistress and Dorcas told her offhandedly what had transpired. Now Eliza was very angry indeed.

'You'd ha' thought she'd ha' come and told me, Mum, wouldn't you? Leavin' you here all on your own and you feeling not so wonderful — why, it's little short of disgraceful.'

'It's not important, Eliza,' Tilly said wearily. 'I am indeed in perfect health. I simply had a — a headache. I am quite fit now. I shall take luncheon here on a tray, if you please. That will suit me perfectly. I shall come down later to see the woman when she fetches back the washing. Let me know when she arrives as I must speak to her about the finish of Duff's shirts. It's not adequate. It is your free afternoon today, though, is it not? Tell Lucy to call me then.'

'Lucy's the kitchen maid, Mum, and has no dealin's with such matters,' Eliza said firmly. 'Afternoon off or no afternoon off, I'll be here to sort out the washerwoman and don't you doubt it. Now you rest here and I'll fetch your luncheon up in no time. Such a carry on. And her not telling me!' And she went away, clearly less entranced with Dorcas than she had been hitherto.

Dorcas herself came into the drawing-room shortly after luncheon. 'I trust you're quite better now? Good. I dare say it was simply that time of the month for you, yes? I know I am sometimes a martyr to the pain. Now my dear, rest yourself and I shall see you at dinner time. I have some shopping to do in Knightsbridge.'

'There cannot be much left for you to buy,' Tilly said with a flash of malice. 'I cannot imagine how you can spend so much time in warehouses and emporia.'

Dorcas laughed. 'Oh, for me shopping is the best sport there is — I have my eye on a darling new bonnet, and also another gown. There are times coming I suspect when I will have more occasions on which to wear such things. I have been in need of a partner for balls and cotillions, but now, now — well, we shall see. Is there anything I can fetch for you, dear? Some silks that need matching perhaps?'

Tilly ignored the bite in the offer; perhaps she did not have such money to spend on clothes but that did not mean she was so dull her only interests were in sewing with well-matched silks.

'Not at present,' she said, and then had a sudden thought. 'You could call in at the jewellers again, of course, and see if he has managed to obtain news of my spoons.'

'Oh, as to that,' Dorcas said, buttoning her gloves with a flourish, 'I doubt it. He said he would ask about the trade, did he not, but he held out small hope of any success. As he told you, dear Tilly, once sold, items do not stay still waiting to be bought again. Perhaps you can buy yourself some new spoons — they cannot be as rare as you say.'

'Those were,' Tilly said sharply. 'My Mamma — well, let be. Ask, all the same, if you please.'

'Oh. I shall,' Dorcas said and, waving one hand and with her broad silk skirts swishing cheerfully, left Tilly quite certain

302

that she would make no shift at all to go to the jewellers. Once Dorcas had her eyes set on an afternoon amongst the milliners and modistes, she was not to be deflected.

The afternoon settled into dullness, after Eliza took away her tray and she stretched herself on her sofa again. Tilly thought sleepily that it might be agreeable to pretend to be an invalid for a little while, even though she knew perfectly well that she was nothing of the sort. Then she was puzzled to hear the knocker far below. And sighed. One of her neighbours making calls, perhaps. A tedium but she had to tolerate it. She sat up and set her gown to rights, glad she had put on one of her prettier ones that morning, in light blue wool cloth, carefully cut and with a nicely trimmed bodice that showed off her lace collar and cuffs.

The door opened and she straightened her shoulders, ready to greet whoever Eliza showed in with a neighbourly smile, but when she turned her head the smile froze on her face.

'Mr Leland! I am surprised to see you again. And you have wasted your visit, for Dor– Mrs Oliver has gone to Knights-bridge shopping, and may well take herself further afield. I am sorry you have been discommoded.'

'I didn't come to see Mrs Oliver, Mrs Quentin. I waited and watched till she had gone and made sure she would not return too soon before I ventured to knock at your door.' He stood and smiled at her and she looked at him more closely. He seemed very pleased with himself, and she frowned at that.

'If you have come because you think I am ill, then let me disabuse you of any such notion,' she said. 'I am perfectly fit. A moment of giddiness is not something over which to exercise yourself greatly.'

'I am glad of it,' he said. 'I was alarmed at the time but I now see that you are perfectly comfortable and will concern myself no more on that point.'

'Thank you,' she said. 'So I bid you good afternoon, Mr Leland. I shall tell Mrs Oliver you called to see her, of course.'

'I told you!' he said. 'I watched and waited till she had gone.

It is you I wish to speak to. I did not come to enquire after your health.'

'Oh? Then why did you come?' She was being very acid with him and she knew it and was puzzled. The man had done her no harm, after all. Why snap at him so? Because she enjoyed doing it, she decided. Anyway, being sharp with him would soon send him packing and she wished to be left in peace.

'I came to disabuse you of a notion and to tell you that Mrs Oliver is not a person over whom you need exercise yourself greatly.' He sounded grave, but there was a note of laughter to match his mocking repetition of her words.

'I cannot imagine what you mean,' she snapped.

'Oh dear. This is difficult! But I dare say it is meant to be so. Otherwise, how could we value what we win?'

'You speak in riddles, Sir, and I have no time for such matters. I have my duties to see to, a washerwoman to interview and my linen cupboard to sort and orders to be got up for the butcher and the grocer — I am surprised that you too do not have duties about your shop to keep you occupied at this time of day.'

'I decided to leave my shop to the care of my shop-boy this afternoon.' There was still laughter in his voice. 'On a matter of importance of the sort I must discuss with you, we trades-people must make what shift we can to cover all our duties.' He smiled widely again. 'Is all this sounding foolish?'

'Indeed it is,' she said tartly.

'Then I must, as they say, address our muttons. I come to tell you, dear Mrs Quentin, that I have no interest whatsoever in your tenant. Mrs Oliver has been for me a means to an end. She has made herself quite ridiculous in my eyes, throwing her hat at me, but I have pretended to field it for my own purposes.'

She opened her mouth to speak but he shook his head. 'Hear me out. I agreed to her transparent invitation to help her with her curtains — and I must tell you she is a *villainous*

304

needlewoman. The stitches in those curtains are no credit to her — I agreed, as I say, in order to see you as often as I might. For me the important part of my visits to this house has always been seeing you in the drawing-room for a few moments before the interminable business of fending off Mrs Oliver's flirtatiousness in her sitting room. Ever since I saw you in the kitchen last Christmas, my mind and feelings have been bent to one end, absurd though I feared my pretensions might be, and silent though I have been in my few — far too few — conversations with you. Now the curtains are finished, for which I must say I will be eternally grateful, the time has come for me to be honest and to tell you that it is you in whom I have an abiding interest. Dear Mrs Quentin, I have come to ask your permission to pay you my addresses. Had you a father or brother to whom I could address myself, of course I would, but in the absence of such persons I must address you directly. I hope you will not spurn my interest, Mrs Quentin, and will permit me to call upon you often. I can assure you that my intentions are of great seriousness, and though my present situation is not precisely affluent, the time will come, I do assure you, when I will be a person of some substance and will be able to —'

'Mr Leland, stop this at once!' Tilly had found her voice at last. 'Are you quite mad?'

'Of course I am, dear Mrs Quentin,' he said. 'I am mad with love for you.'

Chapter Twenty-nine

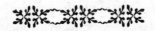

IT WAS DIFFICULT to be sure, Tilly had to admit to herself, why she had agreed to accept Jem Leland's attentions. She liked him well enough; he had a serenity and security about him that was very comforting and he was easy company, but was that the only reason? Could there be an element of malice in her, she would ask her pillow in the darker watches of the night when her sleep was disturbed by such ponderings, that made it agreeable for her to score over Dorcas? The fact that Jem himself was well aware of this possibility did not help. He was amused by Dorcas's interest in him but far from flattered by it.

'I do not,' he assured Tilly, 'regard myself as so well set up a man that ladies find me irresistible. I have much too clear a vision of my own shortcomings to permit myself any such fantastic notions. I am sure Mrs Oliver's interest in me was from the start based on boredom. She is a person who likes to adorn herself, and enjoys displaying her latest attire. I now know the reason she set her cap at me that morning at the shop was that she had a new toilette – and you knew me, and I clearly was pleased to see *you*. She likes to exercise power over others, you see. To distract me from you merely amused her. Not that it was not easy for her to, shall we say, make you step back. I have seen her with you, my dear, and it saddens me to see how easily she is able to get her own way.'

Tilly defended herself vigorously at that accusation. 'I am as aware as you of the way Dorcas likes to – well, twist people to her own designs. But she does not twist me. That morning, to be truthful, I was not concerned about the way she flirted with you. It did not matter unduly, I regret to tell you, and I hope you don't mind my doing so! For the rest, I allow her to do the things she wants only if they are of benefit to me or mine.'

'Are you sure?' he said gently and she felt herself redden a little.

'As sure as it is possible to be,' she said and he nodded.

'You see what I mean? She is a most beguiling and clever person.'

Tilly was much struck. 'Beguiling? That is the word I used to describe her.'

'So we are in agreement, are we not? How very pleasant!' And he beamed at her and proffered his cup for more tea.

Their lives had fallen into a pleasant pattern. She spent her mornings busying herself about the house, ensuring that the kitchen ran smoothly, ordering her meals, dealing with the buying of necessary goods and paying the bills precisely when they were due; mending her linen as well as caring for her ornaments and flowers, as did any lady of a household; and her afternoons she spent with her small son. Once the weather eased into a warm spring he stopped having his nap and he and Sophie played in the garden most afternoons under Tilly's eye. After the children's supper and bedtime there was dinner at which Dorcas would sit and chatter away, pretending she did not know that Jem Leland would appear soon afterwards, and then would disappear about her own interests.

She had taken to visiting the theatre a great deal with an old friend from her Fulham days, a Mrs Dangerfield, or so she told Tilly. ('She has no time to come so far to visit me here,' she said offhandedly. 'So I go to her house and then we go into town.') That left the field clear for Jem to arrive.

Which he did at about half past eight, with the shop safely shut and his day's work done, including his counting house duties. He would settle himself in the other armchair by Tilly's fireside, for spring or not she still felt the need for an evening fire, and tell her of his day's work, as she told him of hers. Quite like old married people, she would think sometimes and then refuse to dwell any more along those lines. They were friends, that was all. It was very agreeable to have a friend, one with whom she could talk in a desultory fashion when she wanted, or be silent if she chose. For so many years she had only had Eliza as a confidante, and though she was a loyal and trustworthy servant, she could not be the truly close friend Jem was becoming; and she cherished him for that. But, she assured herself stoutly, no more.

Both had expected trouble from Dorcas. 'She will become very angry when she realizes that you are not interested in her,' Tilly had told him when he first made his declaration. 'I really do not think I can face the fuss and noise that will result.'

He was very firm about that. 'You cannot permit such a person to dictate how your life will be run. I offer you my undying affection, and ask only that you permit me to visit you often in the hope that in time you will come to reciprocate my feelings. You cannot, you really cannot, refuse me that on the grounds of the possible ill opinion and bad behaviour of Mrs Oliver!' He sounded positively scandalized. 'That would be the outside of enough!'

After a great deal of thought, she had agreed that he might visit her often and pay his respects, while making no promises about the outcome of his devotion.

'I must tell you, Mr Leland — very well then — Jem,' as he had protested, 'that I do not know what my feelings for you might be. I regard you as clearly a man of worth and all that is good. But I have not thought of myself except as a widow, you see, these many years. I don't know, I truly don't, what I wish to — I can make no promises.'

'I ask none,' he said. 'Only the right to visit you and to be sure that you know of my unswerving devotion. That's all.'

'As long as you don't speak of it too often,' she said, alarmed. 'I don't think I could be comfortable if you did that.'

He laughed. 'I know what you mean, my dear Tilly. You will, I hope, permit me that degree of familiarity? No, I'm not made of the sort of stuff that permits dying falls and eternal swearings. I love you and I have said so. I want no reply more than you can bear. We will deal very comfortably together. I'm sure if you stand up to Mrs Oliver and tell her firmly that it is the way you wish it, she will accept it. I too, of course, will speak to her and make it clear that —'

'No!' she said quickly. 'Oh, no. I must deal with her. I know how to — it will be best. No, I will not be dissuaded,' for he had opened his mouth to try. 'I know how to save her face, you see. That is important to her.'

He agreed unwillingly and then she had to decide how to do the face-saving, for she had in truth no notion how to, and decided in the end to come out with the truth baldly and leave it to Dorcas to find her own way out of any embarrassment. And the following day she did just that.

Dorcas listened in stony silence until she had finished, and then lifted her brows superciliously. 'You are saying this man agreed to help me make those stupid curtains simply in order to be in the same house as *you* and look at you for a few moments each evening?'

'Yes,' Tilly said.

There was a long silence and then Dorcas had laughed, loudly, musically and with, to Tilly's ear, obvious falsity. 'And here was I trying to let the poor creature down lightly! I knew he had a *tendresse* somewhere. He came in the house so often I could not fail to know that. I cannot pretend I did not think for a moment it could be *you* he yearned for. You are, after all, such a mouse, my dear Tilly; are you not? You always were! So, I was kind to him and did what I could to let him know I had no interest in him of the sort I imagine he required. Indeed it is a great relief that I need not have worried myself. You may have him and welcome. I do assure you that a linen

309

draper in a small way of business in a village like Brompton is not *my* idea of good *parti!*' And she laughed even more merrily and disappeared off to her own room.

And so it had been ever since. Spring folded itself into a warm and languorous summer and the house was busy with the noise of the children; and of a new development. The Misses K and F asked Tilly if a young protégée of theirs, a music teacher, might come and live with them. Would Mrs Quentin object, they asked, if they purchased a larger piano for their sitting room and brought her pupils to the house? They would of course pay accordingly.

Mrs Quentin did not object and after some discussion with a builder from Knightsbridge, who had some time to spare now that the main buildings in the area had been completed and all the new houses taken, had come to make necessary changes to the Misses K and F's apartment. Two bedrooms, by dint of careful rearrangement of room walls, became three with one being rather small but habitable none the less and a new piano arrived in their sitting room. The young protégée turned out to be a thin, curl-bedecked woman with bulging blue eyes. Tilly estimated her to be close on forty years. She was much given to giggling and throwing arch glances at her two benefactresses, who clearly adored her and fought jealously for her approval, a situation that seemed to give all three of them enthralling satisfaction.

Soon piano pupils, children aged between ten and sixteen, were climbing the stairs looking glum as they prepared for their lessons. Miss Cynthia Barnetsen appeared to be a good enough music teacher and took on Sophie and Duff as well, much to Duff's disgust. ('Boys don't have to play pianos,' he cried in despair. 'Or they shouldn't.' The house not only hummed with people but rang with music and the sounds of practised scales. Not unpleasant from Tilly's point of view, though Eliza sometimes complained. However, since she now had a second maid to help her and Lucy, a rather sullen young woman called Kate, with large feet over which she tended to fall easily and a tendency to being slapdash which demanded much supervisory scolding, she was happy enough.

As time passed, Tilly found herself becoming more and more comfortable with Jem Leland. He was capable of understanding without being told when she was tired and disinclined for speech; and equally knew when she was feeling lively and in the mood for chatter. Duff, who had been scornful of him at first, seeing him as too much in his way when he wished to have his mother to himself on a Sunday afternoon (the other time when Jem came as a matter of custom to number seventeen), learned to like him a great deal since he discovered that he knew a lot about such things as worms and caterpillars and snails and was not averse to handling them and discussing their finer points. Sophie, who had started by ignoring Jem completely, came to like him too, once he displayed an undoubted talent for inventing stories to tell them on the long summer evenings in the garden.

Dorcas was rarely visible, keeping to her rooms most of the day and going out after dinner most evenings. There were no problems about her rent for she was, as she had told Tilly from the start, too lazy to remember when to pay her bills and had made arrangements with Mr Cobbold to see to it that each month the rent would be sent. And it was, arriving by messenger on the first Monday of each month like clockwork. So life should have been tranquil and good for Tilly.

But somehow it was not entirely. It was hard for her to say quite what her problem was, but it was there. She did not feel ill precisely but she did not feel well either. There were vague pains in her middle that sometimes made her catch her breath and want to bend double, and there were very unpleasant attacks of the flux that made her keep to her room, grateful for the fact that her father had installed one of the new-fangled water closets in the house before his death. These attacks left her weak and sweating and caused Eliza much concern.

'You should talk to Mr Fildes, Mum,' she said earnestly. 'It ain't right to have you ill like this. And it makes me feel bad.

I'm as careful as can be to give you food that's not been spoiled, and it ain't always easy in this hot weather. I can promise you. So it worries me, I tell you straight.'

'Oh, Eliza, don't be silly,' Tilly said. 'If it were spoiled food we would all be ill, would we not? No, it is just a tiresome thing – it goes away as fast as it comes.'

And so it did; usually just at the point when she determined she should, after all, ask Mr Fildes to call; and then she would forget about it until it happened again. Jem fretted over her health a good deal, but she told him firmly that was due to his exaggerated feelings for her.

'You really must not let your mind run away with you,' she said. 'I am perfectly fit, but sometimes I am more susceptible than most people. It is perhaps a remaining weakness from the illness I had all those years ago, before Duff was born.'

Even Dorcas took an interest, if only out of irritation. 'I find it very boring to sit with you at table when you refuse every other dish,' she told Tilly firmly. 'It makes me feel as though I'm some sort of glutton, to eat when you refuse. I wish you wouldn't do it to me!'

'I don't do it on purpose,' Tilly retorted. 'I just have a degree of indigestion. It's no more than that.'

'Then you should try taking a little brandy. It settles the stomach amazingly.' Dorcas insisted and poured some for her from the decanter that still stood where Austen Kingsley had left it, all those years before. And to Tilly's surprise it was comforting and now, when she had an attack of pain, she would let Dorcas pour her a little brandy from the decanter, and eventually would feel better. And so it went on all through the summer.

In August Dorcas planned to go away to Brighton and take Sophie with her. Duff was bereft at the very idea and when Dorcas offered to take the boy as well, he was incandescent with joy.

'Oh, Mamma, please let me! I couldn't bear it if you said no. You can't say no, Mamma, it would be too much! Oh, please,

Mamma! Sophie says they play on the beach and paddle in the water and it's the best sort of fun in the whole world. You must let me go, Mamma – and it's a train journey too.'

'But Duff, it's not right that you should live with someone else for so long! I cannot allow it. I know you would like the seaside but –'

Duff burst into tears – a rare thing for him – and fled from her. He refused to be comforted for the rest of the day. It almost tore her in two; and she felt a deep and powerful hatred for Dorcas for putting her in such a position.

It was clearly absurd to expect Dorcas to care for both children for a whole month. She was far too casual a mother in Tilly's estimation to care for her own, let alone two. 'Indeed,' Tilly told Jem. 'If I were not here to take care that Sophie goes to bed at the right time and eats what she should, I don't know what would happen to her. How can I let Dorcas take Duff away?'

'You can't,' Jem said. 'But you could go as well.'

'I go as – oh, please, Jem, don't be absurd! I can't do that! There is the house to run and –'

'Now, let's think about this,' Jem said in his usual stolid fashion. 'Is there anything here Eliza could not do, especially with both you and Mrs Oliver and the children away? She could run the house well enough and take care of the Misses K and F as well as you do. She has Lucy and Kate, after all! I will be here to watch over her, if you wish – I could call most days and be sure all is done as you would like, though I doubt that Eliza would need such supervision.'

'The cost,' Tilly said a little helplessly but knew that wasn't really a problem. The savings made by taking Duff away and having Dorcas and Sophie out of the house as well would just cover the costs of seaside lodgings and she had by now also saved a sufficient sum for modest accommodation in Brighton.

She put the idea to Eliza tentatively after some prodding from Jem. While she was not certain at first because Jem had suggested it (Eliza was still disapproving of the lack of propriety in her mistress's friendship with a shopkeeper, but was slowly becoming accustomed to it), when her much adored Duff threw himself at her, having heard from Sophie, an inveterate eavesdropper, that the possibility was being discussed, she agreed that it was an excellent idea.

'It'll get rid of that peaky look you got, Mum,' she said. 'If you rest easy and take care of yourself, and take some gentle exercise by the sea, you'll come back as good as new. And as for Master Duff – well – he'll have as happy a time as a boy can have. So go and have all the rest you can.'

Tilly capitulated, and took a pair of modestly-priced rooms in a small house in Montpelier Terrace, which was convenient for the sea as well as for Dorcas's far more expensive lodgings on the front, and not too far from the shops in the town. So on a hot morning in the first week of August she shepherded Duff and a multitude of bags and boxes into the train bound for Brighton. Jem, who had insisted on coming to the station to see them on their way, helped her with it all, and she bade him goodbye there.

He looked up at her from the platform, his face tilted towards her as she stood at the carriage window looking out, and for the first time she was aware of how dear a face it had become to her. There was none of the excitement she remembered feeling with Frank all those years ago when she had become engaged, but something better. He looked warm and kindly and utterly dependable and on an impulse she leaned through the window and kissed his forehead.

'Dear Jem,' she said. 'You are so very good to me. I am grateful.'

When she lifted her head and looked at him again she was startled. There were tears in his eyes, and she bit her lip as he mopped them away quite unselfconsciously and said, 'You see? It is just a matter of time, dear Tilly. Soon you will love me half as much as I love you, and that will be enough for me. Goodbye, dearest one. I wish you the happiest of holidays. And don't be surprised if one Sunday I come to see you both.'

314

The train shuddered and there was a loud shriek of whistle and a roar of steam and voices lifted in excitement and he stepped back. 'Take care, dear Tilly,' he called and waved as the train dragged itself with majestic slowness out of the station, and she stood and watched him as his figure diminished on the receding platform. He never stopped waving until the train was out of sight.

Brighton was indeed delightful. The sun shone on a glittering sea and the pebbles on the beach reflected back the glitter with an enthusiasm all their own. Children ran and whooped and wept bitterly when they fell and skinned their knees, donkeys brayed as they trotted along the front pulling governess carts, and fashionable ladies paraded daily in one extraordinary toilette after another.

Tilly would spend the mornings sitting on a bench on the promenade beneath a parasol, a novel on her lap, but rarely reading. She would watch the children and listen to Dorcas's desultory chatter on the days when she kept her company (not a great many, in fact, for now that Tilly had joined her and was able to care for Sophie, Dorcas could visit the many new friends she had made, she told Tilly, and would vanish early in the day). It was as agreeable a way to spend time as she could have imagined. She enjoyed watching the children slowly brown until they looked like hot buttered toast, with fine golden hair glinting on their arms and legs, and her own indigestion and flux vanished completely.

It was not only her physical strength that increased; so did her feelings for Jem. When he had first declared himself she had of course been flattered and as she now freely admitted to herself, gleeful at having succeeded in fixing a man's interest when Dorcas had so signally failed. But now it was different. The long evenings spent with him, the tranquil Sunday afternoons, had become important to her. She did more than enjoy his company and friendship now, she realized; she actually needed it. And that made her think a great deal about the future, and sometimes drift into a daydream in which she was no longer Mrs Quentin but had become Mrs Leland.

But that was dangerous thinking, she told herself. There was plenty of time to let matters run as they chose. She must not hurry them, for that could lead to precipitous actions, which were never wise; and she would look about her for the children and not settle again until she had identified them among the many who played on the pebbles, building stone castles and digging for crabs. Once she had done that she would settle again to her novel and determinedly not think about Jem.

It was on one such occasion that it happened. She was not at first able to see the children and alarm lifted in her and she jumped to her feet and walked further along the promenade to seek them; and then at last saw them down the beach near the water's edge. The sea was tranquil this warm morning, but the tide was coming in and that worried her and she beckoned the children to come closer to the shore, calling to them loudly above the hubbub. At last they heard and obediently came back up the beach to a point she regarded as safe, and she turned to walk back to her seat.

And stopped short. Standing in her way was a nurse with a Bath chair. She was leaning forwards and listening to her patient, who was wearing a straw hat with a broad brim and was wrapped in a blanket despite the warm sunshine. Tilly stepped aside to allow the nurse to push the chair on its way, but she did not. She straightened up, looked sharply at Tilly and then reached down and set the brake on the back wheels. Then she walked away to lean a little obviously out of hearing, but well within sight, against the railings that lined the promenade.

'I would have known your voice anywhere,' the figure in the chair said in a hoarse croak. 'How are you, my dear Tilly?'

She frowned, startled, and tilting her sunshade to give her less light against which to squint, she tried to identify the face under the hat brim. He lifted his head in response, with what seemed a huge effort, and it was then that she recognized him. The cheeks were sunken and the eyes glittered far too brightly, and she caught her breath and said, 'Freddy? *Freddy?* Is it really you? What has happened to you? I cannot believe how dreadful you look!'

Chapter Thirty

THE NURSE FUSSED a little at Freddy's demands but eventually agreed, and went away up the promenade with a disapproving waddle, leaving the chair firmly braked beside Tilly's bench; and at last they could talk.

It was clearly very difficult for him, for his voice seemed quite destroyed. He was hoarse in a way that hurt her to listen to it, making her want to cough for him, and it was clear that every breath he drew was an effort. But he was determined to speak and she realized quickly that preventing him from doing so would cause him even more distress than letting him have his way.

'I have prayed and hoped something like this would happen,' he whispered. 'Prayed and – and –' He was interrupted by a spasm of coughing that racked his body and she put out one hand to steady him. He seemed grateful.

'I am sorry about this. It is the condition, you see.'

'The condition –' she said carefully and he turned his head towards her and managed a smile. It was heartrending to see the shadow of the old transformation to his smile; now the face was so cadaverous and the sockets so pronounced that the smile could only flicker.

'It is not obvious? Consumption – I did not think you could imagine it was anything else.'

'Oh, Freddy, I am so sorry! Should you not be somewhere more suitable for chest complaints? Switzerland, perhaps.'

'It is too late to consider that.' He rested his chin on his chest for a moment. 'We did speak of it, but I would not go while Alice still lived.'

'Alice? Oh, no.'

'I'm afraid so. She took ill first. It was Mary. The maid, you remember, who had looked after Alice for so long? She died quite suddenly, coughing blood one night, until — well, she died. And not a month later it started in Alice, though I suspected it had been there long before. I, of course, returned to her as soon as her cousin called for me, and she seemed glad enough to have me there. We were not precisely reconciled, but she allowed me to stand her friend, even if she could no longer regard me as a husband. Not that it was for long. She went down so fast — so very fast. I stayed with her, of course, even though I knew that the disease had touched me too.' He shook his head, slowly and with difficulty. 'Our family, such as it was, was afflicted sorely. It does so with consumption, as you well know.'

'I don't know what to say, Freddy. Only to tell you that I am so, so sorry.'

'Oh, it doesn't matter any more. I'm so tired, you see, that I just don't mind any more. At first I was so angry . . .' His voice fluttered away like a sigh and they both sat in silence, staring at the light-dancing, restless sea, and then he stirred himself. 'I went away from Staffordshire where Alice had lived, and came back to London and thought of coming to see you and telling you of Alice's death, but how could I? I was touched with the disease too, and I knew I was too far gone with it to speak to you of my — to speak to you. If I were not fit to travel to improve my health, as my doctors assured me was the case, how could I be fit to speak to you?'

'But I am your friend, Freddy! Of course you should have come to me. I might never have known of your distress had there not been this fortunate meeting.'

'It is what I prayed for,' he said simply, his voice seeming stronger for a moment. 'I could not come to you, it would not have been right. But if providence sent you to me – ah, then, it would be permissible to speak to you. That was what I believed. And I was right to do so, wasn't I? For here you are.'

'Here I am,' she said, and reached beneath the rug to take his hand. It was hot and moist and breathtakingly thin and she held it close but lightly for fear of hurting those sticklike bones.

'I have never stopped thinking about you, Tilly,' he said. 'I yearned – oh, you will never know how much – to know of you and how you were and what had happened to you.'

'Oh, as to that, I can tell you very shortly,' she said. 'I lead a quiet and insignificant life and –'

'Never insignificant. To me you are all the significance there is.'

She let that pass, feeling her face flush and glad of the shadow thrown by her parasol. 'You must not say so.'

'I tried to ask the tenants who took our house after we left how you were, but they would not speak to me. They were Alice's tenants, you see, in law, not mine, and she had told them tales of me that – well, it matters not a whit now.'

Again he stopped for some time, clearly marshalling his strength, and then began again, 'But they have left the house now.'

'I know,' she said. 'It has been empty for some time. I did wonder why.'

'I kept hoping for a while that perhaps I could return and live there myself. To see you and watch you and – well, it is not to be. I have been here in Brighton in the care of a doctor who is supposed to have answers to consumption, but he has not. I believe the time left to me is to be measured in days rather than weeks, or at best weeks rather than months.'

'Oh, please don't say so, Freddy.'

'I was always a realist and so, I believe, are you, Tilly. It is a foul disease and no chooser of its victims. It has its grip on me, and I must be ready for its final tightening. Please don't be distressed. Now I have found you again I feel – oh, so much better.'

She looked at him and shook her head. 'But why, Freddy? Why should that make any difference?'

'I learned to love you so quickly,' he said. 'It was only a short time, wasn't it, that we spent together? But your gentleness and — and your good sense — slipped into my heart and stayed there. They are there still.'

She laughed in spite of her anxiety about him. 'Oh, dear! I cannot believe all this. It is so absurd. I am a widow, a plain and ordinary enough person and yet first Jem and now you — I really cannot —' And again she shook her head.

'Jem?' His voice sharpened slightly in spite of its weakness, and she bit her lip at her own stupid tactlessness.

'He is but a friend, Freddy. Truly. He is a shopkeeper in Brompton who — well, he has a *tendresse* for me, I can't deny that. I have told him he is my friend and no more — although —'

'Although you are coming to like him well,' he said a little oddly, and she thought for a moment and then nodded.

'I could not lie on such a matter to you — not when you have — well, yes. In the past months his company has become very agreeable to me.'

He smiled, a faint ghost again of the old look. 'Well, I am glad to hear it. I am jealous of course and there is some of the old anger in me again, but I am glad you have him. I shall feel the happier knowing you are in good hands.'

'I am in my own hands, Freddy,' she said with a sudden edge to her voice. 'I have been these many years now. I have run my house, and reared my small boy and —'

'Oh, forgive me. I did not ask after his welfare. That beautiful baby. I can never forget how I first saw him — in your garden.'

She reddened again, 'You must not remind me of that day. I continue to be embarrassed.'

'You should not be. A mother and her baby is a beautiful sight.'

'Well, he is not a baby now.' She turned her head purposefully to look down the beach to the children who were clearly in her sight and busy about the building of the most massive of pebble boats. Sophie, her gown pulled up to her brown knees, was sitting in it in a very imperious manner as Duff toiled away at the side, shoring up the walls which persisted in collapsing. 'There he is. The two in the pebble boats — by the breakwater. The girl is the child of my tenant. The boy is mine — you see?'

He squinted and then managed to nod. 'Yes.'

'So you see, you must not consider me in need of care,' she said as lightly as she could. 'I may seem frail and — and small, but I am a strong person and well able to care for myself.'

'But how much more agreeable it is to be cared for,' he said and again coughed, though not so painfully this time.

'I wish I could care for you,' she said impulsively. 'Can you not come to my house and let me look after you there? We have good enough doctors in Brompton now. I can arrange matters to accommodate you easily.' Already she was surveying her house inside her head, and seeing how she could contrive it; if she put a truckle bed in Duff's room for herself she could care for Freddy in her own and —

'No!' He spoke so loudly that she almost jumped. For a moment he sounded like his old self again, but then he coughed once more. When he had recovered he looked at her very directly.

'I prayed to see you again not because I wished for you to be burdened with me but because I just wanted to be sure you were well and that — and that you did not remember me with disgust.'

'How could I? You were so very kind to me.'

'There were reasons enough for me to arouse disgust in you,' he said.

She shook her head. 'Do not think such a thing. I remember you entirely with gratitude.'

He was silent for a while, and then said carefully, 'It would be agreeable to see a little more of you, if I am able. Soon that

322

wretched nurse will be back and I will not be able to argue when she insists on returning me to my bed. But I will be here again tomorrow, Tilly. Each morning I am fetched here. It is my only pleasure and the doctor who is, like me, a realist, agrees it will make no difference to the outcome and permits it. Will you be here a while longer in Brighton? Can I see you here tomorrow, perhaps? It would be so wonderful to have something to look forward to with pleasure.'

'I am here for about three weeks altogether,' she said. 'We arrived only at the end of last week. I have another twelve days.'

'That, I rather think, will be enough.' He breathed it in what was now clearly a totally exhausted voice. 'Please, can you be here tomorrow? I ask no more.'

'Of course, Freddy,' she said gently and at last let go of his hand as the nurse came back very purposefully and looked at her sternly.

'Mr Compton ain't fit for chatters, Madam,' she said.

'I know,' Tilly said and stood up. 'But he is able to listen without effort and I hope he may find some pleasure in that.'

'Yes,' Freddy murmured. 'She understands, Mrs Friel. There is no need to be disagreeable with her.'

'I am never disagreeable,' Mrs Friel said in the most disagreeable voice possible. 'I wish only to do my duty as the doctors say I must for you.'

'Then you will take me back now, and bring me here tomorrow,' Freddy said. 'I will wait with pleasure for tomorrow, Tilly. I am so glad we met again.'

'And so am I,' she said gently, and watched Mrs Friel push the Bath chair away along the promenade.

Each day they met at the same time and at the same bench, where Tilly sat and waited for him with her parasol. Mrs Friel would secure the Bath chair and then waddle away about her own concerns. After a couple of days she was clearly well content to have this unexpected free time for herself. Freddy

323

would sit hunched in his blanket staring out under his hat brim and saying little, for each day he seemed a little weaker and a little less able to talk. She learned to chatter in a way that demanded nothing in the way of answer from him. She still felt guilty about the amount of speech he had wrung from his depleted frame on the first morning; she would not let him fritter away his strength so again.

But he seemed happy enough. He did not want to speak, was content to sit there beside her and feel her hand on his and listen to her talk. Sometimes a street musician came by with a barrel organ and the children would come running up the beach to dance to his tunes and play with his monkey. Freddy seemed to enjoy that, so she took to enticing the man to come by at the same time each morning. She did all she could to make the brief hour they shared together as pleasant as possible.

Being sure that Dorcas was not with her when he arrived seemed important to Tilly. She felt uneasily aware that Dorcas would be troublesome if she knew of his reappearance in Tilly's life; and she puzzled about that at first, lying in the rather lumpy bed in her lodgings, and came to the conclusion that it was Jem she was really worried about. Indeed Dorcas never rose before eleven if she could help it, now she had Tilly in Brighton to care for Sophie, and so was at no risk of appearing at the beach early enough to see Freddy. But Jem – Jem *did* worry Tilly. She could not see any logical reason why he should be distressed in any way by Freddy's reappearance; but there was always the possibility and because Jem had been kind to her and was a good friend she did not wish to hurt him in any way.

But, she reminded herself one night, it is no business of his. Freddy is dying. There can be no doubt of that. Why burden someone else with that knowledge if it is not necessary?

The matter was, however, taken out of her hands. The fifth day after Freddy had first found her on the promenade was a Sunday and she took the children to church, feeling that they had run quite wild enough all week and putting on proper clothes and being polite and quiet and well-behaved for a morning would be good for them. When they returned to their lodgings, just before half past ten, she was startled though not unduly surprised to find Jem waiting in her stuffy little sitting room on one of the landlady's uncomfortable, ugly chairs.

He jumped to his feet as she and the children came in and smiled broadly at her. 'I hope you are glad to see me? I took the first train there was – I said I might come one Sunday.'

'Indeed you did. And I am delighted to see you. Children, you may go upstairs and change into your beach clothes if you wish. I will take you there shortly.' And the children ran whooping joyously upstairs as she came into the sitting room, pulling off her gloves.

'Is all well at home?'

'Excellent,' he said and produced a number of messages from Eliza, none of which was particularly important. 'The only problem is that the roses on the bush at the end of your garden, which have been so stubborn and refused to show themselves, are suddenly most exuberant and you are missing them. I brought you some to make up for that.' He showed her the vase of full-blown cabbage roses on the small table in the centre of the room. 'I am afraid they are already falling though I brought you the most budlike I could find.'

'You are so thoughtful, Jem!' she said and reached out a hand to him and decided in a moment of impulse to explain all. She could not lie, even by omission. 'I must tell you of a most remarkable happening.'

He listened carefully as she spoke and then nodded slowly.

'I see – it is very sad.'

'Very,' she said and felt the tears prick her eyes and was surprised. So far she had not wept at all for Freddy and now, suddenly, she had a strong desire to do so.

'He is someone for whom you care a great deal,' Jem said. It was a statement rather than a question.

'He was my friend,' Tilly said. '*Is* my friend. No more than any friend, but a very good one.'

'I am your friend, Tilly,' he said. 'Is it the same as it is with me? I had hoped that you were beginning to care for me a little more than in simple friendship. When we parted at the station – well, I thought it possible. I have to ask you now if the friendship you feel for this sad man is the same.'

She tried to think and could not and put both hands to her face in some distress. He reached for her, his own face crumpled in sympathy and without seeming to think about it, put both arms about her and she, equally instinctively, let him do it, and set her hands against his chest and rested her head on them. She felt safe and comfortable and at last let the emotions that had been so well-controlled all week have their way. She wept.

It was not painful weeping. The tears came gently and easily and washed the pain from her, and after a few moments she sniffed hard and lifted her head and at once he let her go and stood back.

'Thank you, Jem,' she said from the depths of the handkerchief she had pulled from her waistband and was now using vigorously on her nose. 'It helps so to –'

'I know,' he said. 'I – well, there it is. I have my answer then.'

'Perhaps. But he is dying and –'

'I do understand. And I am sad for you.' She looked at him and could see the sadness there; but knew it was as much for himself as for Freddy.

'I must go,' she said. 'I am sorry. You are here just for one day and I – well, I cannot let him down, can I? It is, I believe, the only joy he has in the day. He'll be there in –' she glanced at the fob watch on her bodice, – 'ten minutes, yes. I must hurry.'

The children came down the stairs, whooping again, and she turned to them, glad of the distraction. There was a deal of fussing over sand shoes and the buttoning of breeches at the knee (Duff) and the polite arrangement of skirts (Sophie) and then they were clamouring at the front door to be away. She picked up her parasol and followed them.

'Will you come too, Jem? I would like to introduce you. If you wish.'

His shoulders lifted and his chin came up. 'Are you sure?'

'Of course I am. I will ask you, perhaps, after you have met him to – well, leave us be. He likes to listen to me chatter. We do not say much but it is all he can manage. You will see.'

'I'll play with the children,' he said, his voice was quite ordinary once more and she felt a wave of warmth for him rise in her. Such a kind, nice man, she thought. So very *good*.

The meeting was not as painful as she had feared. She had not precisely expected Freddy to be angry at Jem intruding on their special time together, but she had thought he might be suspicious. In the event his reaction surprised her, for he was clearly relieved to see Jem. An odd reaction, surely? she thought. 'Don't go away,' he whispered, after they had been introduced and he was looking up at Jem with close scrutiny. 'I would wish to speak to you.'

'I would not wish you to tire yourself,' Jem said. 'It is clear that you find it a little difficult to –'

'Then don't argue with me,' Freddy said, with a flash of laughter in his eyes and Jem grinned and sat down on the bench where Tilly was already ensconced with her parasol. She had put on a yellow muslin gown this morning, for it was as hot as ever, and a bonnet in pale straw trimmed with yellow roses. It had seemed important to her to make a real effort to look appealing in Freddy's eyes. Whether it mattered to Jem she did not think about at all.

Freddy looked at her now, and tried to smile. 'You are so pretty today,' he murmured. 'But go away for a little while, my dear.'

She gawped at him. 'Go away? Why?'

'I wish to speak to your friend Mr Leland,' Freddy whispered. 'Please, Tilly. Don't make me argue.'

She got to her feet at once, puzzled but obedient. 'If you insist. For how long?'

'I hope ten minutes will suffice. Mr Leland looks an intelligent person. He will not need more.'

Jem looked at her and lifted his brows in puzzlement, and the wraith of a chuckle escaped Freddy's lips.

'You will understand soon enough,' he managed. 'Please, ten minutes only, Tilly –'

She went, looking back over her shoulder as Jem bent closer to hear more clearly the words that Freddy was producing, clearly with great effort. Ahead of her on the beach, the children waved and gestured for her to come and look at their newest piece of pebble engineering, a carriage this time, and she waved back to them and set out across the stones, slipping and wincing on the painful edges.

She was surprisingly irritated. How dare those two men discuss a matter and exclude her? How typical! Even at death's door they still behave like men; and she let the anger slide through her, relishing it. It was a much less unpleasant emotion than the sadness about Freddy that had filled her all week.

Chapter Thirty-one

WHEN SHE RETURNED fifteen minutes later, the children came with her. They had fallen out over the design of the pebble carriage and Duff was sulky and Sophie furious about it. They came stumping along, one on each side of her, to the bench where Freddy and Jem still sat head to head, and she thought absurdly – now they'll be sorry. They'll have to pay attention to the children.

But as soon as she reached the bench Jem jumped up with real pleasure at the sight of the two cross children.

'Ah, there you are!' he said heartily. 'Now, children, I'm glad you're here for I have a plan and you will, I think, like it. I am going to take you to the end of the pier. There, you see? There's a man selling coconut ice and another selling oranges and there's to be a Punch and Judy show. I want to see that very much. I don't suppose you do, but I'd take it kindly in you if you'd keep me company while I enjoy it.'

The children were at once all smiles, their argument forgotten, and they set about tidying themselves with great enthusiasm. While they were doing it, Jem took Tilly to one side, to be out of Freddy's earshot.

'Tilly, this is going to be difficult. I – I may not tell you why, or how, but I beg you to think carefully of how you will respond to what will be asked of you. Don't say the first thing that occurs to you. I wish you to know that – oh, this is difficult – I wish you to know that I have no doubt you will do the kind and – the *kind* thing. Please don't think of me at all, whatever you do.'

She gaped at him and he nodded his head seriously and set his straw hat in place, and turned to the children and took them each by a hand. 'Now,' he said. 'I am in need of some preparation for the event I am to attend and the best preparation for me is to tell you the story of how Punch and Judy came to Brighton from Italy, where they were born. It happened like this. Once upon a time –'

They were away along the promenade, their faces upturned to Jem and she watched them, dissolving inside a little at the expression on Duff's face. He was rapt and clearly as happy as a boy could be, and she thought – may he never be less happy than he is at this moment. And knew that to be a foolish prayer, for he was but a little boy and had to grow up in a world that was cruel and in which good people died before their time.

She turned and looked at Freddy who was gazing at her with eyes now so deepset it seemed as though they could barely remain in his head. He looked, she thought as dispassionately as she could, like a dead person already. Surely, it is not possible for someone so thin, so consumed by fire, to cling to life like this? But he was clinging. Hard. He lifted a hand to beckon her with remarkable energy, considering his frailty, and obediently she sat down beside him.

'Tilly, I like your friend Jem very much,' he said.

She smiled. 'I do too. He is a kind and good man.'

'He is more. He is a wise man.'

'I am glad to hear you say so.' She was mystified now. 'But why?'

'Because he listened to what I had to say to him, and did not argue with me. I hope you will do the same.'

She frowned. 'I can't see, Freddy, what you might have to say to him that was of importance. You have never met him before today, and anyway you couldn't have known he would be here this morning. I didn't know myself that he was coming.'

330

'It's a strange thing,' he said and she was aware that his voice seemed less painful this morning. 'But providence, once she decides to treat you kindly, persists in her care for a while however wayward she may have been in the past. Just as she brought you here to me in Brighton, so she brought your friend Jem this morning. I would have said what I am to say to you anyway, but it comforts me greatly to have seen what a good man he is and to know that he agrees with my plan.'

'Your plan,' she said, giving up all attempts to understand and even wondering briefly if his disease had, as sometimes did occur she knew, invaded his brain. Was he talking like this from his condition rather than from rational thought?

'Yes. My plan.' There was a silence of the sort she had become used to during this past week in his company, as he gathered his strength again.

'My plan,' he began once more, 'is this. I would wish you, my dearest Tilly, to wed me.'

She gaped at him. 'Are you quite mad, Freddy?' she managed at last. 'Or did I hear you right.'

'You heard me right and I am far from mad. I am thinking sensibly indeed. Your friend Jem agrees with me. He had some doubts, of course, but I was able to dispel them as I am sure I will yours.'

'You asked Jem if — you asked his opinion of this plan, as you call it?' She stared at him aghast. 'Before you spoke to me?'

'Yes. You have no father and no brother and –'

'I have my own mind and my own control!' she said spiritedly, quite forgetting how fragile his hold on life was, and treating him as though he were as he had always been. 'By what right do you sit there and tell me that you have discussed a matter such as a proposal of marriage – a perfectly absurd proposal, I might add – with a man who is only a friend, however good a friend, before speaking to me of it? You take too much on yourself, Freddy, indeed you do!'

'I have so little time left that I have to.'

She was silenced by that and bit her lip. But not for long. 'It is not fair,' she burst out. 'You cannot use your sad situation to – to treat me so.'

He managed one of his smiles. 'I am being outrageous, am I not? But all is fair in love and war.'

'Freddy.' She leaned towards him. 'I am quite destroyed by what is happening to you, my dear. But I cannot possibly allow you to speak as you have of –'

'Hear me, Tilly,' he said with a sharp and commanding air, so loudly that she was taken aback and fell silent.

'Tilly, ever since I lost – ever since we said goodbye in your garden that day all those years ago, and I left you there with your baby at your breast, I have thought of you and longed for you. I knew, or believed at first, that it was a dream and it could never be. There was Alice, after all – but then Alice died, and for a little while, a very little while, I believed I might be well again myself and be free to come to you and court you as any man might. Well, it has not turned out so.'

His voice trailed away to a flutter and she held his hand and waited. She longed to jump in to tell him she had never ever thought of such a possibility; that even had he been well enough to speak to her after Alice's death she would not have entertained his proposal. She cared for him as a friend, of course she did, but no more. But how could she say all that to this desperately struggling creature beside her? She could not, so she held her tongue.

'But now I have found you again. Just in time.' His voice was back, like a flickering candle's wick finding a new pool of wax to burn. 'I have inherited Alice's property, Tilly, especially the house next door to yours. After Alice died, I went to Mr Cobbold and tried to change my will – I wished then to leave my property to you, including that house. But the way Alice's property was left by her father, it is not possible for me to will it out of my family. If I die married, Mr Cobbold agreed, I may leave the house to my wife. She is then, of course, my family. If I die unmarried, then whatever my will says the house must go to Alice's distant cousin.'

332

He looked at her with those huge sunken eyes. 'You understand? I wish to give this to you. You have suffered enough hardship. If you own another house, you may sell your own and live in the one next door – which will remain in trust for members of your family, of course – and no longer struggle to make a living letting rooms. Do you understand, Tilly? This will be a marriage of days only. I know that in my bones. Let me die happy, providing for you as someone I love. Alice's cousin is rich enough – he owns half Staffordshire! He will not be deprived by such an arrangement. Oh, dearest Tilly, my power is leaving me so fast. We cannot waste time. I have told my doctor of my plan and he says it may just be possible – he is making what arrangements he can for the necessary licence. Try to understand, my dear one.'

She understood, well enough. Too well. She tried all she could to explain how it would be anathema to her to marry a man simply to obtain his property, however dearly he wanted her to have it. She tried to make him understand that such an action was foreign to her nature in every way. She told him it was quite out of the question. But he clung to his determination with the same tenacity with which he clung to life; and whatever she said he stared at her and merely repeated, 'Dearest Tilly. Try to understand. Please let me die happy. Please, Tilly.'

Until at last both were exhausted and could only sit there amid the strolling holiday-makers in their bright summer gowns and hats, hearing the children on the beach shouting and playing and the distant sound of Mr Punch's shrill piping and the barrel organ's silly jigging tunes. Sit there in silence, staring at the sea.

It was as though she no longer had any control over what was happening to her. Jem came back with the children a half hour after the nurse had taken Freddy back to his doctor's establishment, bearing with him the promise that she would send her final answer that afternoon, and refusing to believe it

333

would be, as she assured him it would, a very firm 'No'. As the children ran back to the beach, all previous animosity quite forgotten, to rebuild their carriage, Jem came and sat beside her on the bench.

'It is a devilish position he has put you in, Tilly,' he said gently. 'I felt it too, and could do nothing about it. He is a dying man and has this notion so firmly in his head that it cannot be eradicated. To gainsay him would clearly be an act of cruelty. Yet to force you into his wishes would be an act of − well, I cannot find words for it.'

She was so enormously grateful for his understanding that she turned to him and seized both of his hands. 'What shall I do, Jem? I have been sitting here turning it over and over in my mind and I feel like a rat caught in a maze with no way out. Whichever way I turn, there he is, looking at me, and I know that is a matter of − of course, he will be looking at eternity. How can I not please him? Yet how can I? It is, as you say, the most devilish of traps.'

'I have been thinking too,' he said in a low voice. 'And I have to say to you what I said to him. Say "Yes", Tilly.'

She stared at him, the wave of gratitude that had filled her slipping away, like the last of the tide. 'You cannot mean that?'

'I am thinking as much of Duff as of you.'

'Duff? But −'

'He is offering you property that will be passed on in due course to Duff. This house, as I understand it, is not entailed precisely but left in a Trust that demands it "always remains in the family". And Freddy himself worked it out and the lawyers had to agree, the word "family" includes his wife and his wife's children. If you marry him, Tilly, as he wishes, this useful property devolves eventually on your son. You have I know been concerned for his future welfare.'

She closed her eyes and tried again to think clearly. It was true that she worried constantly over Duff's future. He was fatherless, and had no other relation apart from herself to care for him. If disease should strike her − and how much reminder

334

did she need of how possible that was in a young life than Freddy himself? – he would be left with little. He would lose his home for lack of an income to support it, and would have nowhere to go but an orphanage. A thought which sent a shudder through her. But if he were to own twice the present amount of property, he could keep his home and have money that could be invested shrewdly for his upkeep and future.

She opened her eyes and looked miserably at Jem. 'I feel dreadful,' she whispered. 'Quite dreadful.'

'I'm sure you do. It's part of the delicacy of your character, Tilly. It is one of the reasons that you are so – that I feel as I do about you, as well as why Mr Compton does. But you must override your natural delicacy for your child's sake. He deserves this.'

'Oh, Jem,' said Tilly, and she burst into tears.

She decided to say as little as possible to Dorcas of the truth of her situation. She had to tell her that she had some occupation on the next afternoon, for it was necessary for the children to be cared for and Tilly could not trust the rather sluttish and very disobliging landlady of her lodgings to watch over them. Jem himself had to be back in Brompton because of the shop – and was clearly torn apart by the fact that he was not free to stand close beside her and support her through what she knew would be a dreadful experience – and so she had no other choice. She lied as gallantly as she could.

Dorcas, listening to her tale of meeting an old friend and wanting to spend some time with her, said sweetly, 'Oh? A different old friend to the gentleman in the Bath chair?'

Tilly went scarlet. 'What do you know of –' And then stopped, understanding too late how foolish she had been. 'Oh, Sophie.'

'Indeed, Sophie. She tells me all that happens to her,' Dorcas said smugly. 'She is my little darling – she tells her Mamma *everything*.'

'Not so much your little darling that you wish to spend

much time in her company,' Tilly said with some acidity, but Dorcas laughed at that.

'Don't be so stuffy! I adore her and she me, but we do not need to live in each other's pockets! So, you are going off with your elderly beau, are you?'

'He is not a beau,' Tilly said hotly. 'That is, I mean –'

'Oh, don't bother to tell tall tales for me,' Dorcas said gaily. 'I don't mind what you do. And yes, I will take care of the children for this afternoon – tomorrow, is it? You have taken care of them often enough after all.'

'I'm glad you've noticed it,' Tilly snapped.

'Of course I have! But if you are good enough to do it, then I'd be a fool not to take advantage of your foolishness.' Dorcas was in a high good humour now, feeling she had caught Tilly out. 'Oh, don't look so sulky, Ma'am! I'll take the children. They'll have a splendid afternoon – I shall take them to tea at the Pavilion and we shall parade and gawp at the other people of fashion.'

'I doubt they'd enjoy that,' Tilly said a little scornfully, and again Dorcas laughed.

'Oh, they will. They will have ices and cakes for tea, and I shall take them on a carriage ride. They will adore it. You cannot deny that.' And Tilly couldn't. Duff had small interest in gawping at people of fashion, but a deep and abiding one in ices and cakes and carriage rides behind handsome high stepping horses.

'Well,' she said, unwillingly, at last. 'It is but one afternoon, I suppose.'

'Precisely,' said Dorcas and went away to take tea with her friends at the Assembly Rooms in Old Steyne, leaving Tilly to prepare herself as best she could for her second wedding day.

She took herself to the address Freddy had given her in a four wheeler cab, sitting silently in its dusty depths as it toiled up the hill on the far side of Montpelier Terrace, marvelling at the way the nurse, Mrs Friel, must have worked to push Freddy's

Bath chair. It was easier to think of that odd waddling shape struggling with the incline than of what lay ahead. She had decided only after much more talk with Jem that this was the only way to deal with it all; to pretend it was a matter only of the moment and to refuse resolutely to think of anything else. But it wasn't easy.

The doctor's establishment was a large yellow brick house of quite amazing modern ugliness, Tilly decided, when she alighted from the cab. The windows were carefully closed and the curtains drawn, even though it was again a hot and indeed rather sultry afternoon, and she went up the front steps and pulled the bell handle with a sense of foreboding.

Inside, the house smelled powerfully of lavender oil and soap and of another disagreeable odour about which she preferred not to think. She held her handkerchief firmly in one hand, so that she could bring it to her mouth at every opportunity and did so, though unobtrusively; she did not want to offend the people in the house, if she could avoid it.

The doctor, a man as round and rosy as his patient Freddy was cadaverous and grey, greeted her with a facial expression nicely balanced between celebration and woe.

'This is a generous action. Ma'am, a most generous action,' he said unctuously. 'These dying men take such notions, you know, and generally we try to disabuse them if we can, but Mr Compton — well, he would not be gainsaid. And if you are willing to stand beside him and go through with this form of marriage — well, it will do no harm. It is not as though it will be a true marriage in any sense, after all.' He smirked unpleasantly and looked at her sideways and she felt as though she had been touched by a dirty slimy hand, and lifted her handkerchief to her nose and pretended to blow it, to hide what she knew was a disgusted expression on her face.

'I am Doctor Beeston, by the by. I have made all the arrangements — you will find the vicar ready for you.'

He nodded to Mrs Friel, who had appeared out of the dimness, and she nodded back, quite unsmiling, and led Tilly to a door on the far side of the hall, which was a large area lavishly fitted with small tables bearing many ornaments. The door led out to a conservatory filled with plants and smelling, much to Tilly's relief, of leaf mould and growing things, and she straightened her shoulders and went in.

Freddy was in his Bath chair, but this time without his hat. His hair, which had been so strong and vigorous, had thinned and faded sadly and that added to his air of pathos, and she looked at the way he was dressed in a jauntily cut frock-coat over sparkling white linen and how it hung on his gaunt frame, and could have wept. The bravery of him, the joy in him, was palpable in the small steamy room and she smiled at him a little tremulously and then shifted her gaze to the other occupant.

'Afternoon, M'm,' he mumbled. 'James Ferrari at your service, M'm. Any impediment to this marriage?'

'I beg your pardon?' she said, taken aback.

'Got to ask you. The law. Got the special licence and all, but got to ask you any impediment.'

He was, she realized, less than sober. He was a thin man but had a protuberant belly thrusting against his cassock and his collar and bands were soiled, but she was too numb to care about any of that. It was all dreadful, quite, quite dreadful, and she thought suddenly and oddly of the brandy tantalus at home and how comforting it might be to take a glass, to deaden the way she was feeling. But her belly lurched nauseously at the idea, and she pushed it away. Brandy makes me ill, she thought, not better. I mustn't think about nasty things. Think of Duff. Think of Duff . . .

She thought of Duff throughout. She stood there beside Freddy, with the doctor and Mrs Friel hovering behind them as witnesses, as the Reverend Mr Ferrari gabbled his way through the service, and held out her hand obediently when told to so that Freddy could slip a ring on to it. It was too big and slithered on her finger and she thought with a sudden wildness – it is like me, lost and wandering and likely to fall off and disappear into perdition.

338

But she took a deep breath and controlled the panic and let the service run to its end, and when instructed bent and kissed Freddy's moist hot cheek. He looked at her with wide eyes and said in the faintest of breaths, 'Thank you, Tilly. Oh, thank you.'

The doctor was rubbing his hands together. 'We have arranged a small collation for you, Mrs *Compton*,' he said with beaming affability, and a most unpleasant air of roguishness as he said the name. 'Once the certificate is signed, we can perhaps — if you feel up to it, dear Mr Compton —'

'I shall sit and watch you,' Freddy said. And so he did. The vicar, who partook eagerly of the sherry that the doctor had provided, and Mrs Friel who was equally eager for the cakes and ratafia biscuits, said little, but the doctor made up for their silence by chattering on at a great rate about the weather and the local flora and fauna, and the healing waters of dear Brighton: 'Good Doctor Brighton, as it was once known and still should be, tee hee!' All the while Freddy watched and she sat next to him, an untouched glass of sherry beside her and her handkerchief clutched in one hand. It was as unlike a wedding as she could imagine, and quite the most extraordinary day of her life.

But she had done it, she prayed, for the right reasons. One day, she told herself, looking down miserably at Freddy beside her, who had drifted into an exhausted sleep and was lying with his head back in his chair and his eyes only partially closed so that a rim of white showed between the lids, one day I will forgive myself for what I have done here today. Oh, Duff, I hope you too will forgive me when you find out. I hope you will understand I did it for you. But I don't know if I will ever forgive myself.

Chapter Thirty-two

THE LEAVES WERE brown and curled and thick on the lawn in the back garden and the trees were almost bare before she could even begin to think about her situation. She had kept herself busy during these painful weeks by adding the making of new sheets for every bed in the house to her normal household duties and by dint of concentrating on every stitch she set, she was able to keep her mind away from her state of confusion.

She had told Jem when she went to the shop to buy the linen for the sheets that she needed time alone. He had looked for a moment as though he would never smile again but then managed, somehow, to compose himself and said gravely that he understood how she felt, but begged permission to visit her occasionally. But she refused him.

'I know you mean kindly, and I know that those times we spent together were agreeable. But all has changed. I cannot feel – I am different. It may seem absurd to say this, but I am. I need time to understand it all. I cannot find that time in the company of others.'

He looked stricken at that. 'I had hoped I was enough of a friend to be able to – well, let be. But I must tell you, Tilly, that I will not let you go on for too long. I wish you to understand that I have not accepted my *congé*.'

'I can't think about the future at all.' She was aware of how weary she felt, wanting to get home as soon as she might.

340

'Don't ask it of me.' And she went out into the street to pay her bill at Charlie Harrod's and then at Spurgeon's the butcher, leaving them both convinced she was ill, for she was so unlike her usual tranquil self.

The children had become subdued as the weeks went on. Dorcas was out a great deal, leaving the children to Tilly's care, but since they really took care of each other all day, being more or less inseparable, and relying on Eliza to see to their meals and to get them to bed, there was little for her to do with them. She did still always read to them each night and heard their prayers; but for the rest, she was left much alone. Eliza, too, seemed to have understood there was something amiss, about which even she might not quiz Tilly, and kept her own counsel.

But today was different. Today she had to think about how she would re-create her life and bring back to it some sort of peace. Mr Cobbold's letter begging permission to wait upon her had come the day before, and ever since, she had been as tightly strung as a violin. Now she stood at her drawing-room window looking out into the Grove, willing herself to think about Mr Cobbold's visit.

She knew of course what he was coming to tell her. Freddy had died three days after their wedding and had been buried in Brighton with just herself and the doctor and Mrs Friel to see him to his last resting place. As well as the sadness, she would remember the sheer discomfort of the day, for it was still and sultry in the extreme. The little cortège had moved through the dusty streets beneath threatening purple-clouded skies to the church; the horses pulling the hearse were streaked with sweat after only a few hundred yards. Her head ached under the heavy black straw hat and veil she had thought it proper to wear, as sweat ran down her own face to mingle with the tears she shed for Freddy. The trees they passed stood with an air of exhaustion as their leaves drooped in the heavy air. In the churchyard the gravediggers stood leaning wearily on their shovels as the vicar, seeming anxious and distracted, gabbled his way through the service. The earth she picked up to throw on the coffin was dry and hard through her glove and she opened her fingers over the open grave stiffly, shrinking with a *frisson* of horror at the rattling sound it made on the wood; and then jumped as the first flash of lightening whitened the churchyard. It was followed a moment or two later by the grumble of thunder.

Burying Freddy in a storm seemed fitting, somehow, for his re-emergence in her life, so short a time ago, had indeed been as violent as any storm could ever be. She stood in the churchyard after the others had gone, watching the grave-diggers hide Freddy for ever. She was glad to be soaked through by the rain which had come at last to cool the air. It seemed a small price to pay for the guilt she felt about Freddy, and the bequest she knew he had made; and at last she had turned and left him there.

Back in London with the children she had locked herself in her own purdah. But now the will had been proved, probate had been granted, and she must consider her next step.

Mr Cobbold was later than he had said he would be. It was now two in the afternoon, when he had assured her he would wait on her at half past the hour of one, and she gnawed her lower lip, wondering what might be amiss. She tried to push away the memories that had flooded her since she had been forced to prepare her mind for this visit.

She had stayed with Freddy on their wedding day until very late. Mrs Friel had put him to bed once the strained and painful merrymaking was mercifully over and Tilly had gone to his room to sit beside him. He had lain there, so reduced in body that it seemed his head hardly made a dent in the pillow, and she had held his hand. He had smiled at her briefly and then closed his eyes and so had remained for the rest of the time she was there. She had not been able to tear herself away, not because of her affection for him, but because of her embarrassment at not knowing what to do. To wake him to say good-night seemed impossibly cruel; to go without saying good-night seemed impossibly ill-mannered. So, she sat and waited and had herself fallen asleep in the chair and woken with a start at four in the morning. He was still in the same position, apparently asleep, and now she threw her doubts away and left him to creep down the stairs in the dark and silent house and let herself out into the street.

She could remember it still. The sky was already greying gently in the east, though it wanted more than an hour to sunrise, and the salty reek of the sea rose to her from the foot of the hill. She had set out to walk to her lodgings, listening to her heels clacking lightly on the cobbles and knowing herself to be the only soul abroad in the blessedly cool air, perhaps the only soul in the entire world. She had lifted her chin to the sky and whispered to it — I had to do it, I had to. What else could I have done? But there was no comfort to be found in the silence, not so much as a bird chirping sleepily. The dawn chorus would have comforted her, told her that she had acted as she should but it was too early for that.

She had slipped into her lodgings with great stealth, grateful for the key her landlady had grudgingly allowed her to have, and crept upstairs to bed. She had stopped for a moment at the children's bedroom door and then looked in. Duff had been sleeping as he always did, sprawled out, the blankets in a tangle at his feet and his hands flung up to curl, with the heartbreaking vulnerability of childhood, on the pillow on each side of his head. She had gently tugged the blankets back to cover him and then looked across the room to the other little truckle bed where Sophie slept when she came to stay with Duff, which was frequently. She was lying tidily as she always did, her hair spread sumptuously on her pillow and her hands neatly on the sheet that covered her, and the blankets folded back carefully at her feet. Clearly she had been too warm when she went to bed, and Tilly hesitated, wondering whether to risk waking her by covering her. And then had shivered a little herself in the cool of the morning and so pulled the blanket up gingerly and covered Sophie, who turned her head and opened her eyes briefly but closed them again immediately and slept on. When Tilly at last went to bed herself, she lay awake watching the sun rise over Brighton and pondering her future as Mrs Compton instead of Mrs Quentin.

She had, however, decided since coming back to London not to use her new name. There was no reason why she should, she told herself. To make a point of announcing it would cause much conjecture and she shrank from that. It was easier to remain as she was. Not until the letter addressed to her as Mrs Compton had arrived had anyone in Brompton, apart from herself and Jem, known of what had happened in Brighton. She had to tell Eliza then of course, but she could be trusted.

She had brought the letter to Tilly in puzzlement and Tilly had taken it, and sighed and bade Eliza sit down and had told her all about it. Eliza had listened and then stood up and straightened her apron and said matter-of-factly, 'Well, Mum, I don't see you could have done any different, seein' as how the poor gentleman was, God rest his poor soul. Will you let me try out some curried salmon for this evening's dinner, Mum? I've got a new recipe from the *Englishwoman's Domestic Magazine* as I think you'll all like. I got the left-over salmon from yesterday you see, and it won't keep good much longer than today. That veal Spurgeon sent will keep perfectly till tomorrow.'

Tilly's gratitude to Eliza had never been greater than at that moment and she smiled tremulously at her and said, 'Yes, that will do very well. Thank you, Eliza.' Eliza had patted her shoulder in what others might have regarded as a familiar way, but which both knew for what it was — a gesture of affection, and Tilly wept for a little while after she left and felt the better for it. Dear good Eliza!

Tilly bent forward to look out of the window and there was Mr Cobbold, in his sombre clothes and tall ugly hat, coming round the corner. She felt a sudden wave of anxiety, and went to her favourite corner beside the fireplace, now filled with a paper fan and an arrangement of ferns, and waited.

344

He seemed shrunken, she thought when she first looked at him closely. He had been a man of rotund appearance, but since being caught up in matters evangelical, clearly his interest in such earthly matters as satisfying a healthy appetite had vanished. He stood in her drawing-room looking half the man he had been and sour of face with it, and bowed to her.

'Good afternoon, Mrs Compton.'

'If you please, Mr Cobbold,' she said firmly. 'I choose to use the name by which I am best known. I did not live for any time with Mr Compton and it is not, I think, necessary for me to take his name.'

'It is customary, Mrs −'

'It may be,' she said firmly, still feeling the tightness of apprehension in her and puzzled by it; why should she be afraid of this man? He was only disagreeable, after all. 'But I prefer to have my way in this.'

'Very well, Ma'am,' he said and smiled involuntarily. Clearly he would never address her by name, ever again. Well, that suited her well enough. 'I have come to you with news of your − ahem − husband's will.'

'I had expected as much,' she said. 'He told me of its contents before he died, of course. I am not likely to be unduly surprised.'

'I must for all that apprise you of its contents and take instructions on the next steps. You will, I imagine, be considering a plan that involves selling this house, since you are not free to sell the adjoining one.'

She was nettled. Freddy had told her that she would not be free to sell, and that the house that had been Alice's must be passed on to a member of her family, just as it had been left to him as a member of Alice's, and of course she should have thought about it by now. But she hadn't, and this man had no right to point out to her that she had been lax. So she snapped at him without stopping to think, her irritability fed by the lingering apprehension she still felt.

'I do not see why I should sell this house, unless I choose to. And anyway, perhaps I have other plans.'

'I hope you have, Ma'am,' he said with a sort of dry triumph. 'Since I must remind you that this house bears precisely the same embargoes that the one adjoining does. You are permitted to change the interior and the usages of the house in any way you choose, but you must not give it or sell it to anyone. It came to you from your mother's estate, and must be passed on to your issue in due course. So you have two houses, Ma'am, each the twin of the other. Your esteemed father and his neighbour might well have discussed their plans and ideas for the future; I do not know. But I can tell you that Mr Spender and Mr Kingsley were of a mind in this. You cannot sell either house, ever. An expensive pair of properties, hmm? For these of course, must be carefully maintained. They will cost you more than you are likely to earn from them.'

She was dumbstruck and stared at him and he clearly enjoyed that, for now he came further into the room and, uninvited, sat down and opened the small case he had been carrying under one arm and took out some documents.

'It is not perhaps as grim as you fear, however.' He seemed to say this with some regret. 'Mr Compton's will also leaves you some money. There is not a great deal; his – ahem – first wife was the one who had the money in the marriage and he was not a sensible man. He permitted her to retain full control of her inheritance after her marriage.'

'And why not?' flashed Tilly, finding her tongue at last, and Mr Cobbold smiled sourly.

'Society will come to a pretty pass if husbands lose control of their families' finances, Ma'am, and so I tell you. See what harm has already been done by this nonsense of allowing females to dictate what will happen to their houses! Their fathers were fools to leave their properties to women who could not find husbands who knew the right way to go about matters. It never does for women to control their own incomes for they are well known to be capricious and extravagant.'

'That is nonsense, Mr Cobbold,' Tilly said through tight lips. 'And well you know it. Many are the households where the wit of the woman and the good sense she displays in dealing with the household's income is vital to the health of that household. And I, in running my small affairs here, am far from extravagant. However, I do not wish to discuss your views on this. Merely tell me what you have to tell me and we may be done.'

He looked pleased with himself, aware that he had touched her on the raw, but contented himself with an inclination of his head.

'Very well. The sum of money that Mr Compton had to leave was seven hundred pounds. It will not go far, of course, but it is yours and quite unencumbered. The fortune that had been Mrs Compton's — the first Mrs Compton — was some twenty-five thousand pounds, a considerable sum. She left that to her cousin in Staffordshire. I tell you this merely out of general interest of course. It is no direct concern of yours.'

'So there was no need to tell me,' Tilly said tartly. 'Is there anything else?'

He tightened his nostrils. 'The cousin, Mr Egbert Spender, is not entirely pleased that the house here in Brompton Grove has gone out of their family, as he sees it.'

'Then he must be displeased, I am afraid, and live with his displeasure as best he can.' Tilly got to her feet. 'Since Freddy made his decision and that is the end of it.'

'I wish only to advise you that he considered going to court to seek to overturn Mr Compton's will on the grounds that it was made under duress,' he said smoothly and she gaped at him.

'Duress? *Duress?* When it was I who — that is outrageous! I will not tolerate such a —'

'I have assured him it is not so, Mrs — um — Ma'am,' Mr Cobbold said. 'I am well aware of the fact that all the decisions were made by Mr Compton of his own free will. He came to me well before he met you again to attempt to leave you his possessions. It was I who had to point out to him that he had no title on the house here in Brompton Grove, and I who further pointed out to him that only if you were his wife would he be able to make that provision to you. So I had to advise Mr Spender that there was no question of any grounds – to my knowledge of course – for him to seek to overturn Mr Compton's will. But I believe it is best if you know he bears a certain animosity towards you. It is understandable.'

'Understandable?' Tilly said with some bitterness. 'I did not want Mr Compton's bequest, I can assure you, but it seems to me disgraceful that Mr Spender, who I am told already owns a large part of Staffordshire and has recently inherited twenty-five thousand pounds into the bargain, should grudge me this far from massive piece of property.'

'If you did not want the inheritance, Ma'am,' Mr Cobbold said in a deceptively soft voice, 'why did you agree to wed him? He was in such a parlous state of health that it seems to me –'

'I dare say, Mr Cobbold,' she said shortly. 'That you could never understand the needs and desires of a dying man and how a woman such as I might feel obliged to defer to them.'

He looked sceptical. 'And the inheritance matters not a whit, then?'

'Not for myself,' she said and then could not bear to be dishonest, even to this dislikable man. 'Although I do have to think of my fatherless son, of course.'

'Ah!' He seemed satisfied and got to his feet. 'Am I to understand then, Ma'am, that you will let the adjoining house? If so perhaps you will need our services.'

'Oh no, Mr Cobbold. I will not need your services at all,' she said, grateful for the chance to be so direct. 'In fact I have decided that I must take all my affairs out of your hands and deal with someone more convenient.' She considered fleetingly the possibility of adding 'and more agreeable' but her innate good manners forbade her. 'Since it is so far from here to the City and Leadenhall Street, I would be grateful therefore if you could send me all documents and details of your bill so that I can make my new arrangements. Good afternoon, Mr Cobbold.'

He looked at her with his eyes narrowed and his face expressionless, and then turned and went, only stopping when he reached the door.

'Good afternoon, Ma'am. I do of course wish you well, in all Christian charity. I must warn you, however, that –'

'I am not concerned with warnings, Mr Cobbold,' she said icily. 'Good afternoon.'

He left and she took a deep shuddering breath. If he had embarked on one of his hell and damnation tirades, she told herself, she would have been driven to distraction and might have done or said something she would regret. Her gratitude that he was gone was all she had to sustain her for a moment and she went back to her chair and sat there, her head resting back on the brocade upholstery, slowly trying to regain full control of herself.

But not for long, because not twenty minutes later her drawing-room door opened and Dorcas was standing there.

'I must talk to you,' she said in a hard and very direct manner and Tilly snapped her eyes open and looked at her. She was wearing one of her newer toilettes; a handsome gown in the richest purple surmounted by a fur pelisse which looked very much to Tilly's admittedly inexpert eye as though it were made of sables, which she was pulling off as she came into the warmth of the firelit drawing-room.

'Is it important, Dorcas? I have a headache – or, well not precisely but there are matters on my mind that I must deal with.'

'I too have matters on my mind,' Dorcas said and threw the pelisse on to a sofa where it lay like a sleeping animal, and then collapsed into the other armchair with a soft swish of her skirts. The gown was silk and Tilly found herself thinking: she is spending so much on clothes, it is amazing she has time to wear them all.

'The subject I must discuss with you is difficult, Tilly, but I have no choice in the matter. I am driven – well, you will see. Now, tell me first what Mr Cobbold came to see you about this afternoon. And then I will tell you what I intend to do.'

'Tell you – but that is no concern of yours!' Tilly sat up very straight and stared at her, amazed. 'How dare you ask me to –'

'Oh, Tilly, do stop your fussing!' Dorcas said testily. 'I know all that is happening! I know about that ridiculous matter of your wedding in Brighton and more besides. You seem to forget that my Sophie is a child of great intelligence who notices things. And that she tells her Mamma everything.' She smiled briefly. 'So, let us have no fuss, I do beg you. Tell me why he was here.'

Chapter Thirty-three

'I WILL NOT TELL you anything at all,' Tilly said with some spirit. 'I don't even know how you knew he was here.' Again Dorcas sighed.

'Will you never understand me, Tilly? I listen, I pry and I watch! I saw him arrive — and if you will not tell me, I will tell *you* and you may correct me. If you can. He said that the house next door which you have inherited from your Frederick Compton is part of the family property of his first wife, Alice Spender. Am I right? Yes. And that you may not sell the house but only use it in your lifetime. After that it may be left to Duff.'

Tilly was stunned and could hardly speak. 'But, but —'

'Am I *right*?' Dorcas sounded impatient.

Tilly found her voice. 'But Sophie could not possibly have known that! It is beyond her comprehension anyway. She could not have told you —'

'No, about the house she did not tell me. She knew only that Mr Compton wanted to marry you. She told me all about the old man in the Bath chair and all the things she heard you say to him. As I say, she is a noticing sort of child.'

'You should not encourage such spying tricks, even if you use them yourself! She is but a child, and it is your duty to teach her otherwise. I could not conceive of my Duff ever behaving so. If he tried to tell me matters that did not concern him I would give him very short shrift.'

'Which is why I am sitting here as your tenant and you are sitting there as a landlady,' Dorcas said and smiled, 'and why my Sophie will go further in the world than your Duff. Oh, it is no special trick of my darling Sophie that told me this much. It is the man I have been seeing these past months.'

She dimpled delightedly and Tilly marvelled at how lovely she looked. However angry Dorcas might make her, however much she distracted her, there could be no question in Tilly's mind that Dorcas was a lovely creature to look at, and she was not at all surprised to hear that she had a man in her life again.

'I cannot see how any man you know is of my concern,' she said at length and Dorcas smiled again.

'He has lived in these parts for some time. He knew the Spender family and spoke to me of them. That's all. Then when Sophie told me of your beau in Brighton, well, I began to be interested. How could you, of all women, have a secret follower? And I thought, let us find out what we can. It was not difficult, dear Tilly. To sit there in the middle of the crowds as you did made you very visible. I stood myself and listened to you talk, out of your sight I agree, but you were so absorbed you never noticed me.'

The apprehension that had filled Tilly earlier thickened and clotted inside her. She felt heavy and dreary in a most unpleasant way and she sounded it when she spoke. 'How can you bear to be so underhand?' she said. 'Why are you so –'

'As to that, Tilly, I must live by my wits. I cannot luxuriate, as you may, in being a good respectable person. That takes great security and peace of mind. For my part I have always had to fight for everything and never had peace of mind! First I had to fight my mother and then I had to fight the world. Now I have to fight you. It is not, you must understand, a personal matter.' She set her head to one side and smiled winningly at her. 'I like you, dear Tilly! I really do. I liked you when you were a silly infant and so gullible I could tell you the moon was made of blue cheese and you expected to eat it.

352

But even though I like you, I cannot forget the need to take care of myself. And if that means that I must make use of my knowledge of your affairs to my own ends, well, so be it.'

Tilly was sitting straighter, the tide of fear slowly receding. At least she now knew where she was. Dorcas was about to make some sort of bargain with her. She would make an offer of some deviant kind and try to beguile her into accepting it. Well, she would not and there was an end of it.

'I have, as I say, met a most interesting gentleman.' Again Dorcas dimpled, this time in a self-satisfied way. 'He is a very charming and agreeable gentleman.'

'I am glad to hear it,' Tilly said and waited.

'He has a plan to make us some money.'

'Us? You are to wed then?' For a moment hope lifted in her. Was Dorcas about to leave her house and get a home of her own? Could there be freedom from this ever difficult woman in the future for her?

'As to that, I cannot say at present.' Dorcas was sharper now, and Tilly knew she had hit a raw nerve. 'It is business we discuss at present. He says that since the Exhibition people have learned a new taste for going out and about, but although there have always been clubs for gentlemen, places they may go to eat their dinners and be relaxed and comfortable, there are no such places for ladies as well. It is our intention to create such an establishment.'

Tilly lifted her brows. 'A place where ladies and gentlemen may dine together? But that is possible in a hotel. Or —'

'Or, you were about to say, a house of assignation? Yes, it is possible in both such establishments for ladies to dine. But there are no respectable clubs where the two sections of society may enjoy a meal and a little gambling perhaps, all in a relaxed and comfortable milieu.' The word tripped off her tongue easily and Tilly thought, somewhere at the back of her mind — this man she is spending her time with is an educated fellow. She never used to speak so.

'So?' she said.

'So,' said Dorcas. 'We are to open one. In Knightsbridge.'

'I see. And what has this to do with Mr Compton's and my house next door?'

'Oh, a great deal.' Dorcas almost purred. 'It will take some time for us to establish our club, and even when we do we will need all the available accommodation for our customers. I must go on living here for a long time yet.'

'Oh,' said Tilly and her hopes melted and vanished like snowflakes at noon.

'But,' Dorcas said sunnily, 'I shall not be able to pay any rent, since all my available money is to be invested in our establishment.'

There was a silence and Tilly said stupidly, 'What?'

'I told you. After this month, no more rent.'

'But you cannot possibly – you must pay! How can I let you have rooms unless you pay for them?'

'You just let me have them,' Dorcas said. 'It is very easy.'

'But why? For what possible reason can you expect me to provide for you, with no recompense at all?'

'I told you.' She spoke as if to a singularly foolish child who would not learn its A B C. 'I am to open an establishment for ladies and gentlemen with Andrew – with my friend. I need all my money – *all* my remaining money – for that.'

Tilly shook her head. 'It is out of the question. There is no reason I can see why I should.'

'There is every reason,' Dorcas said sharply. 'Mr Egbert Spender is one of them.'

'Mr – what do you know of him?'

'That he would if he could overturn the will that gave you the house next door.'

'He cannot. I am – was married to Freddy and even Mr Cobbold agrees that the house was left to me as I in turn may pass it on to Duff. Oh, Dorcas, don't be stupid. Why else do you suppose I agreed to such a marriage but for Duff?'

Dorcas shrugged. 'I don't know. I thought it one of your nonsenses. The man had been kind to you once, I supposed, and you could not refuse him. You are very easy to push along the road of others' choice, Tilly.' She laughed merrily. 'Why, I am doing it now, am I not?'

'Not this time,' Tilly said grimly. 'Oh, no. Not this time.'

'I think I am.' Dorcas was serious now. 'I can make it possible for Mr Spender to challenge that will, you see. Successfully.'

'I have my marriage certificate from Freddy,' Tilly said. 'Mr Cobbold has agreed that it is quite legal.'

'Oh, it is a legal document, no doubt. But is it a legal marriage?'

Once more the chill of fear was gathering inside Tilly. 'Of course it is! Or rather was.'

Dorcas shook her head. 'It is of itself legal, that document. But the marriage — ah, that is something else.'

Tilly shook her head, weary now. 'You speak in riddles.'

'Do I? Perhaps so. Well then, let me put it in clear terms to you. Did you and your Freddy ever share a bed? Did you make the beast with two backs?'

'He was dying!' Tilly cried. 'The man was in despair! Such a question to ask. You are a disgusting creature, Dorcas, and I do not shame to tell you so. You lack every attribute of decent womanhood.'

'I'm glad to hear it. Indecent women like me do much better for themselves. Oh, Tilly, you stupid creature! If you did not share the normal experience of a married pair with him then the union is unconsummated and may be set aside in law. If Mr Spender knew of the truth of that marriage do you not think he would take you to court as fast as may be?'

Tilly stared at her, this time totally unable to speak and Dorcas leaned back in her chair and laughed delightedly.

'Tilly, my dear, I have but to tell Mr Spender, through my dear friend Andrew, that your marriage was unconsummated and you lose your house. Now, I don't think you'll want to do that. For Duff's sake, if not for your own.'

'I don't believe you,' Tilly said after a moment. 'That cannot be true.'

'But I assure you that it is. And anyway, how are you to find out if it is not? If you enquire about such a matter, do you not think that people will immediately consider why you are asking? And ask questions themselves? And is it not inevitable that such questions will come to the attention of Mr Spender? Oh, Tilly, do be sensible. I hold the whip hand in this matter. You can do nothing.'

Tilly's head was spinning. To let the house go entirely would be no loss to her. She had her own house; what did she want with another which, as Mr Cobbold said, would be costly to upkeep? Let this woman threaten and try her menaces; she, Tilly, had but to sit still and refuse to listen and that would be an end of it.

Suddenly the door flew open and the children burst in, Duff first, and Sophie trailing a little behind.

'Mamma,' he cried. 'Oh, Mamma, there is a puppet show in the park, just like Mr Punch and Judy at the seaside! The muffin man came by and he told us. He said it is a rare treat for they never come in winter time, and it is the best fun. Oh, Mamma, take us to the park, please take us. Sophie wants to go too, don't you Sophie? She wants to go so badly, Mamma, so we must, please, please, please!'

'Hush,' Tilly said. 'Don't shout so, Duff. It is not necessary. Now, wait a moment. You wish to go to the park?'

'Oh yes, and I asked Eliza but she can't for she has the cooking and says anyway it will soon be dark, and we may get there and find the man gone but I do so want –'

'Eliza is right,' Tilly said, and got to her feet. 'No, I am sorry, Duff. No. There is no need to chatter on. I have said no and no it is. Off you go now and play by the fire in your room until bath and bedtime. It is absurd to speak of the park now – it is almost four o'clock.'

'Oh, Mamma!' he cried, but she held up her hand and he subsided and Sophie, who had said nothing but was still standing by the door, looked at her mother.

'*My* Mamma will take us if I ask her,' she said and her voice was very collected and clear. 'Won't you, Mamma?'

'Indeed, I won't,' Dorcas said and smiled at her daughter. 'But I will take you to the pastry cook's shop in Brompton and buy you some jam tarts. That will be just as agreeable, will it not?'

Duff whirled and looked at her eagerly. 'Will you, dear Aunt Dorcas, will you? I would like that above all things!'

'I am sure you would.' Dorcas got to her feet and stretched, catlike, and then picked up her pelisse. 'Well, Tilly, I will take the children to have their jam tarts. You may stay here and think of all I have said. It is very simple, is it not? And think how delighted the children will be. They will have each other now as playmates – and for always. Duff's future is what you have considered, I know. I shall speak to you again at dinner, dear Tilly. Now children, away to fetch your coats, or there will be no time for jam tarts!'

She was gone, closing the door behind the eagerly chattering children and Tilly sat there in her now rapidly darkening drawing-room, for the fire had died low at the same time as the sun had given up its short stay in the winter sky, and tried to collect her thoughts. It was very difficult to do so.

By the half hour before dinner time she had exhausted all possibilities. Whichever way she turned, she faced yet another insuperable hurdle. Refuse to be intimated by Dorcas's threats and Duff would lose his future security. Agree to let her stay without paying rent and their income would be sorely diminished, and she would not be able to restore it by letting the rooms to someone else. There seemed so little remedy.

Even when she began to consider what she might do about the adjoining house, she found herself baulked. If she let it for the rent it would fetch, that would give her some income of course, but would it be enough? In the years since Alice and Freddy had decorated it and made it fresh and new there had obviously been deterioration. No doubt any new tenants would demand a repairing lease from her and she would have to spend money she could ill afford on doing it up. It would swallow much of the seven hundred pounds Freddy had left her.

It was then that the idea came to her. There was no getting rid of Dorcas, that was clear. She had to stay, whether Tilly liked it or not. Duff could not have his future security taken from him. She had acted against all her deeper instincts in order to obtain it for him; to let Dorcas beguile her out of it now would be more than she could bear.

But she could earn more from the adjoining house than letting it to a single tenant; and she began to make some drawings and calculations on a piece of paper from her small escritoire, remembering as she did the details of that house. Her visits there had been few, but the memory of them was engraved in her mind as deeply as acid engraved steel.

When she had completed her calculations she went down to the kitchen where Eliza, with both her assistants being chivvied from place to place, was happily sweating over her dinner.

'I done the curry, Mum,' she announced as soon as Tilly appeared in the doorway. 'A few onions and as good a sauce as you'll taste anywhere, and I do beg you'll try it. Now, here's a clean spoon — Lucy, get a plate at once — hurry now, you snail!'

She settled Tilly at the scrubbed table and set the spoonful of curry on the plate the panting Lucy fetched and then stood back to watch her as she tasted it. It was excellent and Tilly said so.

'There!' said Eliza in high satisfaction. 'Did you hear that, you two? You do as I teach you and you'll make cooks yet. If you wake your ideas up a bit.'

'I think, Lucy, that you and Kate may take yourselves up to your room for a little while to rest before you must set about the dining-room. I wish to speak to Eliza,' Tilly said, and Eliza, torn between wanting her acolytes there to dance attendance and gratification at being needed as confidante, nodded and muttered gruffly at them, 'Off you go!' and then at Tilly's invitation sat down at the table beside her.

'I have a plan, Eliza, that will involve a great deal of work for you,' she said. 'It will not be easy, but I cannot think of a better way to go forward.'

'Anything you wants to do, Mum, and I'll do it. You know that.' Eliza folded her arms on the table and looked at Tilly expectantly. 'Well?'

In the shortest words she could find Tilly told her of the house next door and Eliza opened her eyes wide and pursed her lips at the news. 'We got two houses? Well, fancy that!'

'I could let it to tenants as it used to be, to one family you understand, but that would not give me enough income from it, to be candid. It will need repairs and care and that costs a good deal. Tenants of the family sort are rarely, in my estimation, of sufficient value. But if,' here she paused. 'If I spend some money on making the sort of alterations inside which we had done when Miss Cynthia came to join the Misses K and F, I estimate we could make for ourselves room for at least eight tenants, depending on whether they wanted sitting rooms or not. The dining-rooms of the two houses march, do they not? The one next door is the mirror of this one, so we may cut right from one to the other and make a dining-room large enough for all to sit and share dinner. I could stop just letting rooms and providing breakfast, you see, and offer them all they could wish for. The district has changed so much of late that there seems to be much demand for such accommodation, and I could, I think, make a very genteel large house out of this pair. It would look the same from outside, of course. That would be important. But here inside it would be one establishment with doors from one to the other. What do you think?'

'I'll need a sight more help, Mum,' Eliza said doubtfully, looking at her sketches. 'And they'd have to have their own rooms 'n' all.'

'I have allowed for that, Eliza. See? There at the top of the other house. There's plenty of room there.'

Eliza looked and nodded and slowly a smile curled her lips

and filled her eyes. 'I'd really be a housekeeper then, Mum, eh? I could wear a housekeeper's black dress and no apron and have the keys at my waist, couldn't I? And take the trouble from you.'

Tilly smiled and touched the raw red hand in front of her. 'Indeed you could, Eliza.'

'Then you do it, Mum. It sounds a good use of the house to me. If it's all right for you to do it. You never know with building works, do you?'

'I agree,' Tilly said and folded her piece of paper neatly. But she was not thinking of building work. First she had to deal with Dorcas.

Chapter Thirty-four

JEM WAS CLEARLY uneasy about her request and she could not blame him. To ask him to be underhand was abhorrent to her, and she said so.

'But who else can I ask, Jem? You are the best friend — indeed, I think the only friend — I have to whom I could turn. And who might know how to go forward on this matter.'

'If I seemed uncertain, Tilly, you must not think it an unwillingness to help you. I would, as you know, do all I could for you. It is just that it is not precisely my way to — to —' He shook his head unhappily and his voice trailed away.

'To pry. I know,' she said. 'But how do you fight such an opponent as Dorcas except with her choice of weapon?'

He straightened his shoulders. 'You are right, of course. I don't know of anything else you could do. It is outrageous that you should suffer so. If I could take all these burdens from you, Tilly, you know I would. If I were your — well, if I were closer to you it might be easier.'

She looked at him and felt a wave of weariness, and the thought came welling up; it would be so comfortable to stop worrying, to stop having to struggle, to have a husband to whom I could turn and say, 'You do it, my dear,' and go back to being peaceful. But I can't do that. I married Freddy for all the wrong reasons and I can't do the same to Jem. He is too good and too kind.

She managed a smile. 'Not now, Jem, please.'

He was all compunction. 'I'm sorry, that was — well, now, let me see what we can do. You say she did not tell you this man's name?'

'Only his first name: Andrew. It seems to me that as a man of business in these parts you will know other men of business. It is like that, isn't it? People who share interests flock together?'

'We're on good terms, most of us here in Brompton,' Jem said. 'I can't pretend to be the close companion of my competitors, of course. Colonel Nichols and his wife are not precisely — well, you will understand. But otherwise, yes. Charlie is my very good friend and so are Mr Spurgeon and Mr Potticary at the chandlery shop.'

'Precisely so. If you ask about, it surely should be possible to find out about any business in Knightsbridge, which is near enough to be of interest to you all? If this man has found suitable premises for the club Dorcas says they are to open, and is a man of some standing, as I imagine he must be, then surely the people in trade in the neighbourhood will know of him?'

'It is very likely,' Jem allowed.

'Well, if you can find out who he is, then perhaps —'

'Then perhaps you can threaten him?'

'No!' she cried. 'Oh, no Jem. I don't even wish to speak to him! It is the last thing I would do. I want only to have this information so that I can — oh, it's a dreadful thought but I must confess it — so that I can threaten Dorcas. I have no other defence, Jem.'

He closed one hand over hers. 'You don't need to apologize to me, Tilly. You explained and I fully concur. You are doing this only because you must. Very well. We shall discover all there is to be discovered.' He laughed then, a rueful little sound. 'I don't know which I would prefer. To find out he is a rogue and a vagabond so that we might run him out of the district and leave your Dorcas with sufficient funds to continue to pay you her rent as she should, or to discover him to be the soul of probity so that she will be afraid of – well, let's see what there is to be revealed. It's no use trying to guess.'

It took him just five days. Dorcas had been serenely happy during this time, after her conversation with Tilly, clearly quite confident that all had been settled to her own satisfaction and that she had nothing about which to concern herself. Tilly would watch her, on the rare occasions when she was within doors at number seventeen, and think – am I plotting to do her down only because she is trying to harm me and mine or because I want to see her suffer? If it is the latter, I'm ashamed of myself. I should not have so mean and hateful a nature. But then suddenly the memory of her mother's spoons came back and she lifted her chin and told herself that it was not perhaps so mean and hateful after all. It was clear the spoons had vanished for ever, for the jeweller had been quite unsuccessful in his search, and for that alone Dorcas deserved every punishment that might be meted out to her.

But when the time came and she had the evidence she needed in her hands, it was not so easy.

Jem came to see her at his usual time, walking through the late summer evening to stand in her drawing-room and her heart lifted as she saw him and she jumped to her feet, genuinely delighted to welcome him, and he smiled a little ruefully.

'I will not ask if your clear pleasure at my arrival is due to your expectation of what I might have to tell you, or to the very fact of my presence. No, don't attempt to answer me. It's easier if I'm left doubtful. And I must tell you at once that I have all the information you wanted.'

'You have? You're a miracle worker,' Tilly cried and led him to the armchair facing hers and then rang the bell. 'I shall ask Eliza to fetch the tea tray at once, and then we shall be comfortable together.'

The tray arrived quickly and Eliza looked at Tilly sharply as she set it on a table beside her, and checked the flame on the little spirit stove beneath the kettle on its chased silver stand.

'I'm glad to see you so contented, Mum,' she said pointedly and even nodded at Jem in a friendly manner. 'I dare say you're better company for my mistress than I'd have expected you to be, Mr Leland.' Tilly bit her lip and considered scolding her for her impertinence and then knew she couldn't. It was a most difficult situation after all; he had first visited this house as a friend of Charlie Harrod's, and had frequented the kitchen. It couldn't be easy for Eliza to serve him up here in the drawing-room. That she had come round to accepting his place in her mistress's life to an extent was clear in that she had addressed him at all; for many months she had quite ignored him, and though it might be a long time before she could bring herself to call him Sir, the fact that she had been able to call him Mr Leland was a step forward. Tilly smiled up at her and said gently, 'You're very kind, Eliza, and indeed, yes, you're right. I do feel that Mr Leland is excellent company for me. Thank you for the tea.'

'Yes, Mum,' Eliza mumbled and went away, clearly well aware of what she was really thanking her for. For a moment Tilly and Jem sat in silence as they heard her footsteps go thudding heavily downstairs.

Then Jem stretched a little and sighed. 'It is difficult for her, I do understand that. It is difficult for me too. Does it concern you?'

'Does what concern me?' Tilly asked, though she knew perfectly well what he meant.

'I think I had better not continue along these lines,' Jem said with a flash of laughter in his voice. 'It will do neither of us any good. Instead, let us speak about the errand you set me.'

She sat up very straight in eager expectation as she passed him the tea she had poured. 'Well?'

'You were right. It is remarkably easy to discover all one needs to know about one's fellow traders if one asks the right questions of the right people. I've never been much given to gossiping about other people's affairs. When Charlie and Spurgeon and I are together we're as likely to discuss our

364

gardens as business, though Charlie has a tendency to talk of the shop a lot – but always his own, not other people's. Well, as I say, I've been surprised to see how much men do enjoy discussing others' affairs, now I've learned how to do it.'

'I thought as much.' She was getting tense now, wanting him to come to the point but uncomfortable about harrying him. 'So, what have you discovered that is of interest?'

'Sir Andrew Ledbetter,' Jem said. 'This is the man of whom Dorcas spoke. Sir Andrew Ledbetter.'

She raised her brows. '*Sir* Andrew? And considering going into trade?'

Jem laughed. 'Oh, it's nothing new for him! He is, it seems, as impecunious a baronet as ever stepped. He's had interests in a number of other people's shops and affairs, but always very quietly. He had a stake in Elgar's building scheme – when he built the Ennismore Gardens houses and so forth – and did quite nicely out of that. When the building was all finished and he could make no more from it, he put some money into Shillibeer's – the omnibus business, you know? – and made a tolerable sum from that. The thing is, he's extravagant, likes to live as though he had an income to match his title and his family history. It's a Devonshire branch of a much richer set of Ledbetters in Nottinghamshire apparently. Includes an Earl, so they say.'

'Then he cares a good deal for appearances,' Tilly said and leaned back in her chair in some relief. 'Perhaps my lines are falling in better places at last. If he is a man who is concerned about others' opinions of him.'

'Oh, he's concerned indeed!' Jem said happily. 'I talked to Elgar's man – old Beamish used to be his foreman for many years until he was injured by falling bricks when the last houses were being done and Elgar, who is an excellent man, truly excellent, settled a pension on him. He lives very comfortably on that in a room above Spurgeon's shop and watches the animals for him when they're in the yard waiting to be killed. He tends to be a touch garrulous when he takes his beer, and he told me it was a great secret that Sir Andrew was a shareholder in Elgar's affairs. Didn't think it would be quite the ticket, it seems, for a connection of an Earl. And when Shillibeer's gave him the chance to invest he swore them to keep quiet, and when one of the Shillibeer clerks made mention of his investment in his presence — showed he knew the man was a shareholder, do you see — he was so incensed he withdrew his investment at once. Cost him a good bit, that did.'

'Is it known that he is to open a club of some sort in Knightsbridge?' she asked and reached for his cup to give him fresh tea. 'Or is he —'

'No, indeed it is not. And it is better than that. What is known is that there is a lady who is to do it. The gossip, I have to tell you, is — well, far from polite. I heard suggestions with which I would not sully your ears, but that is perhaps inevitable, when it is a lady who chooses to open such an establishment. The *on dits* are that there is this lady who will open the place and that she enjoys the company of a well-placed gentleman. But no one knew — or said they knew — who the well-placed gentleman might be. Now I may be quite wrong but it seems to me more than possible that the lady in question is Dorcas, and the gentleman with whom she is connected is Sir Andrew. There cannot be two such pairs in one small village like Knightsbridge, after all! But both have been able to keep their names well out of sight, it seems.'

'Then I have her,' Tilly said and put down her cup and saucer. 'I can deal with her.'

'Indeed you can.' Jem looked very pleased. 'I wish I could be here to listen to you do it. It will be a famous victory. I've not the least doubt.'

'Will it?' Tilly said and bent her head to stare down at her fingers, interlaced now on her lap. 'I think it will be horrid.'

He got to his feet and came to crouch before her. 'Oh, I am sorry, Tilly. I should have more feeling. Of course it will be horrid for you to have to deal in such matters. You are not like Dorcas, taking pleasure in triumphing over others. But as you said yourself, what else can you do?'

She lifted her chin and looked back at him as directly as she could. 'You're right. Of course you're right. But I wish – well, never mind. Please, Jem, go home now. I have all the information I need, and I shall wait up for her and use it tonight. I can't sleep until I've done it. But I couldn't do it if you were still here. And anyway –' She shivered a little, for all the warmth of the September evening. 'Anyway I should be ashamed to let you see me behaving like the sort of – like a person who uses such methods of dealing. So go away and leave me be and I promise I'll tell you what transpires.'

He remained where he was for a while, staring up at her, and then slowly got to his feet and almost absently dusted down his trousers.

'I think perhaps I am wasting my heart,' he said abruptly after a while. 'You can't care for me as I do for you, can you? Not ever?'

She was startled and gaped at him. 'But Jem, I think so highly of you that you can't imagine! I think of you as the best friend I could possibly have.'

'But never as anything more. Never as someone to whom you could be close and warm and – and comfortable. Never as a person you could allow to see you except when you are carefully prepared to be seen. Never as one to whom you could display any side of yourself that is less charming than you would like it to be. Not, in short, as a *lover*.'

There was a silence, and she tried to think honestly of all he had said, and to be as truthful with him as she could, and as he deserved; and knew she could not say other than the words that came to her lips now. 'You are right, I suppose,' she said quietly. 'I've tried so hard, truly I have. You're good and kind and I enjoy your company greatly, and value your friendship and your concern and your support. But if you ask me if I feel that freedom that is part of truly loving someone, if I have that sense of – of being one person and with no fear of self-exposure then I have to say — no, Jem. And I don't know if I ever will.'

'I fear you won't,' he said in a low voice and straightened his back. 'I fear deeply that you can't.'

'I thought it would be enough that we were the friends we are,' she said almost timidly. 'You said it would be.'

He smiled that slightly twisted smile of his again. 'I thought it would. But I was wrong. Well, good-night Tilly. I hope you get all you want from your conversation with Dorcas. I wish you all you wish yourself. Good-night.'

And he was gone, leaving her watching the light drain out of the sky outside her drawing-room windows and feeling both bereft and relieved at the same time. Which was a very odd way to feel. She was also deeply apprehensive, for there was still the matter of Dorcas to settle, and she shook her head at her own confusion and told herself sternly that she would think about Jem another time. Now she had to concentrate on the matter of her house and Dorcas and her plans for the future. Hers and Duff's. That was quite enough to occupy her at present. And she settled in her high backed armchair to wait for Dorcas to return home.

She woke startled, not quite sure where she was, nor why, and then looked up at the clock on the mantel as she remembered. The small gilt hands gave her a triangular smile and she thought — almost one in the morning! How much longer can I sit here and wait for her?

But then she realized what it had been that had woken her in the first place: the soft sound of footsteps on the creaking old stairs, and she got to her feet and hurried across the drawing-room, her skirts billowing and sending riffles of draught through the warm room.

The light from the drawing-room door spilled out into the dark hall and she stood there, framing herself in the doorway and said as firmly as she could, 'Dorcas, I have been waiting for you and it is important I speak to you at once. You will come in here, if you please.'

The sounds stopped and after a long pause, Dorcas's voice came out of the darkness above her. She was clearly halfway up the next flight of stairs.

'Oh, not now, Tilly! I am dreadfully weary – not to say a little bosky.' She gave a soft breathy little giggle. 'I have been dining with my partner and drinking quantities of champagne to celebrate the plans we have finished today. We sign the lease tomorrow afternoon and all's going as merry as a marriage bell. And it will be the real thing. You see if I don't bring the man up to scratch!'

'Please come in, Dorcas,' Tilly said again and stepped back in the doorway, willing Dorcas to obey her. If she refused and went upstairs, she would have to follow her and she knew that would put her at a disadvantage. Dorcas must agree to come to her, Tilly's, drawing-room. There, she knew she could make it all work out right. And she stared implacably out into the dark hallway, her face as hard as she could make it, and wondered a little wildly if Dorcas could hear the heavy thumping of her pulses.

There was a long silence again and then Dorcas made an odd little sound, part laugh, part snort, part sigh and said, 'Well, I suppose so – I can't be long though! I yearn for my chamber pot as well as for my chamber, and I am not ashamed to say it! What is it then? Some crime of my little Sophie? She's only a child so don't tell me tales of her, for I shan't listen!' But she came down the stairs and into the light and Tilly made way for her.

She was wearing gold tissue and lace and looked dishevelled, for her hair had tumbled from its careful knots and sweeps and curls and was tangled on her shoulders, and she was flushed and sweating too; but Tilly did not concern herself with that. She just looked at her and said firmly, 'Sit down, I have something to tell you.'

'Well, whatever it is, do make haste.' Dorcas threw herself on to the sofa, spreading her golden skirts and looking like a heap of coins. Tilly found herself thinking – how very apt, under the circumstances.

'It won't take long,' Tilly said steadily. 'I have to tell you this. I know that your partner is Sir Andrew Ledbetter. I also know him to be a man of considerable pride. I know that he is disinclined to do anything that will in any way mark his name. If he discovers that you and your mother lived in a bawdy house, that you were brought up in a common brothel and that you worked as a housemaid here, he will, I am certain, sever his connections with you, and you will not be signing a lease tomorrow or any other time. Now, unless you arrange to leave this house forthwith and agree never to attempt to have any dealings with me or mine, ever again, I shall tell him all I know of you. I can do this with great ease and very quickly; I know not only his name but where he lives and can see him first thing tomorrow morning. And see him I shall. It is entirely up to you what you do. But you must decide soon – now in fact. For unless you are out of this house at first light tomorrow I shall go and see him before noon. The choice is entirely yours.'

Epilogue

THE SMELL OF PAINT was quite qualmish. Tilly thought; no wonder Duff looked so pale. And she stopped beside where he was sitting on the top step of the second flight staring down into the hallway and touched his forehead.

'Are you all right, my dear one? Would you not be better if you played in the garden for a while? If you wrap up warmly it will be quite –'

He shook his head pettishly to rid himself of her touch and said crossly, 'I don't want to go into the garden.'

'But it is so big now, Duff! They finished the new paths yesterday and the lawn has been rolled to perfection. You could play with your ball on it so easily and it will be much better for you than sitting here amid all the paint smells.'

'There's no one in the garden to play with,' Duff said gruffly, hugging his knees even more tightly and he scowled down to where the painter was putting the final touches to the morning room door. 'I'm all right, Mother. Do leave me be.'

'But –' she began and then stopped. The last time she had tried to persuade him against his will to do something he had suddenly jumped up and kicked out at her, missing her most narrowly, and then had burst into floods of tears and fled to his bedroom, refusing to re-emerge until Eliza coaxed him out. He had hardly spoken to Tilly for days after that, and only in the last week or two had he brought himself to be a little more like his old friendly self. The last thing she wanted to do was to start another such episode just because he had sunk back into a gloomy mood again, and she sighed and pulled her skirts to one side so that she could go down the stairs past him, contenting herself only with looking back as she reached the landing and saying, 'Eliza will have your supper ready at the usual time, darling. Now the workmen are almost done we can be as we used to be again.'

He stared at her with eyes as blank and opaque as pebbles, his pointed little chin buried between his knees as he sat curled up on the step, and she sighed again and continued down the stairs.

It was still difficult to be quite comfortable with the changes in her house. Most of the rooms were the same size, of course, except for the dining-room on the ground floor, which had been provided with a great arch that connected it to the dining-room next door. This had created a most impressive chamber, and she stopped now and looked in, and bit her lip at the sight of it. It really was very splendid, almost too splendid, and she felt quite strange as she gazed at the great table, which would comfortably accommodate twenty diners at a time; the vast sideboard with its handsome mirrored back and the shelves so carefully laden with pieces of highly polished silver and sparkling crystal decanters, and the rows of chairs at the table to match those set against the walls. The rest of the room had the same effect; there were palms in pots between the two great windows, and heavily swagged and draped curtains made of the best red plush Jem Leland's shop had been able to supply which framed them sumptuously so that the whole room breathed luxury at her. She was very proud of it, but oddly uncomfortable as well. It did not feel at all like home and she went on down to the kitchen, needing some sort of corrective to her state of mind.

Eliza was busy at the stove, with Lucy beside her, as they pored over a large pot and Eliza raised a flushed face and said in a satisfied voice, 'This is the best leg of mutton we've had from Mr Spurgeon this twelve month, and braising up a treat – it's as tender as can be! And we've a lovely pair of roast fowl for a second course and lovely veal collops – they'll be well found, I'll be bound and more than satisfied. Come and look, Mum, and you'll see –'

'I'm sure it is excellent, Eliza,' Tilly said absently. 'And the burned creams too?'

'Ready this past three hours, Mum, and cooling nicely in the larder. I got some ice for them from the fish man. And the apple pies, they're baking now.' She bent and opened the door of one of her ovens gingerly and peered in and a scent of hot apples and cloves drifted into the room. 'Yes, that'll do very nicely. Now, as to the breakfast ham – I've sent it back and told Mr Spurgeon it ain't good enough, too fat by far. I'll take a plate of cold veal collops to table tomorrow instead, Mum, but we'll have an excellent ham by Friday and no one'll be hard done by at all.' She wiped her hands on her apron and jerked her head at Lucy. 'Be on your way now, you and Kate, and see to it the extra bedrooms next door is all ready. They'll be arriving any time now, will they not, Mum?'

'Yes,' Tilly sat at the table. 'Any time now. I hope they are not late. The dinner will be spoiled if they are.'

'Not it, Mum,' Eliza said comfortably and set to making a pot of tea though Tilly had not asked for it. 'I chose to do a braised leg of mutton, like I told you, on account it can't be spoiled with waiting and the same is so for the fowls. They'll sit nice as you like keeping hot and not drying out if you set a good gravy to them. As to the vegetables, well, a little extra stewing of potatoes never did them no harm. There Mum, there's your tea, now.'

'Eliza, is Duff – does he ever speak to you of how he regards all this?' She waved a comprehensive hand. 'I've been so busy since the alterations began I've had little time to speak to him and even when I have he won't – well, he seems not to wish to talk too much.'

Eliza was silent for a moment and then said candidly, 'Well, he's angry with you, Mum, and there's the truth of it. I've told him it's wicked in a boy of barely seven to be angry with his good Mamma and he says as he ain't, but he is, Mum, you take it from me. It's her, do you see. They was good friends and he misses her.'

'I know he does, I knew he would, but what else could I do?' Tilly looked up at Eliza almost piteously and she patted her shoulder awkwardly.

'Not a thing, Mum. I've told you over and over. You was right to do it and it'd have been a sight worse for all of us if you hadn't got rid of her.' She shook her head reminiscently. 'Funny, ain't it? Mr Freddy getting rid of her Ma the way he did and then you getting rid of her herself. I never did know the ins and outs of all that.' And she looked sideways at Tilly a little hopefully.

Tilly shook her head. 'And you never will, Eliza, so you may stop your prying. Enough that she went when she did and we are left free of her. I only wish we had been able to keep Sophie here. The child would have been better with us, I suspect, than with such a mother —' she stopped then and added doubtfully '— I think.'

'I don't,' Eliza said stoutly. 'She was a sly boots if ever there was one. But don't you fret, Mum. Master Duff'll get over her going when he moves on to his proper school, like the Misses K and F said. He's a clever boy and learned his letters and his books that fast they was amazed. He'll be away to his big school and meet other boys and it'll all be different then.'

'I hope so,' Tilly said and drank her tea in silence. And then as she realized her mind was dwelling again on the long departed Dorcas, she shook her head and straightened her back.

'Now, Eliza, let me be clear. We will be eleven tonight for dinner, will we not? There's the new gentleman from the hospital here.'

'Yes. And Mr and Mrs Grayling what's arriving this afternoon at about six, they said. With the rest —' and she began

374

to count on her fingers: 'The Misses K and F and Miss Cynthia and you – that's four. And never did I think to see the day as those three would sit to table with gentlemen, but there you go! People do change their minds, and no error. Now, where was I? Oh, yes, and Mr and Mrs Grayling and Doctor Charnock, that's seven, and Miss Barton and Miss Duke, that's nine and who else is it? Oh yes, Mr Cotton and Mr Gee, that's eleven. After tomorrow of course, it'll be even more –' And she took a deep breath. 'It'll be hard work, Mum, but don't it do your heart good to see how well we're getting on? Why, I said to Charlie Harrod only today when he came himself with the order, on account of it was such a big one. "Charlie," I said. "We'll be your best customer yet," and he said, "Eliza, my girl, you're our best customer already. If it's for Quentin's, I tell my shop-boys that it's got to be the best of the best." "And so it ought to be," I told him, "Or I'll know the reason why." Now, Mum, you go and rest a bit. There's no more you can do now the builders is all done at last. That painter, he's just touching up and they'll be gone in half an hour. You go and rest and don't you fret more about Master Duff. I'll see to his supper and cozen him out of his megrims in a trice. He'll get over that Sophie – he's only a child and they forget soon enough.'

'It's been six months already, Eliza,' Tilly said. 'And he hasn't forgotten yet.' But she got to her feet obediently. 'Six months since they went.'

'And good riddance,' Eliza said. 'And so Master Duff'll learn all in good time. Now, just you –'

'I'm going. I'm going,' Tilly laughed. 'You must not bully me so, Eliza! You may be housekeeper now as well as cook, but you really cannot bully me so!'

'Someone's got to, Mum, when you're set on working too hard,' Eliza said and shook her head irritably as the bell to the back door jangled. 'Now, who can that be at this time of the day? All the orders in and none to come till tomorrow when the fish man's due – oh, all right, all right. I'm coming!' For the bell jangled again.

Quite why Tilly lingered, she didn't know. The comings and goings at the back door were very much Eliza's affair and not hers and she knew better than to meddle. But for some reason she was interested now, and she stood and watched as Eliza opened the door. She couldn't see the man outside on the doorstep but she could hear his voice.

'Is this Quentin's, Miss? Yes? I bin told the lady what lives 'ere was 'askin' after some items she was interested in. And I think I might just 'ave what it is she's after.'

'There's no one here to buy any nonsense from pedlars!' Eliza snapped. 'We don't want any trumpery jewellery here — be off with you.'

Tilly frowned and moved back into the kitchen.

'Oh, I don't mean the stuff you can see 'ere, Miss! No, none of that. This is somethin' special. I just thought as 'ow if I could talk to the lady she might be interested.'

'Well, she isn't,' Eliza said and began to push the door to, but Tilly was too quick for her. She came to stand at the door and look at the man on the step.

He was thin and far from young, bent of back and wearing a suit of so rusty a black that it seemed to glow in the late afternoon light. His hat was battered, worn well to the back of his head and his face could have been much improved by soap and water. He was carrying a tray before him on which glittering glass beads and brassy chains and crumpled ribbons had been set out in a would-be tempting array and Tilly looked at the tray and then at the man.

'What is it you want to show me?' she asked bluntly. 'And who sent you?'

'As to what I have to show you, if you're the lady of the house, Mum?' and Tilly nodded impatiently. 'Well, as to who told me you might be interested, it was a colleague in the same line of business, you might say. Only a bit more suited as to accommodation than what I am. And what I got to show you is this.'

He reached into a pocket inside his battered old coat and

pulled out his hand with the fist firmly closed, and he held it out towards Tilly with his head on one side and an ingratiating grin on his face.

'Now, lady, shall I show you, or shall I not? That is the question. Are you in the market for such a posy of pretties?'

'I can hardly say until I've seen what it is you have to offer,' Tilly said tartly and Eliza pulled on her elbow.

'Come away, Mum, and let me shut the door in his face. Nasty street pedlar like what he is, he won't have nothing that'd be of any good to a lady like you! Look at that stuff — crumpled ribbons I wouldn't let even Lucy set her fingers on!'

'But these ain't ribbons, Mum,' the man said and at last opened his fist and Tilly stared down at the grubby palm and caught her breath.

There, glinting in the afternoon light, were the gleaming jewel colours, the fine ribbing, the soft gentle shapeliness of her mother's spoons. And she put out her hand and took them and held them close and started to laugh, and then to weep. Eliza shook her head in great distress and led her inside. She reached into her pocket to give the man money and push him away from the door after some noisy bargaining, then came back to crouch beside Tilly at the table where she was now sitting with the spoons spread in front of her and tears rolling down her cheeks.

'Oh, Mum,' said Eliza. 'I don't know why you're takin' on so, but I wish you'd stop! Why should these silly spoons upset you so? Everything's so good now, compared to what it was! You've got your lovely big house, well filled with tenants and safe as you like and me to look after you and there you sit, crying over a few spoons! There's no need, Mum, truly there ain't.'

'Oh, Eliza,' Tilly said and lifted her wet face to her, her eyes wide and shining. 'Oh, Eliza, I know! I've never been so happy in all my life as I am at this moment. Because now I know it is all going to be all right. For Duff and for you and for me and for — oh, Eliza! Isn't everything quite splendid? Quite perfectly splendid?'

'Yes, Mum,' Eliza said, as mystified as ever, but more than

happy to agree. 'Perfectly splendid. Now will you go and get yourself rested and changed for your dinner? Because Quentin's won't run itself, you know, and I've got work to do.'

'Yes,' said Tilly. 'Yes, Eliza. You're quite right.' And she picked up her spoons and went away upstairs.

She stood in the doorway of her magnificent new dining-room, watching them; the Misses K and F positively flirting with Doctor Charnock from St George's Hospital, as Cynthia Barnetsen watched with a sulky expression on her face; Mr and Mrs Grayling clearly enchanted with Mr Cotton, a tall and exceedingly cheerful man who dealt in the City in what he called loftily, 'commodities' and who shared with Mr Grayling a passion for the game of backgammon, which they were discussing in a very sprightly manner; Mr Gee who, despite his shyness, which Tilly had found very endearing in him when he had first enquired after a room for himself, ingratiating himself most successfully with Miss Barton and Miss Duke; and felt a great wave of affection for them all. They were the bedrock of her fortunes, she told herself, her own dear guests who offered her beloved Duff the future he was entitled to have. All her problems, all her worries, all her efforts, had been worthwhile. She had an establishment to be proud of, at last, and only peace and prosperity to come. It was a superb feeling and she revelled in it.

Eliza appeared at her shoulder. 'Now, Mum, get to your place, do, so's I can send Lucy in with the stewed asparagus. I got them all done up fancy, I have, a real piece of resistance like what it says in the *Englishwoman's Domestic Magazine*. You'll be real proud, you see if you aren't! But I can't bring 'em till you're in your place, now, can I? It ain't Quentin's unless Mrs Quentin's set in her place at table.'

'I suppose not, Eliza.' Tilly turned to smile at her. 'And it must be Quentin's, after all!'

'Course it must,' said Eliza, and lifted her chin at Lucy, who scuttled off to do as she was bid. 'So take your place, Mum, do.'

And Tilly did.